MW00513113

TANNADEE

TANNADEE

MAURICE GRAY

Copyright © 2020 Maurice Gray

The moral right of the author has been asserted.

Apart from any fair dealing for the purposes of research or private study, or criticism or review, as permitted under the Copyright, Designs and Patents Act 1988, this publication may only be reproduced, stored or transmitted, in any form or by any means, with the prior permission in writing of the publishers, or in the case of reprographic reproduction in accordance with the terms of licences issued by the Copyright Licensing Agency. Enquiries concerning reproduction outside those terms should be sent to the publishers.

This is a work of fiction. Names, characters, businesses, places, events and incidents are either the products of the author's imagination or used in a fictitious manner. Any resemblance to actual persons, living or dead, or actual events is purely coincidental.

Matador
9 Priory Business Park,
Wistow Road, Kibworth Beauchamp,
Leicestershire. LE8 0RX
Tel: 0116 279 2299
Email: books@troubador.co.uk
Web: www.troubador.co.uk/matador
Twitter: @matadorbooks

ISBN 978 1838592 332

British Library Cataloguing in Publication Data.
A catalogue record for this book is available from the British Library.

Typeset in 11pt Adobe Jenson Pro by Troubador Publishing Ltd, Leicester, UK

Matador is an imprint of Troubador Publishing Ltd

For Cathy

CHAPTER 1

"Look! That cloud – it's just like you, Dad," said Chizzie Bryson as he and his father stood on the front lawn of their family hotel, overlooking the little town of Tannadee in the Scottish Highlands.

"Where?" asked his dad.

"Straight ahead, over the loch there. It could be an omen."

"It's nothing like me."

"'Course it is; it's got a broad head, chubby cheeks, a bit of a paunch, big shoulders and little legs."

"It's got hair."

"That's the omen! Your hair restorer's actually going to work this time."

Johnny Bryson eyed his son sternly. Baldness was a touchy subject. "I'd have hair as thick as your mop," he grumbled, "and be just as slim, but for a lifetime of work and worry. And now, on top of it all, I've got Weever coming."

Chizzie laid a hand on his father's shoulder in mock sympathy. "Sorry, Dad, you've had it very tough, I know."

"If only you did know. I've worked all the hours God sent and, finally, when I get the hotel refurbished and fabulous, along comes that fancy billionaire Weever to sweep me away. I tell you, some nights when I put the tea towel over the budgie's cage, I wish I could just climb in there and spend my days chirping away with not a care in the world."

Chizzie smiled, unsure whether there was more to this than just wild imagining.

1

"I mean," continued Johnny, "there's that little ball of feathers, with nothing but seed and water. And is he happy? You bet he is! A million times happier than I am, and I'm a bloody human being with private health insurance!"

"You're not thinking of selling up, surely?"

"Selling up! Are you nuts? No! I know you'd like me to, though, but it's not going to happen, Chisholm. It's not going to happen. No way."

Chizzie looked away. He hated seeing his father's plaintive look – the look of the martyr; it was a look he knew could snare him for life. "I wasn't suggesting you sell up, Dad, but you know my position: I enjoy helping in the hotel, but I also enjoy teaching part-time. It's the modern way, having a varied career."

"You can't run a hotel part-time. It's a one hundred per cent commitment. It needs passion. You've got to love it. I really can't understand you, son; all the Brysons – every one of us – has been passionate about what we do. We're a passionate breed. We always have been. I blame your mother's side of the family, God rest her soul. And God rest my father's soul. If ever a man had passion, it was him. D'you know what he told me just before he passed away?"

"Yep."

Johnny took no notice; he was lost in nostalgia. "He said, 'If you can lose your head while all about you are keeping theirs, you'll be a football manager, my son.' And d'you know what? He was right! I became that football manager."

"For a little time."

"The point is that passion got me a career that could've seen me rich and famous."

"So what happened?"

"I wasn't good at it. Or, at least, it wasn't good for me. All that sittin' out in the cold, gettin' jaws like a hippopotamus with all that chewin' and my blood pressure rocketing. So I looked around for something easy. *What's easier than hotels?* I thought. But, oh God, how wrong can you be?"

"And that's what you want for me, is it?"

"No, I've done all the spade work. You get all the benefits; they're right here, waiting for you – you know that."

Chizzie looked back at the hotel, a solid piece of Scottish baronial architecture built in sandstone block. It had fourteen guest rooms, a dining room and a lounge, set in large lawns and shrubby gardens: the perfect country retreat. With its big windows and ivy-clad walls, it even seemed to exude an expression that changed with the weather: in sunshine it smiled, but in gloom it could mope dismally. The thought of sharing a future with it brought on a faint feeling of dizziness in Chizzie, as conflicting emotions swirled in his head. In some ways, the hotel presented the perfect life, but there was also an air of stuffy, dull existence about it. He turned to his father, whose plaintive look hung on.

"You could love it; I know you could," Johnny insisted. "You just need commitment and a bit of passion. It's in you somewhere; it must be."

Chizzie tried to change the subject: "We've got Weever to deal with first."

Johnny groaned.

"Maybe we should see this as an opportunity, actually," Chizzie suggested cautiously. "Maybe we could live alongside him. His investment might just be the best thing for Tannadee and even us. Maybe there's spin-off for everyone."

Johnny clenched his fists and faced the hills in silence.

Chizzie knew what was coming; he could almost hear the fuse fizzing; he had to head off his father. "I just like to review the options now and again, Dad, that's all. There's no harm in it," he said calmly.

3

"He'll ruin us. He's an operator. We can't trust him," insisted Johnny.

"He'd be investing millions in the area, and there's no denying that we need houses, we need mobile coverage, we need decent broadband, we need the bank open more often, we—"

"Sure, sure; we need these things, but on our terms, not his. Can you imagine what his price would be? He'd have a gun at our heads. Lord and master, he would be. No, we don't need his millions; we've got things he can't buy. We've got traditional values here, things he can only wish for."

"Tradition isn't everything, Dad; most of human existence has been in the Stone Age – nothing's more traditional than stone tools. But we've moved on. The greatest tradition of all is change. Without it, we'd have no hotel: we'd be living in a cave; you'd be called Ug and I'd be called Wah – probably the most traditional names ever uttered."

Johnny shook his head. "I will move with the times as far as I need to, but no further. Tradition is our bread and butter. And d'you know something? I don't like your—"

Suddenly, Chizzie caught sight of an osprey and seized the chance to escape Johnny's rising wrath. "Look! There's an osprey on the loch and it's going for a fish. Fantastic!"

They watched as the osprey splashed into the water and half-disappeared below the surface. Then, flapping frantically, it hauled itself back into the air, with a fish slung below it, which it turned head first into the wind.

A wry smile crossed Johnny's face. "Well, well, well, there you are. You see that? A bird with a brain the size of a pea and it gets a fish. Surely to God, some of our guests can manage it too. It's just like I said: there's no shortage of fish in that loch; there's only—"

"Don't insult the guests now, Dad, they're your passion remember," warned Chizzie.

"Go and get your camera, son, in case that bird comes back. If you get a good picture, I'll stick it on the reception desk, and then no one could argue about a lack of fish."

"Yeah, we could use it for marketing and publicity – Tannadee the osprey town. Home of the osprey!"

"Better still, the trout and osprey town. That could see us into better days again."

Better days had certainly come and gone in Tannadee. In the nineteenth century, Tannadee had been a celebrated spa resort. Throughout the affluent world, the spa water of Tannadee had been renowned for its healing powers, and – for nearly fifty years – those who could afford to make the voyage bathed in its water and drank it. Then, in the 1930s, a new hydroelectric scheme on a nearby loch altered the water table, causing the spa water to turn brown. For years after that, enterprising locals trawled the loch trying to find a monster that would boost their economy, but none could be found. None that bore sober scrutiny, at any rate.

It seemed that the spa town was doomed. But then a miracle occurred: a local hotelier discovered that persistent application of the brown water on the skin conferred a fashionable tan. Soon the word spread, and Tannadee was once again back in business. The Tannadee tan – the Tan-tan, as it was known – became highly prized among people of quality throughout the Great Depression and the war years.

Then catastrophe once again. In the1950s came acid rain, and the tan turned grey and smelled horrible; something to do with sulphites, they said. Unsurprisingly, this development proved very unfashionable and it killed off Tannadee as a spa resort once and for all.

Since then, things had remained very quiet, despite an attempt in the 1960s by the local Lord Lieutenant to raise the profile of Tannadee by attracting royal personages to a local shooting estate. The attempt foundered when that very rare beast, a Highland communist, and a local one at that, got on national radio and told the proletariat that the royals and their lackeys came north for nothing more than the love of slaughtering local residents. An opinion which, though arguably true, did nothing to attract the guns and royal personages to Tannadee.

As the fortunes of Tannadee faded, the Tannadee Hotel became the only hotel in the area to remain open all year round, though its popularity had dwindled along with the population, which was by then around one thousand six hundred. In spite of their fading fortunes, the inhabitants, particularly the older ones, never relinquished the idea that Tannadee was a spa town with a noble history: to them it was more than a mere village.

The likelihood of getting a good photo of an osprey was extremely remote, so when Johnny went off to meet a news-reporter come to obtain the hotelier's views on Weever's plan, Chizzie simply lifted his head to the sky. He drank in the atmosphere before gazing idly at the big, white clouds floating over the loch and the green-gold hills that surrounded Tannadee. The clouds were the only things moving. Tannadee, as usual, was a village of little bustle.

Change was afoot, though. For up that loch in a few hours' time would come the force that was Gordon Weever, billionaire and international property developer.

But was he a force for good or for ill? This was the question in Chizzie's mind as he searched the burgeoning clouds for a sign. Several cumulus seemed to offer human faces, some grotesque and some almost familiar – in the east there was a young Queen Victoria up to her neck in a foaming bath. Then, flat on his back, came a very relaxed-looking Prince Charles gazing at the heavens. Switching to the west, Chizzie's gaze met a towering cloud uncannily like Gordon Weever with a boxing glove jabbed on his puffy left ear. To the north-west, a massive pair of cauliflowers shaped up before morphing into a huge pair of bulbous buttocks. Chizzie looked away, as much through confusion as modesty.

Was this a premonition of conflict to come? Though he'd spent nine of his twenty-seven years away from Tannadee, the village still felt very much like home. And yet it was awfully small for a man who'd travelled widely and had recently returned from Africa, where he'd spent an eventful two years teaching rural science in a remote secondary school. He didn't miss the riots or the mealie-meal-based cuisine, but he did miss the satisfaction of knowing that his lessons made a real difference to the lives of his students, some of whom were more than thirty years old and barely literate.

Now, looking down at Tannadee, he felt he had grown, but, alas, it seemed Tannadee had not. He turned his gaze to the hills to think of other things, but his eyes soon wandered skywards again, hungry for information on the soaring screens. This time there came cause for cheer: away on the southern horizon, the clouds parted slightly and a shaft of golden sunlight swung slowly through the glen. Seconds later, there was another sunray, then more sunrays burst out, forming what seemed like a giant hairbrush made of light sweeping along the loch. Though made only of light, it seemed very real. Had it come to sweep out old ideas and clear the way for Weever?

On Loch Skein, six miles away and on the other side of the mountain that lay to the south of Tannadee, waves sloshed and walloped against the wooden struts of the jetty as a seaplane came alongside. The pilot cut the engines quickly. The door of the seaplane burst open, and out stepped Gordon Weever. A group of onlookers broke into spontaneous applause as he set foot on the gangway. Weever knew exactly why they were applauding – he was something else. Only a small boy seemed unimpressed: he was around four years old, and was crying and stamping his feet.

"Jamie, stop it," his mother hissed, "you've been on a plane before."

"Not one wi' wellies," the youngster wailed.

Weever, grinning, heard him and responded instinctively. Being tall, broad-shouldered and turgid with people skills, Weever walked up to the boy and leaned over him. "Be sweet to your mom, little fella," Weever advised, wagging an admonishing finger, "She's the best friend you'll ever have. Now, if you want to be on my airplane, you need to go ahead and ask me. I might say yes; I might say no. You need to ask me to find out."

"He doesn't understand," said the boy's mother.

"Never underestimate, ma'am. When I was that boy's age, I was doing deals. Now what d'you say, son?"

"May I get on your plane, please?" said the little boy, demure suddenly.

"You certainly may, young man," replied Weever. "I like your nerve. You go right on ahead and talk to the pilot there."

The boy's mother made to protest, but Weever laid a reassuring hand on her shoulder. "He won't be flying, ma'am. Don't worry."

This was bad news to the boy, who looked shocked and was about to burst into tears again, so Weever knelt down and spoke to him eye to eye. "You asked to get on the airplane, son, and guess what? That's what you got. If you wanted to fly, that's what you should've asked for. But then I would've said no. You see, asking can get you things sometimes, but it doesn't always get you all you want. Life is tough; sometimes, you need to play real smart."

"He doesn't understand," his mother broke in again, pleading.

Weever stood up. "I hope he does understand, ma'am. I really do hope he does," he said ominously. "Now you go right ahead, son, and enjoy what you got."

If no one could place Weever's accent, it was hardly surprising: he'd grown up in eight countries, forever on the move, as his father built up the family shipping business before getting into property development. Now based in Texas, Gordon Weever mostly affected what he thought was an authentic American accent, though Americans mostly thought it was something else. As yet he had not attempted a Scottish accent, but there was plenty of time for that.

He claimed he loved Scotland. His maternal grandfather had been born in the Highlands, and now, at the age of sixty-five, he had begun to look back on his life in search of a meaning that went beyond his financial wealth. Here, in the Tannadee area, there was a wealth that was completely new to him, a wealth that touched him like no other: a wealth of spirit – the spirit of his ancestors. Though it touched him deeply, this spirit nevertheless had to fight for space in the Weever head, a head so attuned to business opportunities that even thoughts of ancestral spirits spawned ideas for new ventures, and this was why he was now heading for Tannadee.

He had made the trip confident in the knowledge that the sheer power of his physical presence would send the local councillors scrambling to approve his plan to construct one of the world's most exclusive hotels, a hotel secreted away in the Highlands where sunshine was not important; the important thing here was a sense of spiritual renewal of the kind he felt awakening inside himself. Important people with busy lives would rest their minds here and breathe restoring air. Apart from golf, there would be gentle pursuits – pony trekking, cultural excursions, hillwalking, and, most importantly, stillness and peace of mind. This was the plan, and the planning meeting was scheduled for that evening.

Now, though, he was taking time out to explore his family's roots in the area. His mother had been a McShellach of Glen Skein, so he and his retinue of two bodyguards and one project manager walked straight to the seat of Clan McShellach – Dunshellach Castle, by the shore of the loch.

Though in need of some repair, the castle was open to the public, and two coach parties were also visiting when Weever arrived. Weever's bodyguards muscled past them, clearing a path for the great man and his project manager, Charlie Fairfoull. People seemed to assume they were the owners and got out of their way without fuss.

Spearheading the foray was Fairfoull; he and Weever could have been father and son, so similar did they look, but Weever wore fair hair while Fairfoull's was natural and black. They were both over six feet tall, and each was dressed immaculately in a white shirt; blue, silk tie; and thick, navy-blue overcoat.

Easing past men, women and children on the winding stone stairway, they arrived at the top floor of the castle. And, here, in this centuries-old place, something extremely rare happened. Weever, tough tycoon though he was, became visibly overcome. Telling everyone to hush, he stared at the wall over the hearth. For nearly a minute he stared at it, completely motionless, lost to all the world in ethereal, stone-still silence. Ancient stone and living Weever were seemingly in rapt communion. Then, suddenly, without a word, Weever lifted a leg, stepped over the rope cordon, and walked slowly towards the hearth, as if hypnotised. The castle warden – a neat, little man in a dark uniform – ordered Weever back. But this was Gordon Weever, and Gordon would go wherever Gordon wanted to go. No one told Gordon Weever where to go.

The great man moved up to the stone hearth and laid his hands gently upon it, as if blessing it. These were hallowed stones: stones that had felt the touch of his kin, had known the sound of their voices, had felt their very breaths and held their shadows. Through all their hardships and occasional joys, these timeless stones had borne witness to the growing and flowering of his forebears. A tear broke from his eye, and he blinked to shove it away.

Then came an ominous creak, the floor boards gave a groan, and a crackle went creeping along the floor like a hairy spider. Weever looked anxiously at his feet, then he stiffened for a moment. A second or two later, the creaking ceased. All went still. Weever looked up, seemingly relieved and almost cocky. He turned to go. Then, bang! The floor burst open and whooshing away went Weever, clean through the hole; in an instant, he was completely gone – all that man, all that importance, snapped and gorged like a mere morsel to some beast. Now the only trace of him was a cloud of dust coiling in the air like a seeking spirit torn from its carcase. For a moment, the air simply froze with shock. Onlookers, stunned and horrified, clung to one other, with some trembling visibly. Then, all at once, people screamed, turned and scrambled for the door before the gates of hell consumed them all.

Death had struck! Or it would have been death for most people. But for Gordon Weever? He was not most people. Through the ceiling of the pink bedchamber he crashed, and he thudded onto the four-poster bed in a smoky cloud of dust. The visitors in the bedchamber, whose guide had just recounted the castle's ghost story, screamed and bolted for the door.

Above it all, Charlie Fairfoull, prostrate on the floor and waving away the dust, peered anxiously through the hole. The screaming panic of the people in the bedchamber he understood, for, as the cloud of dust thinned, it revealed the grey-plastered face of Gordon Weever looking ghostly enough to send any sane person zooming down the spiral stairway.

On the stairway, above those heading down, Weever's bodyguards raced to attend their fallen angel. Charlie dragged himself across the floor then leaped to his feet and ran to join the others.

What they found in the stricken bedchamber was not exactly a complete surprise, for the great man – though limping, coughing and looking a little crestfallen – was on his feet and moving about. This was a man who, despite having just plummeted through a floor, had self-belief that was second to none. It was even widely believed that one day he would actually attempt to walk on water. Nevertheless – covered in dust, with his trousers torn and his coat ripped at the back – he'd rarely looked worse. Most worryingly of all, Weever's toupee had moved – not much, nearly half an inch, but it could feel like a lot – and this from a hairpiece guaranteed not to fail in an earthquake; though, in fairness, no one made any claims about it not failing when it went through floors in ancient monuments.

Charlie Fairfoull pushed his way through to Weever's side and took hold of his arm. "Are you okay?" he asked, like everyone else.

The great man did not respond immediately: he was clearly a little shocked and in some discomfort, but there would be no sign of weakness.

Rubbing his shins, Weever nodded and assured everyone he was fine; that he had rather enjoyed it, in fact; it was quite an adventure; and it might even be a business opportunity here in the form of a value-added experience for castle visitors – there was quite a thrill to be had from floor drops.

But the toupee was a problem, and Charlie knew it. Pretending to dust the great man down, he shepherded the toupee discreetly to its correct position. Weever muttered his gratitude. He was further grateful when Charlie elbowed the outraged castle warden in the chest accidentally, winding the man, while Weever and his retinue made their getaway back to the seaplane.

For the average man, or even the average businessman, falling through a castle floor would have been enough to see them retreat from the Highlands altogether and seek gentler comforts in the Lowlands. But Gordon Weever was not average. This was a man who had fallen through floors before – financial floors, that is. Having been bankrupted more than once, he'd always bounced back. No Highland haunt would dent the ego of Gordon Weever. Now it was time to turn his sights on the Highland councillors.

However, there was a problem.

CHAPTER 2

When Weever reached the seaplane, he found the little boy he'd allowed into his aircraft had locked himself in its tiny toilet and was refusing to come out until the plane took off. His mother's pleadings were met only with screams.

"See where kindness gets you," groaned Weever. "You get shit on. I let my guard down, and look what happens. Well, it won't happen again, no way." With that, Weever stepped forwards, kicked the door in and pulled the boy out by the collar. Then, with the lad cradled in his arms, he stepped outside.

"He called me bastard!" yelled the boy.

"Who did?" asked a news reporter.

"*He* did."

Weever laughed. "I called the door a bastard. It was the door. The goddamn thing was stuck an' he was cryin' so hard to get out. It was pitiful."

Fairfoull nodded towards the aircraft and flapped his hands as if juggling balls in the air, and the pilot responded by revving the engines fiercely, almost to deafening.

The child yelled out, "No. No. He called me bastard. Him. He did."

But the little voice was no match for the roaring engine noise. Weever shoved the child into its mother's arms, and, turning away swiftly, he stepped into the aircraft with his hands clamped on his hair. Fairfoull and his retinue followed him in. The seaplane turned, then taxied away with a roar out of all proportion to its size. But only a few moments later, spluttering could be heard, with the engine seemingly misfiring. The seaplane turned around and headed back to the jetty where it docked once more.

They all got out, and, while Weever cursed the little boy for wrecking the engine, Charlie went off in search of a mobile phone signal.

By the time Charlie returned, Weever, who was not used to hanging around, was now venting his anger on the pilot.

The pilot, however, remained annoyingly calm. "I could fix it," he said with a smile, "but I'm not allowed, as I'm not a qualified technician. The Civil Aviation Authority would have my licence, and I'd be grounded. Sorry."

Seeing Charlie return, Weever drew off his attack, but Charlie was grim-faced.

"Okay, Charlie, what've we got?" asked Weever.

"Bad news. All the hire cars are out and they're miles away from here – there's not even a van for hire." Charlie smiled wryly. "This is the Highlands."

"What about the coaches we saw at the castle?"

"Gone. They left in a hurry for some reason. But it's not all gloom. There is transport."

"Good."

"A horse."

"A *what*?"

"A horse."

"A horse and carriage?"

"No, just a horse. There's six horses at the local trekking centre."

Weever ignited. "Who'd they think I am, Buffalo fucking Bill? Forget the fucking horse. Go find a car somewhere and wave some money around."

"I was advised against that; car insurance and licensing are a bit patchy in these parts, and reliability is another grey area. Basically, you're looking at a seventeen-mile trip in a dodgy car or six miles through the hills on a horse that could do the journey in its sleep. That's the choice – it's a pig in a poke or a horse on the trail."

Weever thought for a moment, then looked up at the sky. The clouds were all white and thin, and forebode no threat. With a customary sudden change of mind, Weever smiled broadly. "Okay. Saddle up, boys!" he barked. "We hit the trail! You know, this could actually look really beautiful and really wonderful; we ride into town Texan style."

"Are you able to do that?"

"'Course I am. We hit town Texas style, like the seventh cavalry."

"Well, not the seventh; they got wiped out at Little Big Horn."

"That was the ninth."

"No, it was—"

"The ninth!"

"Actually, they're not strictly horses – they're ponies," said Charlie with a hint of apology. "They're Highland ponies."

"Highland ponies? What's that mean? Not teeny toy ponies?"

"No, no, they're strong, hardy creatures, built for the Highland terrain. The horse equivalent of, say, a jeep. And riding into town on Highland ponies means we're not too Texan, so we don't alienate the natives. We come in the Texan way, but with a touch of the Highlands – a neat marriage between Texan and Highland."

"Well, it'll be the first neat marriage I've ever known," Weever replied. "Let's go see."

When they arrived at the trekking centre, Weever chose the biggest of the ponies, a doleful looking grey. Charlie, keen to make the most of the change of circumstances, phoned the car-hire company to arrange for a piper to greet the riders as they arrived at the community hall in Tannadee. Here was a chance to turn adversity into good fortune.

After bathing and doing some minor repairs to himself at the trekking centre, Weever and his gang were ready to hit the trail. The obligatory riding helmets were rejected on the grounds that health and safety never built Texas. But the resolute lady of the trekking centre insisted they take them, so they put them on, though once they got half a mile up the track they took them off. Their trek guides, two young students, looked at each other, shrugged and were about to resume the trek when Weever took a fancy to the blue bonnet worn by one of them.

"Young man," Weever said, "you give me that hat of yours before we hit town, and I'll give you fifty pounds. Deal?"

Astonished, the young man hesitated for a second, then replied eagerly, "Yeah. Deal!"

"*Good man!*" shouted Weever, smiling. "We're going to hit town like Bonnie Prince Charlie and his merry men!"

CHAPTER 3

More than a hundred members of the Tannadee public were assembled in the community hall – it was the largest turnout in living memory. On stage sat twelve councillors from the planning committee, who were all very pensive. In the front row of the audience sat Chizzie Bryson and his father. Chizzie turned in his seat and scanned the room, hoping to see a majority of friendly faces, people he could count on for support. At a rough guess, it looked fairly even, with as many supporters as opponents in attendance. On the plus side, there was Ken McIntyre with some of his regulars from the Commercial Inn, and there were some ladies of the bed-and-breakfast fraternity, who smiled back reassuringly.

The chairman of the planning committee stood up and announced that Mr Weever had been delayed and that, out of courtesy to him, they would wait until he arrived. The councillors left the stage quickly, and headed for the tea and biscuits laid on by the Royal Voluntary Service.

Johnny leaned in close to Chizzie's ear. "Now's your chance for a bit of canvassing," he said. "Go and press some flesh and convert some of these bloody councillors. I'd do it myself, but it wouldn't do any good; I've got too many enemies." Johnny was red-faced and agitated. He detested councillors, for they seemed to thwart his every move. Just the very sight of them was enough to make his blood race. Sharing a room with them, albeit a large one, all but overwhelmed him.

Chizzie cast his eye over the hall for likely targets. His eye alighted on a small group chatting by the tea urn.

Johnny saw them too. "Over there," he whispered, pointing, "a twaddle of politicians."

"A what?" asked Chizzie.

"An opportunity. Make sure there's no backsliding. Go over there and say how d'you do, wonderful weather – that kind of thing, nothing important. Then look them in the eye like you know their secrets. Everybody's got secrets, especially these devils. Then let them know what a disaster Weever would be for them and us."

Ingratiating himself with politicians was well outside Chizzie's comfort zone. Nerves kicked in at the very thought of trying to impress these people, who seemed to revel in rough and tumble, being loud, and pressing their opinions on others, no matter how daft those opinions might be. But duty called, and he took a deep breath and made his way to the tea urn.

Just as he got there, though, most of the group – including Mr Dunkie, the gamekeeper – peeled away and headed further up the hall, leaving Chizzie with only three 'opportunities', who were very 'county set': two men and a woman, who were rather distinguished-looking people it seemed to Chizzie. It was looking like a tough ordeal, but, resolutely, Chizzie filled his cup, took some milk and listened in on the conversation, ready to time his entry neatly without seeming rude. Crime and punishment appeared to be the subject under discussion.

The woman was advocating an innovative way of dealing with criminals – something to do with sucking their blood, it seemed. "The aim being," she confided, "to keep your criminal reasonably vital without being in any way vigorous enough to slip his hand in your pocket."

"Not sucked dry then?" enquired the larger of the two men, with the white, close-cropped head and pointed face.

"No, no," she confirmed.

"Pity! Pity!" the large man exclaimed.

"Sucked senseless, that's all?" chirped the smaller chap with a grey, puffy hairdo and a furrow up the middle that put Chizzie in mind of Moses and the parting of the Red Sea.

"Sucked senseless! I like the sound of that!" sniggered the larger man.

"A couple of pints sucked, and they're husks!" cried the smaller chap with the big hair, almost spilling his tea with laughter.

"And serve 'em bloody right too. Let 'em be sucked, I say. Suck 'em. Suck 'em all. Suck 'em senseless!"

"Suck! Suck! And suck 'em again!" declared the smaller man.

"There's nobody with the guts to do it, though," grumbled the woman.

"I'd bloody do it! Too right. Do it in a flash. Bloody sure I would!" declared the larger man. "Suck 'em within an inch of their damn lives, I would."

"Me too!" chirped the smaller chap. "It's entirely sensible; the blood transfusion service never runs dry, and the criminals are rendered too weak to bother anyone for months. It makes perfect sense."

"There's not a cat in hell's chance of it happening, though – it's not pc," added the larger chap. "No, no. But great thinking, Letitia. You have balls, if I may say so. Yes! More balls than most men! If this tea was something stronger I'd offer you a bloody toast, I would. Oh yes."

This was not quite the level of conversation that Chizzie had anticipated, but it was clearly now or never. "Hello," he ventured, stepping into their little semicircle. "I'm Chizzie Bryson."

Barely had he heard himself speak, when the larger of the two men suddenly saw someone who was apparently much more interesting and blared a greeting across the room, straight over Chizzie's head.

Undeterred, Chizzie latched onto the badge all three were sporting on their tweedy lapels. "LA? What's that stand for?" he enquired.

"You don't know?" asked the big chap, incredulously.

"No," replied Chizzie.

"Landsmen's Alliance," the woman informed him dryly.

"Of course," said Chizzie, none the wiser, but adding cheerily, "Is there a Landswomen's Alliance?"

"No," said the big chap, snorting with scorn.

"There's no need," said the smaller chap.

"It's an alliance – a proper kind of alliance – all under one roof and one banner. One for all, and all for one. Male or female, we're all landsmen together. Isn't that right, Letitia?"

"Absolutely!" she declared.

"Isn't that just a little bit sexist?" asked Chizzie tentatively, while his mind screamed, *You idiot! Get out while you still can.*

"What?" asked the little chap with the hairdo, squeezing his eyebrows together.

Chizzie replied with a nervous smile, "Lands men. Wouldn't it be better to say 'landspeople'?"

"The LA is not sexist," declared the big chap. "Not in the least. It's a party with balls. In the LA, even the women have balls, and we are proud of that! We are not pc, and we are proud of that too. We are above pc. Above it!" he insisted.

"There's no room for namby-pambies in the LA," added Mr Hairdo.

"Well said, Julian!" chimed the big man. "This woman here is as good as any man I know, and, frankly, better than most. I can pay her no finer compliment than to say – quite simply

21

and in all sincerity – to all intents and purposes, you are a man, my gal." Clearly inspired and getting quite emotional, his chin wobbled and his lips wavered as he repeated his mighty compliment.

The honorary man, however, looked uncomfortable. Her lips twitched and a slight spasm jolted her head, but, raising it defiantly, she replied, "I know exactly what you mean, Willie, and I am proud to accept your compliment in the spirit in which it is given."

"What a girl! What a man!" cried the big chap.

"Politics is a man's world," observed Mr Hairdo sagely. "If women wish to compete, the very least they must do is man up."

"Be more than a man," protested the woman.

"Steady, old girl," advised the big chap. "Steady. More than some men – that would be fair to say; that's the way to put it, eh?"

"My honorary manhood is taken in the spirit in which it is given," confirmed Letitia.

"Of course. Well said! Good girl," commended the big chap.

"Hear, hear. Spoken like a true man, Letitia!" interjected Mr Hairdo.

"Thank you," she demurred

Bewildered, Chizzie found himself speechless.

Then, suddenly, the big man looked Chizzie straight in the eye and brayed, "I say, you're one of these new people trying to bring in this Weever thing, aren't you? Is that right?"

This sudden change of tack caught Chizzie off guard, and he found himself replying meekly, "Well, not exactly. We're not for Weever and we're not new – my family have lived here for quite some time now. We think there is a case for carefully managed change in Tannadee. For example—"

"What's your name again?" asked the big chap.

When Chizzie told them, all three landsmen winced.

"Oh... oh so," said the big chap, nodding gravely. "Actually, it's time we took our seats, I think."

"Indeed," affirmed the honorary man. The little-big-hair agreed, and off they went.

Chizzie watched them go, and gave an involuntary sigh of relief. Clearly, there were minds he could never reach. Nevertheless, he felt inadequate for not having fought his corner more robustly. He shouldn't have allowed himself to be batted away by people with daft ideas.

He looked across the hall to see if Johnny was watching. He was, but there was no note of censure. Johnny merely shook his head before gesturing in the direction of two young men in dark suits. They were clearly excited about something, perhaps it was Weever's plan. Chizzie took another deep breath and, feeling like one of the Light Brigade, put his best foot forward and prepared to employ the same unsuccessful tactic as before. It was the only one he knew: get there and dive in at the first opportunity.

When he reached the gents in question, he saw his moment quickly and dived in. "Ah stocks and shares! Interesting!" he declared as sincerely as he could.

One of the young men turned sharply and introduced himself, offering his hand. They exchanged introductions, and Chizzie was brought straight into the conversation.

"You have a portfolio?" asked Alistair.

"Well, sort of," replied Chizzie, without conviction.

"Are you a bull or a bear? I'm a bull myself," continued the young man. "Danny's a bear."

"Well..."

"I mean, you've only got to look at stock market valuations. In absolute terms and relative to bonds, it's a bull market no question."

23

"Yes, Alistair," said Danny, "but there's continuing structural weakness in the US economy, plus the recessionary impact of sharply rising oil prices, and corporate profit margins are likely close to their peak."

"But risk appetite is back. The tide's on the turn. Mid and small cap indices have both shot up. Balance sheets are on the mend, and debt and costs are down. Any uptick in the economy is bound to impact the bottom line. And, on the macro front, we have a return to trend growth in the US of three per cent anticipated for Q3. I expect a ladle-shaped recovery environment creating a hippo-type market. You?" asked Alastair.

Chizzie, feeling quite dizzy, struggled to answer. "Eh, me? Eh well, erm..."

Fortunately, Danny couldn't wait. "Only if you follow a barbell strategy retaining a defensive core of resilient, cash-generative companies, while building stakes in recovery stocks. D'you agree?"

"Er, yeah... it sounds good to me," whimpered Chizzie. "Sorry, I have to go now." Without waiting for a response, Chizzie hightailed it out of stocks and shares, and went back to the sanctity of his chair. Clearly, politics was a strange world, replete with people he could probably never reach – ladies with balls, and bulls and bears that were mostly bores. More than ever, he was convinced that big is not always better.

By then, the Weever gang were riding into town, but only a handful of people were around to notice. The mounted men clattered along Lochside Road, enjoying the cool breeze off the loch, and scattering some ducks and stray sheep, before turning into Hill Street within sight of the community hall.

The smokers outside the hall were the first to see the riders approach.

"It's Weever!" one declared, peering down the street. "He's coming. He's riding into town!"

Another dashed indoors to alert the people inside, and yet another dashed off to summon the piper, who was practising round the back of the hall.

Chizzie and Johnny joined the throng as it gathered to watch Weever ride into town.

Approaching the hall like the commander of some conquering army, Weever saluted then raised his blue bonnet. The piper struck up 'Hail To The Chief' and the effect was cathartic. Weever's mount might've been a Highland pony, but it had no love of the bagpipes: first, it whinnied and jolted, and then, farting like a tuba, it reared up and dashed off towards West High Street with Weever clutching it around the neck and trying to cover its eyes with his bonnet. Galloping round the corner, it capped its departure with a rasping flurry of dung balls – an eruption that panicked Charlie Fairfoull's mount, which reared up and shot off in the opposite direction towards East High Street. It took a few seconds for everyone to realise quite what had happened. The other ponies looked stunned, seemingly frozen with fear – a fear shared and welcomed by their riders, who quickly dismounted.

It was one of the trek guides who took the initiative: "*Kyle!*" he shouted to his companion, "*You get Mr Fairfoull, and I'll get Mr Weever!*" and off they galloped in search of their hapless guests.

"Well, that was a resounding entrance," quipped one onlooker.

"In more ways than one," replied another, sharing a little giggle.

Panic set in among Weever's supporters. Some suggested getting into cars and going after him, then they decided that might just spook the pony further. People fretted and smokers drew on cigarettes. Others – like Chizzie and Johnny, who were opponents of Weever's plan – exchanged looks of pleasant surprise. The chairman of the planning committee announced a further delay of ten minutes to give Weever a final chance to attend the meeting before it began. But, with the air in the hall buzzing like an electricity substation, the ten minutes came and went, so they started without the galloping billionaire.

Minutes in, a cry went up from a man looking out of a side window: *"Weever's here!"* he shouted, *"He's here!"* Then, *"No, no – no – he's gone again!"*

Weever's pony sped past the window and round to the back of the hall.

Seconds later came a cry, *"He's back again!"*

Chizzie rushed to a window and watched as the trek guide took hold of the exhausted pony's halter, ending the circus.

The half-demolished Weever slid heavily off his mount, with a hand on his hairpiece, which showed no displacement – confirming its earthquake-fighting claims. Then, looking angrily at his pony, he cursed and swore, and seemed about to kick it, till Charlie drew his attention to the many eyeballs glaring at him through the windows. At which point, Weever managed to affect a wan smile and dusted himself down once again.

After a lengthy visit to the toilet, Weever – looking very weary and sore – joined his retinue in their reserved seats in the front row of the audience.

The hall settled down again to hear the contributions from the planning officer, and one each from the supporters and objectors. The planning officer outlined the plans submitted to him, receiving sporadic applause from parts of the audience, then it was the turn of Weever to take the stage and make the case for his plans.

But Weever did not mount the stage: he only grunted, as he was fast asleep. Charlie nudged him, eliciting a snore, and Weever's head fell to the side. Discreetly gripping Weever's coat, Charlie shook the great man, but the only response was another snore.

"Is Mr Weever all right?" asked the chairman, with a look of concern.

A murmur rose in the hall, and some stood up to get a better view of the sleeping giant.

"It's all right," replied Charlie. "Mr Weever's just a little tired – he's had a very busy day."

At that came a loud snore. Weever's head jerked, and he woke up looking a little dazed.

"Ah, aha, jolly good," cried the chairman looking relieved.

But he was not half as relieved as Charlie, who informed Weever it was his turn to speak.

However, Weever thought for a moment, then shook his head. "No, no, I'm too tired; I can't think," he whispered, "You go up, Charlie. Sock it to 'em."

Charlie stood up and addressed the chairman, "I'll speak for Mr Weever."

"That's fine," agreed the chairman, adding, "Perhaps someone could take Mr Weever out for some fresh air?"

Charlie nodded. "Thank you, Mr Chairman—" He was interrupted by Weever.

"The last thing I need is more fresh air," insisted Weever. "I've swallowed nearly half the Highlands already. I just need a little rest. Carry on."

And, with that, Charlie mounted the stage.

"Ladies and gentlemen," Charlie began. "I stand on this platform here tonight because I know that Mr Weever's investment will not only benefit our clients but will secure the future of Tannadee. Some of you, I know, will not welcome the change. You want to be left alone to continue in your traditional, time-honoured ways. I respect that, but it is a fundamental truth that those who stand still do not prosper: they wither and they die. With our plan, Tannadee will not only survive but it will thrive. People will come here from all over the world – from the US, from Canada, from Australia, from New Zealand, from Europe—"

"*From hell, more like!*" shouted someone in the back row, prompting hoots of laughter there.

Amid further sporadic heckling, Charlie went on to assert that the Weever Organisation was investing in the community, halting the drifting away of the young people, and stemming the probable closure of shops, the bank, the post office and pubs.

Finally, in closing, Charlie declared, "You need something of your own in Tannadee, something unique. And that something needn't be small. 'Small town' does not need to mean 'small time'. Ladies and gentlemen, I call upon your ambition and concerns for the future of your small community. Let it be small, but let it be big-hearted. Let Tannadee flourish for ever and a day! Thank you."

Then it was the turn of the objectors' representative in the shape of Robert Barrington.

"Are you sure Barrington's up to this?" Johnny whispered to Chizzie. "Fairfoull looks a helluva lot more impressive than Barrington." It was undoubtedly the case that, whatever qualities Mr Barrington might be offering, charm and charisma were not among them. "He looks like an off-duty hangman from the 1950s."

"Now, now, Dad, keep your heid," Chizzie advised warmly. "Just because the community council preferred him, there's no need to get testy."

"I am not testy."

Chizzie took a deep breath and hoped those around them had failed to hear the testy response.

"He looks such a fuddy-duddy," insisted Johnny.

"Traditional, you mean."

Johnny growled.

Barrington stepped onto the stage carrying his notes and running his fingers through his greying, bushy black hair. In his early thirties now, he'd been the school bursar for nearly six years. In fashion he was one of the old school. Attired in a brown, dogstooth tweed jacket; beige, cavalry twill trousers; and a club tie, he bore a facial expression that struggled to invite admiration and suggested that smell was chief among his senses. At the lectern, he lowered his hairy eyebrows and affected a Churchillian stoop. Then he lifted his head and greeted his audience with, "Ladies and gentlemen, good evening."

"Good evening," returned the supporters in chorus.

Barrington smiled. "What a blessed comfort it is to see so many friends gathered here this evening."

"*Welcome, friend!*" barked a supporter.

"Your presence affords me strength," continued Barrington. "The spirit of our community is real and vital. It means so much to me and to so many others. Yet, sadly, to our opponents it means so little. To them, I, and those of you like me, are the living past. Well, I ask you, ladies and gentlemen, what is so wrong with the past? It got us here, did it not?"

"*Hear, hear!*" yelled one.

"*Well said!*" cried another.

Then, adopting a look of hawk-eyed resolve, Barrington continued, "I say to you, ladies and gentlemen, that I am proud to be the living past! Proud to value peace and tranquillity; and proud to value friendship, neighbours, our community, our environment and our traditional way of life. I say tradition is no bad thing. By all means, let us reject the obsolete, the nasty and the downright hopeless – but, in the name of heaven, let us not be so blind as to rush at the rainbow for a pot of gold that is no more than a figment."

A section of the audience reacted with applause, and cries of "*No! No!*" and "*Only fools rush in!*"

Barrington nodded sagely. "We are told that we stand in the way of progress. I say let no one stand in the way of progress, but be not hasty – for there is madness here too. False prophets abound. The price of democracy, they say, is eternal vigilance. We must, therefore, be vigilant and discerning. If our wariness be mistaken for ignorance and backwardness, then more fool them, I say. We will not be swayed. Our duty is clear."

"Hear, hear!" echoed the supporters.

Barrington waited for complete silence before proceeding, "My friends, the argument levelled against us is that our quiet life has no future. Our opponents tell us we are fuddy-duddies, that we are gutless and without ambition, and that we are ordinary and we are dull. Well, I tell you this: that view is not only wrong, it is barefaced inveterate prejudice! How dare they? How dare they presume a monopoly on forward-thinking!"

"*Yeah, prejudice!*" yelled one, who was, by then, almost hoarse.

"*Outrageous!*" cried another.

"Not good!" exclaimed a third.

"Bad!" proclaimed yet one more.

Emboldened, Barrington felt confident enough to drop his voice to a more intimate and tuneful tone. "But, I ask you – must everyone lust after frenzy and excitement? The rat race?"

"*No!*" bawled a man.

"No rat race here!" called another.

"Billions, like us, delight in the quiet life," declared Barrington. "For us, people are not mere consumers, not reference numbers and not units on some credit-rating sheet. For us, what matters is friends, neighbours and family – a band of people who know us and who care about us, just as we care for them. We are community!"

"*Community!*" shouted a very hoarse man.

"Yes," ventured another.

"In Tannadee," declared Barrington, getting louder, "community spirit thrives undecayed by the lapse of time. It is a spirit of peace, a legacy of tranquillity, a legacy beloved of plain people and a legacy held dear by none other than the great Abraham Lincoln. In his magisterial way, he proclaimed our legacy fair and unprofaned by the foot of an invader. I say to you, ladies and gentlemen, if it was good enough for the great Abe Lincoln, it is assuredly good enough for us!"

"Yeah!" interjected a faithful supporter.

"Glory hallelujah!" cried another.

"We are sure and fast in our tranquillity, and no power on earth will unbind us, save effluxion of time!" Barrington declared.

"Yeah! Fluckshing!" cried an extremely hoarse individual.

"What's 'fluckshing'?" enquired another.

"God knows, but it's surely great stuff," advised his companion.

Barrington continued, "Let the usurpers know that we will not be cast asunder by wild-eyed dreams of a world stage!"

"Time's up!" called the chairman.

But Barrington was in no mood to stop. "If Mr Weever wants the whole wide world to come knocking at his door, I say: good. Good for you, Mr Weever. Find your peace of mind, but find it in your own place, not ours."

"Yeah! Yer own place, Weever! Leave us alone!" cried someone new.

"Time's up!" cried the chairman once more.

"Three cheers for Mr Barrington!" bawled an admirer.

"*Time!*" yelled the chairman, heatedly.

Barrington held up both hands, seemingly signalling he was about to finish, or possibly that he was offering some kind of blessing. "We say the gates of hell shall not prevail against us! We say, usurper – get ye hence! Be gone!"

"*John Knox yet lives!*" shouted a voice from the back.

Amid the uproar, Barrington stepped away from the microphone and walked confidently to his seat.

The committee chairman sprang to his feet, waving his arms for calm. "Well, there we have it, ladies and gentlemen; there we have it: support for the development and objections to it." Then, turning to his fellow councillors, he asked, "Which will it be? What do you say, councillors?"

Weever glared at the disconsolate councillors, who stirred into life. The noise that followed seemed to Chizzie more like an exchange of artillery fire than reasoned debate. No argument on earth, it seemed, could shift any councillor out of the trenches of prejudice and self-interest. The Landsmen's Alliance group vehemently opposed Weever's plan, while the young investors welcomed it cheerily. Then, with all opinions and prejudices loosed, and the echoes fading, silence gradually fell. Eerily, it hung in the air before the chairman, appearing a little perplexed, got off his seat and called for the vote. Up went the hands: six votes to six – a tie. Now it was up to the chairman, as he had the casting vote. By custom and common practice, he was expected to vote for the status quo. But would he? Would he have the nerve? He hesitated. A murmur grew. Tension simmered in the air.

Finally, with an audible gulp, the chairman spoke. "I vote to refuse," he said quickly.

Cheering erupted. Booing followed, and the chairman's closing words were lost to all but a few.

"*This does not mean the project is refused,*" he yelled anxiously, "*it only means it is refused in its present form.*"

Weever shot to his feet and, spinning round to face the audience, he cut loose: "What is this? Eh? Is this the Soviet Union? Is this Nazi Germany? I'm a guest in this country, right? A guest. And, in a civilised country, that means respect, right? Absolutely right, it's right. So, why am I being treated like a pile of crap here? Why am I having to sit here and take a load of bullshit? It's terrible; it's disgusting. I came here because my roots are here. And you know what? I am ashamed to say that now. Ashamed to say that. And – as my wonderful grandparents and all my lovely ancestors, all those lovely, lovely people – look down on this place now, I know they're in tears. And I mean tears. Big tears. Big time. And you know why? Because they are nice people, believe me. Very nice people. But now it's looking like all the nice people got the hell out of here a long time ago and it ain't difficult to see why. What a bunch of stupid halfwits!"

"Boo!" cried several in the audience.

"*There's good people here,*" yelled another, "*or you'd be talking to yourself.*"

"Yeah, okay, okay, wise guy," replied Weever, "not all of you, not all of you – but too many of you are bad; you are very, very bad."

"You've said quite enough!" advised an onlooker.

"I've only just begun, dummy!" continued Weever. "Look, people of Tannadee, ask yourself this: are you going to let halfwits walk all over you? Do they get away with one of the worst decisions ever seen in all of Scotland? It's stupid – and I mean big stupid. And I'm being very polite here. It's bullcrap! And that's polite too. I say it politely because that's what I am: I am a polite person – the politest person I know. So, I won't say what it really is. But it's so, so completely lousy that it's disgusting. It's also very, very childish and it stinks; it stinks like hell. Smell the roses, dummies! This is a beautiful, beautiful place, and I should know. I've been through all of it today."

The chairman leaned over the stage and said, "Mr Weever. Mr Weever, please; the decision stands, but—"

"Shut up, will ya!" came the reply. "I'm too big a fish for your little committee to fry. Get back, small fry. My reputation will get me approval. So you go away! Just get away!"

The chairman tried again. "But there is an opportunity—"

"Are you thick? I don't care about your opportunities. This is your opportunity. I'm the one giving opportunities, not you. I can walk away; I can walk out that door. I can leave all you sleepy little groundhogs to fend for yourselves in your teensy weensy hell holes, if that's what you want. Is that what you want?"

"*No! No!*" shouted some.

"Yeth, yeth, thay what you like," lisped another, "I like it the way it ith."

Weever scoffed, grinning and pointing at the man. "You hear that? You hear that? 'Yeth, yeth,' he thays. 'Yeth, yeth.' For the love of Christ! Ith that the voithe of Thannadee?"

Johnny leaped to his feet. "Right, that's enough of you, Mr Bigshot! You lost the vote, now clear off back to where you came from! And take your foul mouth with you! You moron!"

The shock nearly toppled Chizzie from his seat. Flabbergasted and flushed with embarrassment, he swung round to see the reaction of the others. Uproar hit like a volcano. A torrent of invective hit a wave of glee. Weever threw up his arms and shouted for quiet. The chairman echoed his plea.

Then, as order was restored, Weever turned to Johnny and asked ominously, "What's your name, little fella?"

"Never you mind, sonny bun," replied Johnny, "and it's certainly not 'little fella'!"

Suddenly, a shabby man in what used to be a suit leaped in front of Weever and swung round to face the audience – it was Daft Willie Duff, who had gone about talking to himself long before the advent of mobile phones and who liked nothing better than a bit of argy-bargy, but he'd never been known to hurt anyone. "*Right, that's it,*" he shouted, presenting both fists and crouching to absorb an attack. "I'll fight any man who bad mouths Mr Weever. Where's your fuckin' manners, eh? He's a guest in our country. An' I happen to love the man; he's got guts – no like some o' you whinos."

Police Constable Tunnock stepped forward, but Weever raised a placating hand. "It's okay, officer," he said, "we've got it covered." Then, turning to Daft Willie, he said, "Thank you. Thank you, sir. Thank you so much, but I have guys who can handle the situation. It's all right. You can sit down now."

Daft Willie hesitated, then nodded, "Yeah, well, I'm standing by if you need me, sir. Just say the word."

"That's good to know," said Weever, "very good to know. You're a good man, sir, and it's an honour to meet you. Thank you." As Daft Willie went back to his seat, looking proud, Weever turned to the audience again. "Go figure, people of Tannadee," he said. "The message you're sendin' out loud and clear is 'If you want to do business, don't come to Tannadee.' That's the message you're—"

Suddenly, a fruit bun bounced off Weever's head. He staggered backwards in shock. In a flash, one of the bodyguards was on his feet and wrapping his arms around

Weever, before pushing him swiftly towards the door, as the other bodyguard rushed to the door and threw it open.

An old lady screamed as Weever was hustled out the door, followed by Charlie Fairfoull. The councillors at the front of the stage scurried to the rear.

Panicking people started scrambling towards the exits, until a stern lady rose up and boomed, *"It's a bun – it's only a bun. I made it! A fruit bun!"* Then she added, pointing at Sven Johansen, "He threw it. He took it off the trolley. I saw him."

Sven got to his feet and, swaying slightly, announced drunkenly, "Yes. I… I threw the fruit bun."

For a moment, there was silence.

Then PC Tunnock stepped forwards and asked, "What the hell d'you do that for?"

Looking rather sheepish, Sven replied, "Gibby Watson said he'd give me fifty quid if I knocked Weever's wig off with a bun. I need the money."

"You drunken fool!" yelled a waspish lady.

The chairman ran towards the door shouting, *"Mr Weever! Mr Weever! Come back! Come back! It's all right!"*

Uproar erupted again. Irate people, some knocking chairs over in their haste, came from all directions to confront Sven, calling him all manner of uncomplimentary things, while others moved to defend him. Chizzie and Johnny were among the defenders that got to him first.

Johnny whispered in Sven's ear, "Well done, son; that could be the bun that saved Tannadee. See me about a job anytime."

"Gee, thanks, Mr Bryson."

But PC Tunnock was not so consoling. He pushed through the scuffling pack surrounding Sven and, addressing him formally, said, "Sven Johansen, I am issuing you with a formal caution. Any more disorderly conduct out of you and… and it'll be more serious."

"It was only a bet," grumbled Sven.

"*It was more than that!*" came a voice from behind the onlookers.

The voice belonged to Charlie Fairfoull, and many in the pack made it clear they agreed with him.

The chairman intervened from the stage. "Mr Fairfoull," he pleaded, "please ask Mr Weever to come back. I'd like to explain things to him."

"He wants to come back, Mr Chairman, but his security team say no. There's clearly no telling what could happen here. The behaviour of some people in here is shocking – truly disgraceful. Mr Weever wasn't to know what came at him. It could've been a bomb!"

Cries of "Yes!" and "Arrest him!" echoed Fairfoull's claim.

PC Tunnock looked slightly vexed.

"You must arrest him as a deterrent to others," insisted Fairfoull. "Charge him with assault."

Johnny spluttered.

But Chizzie acted faster. "Don't be ridiculous!" he exclaimed. "He did a very silly thing, but he meant no harm and no harm came to Mr Weever. Sven's been cautioned, and I'm sure he'll apologise."

Fairfoull replied angrily, "How d'you know there's been no harm done? Mr Weever is shocked, he's not a young man and he's had one helluva day. The last thing he needed was to be assaulted."

The stern lady reacted. "Assaulted? With my bun? How dare you!"

Fairfoull ignored her. "You have to arrest the goon."

"No," insisted Chizzie, turning to Sven, "You hear that, Sven? D'you see what you've done? I'm sure you'll want Mr Fairfoull to convey your sincere apologies to Mr Weever."

"I do, yes. I was very silly. I'm very sorry," replied Sven sombrely.

"That won't do," insisted Fairfoull, "Mr Weever wants him arrested and charged; it could've been a bomb he threw."

"Listen, chum," said Johnny, leaning in towards Fairfoull, "It was a bun; it was not a bomb, not manna from heaven, not a fallen star and not a lot of things. It was a bun – a farruit bun!"

All eyes turned to PC Tunnock, who drew in his lips. "Stand back everybody," he cried. "Where is the bun?"

"Here!" shouted a voice. And the bun arrived, bouncing off Johnny's head.

Sven, with lightning reflexes, caught it, shoved it in his mouth and began eating it.

"He's tampered with the evidence!" yelled an onlooker.

"I'm only showing it's a bun," mumbled Sven.

"Give it to me," demanded PC Tunnock. He examined what was left of it, then called on the stern lady to examine it.

Without touching it, she confirmed it was indeed hers.

"Arrest him!" insisted some.

"Leave him alone!" cried others, most of them ladies.

Then, addressing Sven, the policeman informed him: "On grounds of drunk and disorderly conduct, you are detained under section… section… section…"

For a moment, there was complete silence.

Then, "He can't remember," said an onlooker.

"When did you last arrest anybody?" asked another.

"Section fourteen," advised Sven. "At least that's what it is in Millburgh when they take me in. It might not be the same here, though."

"It's the same here," replied PC Tunnock. "Section fourteen of the Criminal Procedures Scotland Act 1995."

"Go with him, Mr Bryson. See he gets a fair deal," said one of the younger ladies, turning to Chizzie, before smiling broadly at Sven.

CHAPTER 4

"You can't go on like this, Sven," said Chizzie as he sat at the fireside next to PC Tunnock. "You need to sort yourself out – get a job and settle down."

"Why? What for? I have great times; I'm as free as a bird. If I need something, I get it. And I sleep under the stars in fresh air. It's very healthy. If the weather ain't so good, I shack up with my police pals in Millburgh, and I get a bed, I get good food and I get a warm shower. The only thing is that I get the advice; it's the same old stuff, but now I know it better than they do, ha ha, so I say it before they do. There's nobody on my back, though. It's great. It's fantastic. I've no troubles. You should do it. Everybody should do it."

Chizzie winced. "You won't get to sit at the policeman's fireside in Millburgh, though."

"No, but they're good to me; they're very good. They see me right. No worries. A great life. Super."

"You're going nowhere, Sven. You used to be so driven, so keen to get on," said Chizzie.

"Yeah, then I wised up and, hey, I found the good life. May I have another fruit bun, Mrs Tunnock? I'd never had fruit buns before today. They're great."

"Of course, Sven; help yourself, and there's more where that came from," replied Mrs Tunnock.

Mrs Tunnock, whose first name was June, was the embodiment of that month with her warm voice, generosity and glowing countenance, and yet she had the ability to turn stormy and douse a fiery hothead or two. She was the head cook at the school and saw to it that her husband was well fed; perhaps too well fed, for he was more the embodiment of bountiful autumn in outlook and appearance, sometimes bright and jolly, other times sombre and brooding. Being two years away from retirement, the burly PC spent most of his spare time attempting to photograph the local wildlife and fighting the flab that hindered him.

Mrs Tunnock offered Sven more tea then waded in. "You're a fine lad, Sven, but you can't live like a tramp forever," she said, looking him straight in the eye. "What would your mother think if she saw you like this?"

"She wouldn't mind," confirmed Sven.

"Really? You sure of that, Sven?"

"Yeah, no problem." Sven leaned back, and then he put his hands to his head suddenly. "Oh God, no," he cried. "It's a terrible life; it's terrible. I'm a bloody fool. You're absolutely right. God, it's awful. I've had fleas, I've had ticks, I've had crabs – no, not crabs, cancel the crabs – horse flies I've had, but no lice and no bed bugs, thank God. Not yet, but it's only a matter of time; only a matter of time."

Startled by the outburst, Chizzie hardly knew what to say and started scratching himself unconsciously and only became aware of it when he saw the Tunnocks scratching too. When they all became aware of it, they started laughing. Then, they eased their chairs back discreetly, a little further away from Sven.

"I need a break," said Sven shaking his head before eyeing Chizzie. "Your dad offered me a job."

"Excellent," said Chizzie, "when d'you start?"

"I don't."

"Why not?"

"I'd feel locked in."

"You're locked in if you spend a night in custody."

"I get out in the morning. But, yes, you're right. I need to sort myself out. I thought I'd got sorted out – I started my own business two months back. I was doing very nicely, thank you. Alpine Meadows Wheelie Bin Care, I named it. Then, one day, it all went belly-up for real. I reach into a bin to get a duster I've dropped and, silly me, I get stuck upside down. I'm in there and just can't get out, I'm in for over an hour; I'm exhausted. Then some drunk guy pulls off my jeans, but I was goin' commando, no underpants – so stark bollock naked I am. Sorry, Mrs Tunnock. Then some kind soul covers my arse with the *Daily Telegraph* and wheels me to Accident & Emergency. An' all those lady nurses looking on. Could be the love of my life there. An' there's me with my arse in the air. What kind of introduction is that? And when they said it's a job for the fire brigade, I got all panicked and started farting. Excuse me, everybody, that's the truth. I'm farting big time, and one guy shouts 'Hey the bin's moving! Pop-arse propulsion is born!' And I hear it in my dreams now, always. It's a nightmare. I gotta shift it. I need a job – somethin' with dignity."

Chizzie smiled reassuringly. "There's work for you at the hotel, Sven; old Dougie needs help in the gardens and—"

"I don't know; I don't know. I'll think it over."

As the three watched Sven wrestle with his demons, Chizzie reflected on what he knew of the tall, well-built Scandinavian, whose fair-haired good looks should have been a sure-fire passport to success. After arriving in Scotland six years ago to make a living on the professional games circuit, for some reason best known to himself, Sven hit the booze and lost his way. In a six-month spell as a New Age traveller and squatter, he became known as the 'Tundra Tinker' and kept his muscles honed by chucking bailiffs out of windows.

That little social experiment and the subsequent court cases straightened him out. Until, once again, he hit the bottle and developed a strange affinity for pavements, being frequently found spreadeagled on one. Fighting the booze was undoubtedly the biggest battle of his life. At that time, not surprisingly, his self-esteem was mostly where his face was – in the dust. And – with the drink robbing him of all his senses, including his sense of direction – on the games circuit, he became known as the 'Viking Hitman' on account of his veering about a lot and lobbing cabers everywhere, mostly towards the crowd. People got the hell out of their seats when Sven bore down on them with a caber. He himself put it down simply to bad timing, but, of course, it was deeper than that – gallons deeper. He was even more dangerous with the hammer, where he did have a genuine timing problem – for a lengthy spell he seemed incapable of letting go of the thing at the right time, all that whirling about seemed to beat his brains in totally. Nowadays, it was simply the booze that set him whirling.

"If you apologise nicely to Mr Weever, maybe he'll offer you a job too, Sven," said PC Tunnock, puffing on his pipe. "Outdoor work."

"Weever won't be offering him any job now," Chizzie said, looking surprised at the officer.

"I'm not taking sides here," PC Tunnock continued, "but, off the record, Weever'll get his plans through, and you, Sven, could do worse than get a job from him; there'll be plenty of overtime. Right now, though, you're one fruit bun short of a job."

Sven nodded. "I'll think it over. I need to lie down now."

"Will you be apologising to Mr Weever?" asked Chizzie.

"Tomorrow," replied Sven.

While Sven slept, Weever and Fairfoull reviewed their position over post-prandial drinks in the large sitting room of Weever's estate house.

"So, what did we win and lose today?" asked Weever.

Fairfoull took a sip of his cherry brandy, then leaned forwards in his chair. "Right, number one, we scored on support – there were some pretty keen guys rooting for us out there. Two, we scored on fear – we can sue the bum that threw the missile. And, three, we scored on pity."

"Pity? Pity! I don't want pity. That's not me. I'm not pitiful!"

"No, of course not; it's a disguise."

"We don't need that. Pitied? Me? Are you kidding?"

"It's not for long; it's just a nice little plus that fell into our lap. All but the worst in Tannadee will think they've done you wrong, they'll be ashamed and they'll want to do right by you."

"I don't care; I won't be pitied. Not by you and not by anybody, got it?"

"Got it. Sympathy."

"No sympathy neither!"

"Empathy."

"That's ugly."

"Understanding."

"That's better."

"So, in total, we're three up on yesterday – we've got support, we've got fear and we've got understanding."

"We've got a red light on planning approval! That's not a plus."

"It's a mere blip. The red will turn, then it's green lights from there on in."

Weever sipped his brandy thoughtfully for a moment. "There's more red out there," he said, helping himself to two chocolates from the box on the coffee table. Then, with his mouth almost full, he slurred, "There's the red dwarf that bawled me out – the little squirt; he called me a moron. He's going down."

"Forget him, Gordon; he's not worth it."

"I'm worth it. I don't take that from anybody – least of all a pint-sized nobody. God, you'll never know how much I wanted to punch that little bastard right in the juicy kisser, right there, to smack him down – him and the bum with the bun."

"We'll see to them when the time is right."

"That time is now. We'll get our plans through toot sweet. We've got all our pluses lined up and we've got our politicos paid up, right?"

"Enough to get us past the post. We're fine."

"You know, it's funny," said Weever, seeking a caramel from the box, "I honestly didn't care too much about this project at the start. I could've let it go; it's small beer. No planning approval? So what? I use the place for myself. I'm looking for somewhere to cool my heels, and here would be just fine. But two things happened. First off, the whole area is amazing, and our kind of folks would just love it here. I know they will."

"And the other thing?"

"The red dwarf and the bun-throwing bum: they've got it comin'. I tell ya, they got it comin'. I ain't taking their shit. I'm kickin' ass!"

"Well, looking at it strictly as a business proposition, I'd say we've nothing to gain by hitting out, but we could lose out if we're not careful. There's no need for a heavy hand. We can simply roll them out of the picture."

"We could, sure we could, but we won't. This is bigger than business; this is personal. I want to kick ass, right? I want to kick the bastards! They insulted me on my home turf. And it's not just me they insulted – they insulted my whole family, everyone. My flesh and blood were raised here, and that means I get respect. My family gets respect, right? But what do we get? We get shit on! I'm not taking that. I'm going to kick their fat asses clean outta here, and I'm going to do my family proud. It's going to be wonderful. I'm going to do a great job here, and I don't want assholes in the way! I wanna kick 'em out! Kick 'em out."

"I'll get you another drink, Gordon. Same again?"

Weever nodded.

When Fairfoull returned from the bar with the drinks, he found Weever fast asleep, his mouth agape and snoring quietly. He laid the brandy on the coffee table and left, closing the door quietly.

As Chizzie lay in bed that night, listening to the shipping forecast in the darkness, hoping to drift off to sleep finally, his head churned with thoughts of the planning meeting and Sven's aimless existence. How could anyone so talented and so handsome become such a slave to drink? How could something as simple as a beverage control something as sophisticated as a human being? Two hundred thousand years of evolution perverted and humiliated by a humble drink. Ironically, it was a very sobering thought. Chizzie switched the light on and reached for his trusty, comforting, old read – the one he could rely on to restore his faith in the goodness of life. After twenty minutes in the company of Rupert the Bear in full colour, Chizzie put the book aside, switched off the light and went to sleep.

Like machine-gun fire, the rapid cackle of a magpie outside his window woke Chizzie just after seven-thirty. Reluctantly, he got up to open the window and see off the annoying bird. As he pulled back the curtains, the bird flew off, but an odd sight met his eyes. In the distance, three men appeared to be bobbing about next to the stream separating the school playing fields from Weever's estate. One of them appeared to be Sven and he was leaping from one side of the stream to the other while the other two men appeared to be trying to catch him. It looked like a game, but it was likely a game only for Sven; the other two were probably some of Weever's security guards and no doubt deadly serious. It looked like it could get very ugly very soon. Thinking Sven might need a witness, Chizzie rushed across the room and grabbed his binoculars from the top of the bookcase. Back at the window, he brought the binoculars quickly to his eyes and was met by a scene rather different to the one he'd left only a few moments ago.

In the school grounds, the security guards had taken hold of Sven's arms and were frogmarching him towards the stream. Sven appeared to be complaining, but to no avail. They crossed the stream and were heading towards the estate house when Sven shot his legs out sideways suddenly, tripping both guards and breaking their grip. He turned about and began jogging back towards the stream, but the guards were quickly on him again. Sven reacted at the first touch; he threw one man clean over his back onto a pile of sand, and, as the other guard made a grab for him, Sven clasped the man's shins and lifted him clean off the ground. The man was now travelling in the position traditionally occupied by a caber about to be tossed.

Chizzie watched in horror. *This isn't going to help Sven's job application*, he thought.

Surely to God, Sven wasn't going to toss the man? But, yes, up the man went, head over heels and clean through the air. By design or good fortune, the man landed feet first in the pile of sand and, looking as winded as his companion beside him, stared open-mouthed at Sven, who – seemingly pleased with his morning's work – waved an admonishing finger then strolled airily away, apparently with not a care in the world.

So much for the job application. Chizzie would have to break the news to his father, whose response could go either way.

Usually, when Chizzie felt hungry in the morning, he crossed the lawn between the house and the hotel kitchen, and helped himself to a full Scottish breakfast. On this occasion, however, he thought it better to breakfast in the house, with his father, and break the news of Sven's morning exertions before anyone else got in with a typically embroidered version of events. Never being entirely certain of his father's response to things, Chizzie went downstairs and entered the kitchen with a broad smile on his face that was designed to draw the heat out of any incandescence that might follow. But incandescence was already present and waiting for him. The moment Chizzie got through the door, Johnny jumped to his feet brandishing a copy of the local paper.

"*Look! Look at this! Numpties!*" he yelled, pointing to the front-page headline. "*Numpties! I'll bloody sue!*"

Chizzie took the paper while his father raged and paced up and down, shaking his head. Stretched across the front-page in big, bold capital letters was one word – that word was "NUMPTIES!" Below it were photographs of three faces – one was the planning committee's chairman, another was Robert Barrington and the third was none other than Johnny himself. The text was uncompromising – all three were idiots who would consign the region to ruin. Three numpties, pilloried for all to see.

"Hmm, that's not very complimentary," said Chizzie trying to achieve both consolation and condemnation.

The effect was lost on Johnny. *"Not complimentary?"* Johnny exploded, *"I'll bloody sue them! That's defamation, that is! They're the numpties!"*

Chizzie, suspecting that his father was walking right into the trap the headline had laid for him, tried desperately to find the right words. "Hmm," he hummed, "it could be considered fair comment – possibly. But, actually, if they're numpties and they're calling us numpties, then we're not numpties. Our people will know that, and so all the paper is doing is preaching to the converted, and it'll all blow over in a matter of days."

Johnny hesitated for a moment, then his eyes narrowed and his voice squeezed out the words, "I hope you're not thinking of going over to the other side."

Chizzie laughed, shook his head in mock disgust and handed back the paper, before helping himself to what was left in a pot of porridge. He scooped it up as rapidly as he could. He would come back and finish his breakfast when Johnny had left.

But it was too late. Johnny, gaping at the paper, let out a yell. *"Argh! Look at this! It's worse! The bastards! They've spelled my name wrong! They've put Byson – I'm Johnny Byson!"*

Chizzie tried to douse the new fury with casual sympathy. "That's the *Millburgh Express* for you," he said through a mouthful of porridge.

"The idiots! The morons!"

"Yep. Let them know that. Write a complaint, Father."

"I bloody well will. The bastards!"

Suddenly, realising what a bad move a letter from his irate father would be, Chizzie changed tack. "Come to think of it, though, you got off lightly," he said calmly. "Remember old Colin Pollock? They named him Bollock, then, by way of correction, he became a Pillock."

"I'll give them bloody Byson. I'm getting on the phone to them, the lazy ba—"

"Whoa there, Father!" Out of control beckoned. Chizzie rose quickly to his feet. "Whoa! Whoa there! We in the hotel-management profession do not express ourselves in such vulgar terms. We leave that kind of thing to plumbers and the like, do we not?" Previous experience had taught Chizzie that one thing to which his father was susceptible was fancy talk from his son. It seemed to confirm the value of his investment in the boy's education.

Johnny simmered down a little. "And look at that: they're quoting me without my permission," he complained peevishly. "They're taking absolute liberties, they are! I didn't say any of this stuff, and it goes on and on. Look! Look at it; you'd think I was a bloody politician. They should've cleared it with me first!"

"The *Millburgh Express*? Are you kidding? It's not called the 'County Coyote' for nothing."

"I'm trying to keep my business afloat, numpties kick me in the teeth, and the paper calls me a numpty and a bison!"

Chizzie saw his chance to consolidate Sven's employment prospects and said, "Actually, Sven has sorted them out for you. He's put one over on Weever today already."

Chizzie went on to recount what he had seen earlier, and Johnny calmed down and looked very pleased.

CHAPTER 5

Fairfoull put down the phone.

Weever chuckled. "So, Barrington's a frightened man, is he?"

"Indeed he is; he half expects a lynch mob to come and beat his door down any minute, he apologises for any hurt we may have suffered and wants us to guarantee his safety. He's already seen his newspaper mugshot nailed to a tree with the word 'Wanted' written on it."

"So, there's no need for persuasion?"

"Nope, he's very keen. One of the keenest I've ever seen. He's very keen for protection too, though. He asked for a bodyguard to be placed in the bushes at his home."

"And you didn't."

"Certainly not. I said we'd keep an eye on his place, which will be so discreet that he won't even know we're there."

"And we won't be."

"No, but he is considerably calmer now."

"It's amazing, the power of the press. Even a diddly squat little rag like the… the…"

"The *Millburgh Express.*"

"Even that can turn a man's head. And all for the promise of buying a couple of full-page ads."

"It's pitiful really."

"There's no room for pity. I want Barrington sown up and in our pay right away."

"We'll get him and we'll get him cheap. He's a big-hat man. Status counts more than money."

51

"So make him the manager of something."

"Anything in particular?"

"Who cares? Car tyres. Lizard control. Whatever."

"Accounts is his thing."

"Okay, give him a client account – a small one. For now, the key thing is—"

"He operates undercover."

"Exactly. And he's coming over straightaway?"

"He is. He can't wait."

"And we have leverage?"

"Oh yes. Digger's team have hit pay dirt. Not on Barrington himself, it's fair to say, but his uncles have some very useful form. Apparently, the Edinburgh police raided a brothel a few years back, and, lo and behold, Barrington's dear, old uncles were hiding on the premises. They were fined a few thou and given thirty days' community service. Also worth mentioning is the fact that the ladies were admonished and thanked for their cooperation."

"Sounds like they and the judge had a good thing going."

"It has been noted."

"Good."

Robert Barrington made it safely to Charlie Fairfoull's office without being noticed. Seemingly, out for a walk in a small wood, he – as instructed by Fairfoull – cut discreetly through a grove of trees to a hedge that ran up to the estate house. At the back porch, Fairfoull waited, reclining in a rocking chair and reading a newspaper while smoking a small cigar. On Barrington's arrival, Fairfoull escorted him to the office immediately.

Fairfoull's office was bigger than Barrington's – much bigger – and Barrington gazed round the room admiringly while Fairfoull fetched him a gin and tonic. He seemed to envision himself operating in similarly impressive surroundings once his employment with the Weever Organisation was up and running. There were no wall-to-wall box files here; on the contrary, there was ample room here for original artwork, and, even if the artwork was exclusively of golf courses owned by Weever, it was colourful, tasteful and refined. The appeal shone in Barrington's eyes. He lowered himself into a sumptuous, dark-brown leather chair, and exchanged pleasantries with Fairfoull.

Ten minutes later, Weever's personal assistant came through to invite the two of them into Weever's office suite. Both men gladly accepted the invitation and entered the office.

Rising from behind his huge walnut desk, Weever offered his hand. "Welcome, Mr Barrington; how are you?"

"It's a privilege and an honour to meet you, sir," responded Barrington.

"My pleasure," said Weever.

"May we call you Robert?" asked Fairfoull.

"Please do," he replied, with a slight shiver.

Weever pointed to a low-but-well-padded wooden chair in front of the desk, then he sat himself down in the throne-like leather chair behind the desk. Fairfoull sat to the side of Weever's desk in a well-upholstered office chair.

"Firstly, I'd like to congratulate you on an excellent speech the other day, Robert," said Weever smiling.

"Oh, thank you; thank you. I almost believed it myself!" exclaimed Barrington.

Weever laughed. "I particularly liked you quoting Abraham Lincoln. It's always good to get good old Abe on your side. Smart move."

"Thank you," Barrington replied.

"Now, time is pressing, so we'll get straight to the point, Robert. We'd like you to swing in behind us on the Tannadee project and, in return, we can offer you a vital role in the

Weever Organisation, a business with global reach that offers a world of opportunities."

Fairfoull broke in, "We see you starting with valued client accounts before assuming a managerial role within the Tannadee Leisure Resort. How's that sound?"

Barrington nodded thoughtfully. "What if the Tannadee project can't go ahead?"

Weever laughed. "Oh, it's going ahead, Robert. Be in no doubt. It's going ahead as we speak."

Barrington looked thoughtful again before bursting into a cheesy smile. "In that case, I'm only too pleased to say yes. It's an honour and a privilege, sir. Thank you; thank you."

"Excellent, Robert, welcome aboard." Without standing up, Weever reached across the desk and shook hands with the new employee.

"When do I start?" asked Barrington.

"Well, Robert," said Fairfoull, "we'd like you to start immediately – by keeping your appointment secret while you remain in your present post for the next couple of months or so. We want you to be seen opposing us continually. Secretly, though, you're passing information to us on any initiatives devised by our opponents."

"Oh… oh, I see – I'm to be a mole?" spluttered Barrington.

"Intelligence manager," insisted Fairfoull. "I'm sure that, with your business background, you'll appreciate the vital role intelligence plays in a modern global business. And think how useful a role in intelligence would look on your CV."

And, with that, Weever held up three sheets of A4 paper.

Barrington leaned forwards to get a better view. "Er… that says it's my CV, but I haven't given it to you yet."

"We obtained it," said Fairfoull.

"Uh. Oh. Gosh. Er... that's... that's rather alarming actually. Ugh, I don't know what to think. A mole, you say? Hmm, that's risky, very risky. Really, I have to say that I just wouldn't be comfortable with that; not at all, in fact."

"It's a risk to a certain extent," admitted Fairfoull, "but it's more than matched by the risk we would be taking. Imagine what our detractors could do with your uncles' indiscretions."

"Eh? Uh. What... what do you mean?"

"Your dear uncle Selwyn – I have a copy of a newspaper article here; let me quote, 'Edinburgh police raided the brothel and discovered Selwyn Barrington MP hiding in an old wardrobe.'"

"Ugh... oh... ah... er... yes, he was in therapy."

"He was in the wardrobe," continued Fairfoull reading aloud. "'Dressed as a bare-buttocked Apache, Barrington – known on the premises as Geronimo – was discovered sharing the wardrobe with a middle-aged lady wearing nothing but a coonskin cap, and clutching a rolled-up copy of the *Daily Telegraph Weekend Supplement*. Before passing out, she confided the amount of torture the man could take was quite astonishing.'"

"Well... hmm, it was just like a sauna really," pleaded Barrington.

"Then there's your uncle Eric, known on the same premises as Colonel Mustard, who was found chained to the wall wearing rubber tights, a corset, a leather mask and a python round his waist—"

"Yes, yes, well, all right. But... but... you can't visit the sins of the uncle on the nephew. You... you—" spluttered Barrington.

"That's true, Robert, true. But, equally, we can't ignore the gene pool and what's swimming in it. You appreciate we're only as good as our people, and we have to be very, very careful about whom we recruit. As things stand, we have nothing to fear… nothing at all… or not until now. But, in your case, we are prepared to take the risk. If, however, you feel the role is beyond you, we'll find someone else – someone who will rise to the challenge."

Barrington looked perplexed and shifted in his chair. "Ah… ah well," he began, "Well… er… yes, fine, yes, I'll do it. I'll do it."

"Excellent!" Weever purred and shot his hand across the desk to cement the deal. "Now Charlie will take you to his office, go through the contract with you and deal with any questions."

A quarter of an hour later, with a farewell gin and tonic taken to set him on his hedgerow path, Barrington left the estate house. Weever and Fairfoull watched him go.

"One numpty down, two to go," said Weever.

"Two down, and one to go," replied Fairfoull, "I've just learned that the chairman of the planning committee has resigned."

"Hah! Oh dear. That is sad. Nothing to do with our friendly councillors, I hope?" Weever asked, laughing.

"Perhaps there was a little bit of pressure here and there."

"Have they had their gifts?"

"Gifts, Mr Weever? Whatever can you mean? Are you referring to expenses?"

Both men laughed heartily.

"Expenses indeed, Mr Fairfoull," said Weever, wryly.

"I'll meet them separately at a hotel in Edinburgh next week, when things are more settled," continued Fairfoull.

"Good, good; keep them warm. We might need them yet. I want that little, red-faced bison rubbed out. I can't stand him or his crummy hotel. See to him, Charlie."

"He'll need careful handling; he's a big fish in his little pond."

"Tempted as I am to kick his ass, I'll give him one last chance. Sound him out and see how much he wants for his little dump. I want that thing flattened and out of sight of my golf course. Either that or I turn it into a castle. I can't decide. What d'you think?"

"Well, it is a listed building – it'd be hard to get planning consent. Not that it's going to stop you."

"It's never stopped me in the past."

"The only fly in the ointment is the bison himself – he seems rather attached to his little hotel."

"Fine. If he stays attached, he can go under with it. I want that ugliness out of my eyeline. We offer them a fair price and they go; that's the future."

"It might not be quite that simple, Gordon. It might be that he's smarter than we think."

"No, no. He's not smart, Charlie. We just relax and let the mob do its stuff. Then we take what we want. They won't stop us. They need the jobs; I don't. I don't need anything from them."

Fairfoull laughed. "Oh, but you do, Gordon. You do. Enough is never enough for you. You're a megalomaniac."

Weever looked hard at Fairfoull, then, gradually, his cheeks crinkled and he burst out laughing.

Fairfoull joined him. "You need it as much as they do!"

"Much more!" Weever replied, almost snorting with delight.

"Megalomaniacs Anonymous! That's where you belong."

Weever wiped the tears from his eyes and sighed heavily. "What a club that would be, eh? Nobody gets mega without being great – that's what 'mega' means, right? The

Mega Club: the most exclusive club in the world. Only for the great people."

"What about the 'maniac' bit, though? Megalomaniac. You want to be with maniacs?"

"What's a maniac, Charlie, eh? He's a guy out of the ordinary, right?"

"Yeah, so far out he's nuts."

"You can't be nuts and successful, Charlie. Not in the long run. All the megas are successful, exceptional people."

"And some are nasty."

"Not to me, they ain't. Yes, call me megalomaniac; I'm proud of that. I'm the best there is."

"A mega claim, to be sure."

"It's the truth, Charlie boy! People say I'm a big mouth. They say I'm a pompous ass. But what I really am is honest. I tell it straight. People don't like that – the truth hurts. I've worked hard. I've used my God-given talents to the full. I'm successful. I don't apologise for that. I don't hide. What do they want? I'm to be humble? A shadow? A guy like me? I'd go nuts. I employ thousands of people – that's livelihoods – thousands of them. You think that's easy? I tell you, night after night, I've gone without sleep. There were times when I just wanted to crawl away and be ordinary. But families – men, women and all their kids – all needed me to put food on their tables. I had to deliver. And you know what saw me through? My vicious streak. Right back to cannibal, I went. Back through evolution to the most basic, basic instinct – the refusal to die, no matter what. The more death wanted me, the more I fought it. I wasn't going down. No way was I going down! You name it, I fought it. Sheer cussedness. Have you ever seen a dogfight? That's what it's like. You're so busy fightin' you feel nothing – no pain, nothing. You get tough as hell. And that's what I am today: cussed and tough. They can jeer all they want, but I don't give a shit, cos I make things happen and they don't. Without me, there is no merry-go-round. I am the centre. I am the sun. I am brilliant. And that's not pompous; that's real. It's in my DNA."

"It must be, and not only *your* DNA: you're not the only billionaire with Scottish heritage, a beautiful daughter, and a new golf course."

"Hah! Sure, sure, there's other megas out there doing great things, but even they are looking to me to light their way."

With that Fairfoull stared for a moment, then smiled, and withdrew.

CHAPTER 6

Three days later, the *Millburgh Express* announced gleefully that an emergency planning meeting would be convened the following week by the full district council, explaining that such a major development was a matter relating to the regional strategic plan and therefore too important for a local planning committee.

The opponents of Weever's plan met at the Tannadee Hotel, with Barrington in the chair. Suggestions for action were raised. Barrington suggested writing to the *Millburgh Express* to demand that their side of the story be heard.

But Johnny was quick to reject the idea. "You know what they'll do, don't you? They'll mangle our words to make us look like idiots. We need national coverage."

"We'll never get that," insisted Barrington.

"We will if we mount a public protest: a demonstration outside the council headquarters before the meeting," insisted Johnny."

"That would make us look worse than ever," replied Barrington. "We'd look like a rabble. I don't want to be a part of any rabble. It's exactly what we're fighting against."

"We need to do something."

"A small, civilised protest through handing in a petition – that's what we want," advised Barrington. "I can get all the stuff – the boards, etc. – and I'll organise the petition, if I can get some volunteers to help. And, by the way, I regret to say that I won't be able to attend the protest myself, as I have important business elsewhere that day."

On Monday, the day of the full council meeting, Chizzie got up early, hitched the trailer to his old Volvo, and drove it round to Barrington's house to pick up the boards and the petition. What he got was a surprise.

"No boards? No petition?" Chizzie asked, looking bewildered.

"I've been badly let down," Barrington explained. "It's not my fault. Their ears are ringing, I can tell you. I gave them a tirade, but the fact is that we've no boards. We'll just have to do without."

"The petition – how can you have lost the petition?"

"I wanted it to be absolutely safe, so I put it away very securely, so securely that I can't remember now where I put it! I've hunted high and low – absolutely everywhere."

"Well, it has to be somewhere; think, man, think. Cast your mind back to last night. What did you have for dinner?"

"You know, I can't remember – my mind's gone completely blank after all this searching. I feel confused; I can't think anymore."

Chizzie had to admit defeat and go on to the hotel with neither boards nor petition.

The news of Barrington's blunders was not received well at the Tannadee Hotel. Johnny, flabbergasted, dropped heavily into his plush office chair, which sighed as he did. "What a complete and utter balloon!" he exclaimed. "He's a total idiot! He might be a good public speaker, but – God Almighty – as an organiser, he's useless; he couldn't organise a fart in a bean factory!"

"Well, it's partly our fault, perhaps," Chizzie said thoughtfully, "We should've had contingency plans."

Johnny sighed heavily again and rubbed his chin. "You know, Barrington's so damn conceited that I actually wouldn't put it past him to have made all this up, purely because he won't be at the protest to shine with his fancy words. There's to be no limelight without him."

"He's conceited all right and sometimes unpleasant, that's fair to say, but even he wouldn't put his own ego above our protest. No way. He wants Weever out just as much as we do and he needs us."

"Well, what do we do now?"

"There's only one thing for it: we get hold of big cardboard boxes, some wood and some old sheets. It won't look too great, but it'll do the job. The homespun look might even have a bigger impact. Who knows?"

As Chizzie and Johnny waited anxiously outside the Tannadee Hotel, the small band of protesters gathered together, looking thoroughly demoralised at the sight of their weapons: six bits of cardboard hewn from boxes, with rough-looking slogans written across them in felt tip, and four improvised banners with even rougher-looking slogans. The light drizzle dampened their spirits further. Was it worth continuing on such a dismal morning with such desperately poor equipment? By a majority of two, they decided it was worth it.

So off they went in four cars. Chizzie took the most enthusiastic-looking ones: Dekker the chip-shop owner, Jessie Taylor, her son Jamie, and their fox terrier, Sparky. To Chizzie's mind, this was the A-team: Dekker was a big, paunchy man with a figure that got noticed, albeit he was slightly musty from the odour of spent chip fat – an odour that Chizzie hoped would have the decency not to cling onto his car upholstery. Jessie Taylor, though small, was a formidable, old-fashioned B&B landlady, who would happily bend the ear of any politician. Her student son, Jamie, brought his guitar and a song freshly penned for the occasion.

Throughout the journey, Sparky Taylor's wagging tail and seemingly irrepressible enthusiasm kept Chizzie's spirits from flagging.

When they reached the car park outside the council offices, Chizzie issued the boards and banners, while Jamie tuned his guitar. Then – with Jessie leading and Johnny bringing up the rear uncharacteristically, as this was really not his thing – the band of militants made its way up to the main door of the building, where they were surprised to find not a single news reporter.

"Where's the media?" Johnny whined as everyone's eyes scanned up and down the pavement. "We've been got at. The big money's put the lid on us."

"Maybe Barrington just forgot to tell them," Chizzie suggested.

Johnny shook his head and clenched his fists. "Not another of his bloody cock-ups!"

Jessie Taylor was undaunted: "All the more reason for us to let the councillors have it when they come," she observed.

As some councillors began to arrive, the protesters went into action. Only Jessie recognised them. She raised her board above her head, and the others followed suit. Jamie struck up his guitar to let rip with his adaptation of a traditional song:

If it wisnae for the Weever, what would we dae?
We would get a livin' in the good ol' country way,
We dinnae need the likes o' Mr Weever…

For the unfortunate councillors, there was no escape; Jamie's nasal baritone rent the air all around them. And, as if that wasn't enough, Jessie joined in the chorus, followed by others. Chizzie got into the swing of things too, literally, swinging his head from side to side and singing heartily. Johnny tried to hide behind his board; with a bit of luck, none of these councillors were on the licensing committee.

When the councillors disappeared into the building, Chizzie stopped performing and got his breath back, as did Jamie; both looked very pleased with themselves, as the councillors had rushed away, so the protest might well have had some impact. Even Johnny seemed a little brighter now.

Then reinforcements arrived, or – more exactly – one reinforcement arrived. It was Sven, and he was clearly delighted to see his friends. But the delight was not mutually held: his friends remembered his boozy antics only too well and greeted him with a muted welcome. Chizzie, though – on seeing the tousled, fallen strongman who'd once given Tannadee something to be proud of – felt a pang of compassion and walked forwards to greet the man. Even at arm's length, he could smell the booze.

Sven explained airily how he'd been meditating on a park bench nearby when he'd heard the singing, and, being one who'd never lose an opportunity to brighten the day with a jolly sing-song, he'd rushed over to join them. He wondered what it was all about.

To avoid overtaxing Sven's addled brain, Chizzie simply told him to sing along when he felt up to it.

It was a mistake: the next batch of councillors got more than just a song, they got a jig – a rather unsteady one – from the swaying Sven, who carried on dancing even after the councillors had gone. Fearing that enthusiasm might spill over into public nuisance, Johnny had a quiet word with the dancing Dane, who reacted loudly with a big belly laugh. Then Sparky weighed in with a growl and loud barking, which seemed to addle Sven's brain even further. He stopped dancing, ran his fingers through his hair for a second or two, then he bolted away suddenly and ran into the middle of the road where, legs akimbo and arms waving in the air, he brought a double-decker bus to a halt.

The bus driver hit the brakes sharply, and the bus screeched to a halt, inches away from Sven. The driver jumped out, seething and demanding to know what the hell was going on. But Sven was so far away in his own little world that he made no reply and took up drumming his big hands on the front of the bus.

Mortified, Chizzie and Dekker ran over to Sven and attempted to pull him away, but, feinting left before springing to the right, he dodged them both and took off again, running straight across the road before swinging open a gate and running into the garden of a bungalow.

Desperate to get hold of Sven, Chizzie and Dekker ran after him. For a moment, it looked like the big Dane was trapped, surrounded by the garden hedge, but he turned quickly and, taking a run at the hedge, scrambled clean over it into the neighbouring garden.

This took Dekker out of the chase, years of chip eating, night after night, precluded any thought of clearing a hedge, but Chizzie dashed out of the gate and into the neighbouring garden.

Sven saw him and was off again, over the next hedge and across the lawn. It was now looking more like the Grand National than a manhunt, and it was clear that further pursuit would only do more harm than good, so Chizzie abandoned the chase and simply watched as Sven, vaulting over hedge after hedge, got clean away. Despite all his booze, the man seemed in very good physical shape.

Chizzie returned to the protest, where he found it was all over, and Johnny was trying to persuade the protesters to pack up and go home before they fell victim to other drunks. However, a final group of councillors arrived, and actually stopped and gazed at the bedraggled band before smiling and turning away. Now it really was all over.

The bedraggled band gathered up its things and made its way home in almost complete silence. It didn't even bother to find out what was happening in the council chambers. They knew they were now a disorderly pariah. Even the dog looked glum.

Later, as they watched the local evening news on TV, it came as no surprise to Chizzie and Johnny that Weever's plans were approved by a large majority. Though there was some relief to be had, for – despite some people snapping pictures of Sven as he held up the bus – there was no mention of it in the local news item covering the council's decision.

There was simply an interview with the leader of the council who explained that, "It is our policy to prioritise investment that meets the wider strategic objectives of the council."

"What's that gobbledegook mean?" asked Johnny.

"Jobs," replied Chizzie. "The councillors bring in more jobs, then they get more votes and they get more power."

"What about our jobs?"

"We bow to the greater good."

"What? I bow to no man. And just how great do you have to be? There's a load of good people out there in Tannadee; don't they count?"

"We've got to stop this guy Weever."

"Not just Weever – the council, the press and some of the good people. That's who we're up against. And if we're not smart, we'll be up against the Government as well. If the big get bigger, the small get smaller. Then we disappear under their feet. Barrington was right – I don't like the man, he's far too cocky – but even he sees the danger. Small doesn't have to mean small-minded. We welcome the right people."

"But Weever isn't the right people – he'll destroy us."

To Weever, the news brought an unusual calmness as he sipped champagne in his large sitting room. Particularly pleasing was the news that many of the councillors virtually had begged for his plans to be approved – begged and pleaded, just like Weever had intended. Mulling things over, he appeared quietly satisfied – until he spoke.

As if addressing a large audience, he angled his head upwards and declared aloud, "Well, thank you, ladies and gentlemen of the council; thank you most kindly. Most sincerely, I thank you, but, actually, it's not quite that simple now. You see, you're gonna get what's good for you now. You're gonna get hit clean out of the ground. Yessir." Then, turning to the only other person in the room, he asked tersely, "Ready to rock, Charlie boy?"

"Ready to rock! You betcha!" replied the good and faithful servant.

Neither man laughed – they were too serious for that now – but they smiled, with smiles intense and full of intent.

"We've got to get the assholes outta the picture first, especially that red-faced dwarf with the horrible hotel! I don't want him anywhere near me! Nowhere near, you hear? He's had his chance."

CHAPTER 7

The next morning saw the red-faced dwarf in his horrible hotel, sitting in his office, only his face was not so red and his hotel was not horrible. On reading the local newspaper, he found it wonderfully free of any reference to the abortive protest. He lay back with a grin, savouring his luck for a few moments. Not many people were as fortunate as he, and he knew it: he was his own boss, he was in his own office and he was surrounded by things he personally had chosen, though few people shared Johnny's taste – opinion ranged from faint praise to downright mockery, behind his back. The kindest thing ever said was that it was cosmopolitan. Less charitably, one observer described it as a conglomeration of styles gathered at random from the floors of county auction rooms when taste was out having its lunch. The prevailing theme was arguably brawn. There was a big, solid oak desk on a red carpet, surrounded by magnolia walls. Dark paintings of Highland scenes hung side by side with sepia 'family' photographs, which bore little if any familial resemblance to Johnny. The tops of the filing cabinets were home to a variety of antique figurines, some tasteful, some not so – like the big, porcelain cabbage with a smiling slug peeping out. Unloved as they were by many, these things brought comfort and joy to the fiery, little man who loved them.

However, this morning, apart from the relief of avoiding public humiliation, there was little comfort and joy to be had in the office. Weever had thrown all the punches, and no doubt more were on the way.

Also coming Johnny's way was Chizzie. He brought news that he knew would require a little tact. "Sven's at the back door asking to take up your offer of a job," Chizzie announced pleasantly.

Johnny jolted. "Job? Doing what? Leading the local foxhunt?"

"There is no local foxhunt – not after their grand master, or whatever they call him, went to prison."

"I can't give him a job – not after that insane display in Millburgh. I can't let that loose on our guests! What if he starts leaping over our hedges?"

"You promised him a job. You can't go back on that, Dad."

"It's Father! I'm your father, dammit!"

"You can't go back on it, Father."

"Oh yes, I can."

"No. No. No way. Paw Baxter has offered Sven accommodation on his croft if he gets a job and gives up the booze. Sven's promised me no more booze come hell or high water, and I believe him. He can help in the garden. You owe it to him. We all do. When he was doing well, we basked in his glory. Now, when he needs us, are we going to turn our backs on him? Give him this chance… please, Father. I'll take full responsibility."

"You're not here all the time. What happens when you're teaching?"

"I place him in the hands of the caring father who made me what I am today – and who makes me so proud to be his son." He knew the remark would meet with a mixture of cynicism and flattery, but he was banking on the latter getting top spot.

Johnny eyed him with raised eyebrows, then looked away. Staring at the far wall, he replied, "You keep him sober, you get him washed and you get rid of his bloody ponytail."

"Thank you, Father. You won't regret it. Oh, I nearly forgot – as luck would have it, there's a party of Danes coming in for an early lunch. They're on Rob McLean's wildlife photography course and they heard about our ospreys."

"Excellent."

"They want to see an osprey catch a fish."

"What? Like we're supposed to phone osprey headquarters and book a swoop?"

"Well, if they get what they want, they might recommend us. I thought Sven could welcome them in Danish and make them feel at home."

"I don't want Sven anywhere near them; he could be all the wildlife they can handle. I'd be worried enough with him talking English, never mind a language I can't understand. Actually, I've had a thought about the ospreys. How about we put some fish out on the loch and attract the ospreys in. See what's in the cold store, then run round to the fish shop – we need whole specimens, a dozen or so."

"Are you serious?"

He was. "Let me know when the Danes arrive. I want to welcome them personally; this could be a great opportunity."

Selecting whole fish for diners was something Chizzie had done occasionally, but selecting fish for ospreys was very new. In fact, selecting was hardly the word, for the cold store yielded nothing and the local fishmonger could offer only two whole herring, one whole mackerel and one whole haddock.

Armed with these, Chizzie set out in the hotel's dinghy, and – though tempted to use full throttle on the outboard motor to get the thing over and done with – he kept the speed down to a modest level in the hope of attracting little attention. He headed for the roadside viewing area that was the most likely to be used by the Danish photographers, but he kept well away from shore to avoid the Danes getting an eyeful of dead fish in their binoculars. He scanned the sky; there were no ospreys, but, just as importantly, no people and no gulls. He slipped the fish carefully into the water and headed back to shore.

Skimming over the water, the wind cooled his cheeks, and as the cold sank into him, his spirits sank too. In the shadow of a cloud, the hotel, as seen in the near distance, looked like a tomb. How could he possibly spend his entire life there? There in the contrived world of hospitality where you were professionally jolly; where customers were called guests – guests whom you sued if they didn't pay up; where you toed a fine line between servility and authority; and where you set out fish on a loch to haul in punters. In his earlier life, Chizzie had thought to become a zookeeper, but, right now, that ambition seemed all but fulfilled – hospitality and zookeeping seemed awfully, awfully similar.

Chizzie docked the boat and got out, and as he walked up the drive and approached the hotel, he saw Johnny taking in the view from the hotel steps while smoking one of his occasional cigars. A small coach was parked in front of him.

Chizzie's heart sank. "The Danes aren't here, are they?" he cried.

"No, no, no; you're safe enough. Did you get the fish out all right?" asked Johnny.

"Yes. Let's just hope the birds don't drop anything. If word gets round that there's haddock, herring and mackerel living in a freshwater loch, the press and half the scientific world'll be all over us."

"That might be a good thing. Think of the occupancy rates."

"Where's Sven? Have you seen him?"

"No, ask Dougie; he's over there."

Chizzie shouted across to Dougie, who was edging the lawn.

"Roddie's strained his shoulder," Dougie replied, "so he asked if Sven could carry the luggage upstairs for him. Billy went too."

"Aw, God, no, no!" wailed Johnny, "Sven shouldn't be anywhere near guests."

"He'll be all right, Father, don't panic. I'll go and see."

Johnny stubbed out his cigar on the wall. "I'm coming too."

*

When they reached the west stairwell, Chizzie called up to the first floor, "Sven! Sven! Are you there?"

"Up here, Chizzie!" Sven replied.

Johnny looked stung. "Why is he calling you Chizzie?"

"I told him to," Chizzie replied matter-of-factly.

"*Come quickly!*" yelled Sven, "*You must see this!*"

Chizzie ran up the stairs, followed more slowly by Johnny. Sven was excited. "Wait till you see this!" he chirped. Then, through cupped hands, he shouted to the other end of the corridor, "Okay, people, bring it on! Bring it on!"

There was no response.

A few seconds passed. Sven rubbed his hands nervously and made as if to peer round the far corner. Then a smile broke across his face as a shuffling sound issued from the far end. "Wait till you see this," he said smiling, his eyes wide.

They watched intently as something resembling a heap of luggage emerged. It rounded the corner at the far end and made its way slowly along the corridor towards them. Behind the heap, Chizzie could discern a couple of heads bobbing about. Then a head became visible atop the heap of luggage – it was Billy Pung's head. The heaving heap of luggage was actually Billy Pung – the schoolboy on work placement!

Johnny's jaw dropped. Then, growling like a dog, he hurried to meet the lumbering heap head on before bawling at it to stop.

For a moment, Billy froze, then he began lowering all the luggage carefully, piece by piece, onto the floor. Though not tall, the young man was broad-shouldered and strongly built, and seemed in no discomfort.

However, Johnny was seething; he counted eleven bags, then turned to Sven. "*What the hell is going on here?*" he roared.

It was a meltdown or so it looked for Sven, who smiled nervously and said, "Well, Mr Bryson, you see, you have just seen the Tannadee Hotel make a new record for carrying luggage from one floor to another floor! Amazing, yeah?" Then, seemingly overwhelmed by nerves, instinctively, he clapped his hands and burst out laughing.

Another head burst out laughing: an older one, behind Billy. This head belonged to the regular porter, old Roddie Pratley, a man whose dry cackle rumbled like a cement mixer.

But Johnny was not laughing. Though more than a foot smaller than Sven, he bristled at him, asking, "Are you insane?"

Chizzie intervened and put a placating hand on Johnny's shoulder. "It's only a bit of fun, Father – just a bit of fun."

Sven agreed nervously, "Yes, a bit of fun, Mr Bryson; that's all. Yes, 'Eleven Bags Bill' we have here, a legend in his own lifetime! Eleven bags he was taking, along the ground floor, up the stairs, then along here. I'm phoning the *Guinness Book of Records!*"

Johnny was dumbstruck for a moment, then he exploded. "*You're phoning nobody, lad!* Eleven Bags Bill? He's a school lad; he's not here to be a laughing stock or a beast of burden!"

The laughing ceased abruptly. Sven looked stunned. He jerked his head and blinked several times.

Chizzie didn't quite know who was right and who was wrong. The old porter, also seemingly at a loss, muttered something before looking away, like he'd never been any part of it.

Billy, however, was as furious as Johnny. "I'm not a beast of burden! No way!" he shouted at Johnny. "And I can do this, no bother! I can do all these bags and the porter too! Look!" and, with that, he grabbed the unsuspecting porter by his shirt front and slung the poor devil onto his left shoulder like a kitbag. Then, with the porter spluttering and yelling to be put down, Billy gathered up all the luggage bags and moved off, with two bags perched flat on his head; one on each shoulder, porter or no porter; two bags held in each hand; one balanced on each foot; and one held by a handle in his mouth. "See, easy! No problem!" he sort of called out, muffled by the bags and the fading appeals of the porter in transit.

Johnny turned to Chizzie and stated, "Get after him and tell him to stop."

Chizzie, slightly confused but inspired by Billy's can-do attitude, simply smiled and shrugged.

Johnny shook his head and blew through his cheeks like a boiler valve about to burst. "*Right, out of the way!*" he yelled and thundered after Billy. He overtook him and swung round in front of him. As he helped the porter off Billy's shoulder, he commanded, "Put the bags down, Billy! Put them down! Now!"

Billy, silently and reluctantly, did as he was told.

Johnny then turned and, wagging his finger, bawled at Sven, "*Never ever do a thing like that again! No more stunts! Understand? Never ever! No more!*"

"It was just a bit of fun, Father; that's all," Chizzie pleaded.

"Fun? What fun? He's made a fool of you and me, and a fool of Billy there!"

At that, Billy flapped his arms and yelled at Johnny, "*It was my idea! I'm not a fool and I'm not a beast!*" Then, he turned and ran off along the corridor and disappeared down the stairs.

The others watched in silence; it wasn't every day that someone shouted at Johnny.

But Billy was Chizzie's main concern. He rushed along the corridor, calling out Billy's name; however, by the time he had reached the bottom of the stairs, Billy was disappearing down the drive. He was the fastest runner Tannadee had ever seen, so there was no point in chasing him. Chizzie watched him go.

"See. See what comes of your nonsense," Johnny called as he stepped off the bottom stair and pointed towards the door.

But Chizzie was outraged. "He was happy, Dad. He was doing something really well. He was confident. He was having a great time. I've never seen him so happy. So what if it was unusual?"

"Happy? That's not happy! How can that be happy? He's run off!"

"Only after you upset him. You need to be careful with him. Jim thinks he's on the autistic spectrum somewhere, despite what the experts say. And I agree with Jim. You have to be careful with Billy."

"Well, he'd better come back pronto or he's fired. I can't run a hotel with runaways."

"You know what he's like. He could be gone for days."

"Well, you should've thought of that before you dropped him in it. You'll need to tell Jim. He'll have your guts for garters now, and rightly so."

Sven stepped forwards. "I resign. I'm the one. I'm to blame."

"Okay, fair enough," agreed Johnny.

Chizzie made to halt Sven. "No, no, Sven, you stay. We're all to blame. We need you here. You stay."

"No, it's me. I'm to blame. I go."

Johnny nodded. "I'll get your pay made up and you can collect it tomorrow."

And, with that, Sven strode towards the door.

Chizzie called after him, but Sven took no notice.

"There's a minibus drawing up," the porter announced.

Johnny crossed quickly to the door and looked out.

"It's Rob McLean and his Danish photographers," confirmed Chizzie.

"Oh my God!" yelped Johnny, "Don't let Sven near them; he can't have a word with them!"

"It's too late; he's spoken to them," observed the porter.

"What'd he say?" demanded Johnny.

"I don't know; it was only a word," the porter replied.

"Bloody hell! If he's spiked them…" began Johnny.

Chizzie shook his head. "Father, you're paranoid."

"Is it any wonder?" Johnny queried. "I'm being attacked on all sides. Weever's out there, Sven's in here and Billy's out there – God knows where! There's—"

"They're happy!" the porter announced suddenly.

Johnny turned on him with a glare. "Who? Who's bloody happy?"

"Your Danish folk. Look, they're smiling," declared the porter.

Johnny spun round to face the doorway. "What? Yes. They are! They're smiling! Christ Almighty, happy people – it's a miracle!" He pulled a big, professional smile, then turned to Chizzie and said, "I'll deal with this. You get Billy sorted out."

Chizzie went to the rear of the hotel and sat down on the bench beside the kitchen garden. Should he see Jim in person or phone him immediately? Phoning seemed a bit cowardly, but speed was important. He steeled himself and rang Jim's number.

As headmaster at Tannadee School, Jim Ferguson was responsible for Billy's work placement at the hotel and he knew Billy better than anyone apart from the lad's grandad. Billy had a long history of running off and disappearing for days, but things had improved greatly in the past six months, thanks largely to the efforts of Jim and Chizzie, who appeared to have gained the lad's confidence.

No one really knew where Billy came from. At the age of around four, he was found in the woods one day by a rambler. But no one ever claimed him. At first, all he said was "Pung!" Hence his name – Billy Pung. Later, Billy claimed to have been raised by foxes, though sometimes it was badgers. Unclaimed and seemingly unloved, he was fostered at first and then adopted by a local shepherd and his wife, whom he called Paw and Granny. Though raising Billy proved a difficult charge, Paw and Granny stuck to it, and – despite Billy's frequent walkabouts and odd habits – the lad grew up law-abiding if not very sociable.

When Granny had died a year ago, it was decided – with Billy's agreement – that it was best for him to board at the school for a while, so he could learn to make friends. The initiative had been partially successful, insofar as Billy hadn't run off for nearly six months. But now that had changed.

For nine nervous seconds Chizzie waited, then he heard Jim's voice. Jim, as usual, took the news calmly, much to Chizzie's relief. After being on the wrong end of his father's ire yet again, it was good to know that placid people like Jim really did exist. It gave him the confidence to tell the whole story about 'Eleven Bags Bill'. They agreed that it had not been a good idea and that Chizzie needed to go looking for Billy right away.

"Dennan Hill is the most likely place," said Jim. "I know he likes it up there. So take yourself up. If you're anywhere near surefooted, a couple of hours should just about be enough."

"Two hours? That's hardly enough time to scour the woods, let alone the moor – a proper search would take at least three hours, including the getting up and getting down," explained Chizzie.

"Chizzie, you won't actually be doing the looking. If Billy is up on Dennan Hill, you will not be the hunter – you will be the hunted. If Billy wants to meet you, he will; if not, give it two hours then come away. Take your mobile phone and don't go falling into peat bogs, you might scare him off. Now, I'd wish you good luck, only it's really not up to you, so just tread carefully and don't look shifty."

After a bit of rummaging, Chizzie found his hillwalking gear, rubbed some waterproofing into his creaking boots, then set off for Dennan Hill to present himself as bait for the 'wild boy', Billy Pung.

Entering the woods that clung to the top of the hill, with his daysack on his back and his boots crackling over fallen twigs, Chizzie found his spirits lifting surprisingly quickly. The air was so fresh that it smelled like it had been scrubbed clean – it was a world away from the stuffiness of hotel rooms down below. Hauling in deep draughts of the pristine air, he felt liberated and free to look about, but that was exactly what he mustn't do. He must train his mind on the primroses, the bluebells, the festooning lichens, the ants and the wood-lice – anything but Billy Pung.

An hour later, he was finding the life of the amateur naturalist surprisingly agreeable. The heavy rain overnight had released the mossy fragrances of the pinewood, and, like a salving elixir, it soothed his body, and seemed to tone his system and give him strength. His mind couldn't rest, though; it was insisting that he find the lad, and no amount of eyeballing bluebells and acquainting himself with ants' nests would exorcise his overpowering feeling of guilt.

Hoping that bodily joy would soon have an easing effect on his mind, Chizzie ventured deeper into the woods. However, after nearly an hour, it seemed things were simply getting worse. It struck him that there was more than just guilt here. The strange feeling of an eye forever on him, always watching him, preyed on his mind. Was it the ants? The buzzards? The pine martens? Or was it the feral boy himself? Deep-down, he knew the answer actually lay in his own head – the eye was only in his mind. He recalled the famous words of Franklin D Roosevelt: "Nothing to fear but fear itself." Certainly, if he was feeling uneasy because he was being watched by ants, it was time to be getting clean out of there.

He glanced at his watch: it was two-ten. He weighed his options. Then, rubbing his chin, he resolved to carry on a bit longer.

Twenty minutes later, he no longer felt he was being watched. Now, he was being stalked. Not far away, a predator was lurking and it was casting its eyes over him. For the sake of his sanity, he took a look around. But, far from helping, the look around proved unnerving. Everything was so very silent: nothing stirred. He took another look. Again, there was nothing; nothing but the trees and the penetrating eyes he could not see. Then the wind blew up very suddenly and branches began to sway. Sunbeams and shadows began to play like piano keys on the forest floor. The wind grew stronger; the dry rustling of leaves in the high branches increased to a loud hiss, like the sound of a waterfall; and then the rain started to fall. It was time to go.

He had felt a presence, but there was no sign of Billy, and now it was one of those situations when no sane person would even think about wandering in the hills. He took a final look round and saw that, in the growing mistiness, everything was merging into one grey mass. It was definitely time to go.

He turned, took a few steps, and then something touched his shoulder. The jolt nearly shot his limbs off. Gasping and wheeling round, he saw right next to him the feral boy – Billy Pung. Rocked by the sudden manifestation, Chizzie stumbled backwards. Even half-knowing what to expect was no proof against shock. The lad looked almost unhuman – his wavy, brown hair was matted and hanging over his eyes; his fuzzy, broad face was dusty; and his dark anorak and jeans were smeared with mud and stains. He smelled faintly of compost, but – amazingly – he was smiling, with his big, square teeth glistening like ivory in the rain.

"Billy!" yelped Chizzie, wide-eyed and sizing up all five feet six inches of the stocky lad.

Billy laughed. "Yeah! Me!" he answered, mockingly, waving his arms in the air. "You found me. Now what?"

Chizzie had prepared for this moment; he had an elaborate apology ready, but right now he couldn't think of it. It was gone, completely gone. His subconscious, it seemed, had never really entertained the idea of actually meeting Billy on the hill and had consigned the little speech to the wind. "How... how are you?" he blurted.

"I'm fine; I'm good. An' you?"

"I'm good, too. Yes." Chizzie replied, stilted and breathless.

"You don't look good. You look cold. We'd better get movin' 'fore you freeze."

Chizzie nodded. "Yes," he muttered. It was the best he could muster as he racked his brain for that elusive little speech, the one that would mean a lot to Billy.

"It sure is great up here, isn't it?" Billy observed, casually waving his hand across the misty view of the hills and glen. "No humans – 'ceptin' you. The middle of the night's the best time, though – there's no humans nowhere."

Billy Pung had long professed a deep dislike of human beings and often regarded himself as some kind of non-human.

"I'm very honoured that you met me up here, Billy. Very honoured indeed. And I thank you for that," explained Chizzie.

"That's okay," Billy said coyly.

"My dad apologises for the misunderstanding."

"He called me a beast."

"No. 'Beast of burden' is what he said; it's an expression that means someone being put upon. He thought you were being bullied. He meant well. So, if you want to come back tomorrow, we'd be delighted to see you again."

"Is Sven okay?"

"Sven's fine, but he's taking time out to clear his head at the moment. He'll be back soon, though," Chizzie said with a degree of confidence that surprised himself. He was very comfortable with the little white lies, since they seemed more beneficial than the truth, and they were arguably educated guesses – a bit like the weather forecasts. Moreover, this wasn't

81

a scientific debate or a court of law; this was one human being helping another on the road to a better life, and that road is rarely straight.

"Yeah, okay. Yeah, I'm back," replied Billy with a smile.

Chizzie returned the smile and placed a hand on Billy's shoulder. "Good; excellent. Are you ready to go now?"

Suddenly, Billy looked over Chizzie's shoulder and whispered tersely, "Somebody's comin'! A woman!"

Chizzie turned to look, peering into the misty sun, but he couldn't see anything or hear anything. He turned back to Billy, but Billy was gone. And, for a moment, there was just a pure eerie silence. Chizzie looked around again. Then, out of the gloom, a young woman appeared. She was running towards him, wearing a crimson sports top and matching shorts. Compared to Billy's square and rugged features, she was elegant and refined. Her coppery-auburn hair was swept straight back to a ponytail. Chizzie watched her in amazement.

Coming closer, she slowed down and greeted him with a slightly wary expression. "Hi there! Lovely weather!" she said in an attractive, melodic voice.

Chizzie gave a wry laugh. "Lovely weather for yaks, eh?"

She stopped and smiled. Her grey-blue eyes had an assured look about them. More trim than slim, she exuded both an outer and an inner strength. Strengths that Chizzie perceived from several feet away.

She spoke confidently with a slight American accent that also hinted at a privileged English education. "Am I right in thinking you're Mr Bryson?"

Chizzie was struck almost speechless. "Uh, you know me?"

"I was at the public planning meeting for my father's development in Tannadee. I'm Yolanda Weever." She held out her hand, smiling. "Nice to meet you."

For Chizzie, the weather seemed to improve suddenly. They shook hands. He introduced himself and returned the greeting. When she smiled again, he could feel the sun shining.

But the wind was in Yolanda's glistening face, and she screwed up her eyes. "It's very nice to meet you, but not exactly a day for standing still, so I'll get going again before the next big cloud opens up."

"Are you holidaying here?" asked Chizzie.

"I thought I'd spend a few days getting to know the area. My ancestors lived round here. And I'm a trail runner, so I like to get out on the hills and stretch my legs."

"Excellent. Me too – well, I'm not exactly a trail runner, but I run a lot up here; I've done a bit of hill running now and again. Might bump into each other again, who knows? Are you staying at the estate house?"

"Yes, McShellach House it's named now. My father named it for our ancestors."

"Well, if you're not too busy some evening, why not pop into the Tannadee Hotel and have a drink on the house? A meal on the house even?"

"Oh, thank you; that's very kind of you. Yes, I'll do that. I'll look in sometime."

"I look forward to it. Ask for Chizzie, that's how everybody knows me."

"I'll do that, Chizzie. It's good to have met you. A word to the wise, though, if I may: I don't want to sound like a Shakespearian hag or something, but do take care in dealing with my father. And I have to say I'm so glad you didn't sell out."

"Sell out?"

"Your hotel. He'll try again, be sure of it."

"Our hotel? The Tannadee Hotel?"

Yolanda winced. "Yes," she said and angled her head away slightly. "You didn't know?"

"No!"

"Oh. Oh, I am sorry. I thought you would've known. I've... I've put my foot in it. I do apologise. It's best I get on my way."

"Wait! When did your father make his offer?"

"A few days ago. I'm sorry, Chizzie; I shouldn't say any more. I've probably said enough. Leave it there."

"How much did he offer?"

"That I don't know. Honest. Look, I'd appreciate it if you didn't tell anyone you heard it from me. Okay?"

Chizzie thought for a moment. "That would be difficult, Yolanda – impossible actually. My dad's going to think it was your dad or one of his team who told me. He could steam right in and cause all sorts of trouble. You don't know my dad. I have to tell him, Yolanda."

She pursed her lips and glared at him, then turned away petulantly. "Right, you say it was from me then."

Instinctively, Chizzie made to call her back, but he checked himself. Then he felt the patter of rain on his face. Billy was gone, Yolanda was gone, and trust in his dad was gone. There was no point in being out on the cold, wet hill anymore. He needed to be down in the hotel confronting his secretive dad. However, then again, he couldn't just leave, knowing that Billy could still be out there on the hill. But where should he go?

The answer came in seconds. There was a tap on his shoulder, and Chizzie spun round. It was Billy again, and he was smiling. The weather didn't improve this time, but emotion and relief welled up in Chizzie, and he hugged the lad. He would even have cuddled him, but for the muddy face; there was no telling where that had been. Billy had very odd tastes at times.

The hug seemed to confuse Billy; he took it like a fence post. But, gathering his wits quickly, he stepped back and strode off down the hill, going so fast that Chizzie had to jog at times to keep up.

CHAPTER 8

At the school, Billy went off to shower and change his clothes. Headmaster Jim was busy with a parent, so Chizzie went to the staffroom to relax and have a cup of tea. Having taken up a part-time supply post as a biology teacher two months ago, he was no stranger to the staffroom. Johnny had bitterly opposed Chizzie's acceptance of the post, but Chizzie had three reasons for taking it. First, the school needed him, as he was the only applicant. Second, he'd enjoyed teaching in Africa and had returned to Scotland with a keen interest in teaching, an interest made all the keener in light of Johnny's plans for the Tannadee Hotel – plans that were very different to Chizzie's vision of the hotel's future. The third reason for taking up the post was quite simply strategic: it told Johnny, loudly and clearly, that if he wanted Chizzie to keep the hotel on, he needed to compromise; no longer could he take his son for granted.

When Chizzie entered the staffroom, he found four members of staff present; two seemed to be engaged in a heated debate, which was the very last thing Chizzie needed. Instantly, he thought about walking straight out, but the fragrant aroma of tea was just too inviting and it reeled him in. One of the debaters was taunting the other, clearly aware that his opponent was excitable and open to every arrow. The taunting one was Robert Barrington, the school bursar and erstwhile orator; the excitable one was the woodwork teacher with the drink problem. Though a school employee,

Barrington was firmly of the belief that those who can, do; and those who can't, teach. A belief not openly expressed but made plain in his so-called joshing.

Chizzie tried to avoid eye contact and made his way discreetly along the side of the room towards the refreshments at the far end. But he was spotted.

"Ah Mr Bryson! Welcome! Thrice welcome!" Barrington declared, pompous as ever. "Perhaps you can add a modicum of fresh thinking to our little exchange of views here. Mr Chalmers opines – mistakenly, in my view – that we should be directing the larger part of our resources to the very poorest performing pupils. I beg to differ. Perhaps we can enjoy the benefit of your special knowledge of the subject, seeing as you seem to be taking the lad Pung under your wing these days. Is he, would you say, worth the greater part of your resources, Mr Bryson?"

Chizzie, well aware that this was nothing more than bait designed to give Barrington a platform from which he could inflict his views on everyone else, ignored the invitation and sought to change the subject. "I was up on Dennan Hill a wee while ago and—"

"Scouring the country for the wayward Pung, I believe!" broke in Barrington.

Chizzie ignored him and carried on, "And, out of the blue, appeared – of all people – Gordon Weever's daughter Yolanda, out running on the hill in all that weather!"

"Ah Yolanda! Yolanda Weever!" cried Barrington. "A spirited young woman, as they say."

"You know her?"

"I've seen her often enough in the news media. By the way, that's my tea caddy you're fingering; the generic teabags are in the white thing adorned with tea stains. If you'll kindly put down my caddy, I'll join you in another cup."

The woodwork teacher took his chance and left swiftly, leaving his mug on the table.

Barrington glanced at it disdainfully, shook his head, reached into his jacket pocket and took out a tissue, which he applied to the handle of the mug before carrying it to the sink.

"I see from your happy demeanour that you found the recalcitrant lad," said Barrington.

"We met," Chizzie replied, aware that the bursar was angling to play him like a fish.

"Oh. We met. I see… a chance meeting on the hill, in all that weather; what a coincidence. You just happened to be up there, and he just happened to be up there too. Happy days indeed."

As Barrington opened his tea caddy, the other two occupants of the staffroom, a young maths teacher and a young chemistry teacher, each let out a muffled laugh, then quickly left the room. Barrington looked over his shoulder and sounded agitated as he said, "Every time I get up to make a cup of tea, those two have a snigger to themselves."

By then, Chizzie was very much aware that he was in the unfortunate position of being Barrington's entire audience. He moved away and headed for the furthest chair.

"Wait a minute!" Barrington exclaimed. "Is there something pinned on my back?"

"Nothing that I can see."

"My trousers?" Barrington fretted, lifting his jacket above the waist. The thought of scrutinising Barrington's buttocks was just too much for Chizzie, and, with hardly a glance at the offending things, he replied in the negative.

"You didn't look. Look properly!" Barrington commanded.

Had Chizzie been in possession of a rat trap, there and then, he would've known exactly where to put it. But, lacking such a device, there was little for it but to oblige the horrible presenter of the horrible buttocks.

"Nope. Nothing at all."

"No chewing gum?"

"Nothing."

"Ink?"

"Nothing at all," insisted Chizzie. But, on closer inspection, he did see something: a little green thing dangling from the crotch of Barrington's trousers. "Hold it," he said, taking a closer look as intrigue overcame revulsion for the moment.

"What is it?" Barrington asked anxiously.

It was a loose thread that was slightly different in colour from the olive green of Barrington's trousers; seemingly, the seam of the trousers had burst at some point, and the man had effected a crude repair with his own creepy hand.

Chizzie faced a dilemma. Should he pull it and see the man's trousers disintegrate? Or should he treat Barrington like a normal human being? To pull or not to pull? That was the question. A picture of the Queen unveiling a plaque at a new art gallery flashed through his mind. In an instant, he could be providing a similar service – declaring a pair of trousers open to the public. But then came the awful thought of the first exhibit. That decided him. No pulling!

Nonetheless, could he allow the great, pompous oracle to get off scot free? Certainly not; that would be going too far. "There's a dark-green thread hanging loose," Chizzie confided as casually as he could. "You've been repairing your trousers yourself?"

The occupant of the unsafe trousers couldn't have moved quicker if an elephant had swiped at his crotch. He whisked his buttocks away, his face bright red. "Are you in on this?" he snapped, glaring at Chizzie.

"In on what?"

"The joke."

"What joke?"

"Whatever it is? There's something going on!"

"Not with me there isn't!" retorted Chizzie angrily. It was typical of Barrington to shoot first and establish the facts later. By then, Chizzie was all for declaring Barrington's trousers open, but humanity got the better of him. "If they snigger every time you go near your tea, perhaps they've put something in your tea. Have you thought of that?"

Barrington froze. Then almost whimpering, he cried, "Oh good Lord!" And, like a terrier after a rat, he peered into his tea caddy. Carefully, with his silver caddy spoon, he sifted through the brittle, aromatic leaves. The meticulous sifting soon yielded results. "Yes! Something's in here," he proclaimed with forensic precision.

Chizzie waited for the finger of suspicion.

Barrington lifted a sample out of the caddy and sniffed it carefully. Bringing his great powers of discernment to bear, the bursar was able to offer a diagnosis immediately. "Rabbit shit!" he declared.

Quite how he could divine rabbit shit from any other type of shit was a mystery to Chizzie, but he of the precarious trousers was, of course, a connoisseur.

Then came the inevitable finger. Turning his gaze now towards Chizzie, Barrington narrowed his eyes and asked firmly, "So what exactly do you know about this?"

In the circumstances, there was but one thing for it; the game was up – Chizzie had to come clean. "It's a fair cop," he confessed. "It's an international conspiracy. Bugs Bunny's the one you want; he's the international big cheese. I was sucked in cos I'm gullible and hooked on carrots!"

Just then, the door opened, and Jim looked in and said quietly, "I'm free now, Chizzie. When you're ready."

"I'm ready now!" Chizzie answered, springing to his feet.

"No, you're not," wailed Barrington.

"Yes I am," replied Chizzie, grabbing his mug of tea hurriedly. "I'll take it with me."

"We have to discuss our next action against Weever," pleaded Barrington.

"You should've thought of that before," Chizzie chided.

A short time later, as Chizzie and Jim sat in Jim's office, they agreed over tea and biscuits that Billy liked working at the hotel, so he would be welcomed back, but he would need more supervision. The discussion then turned to Barrington.

"I think it worth mentioning that Robert Barrington seems to have it in for Billy," said Chizzie, "It might warrant a bit of watching there."

Jim smiled. "Oh, you know what Robert's like – he's a traditionalist, he thinks the future lies in the past and he hates everybody who's not like him. It's not just Billy he dislikes; it's you, me and everybody."

"It's not for me to say, of course, but – frankly – I think he's very lucky to have a job here."

"Actually, I think we're quite lucky to have him: he does his job well and he'd be difficult to replace. Out here, choice isn't a luxury. And, in a perverse sort of way, he's actually good for the school – and good for morale. If you're feeling down and you see Robert, your own problems don't seem half as bad suddenly, and you're perked up. Schadenfreude and all that."

"And, in fairness, it has to be said he did do a good job at the planning meeting; he got a lot of support."

"That is very commendable for someone who doesn't like people. Or maybe change is something he hates even more."

"Maybe, but we have to embrace it," said Chizzie. "As I recall, our Mr Barrington said at the meeting that he wanted to embrace change."

"Yes, I had to laugh when he was playing to the gallery like that and taking his big chance to pretend he's Churchill. The reality is that Robert would embrace a grizzly bear before he'd embrace change. As far as he's concerned, Tannadee ain't broke, so there's no need to fix it."

"I don't object to change, and neither does Dad; we simply object to Weever, as he's not the right change. He won't work with what's here; he'll destroy it."

"Absolutely. At first, I was all for him – a bigger school roll, and more opportunities for our pupils and staff alike – but the reality is that we would find it difficult to attract enough staff. And if Weever helped us out with cash, he'd want a say in how we ran things. You can imagine where that would lead."

"We can't let Weever just take us over like a herd of cattle. We need to do something."

"We could mount a legal challenge, but that takes a lot of money, which we don't have, and Weever's done nothing illegal anyway. The other option is that we ask for a public inquiry, but there's no chance of that happening. All we can do is keep an eye on Weever. Somehow, I think we haven't seen the last of his plans."

Both men groaned thoughtfully.

Chizzie's mind wandered to Yolanda and her news about Weever seeking to buy the hotel. Why hadn't his dad told him? What kind of money was offered? With a good offer, Chizzie could be set for life, and never have to work purely for the money. Weever's offer played on his mind so much he couldn't keep it to himself any longer. "You know what, Jim?" he said, "Keep this to yourself: Weever's offered to buy our hotel. But Dad's turned him down flat."

"Yes, I was aware of that, Chizzie."

Chizzie jolted. "You knew?"

"So your dad told you after all?"

"No. No, he didn't. And I'm the last to know, it seems."

Jim laughed. "Chizzie, a secret in Tannadee is like a fly; it gets around."

"How much did he offer? D'you know?"

"That's not for me to say, Chizzie. You'll have to ask your dad about that. But, for what it's worth, I can tell you that Weever has also offered to buy the school."

"Really?"

"Yep. It seems the man won't be happy till he owns us all."

"It's sounding like a game of Monopoly now."

"Without the jail, hopefully."

CHAPTER 9

Reclining on the sofa in the conservatory of McShellach House, Charlie Fairfoull was on the phone to his boss, who'd flown to Texas. "She won't speak to me, so I didn't know if you knew or not," said Charlie.

"For definite? She's taken over the lodge for definite?" asked Weever sounding very peeved.

"She has, yep."

"Yolanda's not actually the problem – it's her mother; she's getting back at me. Take it from me, Charlie, when you have kids, make sure they hear more than just their mother's mouth. Get involved from day one. Yolanda's mother took her from me, and she's used her against me ever since – in sheer spite. That's the kind of woman she is: a viper. And that's why I dumped her. Well, that and I found someone better looking and only half as bitchy. Yeah, Yolanda's mother's a spiteful cobra and she's poisoned my beautiful baby against me. I gotta come over there, Charlie, but I gotta sort things out here first. I'll see you tomorrow."

"Right, see you then. Oh, by the way, the old Paw guy simply won't sell; he said he'd rather die than sell his croft."

"That's not a croft; it's a slum, it's an eyesore, and I'm not having it next to my golf course."

"So what do we do, Gordon?"

"We run him out. We mound up dirt around him, and we shut off his water, then he'll quit. Goodbye Mr Paw or whatever they call him. Get the bulldozers in at sun up and

94

throw a mound up all round that hovel. Put it right on the fence line, right up. I want him squeezed out. Three good offers I've put on the table and he's refused them all, so he's had his chance."

"There'll be trouble."

"You know what? Who cares? It's our property, and we've every right to wipe out that eyesore. We can't have our clients looking at a slum, and the mound'll divert attention from clearing out those scrubby 'dumplins' or whatever they're called."

"The wooded drumlins."

"Drumlins, right. What the hell, call 'em dumps; it's what they are. They're an eyesore, but – cleared and covered in beautiful bluegrass – they'll make one helluva great eighth hole. They'll be truly amazing. No question. They'll feature in our marketing. So get it done real quick, Charlie, before any bug-ugly tree huggers come swarmin' in. Wouldn't surprise me one bit if Yolanda's tipped 'em off."

"It will attract attention, that's for certain."

"Well, let them howl. I don't care if these hillocks are special scientific interest or whatever – the truth is they're scrub, and we're doin' the place a favour by clearin' out some of that stuff. There's enough scrub up there for every scrubber in Bonnie Scotland. And have you ever seen any scientists up there, Charlie?"

"No, sir."

"Me neither. So, we get on with the good work right away. No pussyfootin'. I'm comin' over. I'll see you tomorrow, Charlie. Goodnight."

Chizzie awoke to the distant roar of rutting stags, or so he thought, until his mind cleared and he remembered that stags don't rut in springtime. When he got out of bed and pulled back the curtains, he discerned tiny figures, who were hard-hatted men, over at the Weever estate, busily chain-sawing trees near the West Woods. Adding to the distant commotion was the deep throb of a bulldozer and some heavy trucks. The trucks seemed to be supplying the bulldozer with soil, which it first spread and then mounded up at the back of the cottage inhabited by Paw, Billy Pung's guardian. Such activity hadn't been seen for years in Tannadee.

Chizzie found his binoculars and took a closer look. He saw the earth rise up and trees fall. Then, a man in a raincoat hove into view: it was Paw. He was animated and shouting at the bulldozer. When he waved his arms, the raincoat opened to reveal a pair of long johns. In view for only a few minutes, Paw disappeared behind the mound of earth as it rose higher. To Chizzie, it seemed surreal.

Lowering his binoculars, he looked around the room to be sure this was no hallucination. He had consumed blue cheese the night before and, unable to sleep, had spent much of the night thinking of his meeting with Yolanda and his father's secrecy, so it was possible his mind was playing tricks.

But, no, a second look through the binoculars confirmed the reality of the earthworks and tree felling. As more trees fell and more earth rose up, Paw emerged again from behind the mound like a glove puppet, waving angrily and shouting like Mr Punch. It made no difference; the bulldozer simply pushed up more earth into places that Paw couldn't get to quickly enough.

Then another figure appeared: a young woman – Yolanda. She was running quickly up to the bulldozer. She seemed to want to talk to the driver. The machine stopped, and the driver jumped out just as Paw scrambled down the mounded earth, shouting and pointing in the direction of his cottage. He was clearly furious and directing his ire at the driver, who stepped back and then further back, as Paw began stabbing him with his finger. Then Yolanda turned and rushed towards the bulldozer, pulled open the door and climbed into the cab.

In seconds, with a huge jet of black smoke from the exhaust pipe, the bulldozer accelerated away, leaving both men looking thunderstruck. The bulldozer sped towards the little bridge over the ditch where the trucks came with their cargo of soil, and there it came to a halt, blocking the bridge. The cab door flew open and Yolanda leaped out. Then she went running back to Paw and the driver.

This was all too much for Chizzie to miss. With a crazed pensioner running around in raincoat and long johns, and a young woman in running kit driving off in a bulldozer, Chizzie lost no time getting into his running kit and headed out to join the commotion.

Running the same routes time and time again had lately become wearisome for Chizzie, and he hardly noticed as the familiar scenery sped by. Firmly in his mind's eye were two things: intrigue and romance, though romance was no more than a possibility – a mere figment that was as likely to be dashed in an instant as bloom and grow, but hope drove him on. Sweating and panting, he leaped over the stream onto the Weever estate and clambered up the shallow green bank, to the delight of the man in the raincoat and long johns, who came running towards him. Yolanda, about twenty metres away, was partly obscured by several men gathered round her, including Charlie Fairfoull.

"*See! See what they've done!*" yelled Paw, pointing to the mounded earth around his home. "*See! They've mounded me up; they're forcin' me out!*"

"Who is?" asked Chizzie, breathing heavily.

"Big man Weever! But the wee lassie Weever, she stopped them. She says it's an accident. But the big lad Charlie there, he says the opposite. It's madness; it's bloody madness! I wouldn't do that to ma worst enemy! Would you? How could anybody do that to anybody?"

Chizzie wiped sweat from his brow. "It's beyond me, Paw. I'll see what they're saying."

"Over my dead body!" Chizzie heard Yolanda say as he approached the circle of men around her. There was no reply. Chizzie squeezed past a hard-hatted man smelling faintly of sweat and diesel, and saw the glaring eyes of Yolanda fixed on the glaring eyes of Charlie Fairfoull. Yolanda looked flushed and was breathing hard, but Fairfoull looked cool. Then, a little smile broke across Fairfoull's lips, seeming to signal that the deadlock was at an end. But Chizzie discerned another message in that smile: it wasn't simply about truce; it was also about warmth – and the knowing look that followed the smile confirmed in Chizzie's mind that his own chances of romance were very much lower than he'd hoped.

"We'll wait and see what your father says," said Fairfoull warmly, as he held out his hand.

Without a word, Yolanda handed him a set of keys, which Fairfoull tossed to the bulldozer driver before turning to the other workmen.

"Okay, men," he said, smiling, "back to the site office and we'll fix a new schedule."

The men peeled away quickly.

"You'll have to teach me to drive one of these things," said Chizzie smiling and pointing to the bulldozer.

"You looking for another job?" replied Yolanda curtly.

"No. I've still got two. And..." He looked over his shoulder. They were alone – Paw was in Fairfoull's face, haranguing him. "And I didn't speak to my dad about your father's offer, so nobody knows I know, except you and me."

"When d'you intend discussing it?"

"When I can do so discreetly without mentioning your name."

Yolanda stepped forwards and, clapping Chizzie on the shoulder, she looked him in the eye and thanked him.

Chizzie, in turn, thanked her for calling off the earthworks. "Why all the mounding? What's this all about?" asked Chizzie.

Yolanda shook her head. "My father apparently regards the farmstead as some kind of eyesore and wants it obliterated. If he could, he'd flatten it, but he can't because the old guy won't sell."

"That's… that's outrageous."

"It's perfectly legal."

"It's immoral."

"My father has done nothing wrong."

"What? Are you kidding?"

"Sadly not. The law's on his side."

"The law's an ass."

"Leave it with me. I'll sort this out, law or no law."

An awkward silence followed before Chizzie spoke. "Well, I'd better continue my run." He hesitated for a second – waiting for her to say, "I'll join you" – but it didn't come, so he turned to go, unsure which direction to take but knowing the important thing was to set off with conviction, and that's what he did, uphill, for no particular reason.

But, only a few strides later, he heard Paw cry out, "Hey look! Look! They're cuttin' through the West Woods. That's not right – they're protected them woods are!"

Chizzie stopped to look.

Yolanda called to Fairfoull who was getting into his Landcruiser, "Should you be cutting into those woods down there?"

"In that area, yeah," replied Fairfoull casually. "That's the eighth hole. We have an avenue going through the trees down there."

"Not through there, you don't!" insisted Paw. "You're off line. That's no ordinary timber; that's the West Woods."

"Kinda hard to say at this distance," Fairfoull observed calmly, screwing up his eyes.

Yolanda looked at Paw, then turned and set off running. "I'm going down there!" she cried.

"Me too," said Chizzie, following quickly.

Sprinting to catch up, Chizzie felt like a wolf chasing a hare. Yolanda was so elegant and nimble. Drawing alongside her, he wanted to say something, but everything he thought of sounded like a cheap chat-up line. Not that his mind was entirely free of the desire to chat her up, it was just the wolf and hare thing; it felt so animal to be chatting her up in the midst of adversity, but the opportunity to know Yolanda better was too good to miss. "You run very well; like a track athlete, I'd say," he began. "Are you a club runner?"

Yolanda seemed to take the comment at face value. "I used to be; I ran the eight hundred metres for county and college. I loved it, but too many other things got in the way. But, now I'm over here, I thought I might get fit again and try my luck in the eight hundred metres at some amateur Highland Games. How about you?"

"I did the four hundred metres for school, then uni, then the national club league."

"I never had quite enough speed for the one lap."

"Neither have I now," he laughed. "Are you American?"

"American and Irish, and Danish and South African and Spanish and German; I've been around. Technically, I'm British; my mom got us naturalised."

"Ow, that sounds harsh."

"Everyone says that," she replied curtly, but then she turned her head and smiled at him almost apologetically. "Mother wanted my formative years spent at an English public school. Hence the accent. Are you a local boy?"

"Aberdeenshire born and bred till I was fourteen, then we came to Tannadee. I went to uni, trained to be a teacher, then went off to Malawi teaching for two years. So I've been around a bit too. Not as much as you, though, obviously."

"What d'you teach?"

"Biology, but I couldn't get a teaching job over here, so I'm working at the hotel, and doing temporary teaching as and when. Dad wants me full time at the hotel, but I don't think it's really for me. We'll see, though. What d'you do?"

"Workwise?"

"Yeah."

"You name it – public relations, account manager, food and beverages, entertainment, conferencing, construction… Say, are these the right trees they're cutting?"

"They can't be. That's the West Woods. Like Paw says, they're protected. There's been a mistake."

"No. There's no mistake. Believe me, these guys will be exactly where they want to be. Hey! Stop! Stop cutting!"

"They can't hear you."

With less than thirty metres to go, a Landcruiser went past them throwing up a little wake of gravy-coloured dust. When the vehicle came to a halt near the tree-fellers, Fairfoull got out and approached the man who seemed to be the chargehand. After a brief word with him, the man called a halt to the cutting. It went so quiet so quickly that

Chizzie became suddenly self-conscious and aware that he was approaching a potentially hostile gang of lumberjacks while chumming around with the big chief's girlfriend. It was a little unnerving, but Yolanda – he was sure – was on his side, and she seemed keen to get among them.

She headed straight for Fairfoull. "What's going on?" she demanded. "You're cutting down all the wrong trees! Those are protected trees!"

Ignoring her, Fairfoull directed himself to the tree-fellers. "Right, guys, we'll finish here now, and I'll meet you up at the teeing area on the fourteenth hole."

The leading lumberjack seemed puzzled. "We've just got a tiny bit to do and then we're done here."

"Well, the thing is, Nick, we seem to have gone off line somewhere."

Nick looked insulted. "That's exactly the—"

Fairfoull cut him short, holding up a placating hand. "I know, I know; it's my fault. Obviously, I didn't make it clear enough, but we'll just call it a day here and we'll meet over at the fourteenth, in say…" he looked at his watch, "twenty-five minutes. Give the guys a break; they've earned it."

"We're on piece-work," replied Nick, "We just want to get on with the job."

"Right. Right. Of course, of course," said Fairfoull, beginning to sound a little flustered. "You just go on up there, and I'll join you very shortly."

As he turned to go, Nick looked at Yolanda as if about to say something, then he changed his mind seemingly, and merely went over to his team and called on them to leave.

Yolanda shook her head, then half-turned to Fairfoull. "You should be shot, you should," she said. "First you give an old man a living nightmare, then you lay waste to this special place."

"Accidents happen all the time on land works; you know that as well as anyone, Yolanda. It's easy to blame."

"I know who's really to blame, but I know you're guilty too."

Fairfoull laughed. "Guilty? Guilty? It's not a murder trial, Yolanda. It's… it's a few trees, for Christ's sake. There's plenty more. Look, there's a whole damn hillside of them! What've we taken? One per cent, maybe? And, let's face it, these things are probably some of the ugliest, scrubbiest-looking things around."

This was like a red rag to Chizzie, and he broke in angrily. "That's in the nature of the West Woods! That's the nature of the habitat; don't you understand these things?"

"Save your breath, Chizzie," said Yolanda, with a fierce look at Fairfoull. "He doesn't care; he doesn't give a damn."

"I'm doing my job, Yolanda, that's all," Fairfoull explained. "If I didn't do it, someone else would – somebody who wouldn't respect your views as much as I do."

"If you valued my views, you wouldn't be working for my father," retorted Yolanda.

"Ho! That's a twisted one, Yolanda," replied Fairfoull, with a shake of his head. "As I say, if we didn't do what we do, somebody else would, and someone who's not half so pretty."

"What? You're pretty?"

"Pretty damn good, I'd say. Call me ugly if you like, but you've changed your tune. Anyways, I'm not saying anymore here."

It didn't escape Chizzie that the two people who were locked on with such intensity, completely oblivious to onlookers, were either overwhelmingly in love or full of all-consuming hatred. Chizzie was rooting for the latter, but hating himself for doing so. Coincidentally, he felt something hanging off his left ear; clearing it with his hand, he found it to be a small spider. A timely symbol of life weaving its tangled web perhaps, or maybe a call to try, try and try again. But a third option also loomed, a more straightforward one – the simple spider, previously at home in a tree now felled, had cast about for new wood and, arriving at Chizzie's head, had seemingly found itself the perfect replacement. Not sure what to make of it, Chizzie lowered the spider onto a branch and watched it scramble away, envying the utter simplicity of its humble life.

"We'll wait till your father comes," said Fairfoull brusquely. "Then we'll see."

"See what?" replied Yolanda.

"The way forward."

Yolanda hesitated for a moment before answering with steely quietness, "I think we already know the way forward, Charles. Do we not?"

"Aw, don't get all negative on me, Yolanda."

"Negative? I'm negative? Have I destroyed these valuable trees? Go, Charlie! Just go! Go away, and take your crew with you. You'll hear more of this when the big boss man shows up."

With a wry smile, Fairfoull shook his head, then got into his Landcruiser and drove off.

Yolanda looked at the felled trees and let out a cry of anguish.

"I'm livid too," groaned Chizzie. "Absolutely bloody outrageous! You're right, he just doesn't seem to give a damn."

"Yep, he couldn't care less. He won't lose any sleep. I used to think he was a good man who'd just fallen in with a bad crowd."

Your dad, you mean, thought Chizzie, but he said nothing.

"But, now, I'm not so sure – a good man with a bad streak, maybe."

"Him and a billion others," said Chizzie. The sheer audacity of Fairfoull seemed beyond belief, but Chizzie found himself struggling to condemn him. "Maybe it wasn't deliberate after all. I mean—"

"What else could it be? You think a global outfit like the Weever Organisation can't find its way through some trees? Look! Look at the view you get now with those trees out of the way. That's the prize – that's what it's about."

"They're not all out of the way."

"They will be tomorrow."

"What? How?"

"I don't know how; I only know they won't be here this time tomorrow."

"They can't touch them; we'll get the planners on to it, and they'll stop them."

"The politicians will flatten the planners. You know there's a by-election in the offing not far from here?"

"Corruption? You're saying they're all corrupt? This isn't Sicily or Naples, Yolanda. This is quiet, wee Scotland."

"I'm not talking Mafia – it's much more subtle; it's you scratch my back, I scratch yours. It's everywhere; it's little people rubbing along in an untidy world, just crimping the rules. A little breach here, a little breach there. Believe me, I know how it goes. You'll hear the politicos soon enough." Adopting a vacant expression and flat tone, she gave her impression of what was to come. "'The economic and social benefits substantially outweigh any environmental impact.' That, Chizzie, is what you're going to hear. A few trees against a few jobs? And an election looming? There's no chance. Anyway, I have to go now, I've got to make some calls. Enjoy your run."

"Remember, you've got a meal on the house waiting for you at the hotel. You just say when, Yolanda."

Yolanda smiled and nodded. "Thanks, Chizzie; I haven't forgotten. Will do. I do look forward to it and I'll be in touch."

Chizzie watched her go. It was clear to him that there was still a place in her heart for Charlie Fairfoull, whatever her misgivings might be. Turmoil seemed to be welling up from all directions; it looked like being one of those days that just crashes in, takes all the stuffing out of you and throws it to the wind. Then, he saw someone who must be feeling even worse than he was. It was Paw – poor, old Paw.

He was digging furiously at the mounded earth enclosing three sides of his house. If the poor man didn't slow up, he'd break his back before he'd made any real inroads on the mound. What a futile gesture. If he ended up in hospital, he'd almost certainly lose everything, and Weever would have crushed him and taken all he wanted from him. When Paw was knocked off his feet with the flu last year, Chizzie had fed and looked after Paw's cattle, and it wasn't easy, even with Billy's help. Life for the small-time hill farmer was tough. Paw needed help.

Chizzie ran up to the mound and called on the old man to stop digging. "It's no use, Paw; stop. Stop digging. You'll just do yourself in, and then where'll you be?"

"I'll show that bloody Weever. I'll show him. He's on his way, they say. Well, he's gonnae see I'm no' havin' it! I'm no' havin' it. I'll shove every bit of it up his backside! I'm flamin'! Absolutely bloody flamin'! The bastard!"

"No, no, Paw; he'll get the police to you for digging his stuff, and you'll get fined."

"No. I've called the police! I've called them. They'll jail the bugger for this! Tunnock's on his way, as soon as he gets his tyres pumped up. His patrol car's blown a gasket and his mountain bike's punctured. It's just as well we dinnae have a bank, or robbers'd be queuing up to have a go."

"I think you'll find that PC Tunnock will be with Weever on this one, Paw. Whatever you and I might think, Weever's within his rights. It's his land."

"He's blocking my light and my view, everything! He doesn't even live here. It's our land."

"It's all legal, Paw. You're not entitled to a view, and you've probably got enough light for the law, believe it or not."

"I've hardly any light at all."

"It'll be enough for the law."

"That can't be right. That's no law at all."

"It's the law of the land, Paw."

"The law for the rich man, you mean. What about my rights? Who could look at this and say it's right?"

"A judge, Paw. A judge will."

"No, I'm no' havin' it. They can stick their stupid law where the sun don't shine!"

"Here's PC Tunnock now. I'd stop digging if I were you, Paw."

"Damn the fear! I'm just gettin' started!" At that, Paw began digging even faster than before.

PC Tunnock, free-wheeling down the slope, came bouncing up to Chizzie, and – with a squeal of his brakes – he came to a halt.

"Find a shovel, Tunnock, an' help us get rid o' this bloody mess here!" Paw shouted, only half-jokingly. "Look at it. It's bloody criminal! How'd ye like this bloody lot in your back garden?"

Tunnock winced and puffed his cheeks. Paw stopped digging and waited for a response. Tunnock looked about as if trying to find even the remotest thing that might be positive. But, evidently, there was nothing to find, and, sadly, he said what he had to say. "Eh... actually, Paw, it looks like there's nothing wrong here – apart from your digging. Unfortunately, you're trespassing. The mound's on Weever land. So, I'm going to have to ask you to stop, I'm afraid."

"Nothing wrong? Nothing wrong! Look at it! It's all bloody wrong! It's mad! *Would you accept this round your house?*"

Tunnock pursed his lips and shook his head. "I can't answer that, Paw. If you want to take things further, you'll have to speak to your solicitor."

"I don't have one. The last one I dealt wi' is deid. Millburgh bloke – Watson, I think his name was. Anyway, I'm no' payin' any fancy lawyer to get this shifted; that's your job."

"It's not my job, Paw. I'm asking you to please stop; no more digging, please."

"I'm no' stoppin'; I'll have this bloody heap finished by midnight."

"Paw, I'm telling you now – you must stop."

"No fear. I won't stop. Shove yer law!"

Exasperated, Tunnock appealed to Chizzie. "For God's sake, Chizzie, tell him to stop, please."

Chizzie took a deep breath then pursed his lips. Reluctantly, he complied. "Paw, the PC's right," he said sheepishly. "We'll sort something out. You're right, it's wrong, but the law's the law, if that makes sense."

"No, it bloody well doesn't!" cried Paw.

"What's goin' on here?" asked a new voice. "Has there been a landslide or something?" It was Denis Dekker, the chip-shop owner. "I saw bulldozers and trucks from my window. Is everybody okay?"

Paw replied quickly, "No they're not, Dekker! I've been shut in by Weever, and the law's here tae make sure I stay shut in. What d'ye make o' that? Eh?"

Dekker looked confused. "What? Is that right? Weever did this?"

"Bloody right he did," answered Paw.

"Are you arresting Weever?" Dekker asked innocently, turning to Tunnock.

"No, he's arrestin' me! The innocent man!" declared Paw.

Dekker looked even more confused. "What? Is that right, PC Tunnock?"

"I haven't arrested anybody," replied Tunnock.

"But you're goin' tae, cos I'm no' stoppin'!" insisted Paw.

"Aw, somebody talk sense into him, for God's sake," pleaded Tunnock.

Chizzie again appealed to Paw, but there was no stopping the old man; he was completely incensed, and the red mist was all over him.

Finally, Tunnock snapped and climbed onto the mound beside Paw. "Right, I'm arresting you under section... section... er, section..."

The others waited, hoping that PC Tunnock couldn't recollect the essential detail.

"Thirteen!" shouted Dekker eventually.

"Thank you. Section fourteen of the Criminal Procedures Scotland Act 1995," said PC Tunnock.

"What'd you shout that for?" Paw asked angrily.

"I shouted thirteen to put him off the scent," replied Dekker.

"You put him on the scent!" cried Paw.

"Sorry, Paw. I thought I was helping," apologised Dekker.

Paw shook his head. "You've got me arrested now. Tunnock hadn't a clue."

"I would've got there," declared Tunnock.

"Yeah, by which time I would've finished digging," insisted Paw. "But now he's jailin' an innocent man!"

Dekker put an arm round Tunnock's shoulder. "Tunny, Tunny man, look—"

Tunnock pulled away. "That's PC Tunnock to you; this is official." Then he turned to Chizzie, "Please Chizzie talk some sense into him."

"No, Chizzie. If he won't let me clear my family home o' that bloody muck, I want the world to know what Weever's done. He can't get away with it. He can't!" ranted Paw.

"Right, Paw, that's it," Tunnock snapped, "Go inside and get yourself changed. You've got five minutes."

"If you're arrestin' me, I'm goin' like this," declared Paw.

"You can't go through the village in long johns and wellies," Tunnock protested.

"I can, and I bloody well will," confirmed Paw. "I want people to see that this is what Weever and the law can do to people. I'm no' tidyin' up for you and your law. You want me? Then here I am. Take me in."

"He's only doing his job, Paw," insisted Chizzie, "Calm down, please."

"I won't bloody calm down. I didn't ask for this!"

Tunnock went quickly up to Paw and grabbed him by the shoulder. "Right, come on then. We're going!" he said pushing him.

"Take a picture somebody!" roared Paw.

Dekker searched his pockets. "I don't have my phone."

Tunnock snapped at Paw, "Button your coat up, man!"

"*Call the press!*" yelled Paw.

"The press are all Weever's men," Dekker informed him.

"Get the national press!" continued Paw. "This needs exposing!"

"You're the one exposing," yelled Tunnock. "If you don't button yer coat, I'm charging you with lewd and libidinous behaviour as well."

"What the hell's that?" asked Paw.

"Just make sure everything's tucked in!" Dekker advised, providing the benefit of his wrestling experience.

"No press," insisted Chizzie. "We can handle it."

"What's going to happen to him?" asked Dekker.

"It depends on him," replied the policeman. "It depends on what he does."

"I'll come with you," said Chizzie.

But Paw waved him away. "No, no, you stay out of it, Chizzie. It's me an' him – Weever's lackey here! People need to see. An innocent man hauled oot o' his bed an' jailed for defendin' himsel' against an international bully boy."

With that, Tunnock nodded in the direction of the village and away they went, with Tunnock pushing his bike, and Paw's wellies slapping against his shins.

Chizzie put his hands to his head. They looked so pitiful, Paw and PC Tunnock. Less than an hour before, Tannadee was a quiet, little haven of everything that civilisation stands for. Then, suddenly, as if in some kind of explosion, everything had turned upside down. A man in his sixties, a good neighbour and a trusty friend – a man who never before, in all his life, had been in trouble with the law – was being led away in his underwear by a policeman respected by everyone in the village and who hardly knew what it was to arrest anybody, let alone Paw.

Feeling utterly confused, weak and strangely vulnerable – like a rabbit driven from cover – Chizzie turned for home. He'd have his breakfast and then go to the police house to find what on earth had become of poor, wretched Paw.

CHAPTER 10

A little later that day, a helicopter landed on the newly completed helipad near McShellach House. No one got out of it while the rotors continued to whirl. Finally, when Weever felt he could disembark with his hair secure, he and his staff got out and walked to the house. Waiting to greet the great man at the door was Fairfoull, wearing an expression of mingled relief and apprehension. It was clear that the great man was in one of his 'glooms'; these were known as the famous 'Gordon Glooms'.

He strode past Fairfoull with hardly a glance. "Twenty minutes, in my office!" he grumbled.

It was no more than Fairfoull had expected. Weever had written several books on business success; none of them contained the word 'subtle'.

Twenty minutes later, Fairfoull entered Weever's office. Weever stood in the far corner, like a boxer ready for the fight to begin.

Before Fairfoull could even utter a greeting, Weever exploded. "You lied to me, Charlie boy! You told me those trees were down and the mound was up. The trees are not down and that mound is nowhere near high enough – it wouldn't hide a turkey! You know what? You're fired! You're fired. Get your things and go!"

Fairfoull made no reply. He just stood there, impassive.

"*Get the hell out!*" Weever yelled. "*Get out dammit!*"

Again, Fairfoull offered no response.

"Do you want me to get security?"

A broad smile crossed Fairfoull's face. "Okay," he said, "I'll go, but, before I do, you'll hear me out."

"I don't want to hear it."

"I have worked with you—"

"I don't want to hear it. Just get out!"

"I have worked with you because – in spite of all the aggro, all the ins and outs, and all the ups and downs – unlike many people, I think you're good. You're good at what you do and you're generally a force for good. You're also a bullshitter, though. No! Hear me out. You're a bullshitter, you are, but you're the best. It's all bullshit out there. But you know how to work it for your own good, and for the good of lots of other people. Sure, you stand on some people, but that's inevitable. That's life. That's the price of progress. Progress is tricky, and I've learned a lot from you. On the other hand, you're older now – wiser too, for sure – but now you're picking fights, not because you have to but because you like it. You've got too used to winning."

"You don't know the half of it, boy. I've come off the floor more than once. I know what it is to lose. I don't forget. It's ugly, it's horrible and it's nasty."

"The truth is that it's all a distant memory, Gordon. You said it yourself – you're not in it for the money anymore. You're shiftin' more money than ever, but you don't care. I see it; you don't."

"I'm an old fart! Is that what you're sayin'?"

"You're older, Gordon. The older you get, the more things you have running. You need a keener pair of eyes about you, and that's where I come in."

"Oh really?"

"Yes. Your two sons don't know how to make money; they only know how to spend it. And Yolanda, well, she's taken against you."

Weever made no reply. He stood motionless, his head up, staring at the door for nearly a minute. Finally, his eyelids moved, blinking rapidly as if in communication with some counsel far beyond the solar system. Barely moving his head, he swivelled his eyes towards Fairfoull, searching the younger man's face. Then he nodded. "Yes. Okay. Good. There's sense in what you say. I don't care as much as I used to. Most of the time, that is. Sometimes, though, I care even more. I'm up and down more. But you're right; you're right. I need a level head sometimes. You're hired."

"Thank you," replied Fairfoull, aware that he was never in any danger; if Weever had really wanted to fire him, he would've arranged for someone else to do it.

"Just one thing, Charlie: Yolanda has not turned against me; her mother has. She's turned Yolanda's head. Yolanda's a good girl. She's a good young woman. But, right now, she's trouble. I know you and she had a thing going, and I don't quite know where it's at, but it seems like she's trouble for the two of us right now. D'you think?"

"Yeah, but we're optimists and we're fighters. We'll win her back."

"Good. So, tell me, what's the plan for the trees I want down?"

"Hand of God, foot of man."

"Uh?"

"We set up a heap of the sandy-soil mix we use to make the greens, and we place it in a shallow gully, like a chute, on the slope above the trees that need taking out. The first heavy downpour shoves the heap down the slope onto the trees, and either takes them out directly or we take them out accidentally with a careless boot on the accelerator while the stuff's being cleared. These things happen; it's an everyday occurrence on construction sites. Either way, they're gone."

"Good thinking, Charlie. Neat. I like it. It's always good to hire old Mother Nature."

"There's no better assassin."

"The grand, old bitch."

"Before that, however, we need some goodwill in the bank. I suggest we lay on a seed-sowing ceremony tomorrow – nothing major, just a little reminder of all the goodies we're bringing to the table. We set things up at the first tee, you sprinkle some seed and then some VIP blesses it with a whisky toast."

"Good thinking again, Charlie. It's good to have you back."

Both men laughed.

"Yep, it's a smart move, Charlie. Not too low key, though. Classy is the bottom line. Our people expect nothing less. Can we hire a royal or something?"

"Not at a day's notice."

"I'm not asking for the Queen – just some classy dude. Surely there's somebody local – a prince or a duke, that kind of thing. I mean, what're they doin' all day, these people? This is a wonderful opportunity for them. I'm helpin' 'em keep their heads on."

"This isn't France, Gordon. Their heads are perfectly safe here. But I could have a word with the Lord Lieutenant and see if there's someone available, even just a quasi-royal, perhaps."

"I don't want a quasi-royal or any lieutenant. Get the mayor from the nearest town; he'll do. Get him to wear his chain and crown if he has one."

"They don't have mayors in Scotland, Gordon; they have provosts. The nearest one's in Millburgh. Unfortunately, he struggles to string two sentences together, so we'd be better with the local MP, Sir Reggie Tallboys; he can talk all day without actually saying anything."

"Is he classy? What's he look like?"

"Well, at first sight, not so good. Frankly, his head wouldn't be out of place mounted on fins. His friends call him Kipper, partly on account of his looks and partly because he spends most of his time in the House of Commons nodding off."

"And he's our man?"

"An odd one, yes, but, weirdly, it's an oddness that actually commands respect. If he can get through life being like he is, he really must be something – that's how people look at it. They vote for him in droves, despite everything. And, frankly, he's probably all we've got, unless you want some local councillors; they'll throw themselves at the opportunity – employment, development and tourism, it's got the lot for them."

"Can they string words together?"

"Not words you'd want to hear at a ceremony, but they will look extremely pleased and provide the necessary counterweight to Tallboys, who, however hard he tries, will look very glum."

"God help us! What a place! What the hell am I doing here?"

"You're building one of the most exclusive resorts in the world, Gordon."

Weever puffed out his cheeks. "That is what I am trying to do, by God. I'm bustin' a gut for that! But it's getting like the trials of Moses here. He could part the Red Sea, but I bet he couldn't build a golf course in this place!"

"We can do it. We'll get there, Gordon."

"Well, get the best you can for tomorrow's thing, but I insist on a big royal for the official opening, Charlie, I really do; I want a big one."

"You can't just book them like soap stars, Gordon."

"You can book anybody if the money's right."

116

"Not the top royals, Gordon. You can only invite them. It would probably help if they had something to shoot."

"To shoot? I can give 'em plenty to shoot."

"Something bigger than rabbits."

"I'll give 'em something much bigger. Something to die for – bear!"

"Bear?"

"Bear. All these wonderful woods here, mile after mile, and not a bear in sight. Have you seen bear here?"

"Not yet, but they used to be here, and there's people working to bring them back."

"Our people?"

"No. Conservationists."

"Eco-nuts you mean?"

"Indeed."

"How many bears have they got coming?"

"None at the moment."

"None?"

"'Fraid so."

"Right, we're on it – we'll speed things up."

"Actually, it might be better if we weren't the prime mover. If we're seen to bring back bears only to shoot them, that wouldn't go down well here. If, on the other hand, we embrace our eco-nut brothers and we give them all the help they need, our bears are on the way. Then, when the bears get to be a problem, as they surely will, we step in and help out; everyone's a winner."

"Great thinking again, Charlie. We go fluffy and we go under the radar. Then boom! Bang! Bang! Bang! We bag 'em!"

"And to speed things along, we create a lobby group something like, say…"

"The Bear Action Group."

"Well… not exactly that. There's an unfortunate acronym there – BAG – which isn't quite the image we're looking for. How about the Bear Conservation Action Society?"

"Excellent. You've got everything there. Good man, Charlie. Good man. How soon will the bears be ready?"

"Well, it could be several—"

"Months?"

"Years."

"What? Years? Hell, make it three months tops. It's your baby now, Charlie. You run with it. I want it. It's great. It's a value-added activity and a unique selling point too."

"Though it can't be a regular thing, Gordon. I mean, golf and shooting – it's not exactly a great mix. You wouldn't want to be the one putting for birdie when a shotgun blasts the air only yards away."

"No problem. We shoot on ladies' days. The ladies won't mind; they only want the social life. Besides, we offer them a value-add – such as, say, a beauty treatment or a spa treatment, that kind of thing; they'll lap it up. Keep the men happy – that's the money shot. We make sure they have a good time. They shoot bear on Thursdays."

CHAPTER 11

Preparing to visit Paw at the police house, Chizzie was in fighting mood and decided to confront his father about Weever's offer for the hotel. At the kitchen table, he waited until Johnny finished his coffee and took up his newspaper. "Seems like the council unleashed some kind of uncontrollable beast when they gave Weever approval," he said. "Imagine if he put a wall of earth around us."

"That'd be different," replied Johnny, lowering his paper, "We're a business, Paw's not."

"He's expendable you mean? He's old and he doesn't work anymore, so throw him to the dogs."

"Let the law handle it. We can't fight everybody's battles. I've got enough on my plate right now with Weever pressing, you walking out on me, and employees going nuts."

"I'm not walking out on you. I'm—"

"Look, I'm not arguing; I'm too busy. Just leave it. Paw can't run the croft anymore, so he's better out of it. And Weever made him a good offer. He didn't take it; he had his chance."

And here was Chizzie's chance; he went for it. "It seems like Weever's trying to bag the whole place. It wouldn't surprise me if he tries us next. What d'you think, Dad? You think he'd be interested in our hotel?"

Johnny's chocolate digestive stopped in mid-air for a second, before continuing on its short journey.

"Father! I'm your father," Johnny mumbled irritably,

concentrating on his paper. "How many times do I have to tell you?"

"What's it matter? There's nobody else here."

"It's got to come natural – and that means sticking to it. Now, I have to go." He pushed back his chair, folded his paper quickly and got to his feet.

"Where?" asked Chizzie, as casually as he could.

"Never mind where," Johnny replied briskly, as he made for the door.

"Has Weever expressed any interest in this place, Father?" Chizzie asked calmly.

Johnny froze, then turned his head with a furtive glance, which, along with the silence, gave him away.

Chizzie delivered his attack: "He's offered. Your face says it all, Dad."

"So, what if he has!" snapped Johnny.

"You didn't tell me. You turned down an offer and you didn't let me know. I had to find out for myself. And you say, what's it matter? How can it not matter that I'm shut out of the family business?" Chizzie shook his head, then, shoving his chair back, he got swiftly to his feet.

"Well, that's it, Dad. That is it! I quit! You want to run this business on your own – fine! It's yours; it's all yours! Your little empire! You keep it!"

Johnny whacked his newspaper on the door. "Right! Right. Okay, okay. I'll tell you why you weren't told. It was because at the first half-decent offer from Weever you'd be shouting 'Accept! Accept!' You don't want this business; you just want the money. Well, Weever can offer the earth, but I won't sell, and if you want to cave in to him, you can go to hell!" With that he strode out of the room.

Chizzie knew his dad could be volatile, but the vehemence behind the reply was exceptional even for him; it came straight from the very atoms of the man, as much an appeal for understanding as a war cry, and Chizzie felt it as much as he heard it. He felt for his dad and all he'd strived for, yet he also knew that, for himself, the hotel would be as much a millstone as a prize.

Then a bang on a window startled him. He swung round. There was a face peering in – it was Billy Pung's face.

"Paw's in jail!" shouted Billy, "Paw's in the jail!"

Chizzie sighed and gestured towards the conservatory door, then walked over and opened it. Billy stepped inside carrying two bulging plastic bags, one in each hand.

"What's in the bags, Billy?" asked Chizzie.

"My things," Billy replied, very agitated.

"What things?"

"My things from school. If I go to jail, I don't want other people using my things."

"You won't be going to jail, Billy. Come in and leave your bags here." Then, calmly, trying to avoid exciting the lad, he asked, "Paw's in jail you say?"

"Yeah. An' they'll be comin' for me next. I'm with Paw; I ain't backin' down."

"Nobody's coming for you, Billy; unless… have you done anything?"

"Any what?"

"Have you been on Weever's land or touched any of his things?"

"I ain't touched nothin'. I've been home an' back to school, then straight here; that's all."

"Right, that's fine; they can't touch you then."

"What's all this touchin'? How come I touch Weever's things an' I'm in jail? Is he the law? How come?"

"He's not the law, Billy, but he has… influence."

"Money you mean – he's got money."

"Well, that's… that's part of it."

"He buys people. That's what Paterson said."

"Who's Paterson?"

"A guy I know. He wants to be prime minister."

"Paterson and half the country. Look, we need to get down to the police house and see exactly what's happening."

The police house wasn't far away, so Chizzie and Billy walked to it very quickly, acknowledging on the way the people who – having seen Paw in the streets – thought Chizzie and Billy should be made aware of his plight, as if they didn't know already. The good intentions served only to make Billy even more anxious.

As they reached the police house, they saw a small group of people shouting sporadically – four women and two men.

When the group saw Chizzie and Billy approaching they all started chanting, "Free Paw! Jail Weever!"

If it was intended to boost Billy's morale, it worked, for Billy's lips parted to reveal a rare smile. Chizzie smiled too, though he doubted the wisdom of the protest, and walked swiftly through the gate and up the crunchy gravel path to the police house. The door swung open before his pointing finger reached the bell, and in the doorway stood Mrs Tunnock.

"Thank goodness you two are here at last," she declared. "In you come; just wipe your feet and follow me, please." She led them down the hallway.

The portents seemed better than expected. Mrs Tunnock was calm, and there were no sounds of ranting and raving, or noises of the sort that accompany the smashing of chairs or kicking of doors. Then again, it occurred to Chizzie that the calmness might be resulting from Paw being laid out unconscious somewhere or possibly in a straitjacket. Chizzie turned and looked at Billy – the lad looked nervous and troubled. But things brightened up when Mrs Tunnock led them into the living room, and the smell of tea and freshly baked scones met their nostrils. And there was Paw, sitting by the fireside, in an easy chair, still in his coat and long johns, sipping a mug of tea.

Paw greeted them sombrely. "Well, well, Mr Bryson," he said with a bitter smile. "It seems we've been taken for a right bunch o' village idiots, wouldn't ye say? Don't cry now, Billy! Dinnae let the bastards grind ye down. Mum wouldn't like that."

Mrs Tunnock retorted, "And she wouldn't like seeing you in the state you're in, Paw – that's for sure. Half the place thinks ye've gone off yer head."

"So ye keep sayin'," muttered Paw. If anyone held sway over Paw it was June Tunnock, a lifetime friend of his beloved wife, Morag.

"Morag would be devastated to see you battling with PC Tunnock there," she continued, "risking who knows what." June continued indignantly, "I keep sayin' it because it's right, and you know it is. So, get out o' those long johns and get into these clothes o' PC Tunnock's; they're clean and fresh, washed and aired only yesterday."

Paw pursed his lips thoughtfully and then glanced at Billy. "Aye. Aye, you're right, June. Right enough. I'll deal with it another way. I'll get changed."

PC Tunnock replied ominously, "You'll stay off the Weever property, Paw."

"Don't give in, Paw!" Billy interjected.

"I'm not givin' in, Billy. I'm just givin' common sense a chance," explained Paw.

"And it'll be legal, Paw; all above board," confirmed PC Tunnock.

"All above board, PC Tunnock; yes, very much above board," Paw conceded.

"What does that mean exactly?" asked the policeman, cautiously.

"Wait an' see," replied Paw.

"He'll put you in jail. Tunnock'll put you in jail," insisted Billy.

Paw looked offended. "Don't be cheeky, Billy; that's a PC you're talkin' to. PC Tunnock is his name, an' he's only doin' his job."

Billy turned fiercely to PC Tunnock. "Who pays you?" he asked. "You've got a big house here. An' nobody's pushin' earth on you. Who pays you?"

"That would be the Scottish police service, Billy," replied Tunnock calmly.

"Who pays them?"

"The Government."

"Who pays them?"

"The taxpayers, Billy."

"Who are they?"

"Well, everybody, Billy. All the men and women in the country: Paw, Chizzie—"

Billy turned to Paw and said, "So you're payin' for him to put you in jail?"

Paw gulped. "Well, only if I break the law."

"Weever's law."

"It's not Weever's law, Billy."

"It is, Paw. Weever's done you, an' his monkey here's puttin' you in jail cos you ain't got no money."

"Don't talk like that, Billy; you're upset an' so am I, but you don't talk like that to PC Tunnock. Now you apologise."

Billy stood motionless for a second, saying nothing, then suddenly he lunged forwards and grabbed PC Tunnock's police hat from the table and clapped it on his head. "Look, I'm the law now!"

124

"Take that off, Billy; put it down!" demanded Paw.

Billy pointed at PC Tunnock, and cried, "No. You're for the jail, Tunnock; you've got the law all wrong." The young lad swivelled round and grabbed the first thing that came to hand – a carriage clock from the sideboard. Then glaring at PC Tunnock, he yelled, "*I'm takin' this. It's not yours, you're a cheat.*" He reached forwards and grabbed a mug from the little table beside PC Tunnock's chair. "An' this." He grabbed another mug. "An' this."

Until then, Chizzie had felt Billy's outburst was a matter for Paw and Billy alone, but he had to intervene before PC Tunnock did. He stepped forwards, but Billy was off – clutching his new belongings, including the police hat. Billy ran down the hall towards the door. Chizzie made to go after him, shouting Billy's name, but Paw stopped him.

"No, Chizzie," stated Paw. "No, you'll never catch him; he'll be down the bottom o' the road afore ye even reach the door. He's fast as lightning. An' the more ye chase him, the further he'll go. Just leave him – he'll calm down eventually." Paw then apologised profusely for Billy's behaviour and promised to pay for any damage.

PC Tunnock and June looked bewildered, but they accepted Paw's apologies graciously before June directed Paw to the spare bedroom, where he changed into the lawman's spare clothes.

CHAPTER 12

Once again, Chizzie had the unenviable task of informing headmaster Jim that Billy had run off into the hills. This time it was even worse; technically, Billy was now a thief on the run, having stolen from none other than the local policeman. By then, even Billy's stoutest advocates would likely struggle to see how he could ever be regarded as fully trustworthy. On the other hand, Billy had not run off with PC Tunnock's property for financial gain: he'd taken the stuff in a moment of desperate confusion. If he would only return the stuff quickly and show genuine remorse, Chizzie felt, Billy might still have a future in Tannadee. Thinking along these lines, and eschewing Paw's advice, Chizzie met Jim at the school again and agreed to go up Dennan Hill to the place where Billy had approached him before.

"I can't say I entirely blame Billy," said Jim. "A mound of earth thrown up around his house is a pretty harsh lesson for him in the ways of the world, and a bloody ruthless thing to do to an old man and a young lad."

"And Weever's carved his way through the West Woods," added Chizzie.

"Yes, which is frankly criminal – and, what's worse, he'll get away with it. When a shark smells blood, as they say, there's no stopping it. And he's smelled it, so the question now is what next?" But it wasn't all bad news. "On a brighter note," Jim continued, "Jill Stewart is thinking of taking a sabbatical year after the holidays if we can find a suitable replacement. She mentioned you."

Chizzie jolted in surprise. "Me? Favourably?"

Jim laughed. "Of course. It could be a chance for you to get your CV on a full-time footing. Have a word with Jill if you're interested, though do discuss it with your dad first. I know he won't be pleased."

"Nope, there's no need for that, Jim," Chizzie insisted. "Dad and I see things very differently now. I want a career in education, and this would be a big step on the ladder for me."

"It would indeed, Chizzie, and I'm glad to hear you want it, but do have a word with your dad first – for my sake, if not yours, I don't want him coming round here and giving me the hairdryer treatment for pinching his star player."

Grudgingly, Chizzie agreed. Then, slightly stunned and slightly ecstatic, he made his way down the corridor towards the school dining room. He hadn't gone far when it occurred to him that Jill Stewart might still be in her lab. It had just gone lunchtime. So, he walked on until he got to the science corridor.

At the science department's office, he found a boy in school uniform looking slightly dishevelled and forlorn; he had a note in his hand.

"Are you waiting for someone?" Chizzie asked.

"I want to give this note to Mr Devine," replied the boy, "I know he's in there. I've knocked lots of times, but he's not answering."

"Maybe he's very busy. I'll give it to him if you like."

The boy thanked Chizzie and handed him the note.

"What's your name?" Chizzie asked.

"Jack Mathieson, sir. I'm the class rep for 3X."

"Oh," replied Chizzie, failing to hide the ominous note in his voice.

"We're not as bad as people say."

Chizzie didn't argue. "I'll see that Mr Devine gets your note. Now, it's best you go and get your lunch, Jack."

As the boy moved away, Chizzie read the note. If it had been written by monks, it could hardly have been more majestic; in a flowing, copperplate hand fit for a wedding invitation it bore the simple message "We are not stick incsets We are human biens. Yours sincerly, Class 3X." The basic thrust of the message escaped Chizzie, but it seemed sufficiently innocuous to pass on, so he knocked on the door and entered.

Inside, he found Mr Devine, who was large and bearded, fast asleep with his head on the table. Radio 2 blared out from the shelf above. A half-filled-in football coupon lay next to his big, snoring nose. Evidently, divining the score draws had robbed the man of all his strength. As the head of science, Devine had this little office all to himself to help him meet the heavy demands of the role. At least, that was the theory. Everyone, including Jim, knew very well that Devine was an increasingly opinionated slacker, but he still got good results – even with difficult pupils – so he retained his role, but only just.

Deciding to let sleeping dogs lie, Chizzie turned to go. Then devilment got the better of him. Moving quietly up to Devine, he stood behind him and clapped his hands together. Devine's head shot into the air.

"Arsenal versus Chelsea," recommended Chizzie, pointing helpfully in the direction of Devine's coupon, while giving him a reproving look. "They're always good for a score draw."

Devine lifted his head and smiled wearily; embarrassment haunted him for less than a second, though. He shook his head. "What time is it?" he enquired.

"Twelve-forty," replied Chizzie, arms folded.

"What may I do you for?"

"Well, actually, I'm just delivering a note on behalf of a young man who knocked on your door several times but failed to gain your attention."

"Less of the sarcasm; I nodded off for a few minutes, that's all. I'll be all the better for it and so will my classes. Now, is that the note?"

Chizzie handed it over.

Devine read it and let out a dismissive laugh, then tossed it in the bin. "No problem," he said. "You've read it no doubt and are desperate to know what it all means."

Chizzie said nothing.

"Well, for the avoidance of confusion, this morning I told class 3X that the stick insect on the nature table was the only thing keeping the IQ of the class in double figures, and it had more chance of getting a job than they had, unless they pulled their fingers out. And now Jack Mathieson – the alpha male of the troop, God bless him – has taken it upon himself to complain."

"I take it you will apologise?"

"What? Apologise? Oh yes, I know. It was totally unprofessional of me. Well, it's too bad; the kids know me by now, and I tell it straight. It's not pc these days, of course. Oh no, very bad, naughty, naughty Mr Devine. But, the thing is, I'm still in the game, Mr Bryson. All the guys I started out with burned out long ago, but not me. I paced myself right from the start and survived to tell the tale. Twenty-three years on the clock and fourteen to go. Fourteen bloody years. Same job, same room and same bloody pupils frankly. Believe me, when you've seen twenty years of them, you've seen 'em all. So don't ask me to inspire anybody. I mean, who's inspiring me? Anyway, if the kids need inspiring, they're not doing their bit, are they? It's not for me to inspire them, any more than it's for them to inspire me. If they come in like wet rags, I'm not going to be leaping off my seat, with my arms in the air, shouting, 'Who's for a go at the Oxbridge entrance exam?' Expect it all on a plate, they do. But it's bad for them. They need to know that. When they come to me, I let them know. And, guess what? They don't like me. But I put the ball in their court, and it's for them to deal with it, and that's a better education than they'll ever get served on a plate."

"Hear, hear," piped a head peering round the door. It was Robert Barrington. "There's no such thing as education anymore!" he opined, shaking his head. "Training's all they get nowadays; training, and nothing more!"

"I couldn't agree more, Mr Barrington; good man," chimed Devine, placing a textbook over his football coupon, "Welcome to the brotherhood of derelict educationists. Now to what do we owe this honour? Not another teabag, surely?"

"Regrettably, I have to respond in the affirmative; not that I mean to cast aspersions on the quality of your teabags, Mr Devine – on the contrary, I can say with all candour that I have in fact found them surprisingly pleasant."

"A teabag?" exclaimed Chizzie. "I find you in reduced circumstances, Mr Barrington."

"And you know very well why that is, Mr Bryson," replied Barrington pointedly.

"I hope you're not still blaming me!" Chizzie protested, barely able to suppress a smile. "I did not put rabbit droppings in your tea caddy."

"I know you didn't, and we both know who did. Teachers they call themselves. Pah! The 'seventh form' I call them. Only marginally better than the pupils, that's your teacher today: a man-child, nothing but a man-child."

"We're teachers!" Chizzie reminded him, indicating Devine and himself with a wave of the hand.

"Present company excepted, of course," replied Barrington with an ingratiating smile. "I can't say I envy you your task, frankly. It's soul-destroying, I should say, having to put up with some of these classes. I've seen more life in molluscs. Yes, you've hit the nail right on the head there, Mr Devine. The only thing pupils want nowadays is adulation for singing about their first sexual experience or who's run off with their bitch, as they would have it these days. Time was when one went to school, got an education and developed thoughts of one's own, but that's all too much for pupils nowadays, apparently. They steal it off the internet and call it their own. I shudder; I truly shudder for the human race. I truly do."

Devine reached into a red cardboard box on the first shelf and pulled out a teabag. "Is one sufficient?" he enquired.

Barrington sighed. Putting the world to rights had taken the air out of him evidently. "Yes. Yes, that'll tide me over; thank you very kindly, Mr Devine."

"It can't be all bad, Mr Barrington," Chizzie insisted, determined not to let cynicism carry the day. "I mean, what's the problem? We're still producing doctors, lawyers, scientists, architects, generals and the like, are we not?"

"That's the top end of the spectrum there, Bryson; excuse me, Mr Bryson. The elite teach themselves. All teachers need do is point them in the right direction. But, at the other end of the spectrum, *ho*, that's another matter – a very different matter. And the truth is that no amount of teaching will turn them into anything better than walking, talking pet food." And, with that, he threw his arms aloft suddenly in a dramatic, defensive pose. "I know, I know – that's not pc; I'm guilty, guilty as charged!" he wailed mockingly, "But it's the truth, unsavoury though it may be! And, between the two extremes, what do we find? We find the vast sweep of humanity, like a seething herd of wildebeest chomping its way across the African plains – an ocean of brute flesh dedicated to nothing more than mere existence. And as for these professionals of whom you speak – they have no character and no class now; there's more to a profession than mere qualifications, Mr Bryson. But that's enough from me. 'Bad Mr Barrington,' I hear you say. You mustn't upset people. Well, that's too bad. Until the day comes, as come it will, when the thought police drag me from my bed at three in the morning, I will neither yield nor stint in my dedication to the truth. So, despair not, Mr Devine; you are not alone! Not alone! Good day to you, and thank you for the teabag. It's most kind of you." Then, at the door, he turned and continued, "Oh, and Mr Bryson, we need to discuss urgently what we're going to do about Mr Weever. He seems to be upsetting people. How do we resist?"

Preferring not to associate with the apparently bungling Barrington, and rather ashamed of his father's attitude, Chizzie felt obliged to dodge the question. "There's not much we can do. So, as far as my father and I are concerned at the moment, we'll just keep an eye on things and give due process a chance."

Barrington drew back slightly. "Oh dear, I didn't think I'd hear that coming from you; it sounds almost defeatist."

"It's nothing of the sort," insisted Chizzie looking angrily at Barrington. "There's no point picking fights when you don't need to."

Barrington paused for a moment with his head inclined upwards, which Chizzie knew to be purely for dramatic effect. Then, with a withering look, Barrington said simply, "I see." After that, he turned and left.

For a few moments, a charged silence hung in the air. Then, almost simultaneously, Chizzie and Devine turned and eyed each other.

"It sounds like the rabbit droppings have gone straight to his head," observed Chizzie. "You agree with that critique of education and world order?" he asked tersely, pointing towards the door.

Devine thought for a moment, then shrugged his shoulders before he ambled towards his shelves. "Not entirely, Chizzie; not entirely. In spite of enjoying free access to my teabags, it seems to me that Mr Barrington is a man without hope. I yet live in hope. Though I have to say I do find him very reassuring in one respect: at least my bloody pension's safe in his hands! The Mr Barringtons of this world do not off with your cash walk." With that, he pulled out a teabag. "Now, d'you fancy a brew?"

"No, thank you. I… I'm going to get some lunch. See you." Chizzie went out quickly, then took a step back and popped his head back round the door. "Personally, I wouldn't be too sure about your cash not walking off. He certainly won't be getting his hands on mine, that's for sure."

As Chizzie approached the dining hall a short while later, a very fine smell wafted towards him, and it made his stomach rumble. It was macaroni cheese, and it proved excellent – very cheesy and very crispy on top. The sago pudding with raisins was also very filling, not least because he had three platefuls on account of Mrs McEwen being unable to dislodge the thought of frog spawn from her mind and the raisins reminding Mr Moffat too much of bluebottles.

Satiated with his meal and feeling rather pleasant, Chizzie reclined and took the time to look round the dining hall for a moment or two. He looked first at the walls, then languidly observed the roof, and – after a minute or so – he watched the flow of people passing by. They were, as Barrington would have it, a mass of wildebeest on the hoof, though it occurred to Chizzie that they were more like a mass of sago pudding and macaroni cheese on the hoof, which suddenly made him feel rather queasy.

He turned his thoughts to his prospective full-time colleagues. Which one would he be in the coming years? A Mr Devine – the cynical, time-serving lag? Or a Mr Moffat, perhaps – who was seemingly eccentric? Or a Jim even – aloof, alone and rather lonely perhaps? Or would he be one of the seventh form, as Barrington would have it: a man but one rung above the pupils – a man-child? These were chastening thoughts.

Commitment is a pretty scary thought and there it was, staring him right in the face – years of it. Was he ready? Ready to be tied down? Maybe he'd been too hasty in accepting Jim's offer. Maybe Billy had the right idea, and perhaps freedom was the most important thing in a young life. He felt his mouth drying, and the noise of the dining hall getting louder.

Then Miss Falconer walked in. Her kingfisher-blue top and her light-blue slacks might not be the last word in fashion, but they were more than merely tasteful, and her fair hair cascaded, not just modestly but majestically, down over her shoulders. Chizzie's doubts began to melt – if such a woman could be a part of Tannadee, then so could Chizzie Bryson. But Chizzie Bryson would have to find another Miss Falconer, for this one was engaged to be married.

She wasn't the only nice thing on view, however. Through the large windows, Chizzie observed Mrs Catriona Hay sitting on the lawn beneath a large beech tree, instructing members of the classical-guitar club. And jovial Dave McDougall was over at the river's edge, putting the pipe band through a practice session that was clearly very committed, though undoubtedly better seen than heard. Out on the loch, members of the sailing club were flowing quietly along with the warm breeze that ruffled the water beyond the emerging flag irises.

A warm feeling arose in Chizzie's body and eased into his mind. Tannadee might be no bustling metropolis, but it was a place of calmness, beauty and contentment. Bliss would not attend it every day, of course, but there would be good times enough. Feeling reassured and quite satisfied, Chizzie rose from the dining table and went outside to enjoy the fresh air.

A sunbeam warmed him as he stepped onto the lawn and pulled in a full draught of Highland air. *If they can bottle water, why not this stuff?* he thought.

Then someone shouted his name. He turned to see who it was. It was Jim, who was leaning out of his office window and pointing to Dennan Hill. "Look! It's Billy! He's coming down the hill by the trees over there!" he exclaimed. "He's with someone. It looks like a woman."

Chizzie screwed his eyelids closer together. "It's Yolanda!" he cried.

As Yolanda and Billy approached, they were jogging, Yolanda in her running gear, and Billy in his shirt and jeans. Yolanda held the police hat, and Billy clutched the carriage clock in one hand and two mugs in the other, his fingers hooked through the handles. Chizzie joined them as they came up to meet Jim, who was standing in the school doorway by then.

As Jim greeted Billy and Yolanda, he reached out for the police hat and insisted that he speak with Billy alone in his office right away. Billy said nothing, he merely glanced at Yolanda, who nodded. Then he shook his head and went with Jim.

Chizzie and Yolanda turned to one another. She looked worried.

"I hope they won't be too hard on him," she said. "He handed himself in. I didn't find him; he found me. He's actually very upset."

"I know," said Chizzie, who by now was fairly sure that he could read Billy quite well. He could also read genuine concern in Yolanda's face, along with evidence of several midge bites, though none had been apparent on Billy's face. "Where'd you find him? Or, rather, where'd he find you?" Chizzie asked.

"Up on Dennan Hill. I was out for a run, but I sat down by the lochan for a little while to have a good think. Then, out of the blue, Billy arrived. I needed the run, partly just to help me think straight and partly to escape my father; he keeps trying to get in touch. He wants to talk, but I don't; not now. I know what he'll say; I've heard it loads of times. I don't know how I'd react. My mom says I should kick him in the nuts, but he's my father; he's my dad. I can't even think of that."

The thought of Weever reeling about clutching his nuts was one that appealed very much to Chizzie. It was a good feeling, but it wasn't right. It might be only human to want to administer summary justice, but it was summary action that was at the root of Billy's problems – summary action from Billy himself and from Weever – so a more considered approach was called for. The trouble was, he couldn't think of one. All he could think of was what his heart desired. "I'm afraid I'm not much help, Yolanda, but perhaps a first-class meal on the house would help you feel better?"

It sounded like a limp chat-up line, and was almost embarrassing, but Yolanda – much to Chizzie's relief – smiled warmly and answered, "Is that a firm invitation?"

"It is. You're most welcome, Yolanda; absolutely," Chizzie replied, returning the warm smile. "Dinner tonight?"

"Dinner for two at seven, shall we say?"

"Excellent," replied Chizzie with a wink that he knew instantly was crass, but it was too late – it was done.

Fortunately, it brought only another smile from Yolanda, rather than the kick in the nuts her mother might have administered.

Then, a man cleared his throat close by; it was Jim. "May I have a word with you both, please?" he asked, gesturing towards his office.

They followed Jim and entered the office. Inside it, Billy was sitting in front of the desk, his arms tightly folded. "Yolanda," said Jim, "I don't want to put you on the spot, but Billy says he came to you and asked you to come with him because he wants to return PC Tunnock's property. I believe him, but I have to ask you if it's true."

"Yes. It is true," Yolanda insisted. "He came to me and explained what had happened. Frankly, I was very impressed by his manner – he seemed very sorry and… very open and honest too, actually."

"He says he won't apologise—"

Billy broke in angrily. "I'm handing the things back, but I'm not saying sorry," he insisted. "If I'm wrong, so's he. An' he started it."

Jim stared at Billy for a moment. "Right, I'll phone PC Tunnock now and tell him you're returning his things, and we'll see what he says."

"He can say what he likes, I'm not going to his house. He knows his things are here," Billy remonstrated.

"You took them away, Billy," replied Jim sternly. "You—"

"I'll return them," said Chizzie. "It's no problem."

CHAPTER 13

When Chizzie arrived at the police house, it was June who came to the door. PC Tunnock was not at home, but June made it clear that the return of the property marked the end of the matter and there would be no further action. With obvious relief, Chizzie expressed his immense gratitude and was on the point of offering the Tunnocks a complimentary dinner when it occurred to him that some people might construe the favour as some kind of bribery. Secrets never survived long in the village; it was even held that an international spy wouldn't last five minutes in Tannadee. So, Chizzie simply reiterated his thanks, then left and walked back to the hotel.

"Father, I left a couple of shopping bags in the conservatory, but they seem to have disappeared. Did you shift them?" Chizzie asked as he looked round the office door.

Johnny thought for a second. "Ah, you mean the rubbish? It's okay; I put it in the bin."

"Rubbish? That wasn't rubbish; that was Billy's stuff."

"What stuff?"

"All his stuff: his property and his prized possessions."

"Prized possessions? You mean old toothpaste and smelly, old trainers? If I hadn't put that junk out, it would've walked out!"

"Is it still out there?"

"No, the truck took it away half an hour ago."

Chizzie closed his eyes, blew out his cheeks and shook his head before letting out an anguished sigh. Partly, it was his own fault, as he ought to have let his dad know. But it had all happened so quickly, and there was so much to think about at the time. Now, he was going to have to test his powers of diplomacy against Billy's often-weird logic. "I'll explain it to him when he comes back."

"Who comes back?"

"Billy. I want to see how he gets on in the kitchen."

"Billy Pung is not going anywhere near my kitchen."

Chizzie raised his head and eyed Johnny sternly.

Johnny got the message suddenly and corrected himself: "Our kitchen."

"Say it often enough and it'll come naturally," said Chizzie, parroting his father's own phrase. "If it's our kitchen, I have a say, and I say he's welcome."

"He's a thief, Chisholm: he steals. I can't – we can't – let him loose in the hotel. If he steals from guests, we're finished."

"He won't steal."

"How d'you know? He stole at school; he even stole from the bloody police, for Christ's sake!"

"I know it sounds odd, but he's no thief. You have to put it in context."

"Aw, for heaven's sake, Jesus wept. All these poor prisoners in jails up and down the land, they're just so misunderstood; get to know them better and you'll find they're really lovely, lovely people! My heart bleeds. How can you be so gullible?"

"Billy's different."

"Oh yes, of course he is."

"He is. He really is. People've put a lot of time and effort into helping Billy get a future. They wouldn't have done that if they didn't believe in him. He's turned a corner, but a little blip backwards and you're down on him. Yes, a little blip it is, and don't wag your finger at me. I am not gullible. We've really turned a corner with Billy, and what he needs now is a little help to navigate the road. It won't be easy. Before we even start, I've got to tell him his treasured stuff's in the dump. Hopefully, he'll trust me, but maybe he won't. Then, after that showdown, I've to tell him he's fired. Not exactly his lucky day, is it? How d'you think it's all going to hit him and all the people who've helped him?"

"You're missing the point. This is a hotel, not a bloody mental institution! I'm bending over backwards to make this business a real success, in spite of Weever, and I can't afford setbacks! And neither can you!"

"I insist that Billy comes back. I'll take full responsibility."

Johnny sighed then drooped his head sideways, staring at the floor. He sighed again, deeply, and thought a little more. Finally, with a wary glance at Chizzie, he said, "You'll keep a beady eye on him."

"Of course I will."

"And I'll get CCTV fitted."

"There's no need for that, Father."

Johnny thought for a moment. "How's the website coming along?"

"Slowly," Chizzie answered sheepishly. He took the hint and went to do some further work on it.

Toiling on his laptop in the conservatory, Chizzie found website production the usual frustrating business; for one thing, the photos supplied by Johnny weren't just dreary, they were aimed exclusively at a mature clientele. Johnny strongly believed, probably correctly, that this was the target market for the Tannadee Hotel, but it left Chizzie with very little scope for innovative fun. Or did it? Just because the guests were mature, it didn't mean they didn't like to let their hair down now and again. Heartened by these afterthoughts, Chizzie wrestled further with the software.

Annoyingly, though, the software seemed to have its own opinions about picture placement – it stoutly refused to accept some photos, while others that had been placed perfectly would jump suddenly and find a new home elsewhere on the screen. Irrational though it might seem, Chizzie felt the computer was somehow empathising with the mood of the operator. With all the frustration, jumpy was certainly how he was feeling.

At the back of his mind lay the explanation that he was going to have to give Billy about the loss of his stuff. It was difficult to know which was better: the truth, or some cobbled-together story about a freak whirlwind, mad dog or a burglar, perhaps. The trouble with lies, though, however white, is that you need to make them real in your mind and to the tiniest detail, or you get caught out, and body language can be a sure giveaway. Billy was probably good at reading body language; he'd certainly demonstrated acute natural awareness at times. Chizzie, on the other hand, had no doubts about his own lack of prowess in this particular field – he was pretty much an open book.

Suddenly, a muffled thud on the window jolted him. But, looking round, he saw no one there. He got up and went over to have a closer look. Outside, a cock sparrow was lying upside down and breathing rapidly on one of the concrete slabs. He considered going outside to pick it up, but then it struggled a bit and righted itself, looking as bewildered as Chizzie felt about the website software. Then, it flew off suddenly. If only all problems were so easily solved.

However, just as he moved away, there was another knock, which was at the opposite window. "Aw God, not another one!" he muttered, but there was no unlucky bird this time: it was unlucky Billy who'd come for his stuff.

Taking a deep breath, Chizzie went to the door and let him in.

Amazingly, and to Chizzie's great relief, Billy wasn't the least bit perturbed about his stuff hitting the dump. Not that Chizzie put it that bluntly: his explanation made no mention of the stuff walking out by itself, but alluded positively to the virtues of recycling and the promise of the stuff being replaced on a new-for-old basis. This approach was fortified by the news that the stuff Billy really valued was actually in Paw's house and the stuff in the shopping bags was simply stuff he didn't want other people throwing about when he was banged up in jail. He was delighted by the new-for-old offer and even more thrilled about the prospect of working in the kitchen. Home economics had been his favourite subject at school, no doubt helped by the fact it was mostly girls in the class. Moreover, the 'beast of burden' tag had struck home.

"I don't want to be carrying other people's things anymore. They can carry their own things. I'm not an animal. And you get more money for cookin'," Billy insisted.

But Billy's dreams of 'big-money cookin'' got off to a faltering start. The chef had phoned in sick, which was always a worrying development for a hotel manager conscious of norovirus, E. coli and all the other bugs that forever seem to stalk the headlines as some poor devil in hospitality cops it. Thankfully, it was only a bout of angina that kept the chef away, and the sous chef, Jeff Proudfoot, was able to welcome Billy on board. But it wasn't actually much of a welcome, and it certainly wasn't a warm one.

Jeff, who was tall and thin, looked pale and nervous. "With Chef out, I'm on my own," he whined, "There's eight reservations, and I haven't got time to help the lad – he'll need to help me with prepping and then help on service. I can't do everything. I'm a good second in command, but I'm not a leader. I need help. I'm on my own. People want everything now, this minute – and that's not me. Everybody's wanting their food *now*. Not in ten minutes, not in five minutes, but *now* – it has to be *now*. Now! Now! Now! People are obsessed with now! Obsessed! Nobody waits no more – they wait an' somehow their life's flashin' past their eyes, all cos there's no steak under their nose in seconds. Good food takes time! They know that, but they don't care. They get what they deserve."

"And what's that?" asked Chizzie apprehensively.

"Food poisoning! It's inevitable."

Chizzie looked alarmed. "Food poisoning is not inevitable," he said sharply.

"I don't want to be hit again," Jeff explained. "The punters, they have a choice. They can have waitin' an' real food, or they can have speed an' salmonella. I know what I'd choose."

"What d'you mean 'hit again'?"

"It wasn't me. I didn't flatten people – it was the bum pâté."

"*Bum pâté?*"

"It was chicken liver pâté, but the fridge went on the blink an' it got warm, so bugs got goin'. I said don't serve it, but it was a big weddin' do, an' Chef said serve it up. So I did."

"What happened?"

"Well, nobody died, but Chef got jailed an' I got admonished. Chef said he'd get even one day, cos I helped the police with their inquiries. Oh, I just wanna get out of this business, you know. It's so depressin'. I don't know why I do it. Well, yeah, I do know – I can't do nothin' else, that's why."

Welcome to 'big-money cookin', Billy, thought Chizzie. "I didn't know about all this," he said.

"Nobody asked me."

"Your references made no mention of it."

"'Course not. If you want rid of somebody, you give 'em a glowing reference, don't you? That's how it's done. Everybody knows that. You gave me the job; I took it. But not head chef; I didn't take that job."

"Let me get this straight: you poisoned people."

"Years ago. Some of them say they'll get me one day. Sue me for every penny. What a laugh. Me? Every penny? What penny?"

Chizzie shook his head in amazement: "Well, Jeff, I'm... I'm stunned... I'm blown away. That's some revelation."

"And my name's not Jeff."

"What?"

"I changed it. It's easy: a few quid and, hey presto, you're somebody else. Some nights I fear a knock at the door, but other nights I can't stop laughing. I'm somebody else now, so how're they goin' to find me?"

"So, who are you really?"

"Wilson Tucker."

Chizzie blew out his cheeks. "Well, Wilson, you've... you've put us all in a right old quandary now. And that's putting it mildly. I don't know what to..."

"Jeff. It's Jeff now. Definitely Jeff. Look, everything'll be fine; let's just stay positive. I'm not a killer. I'm actually a pretty fine cook. If we just take our time, we can come out of this just fine. But I need time. Just don't rush me."

"I can help. I cook a little."

"Oh no, no, no. Having the boss under me – that would scramble my brain. Turn it to complete mush. I'll manage okay on my own. Just no rushin', okay?"

"I'll offer complimentary drinks to diners," said Chizzie. Jeff nodded approvingly.

Chizzie took a deep breath. "Well, Billy," he said, turning to the aghast novice, "welcome... welcome to... to cooking."

CHAPTER 14

A quarter of an hour before Yolanda was due to arrive, Chizzie was at the front door of the hotel, waiting. Some of Jeff's nervousness seemed to have affected him. He shuffled aimlessly backwards and forwards on the top step, craning his neck now and again to see who was approaching. He mused on what Yolanda would wear; how much trouble would she go to? Too casual would signal little interest in developing a relationship. Too much trouble would suggest a person who was rather self-absorbed. *It must be difficult being a woman,* he thought, *with so many different options and so many different signals.*

And Yolanda's range was wider than most: it wasn't beyond the realms of possibility that she'd turn up jogging or even driving a tractor. In the event, she arrived in a car; however, the car was driven by none other than Charlie Fairfoull.

It was a heart-stopping moment for Chizzie. He thought, *She's come to say sorry, but no thanks. My evening is over. It's time for the brave face and the quiet understanding. There're plenty more fish in the sea, but who wants to kiss a fish? It probably wouldn't've worked out anyway. It's a bit of a cheek turning up with the boyfriend, though. That's rubbing it in. She's definitely not worth it. She's doing me a favour really.*

When she got out of the car, she turned and spoke briefly to Charlie. Chizzie couldn't hear what she said, but he imagined it was something like keep the engine running. What a rat. Evidently, the Weever blood was coursing. She came up the steps purposefully; it was nothing to her. Charlie watched her intently, and, catching Chizzie's eye, he smiled in a manner that seemed almost contemptuous. Chizzie swallowed and braced himself, feeling like an interloper. He tried hard to think of something pithy yet casual to say, but he really couldn't be sure what he'd say. This was awkward.

"Hi. Sorry I'm late," Yolanda called breezily, "I like to be punctual normally, but something came up; I'll explain inside. How are you?"

Chizzie nearly fell backwards. While he was looking for the left hook, she'd caught him with the right. "Oh, great!" he spluttered. "I'm... I'm very well actually, thank you." Over Yolanda's shoulder, he saw Charlie drive away. "How are you?"

"I'll be fine after a good meal and some wine. It's been quite a day."

He led her inside, and – once they were seated at the table – Chizzie opened his mouth to compliment Yolanda on her appearance, but she got in first and complimented him. It seemed genuine rather than merely polite, and he grew in confidence and returned the compliment with equal sincerity. Yolanda seemed keen to explain how she came to arrive at the hotel in Fairfoull's car. But, before she got started with the explanation, the head waitress arrived and introduced Billy, who produced the menus and the wine list mechanically. On Billy's departure, Yolanda explained that her father had been trying to get hold of her all afternoon, but she was in no mood to meet him and, even when he sent Charlie out to inveigle her, she defied him.

Chizzie felt like leaping to his feet and ordering champagne for everyone, but he kept his head and thanked his guest for coming despite all her troubles.

She told Chizzie that the thought of tonight's meal had helped her stay positive. It was all going very well, better even than Chizzie had hoped; until, suddenly, Yolanda noticed that the menu offered her nothing. "I'm a vegetarian, and there's no vegetarian option here."

Chizzie's heart hit the floor. He apologised, called Billy over and told him to ask Chef what the vegetarian options were. Billy picked up on the urgency in Chizzie's voice and ran to the kitchen, prompting looks of concern from some of the diners. No one needed to tell Chizzie that things were now back on a knife edge – his future with Yolanda was now in the hands of a reformed food poisoner who was about as stable as nitroglycerine. As he made polite conversation nervously about his website travails, Chizzie's mind was in the kitchen, hoping against hope that his chef would remain a coherent entity. When Billy returned briskly, relief and apprehension mingled in Chizzie's breast. The omens were not good – Billy had neither a menu nor a note in his hands. Chizzie strove hard to put on a cheery façade.

"Well, Billy, what's the good news?" he asked.

"Chef said, 'Bloody hell. She'll have to make do with ham salad,'" said Billy.

In the circumstances, a lesser man would have hit the floor, but Chizzie merely recoiled, winced and wished he was dead. With a pained smile, he cast a furtive glance at Yolanda. She half-winced and half-laughed.

Reddening with embarrassment, Chizzie gulped and looked sternly at Billy. "Billy, you don't tell the diners exactly what—"

"And he's havin' a heart attack, he said," added the young waiter.

"*He's what?*" gasped Chizzie.

"Having a heart attack. He told me to get away."

Chizzie leaped from his chair, almost knocking it over. "Hell's teeth!" he hissed and ran towards the kitchen door.

The diners looked alarmed. Here was yet another man making a fast exit; could they be next?

When he reached the kitchen, Chizzie found the ventilation fans full on and the chef slouched over a sink, sipping water from a glass. "*Jeff! Jeff! Are you okay?*" Chizzie bawled as he dashed over to the stricken man.

Jeff, looking drained, nodded in the affirmative and straightened up. "Just trying to settle things down with sips of water," he answered.

"You had a heart attack?"

Jeff looked puzzled and shook his head. "Heart attack? No. Why?"

"Billy said you did. You told him you were having a heart attack."

"A fart attack. A fart attack's what I said, not a heart attack. I get terrible wind when I'm nervous. The pills don't work. It's blighted my whole career. I've cleared kitchens in the past. I'm feeling pressure now, an' it's all kicking off. I need help. Billy's no help; he's too slow – far too slow."

"I'll help!" came a voice from the doorway. It was Yolanda. "I've cooked in hotels. Get me some whites and tell me what you need doing."

Chizzie and Jeff fell silent in astonishment.

"Well, come on," Yolanda insisted. "There's people waiting out there. Move it!"

"Right. I'll get the whites," replied Jeff, hurrying to a cupboard just outside the door. "Breakfast Susie's stuff'll fit you."

As he took out the clothing, there was a clatter at the rear door, then the fly screen swung open and a young man with Down's syndrome entered, carrying two bulging shopping bags.

"Good man, Plato," Jeff cried as the young man hoisted the bags onto a work surface.

Chizzie was as baffled as he looked: "What's this?" he asked.

"It's fish and chips!" explained Jeff, "The fryer went on the blink, so we had to send out."

Then, the fly screen swung open again, and in came a big man carrying a rather large cooking appliance. It was Denis Dekker, from the chip shop. "I've got a mobile fryer for you," he announced. "It'll keep you going till yours is fixed. There's no charge. Just make sure it's clean when you bring it back."

"I'll do that, sir," replied Plato, the kitchen porter, saluting, "Don't you worry, sir."

Chizzie began to feel totally overwhelmed, and his thoughts swirled in all directions. "It's good of you to help us out, Denis, but… but we can't sell your chips as ours."

"Not good enough, you mean?" enquired Denis.

"No, no. Your stuff's great, Denis – as always – but they're simply not ours."

"They are now," insisted Yolanda, "Come on, set up the fryer, Denis, and see if the fish and chips are hot enough. I'll get into my whites. Where may I change?"

Chizzie directed her to the locker room.

But seeds of doubt had sprouted in Jeff's mind. "You're right; you're right," he said turning anxiously to Chizzie, "Reheating fish and chips – that could mean food poisoning."

"No, no," insisted Dekker, "I do it all the time. In any case, open these cartons and you'll find they're well hot enough. Look, try one." He pulled open one of the cartons, steam rose up, and Dekker's big fingers thrust a chip into Jeff's mouth.

It was clearly hot enough, for Jeff gasped and waggled his tongue trying to ventilate the scalding chip. "Well, dat one's hod enough," he acknowledged. "Wha' aboud the rest dough?"

"Well, we're not testing them all," replied Dekker, "or you won't have any to serve up."

Jeff took another sip of water, then rubbed his chin. He looked perplexed. "Oh, I don't know. I don't know," he muttered.

"Right, let's get a-cookin'!" cried Yolanda, striding in. "What's first?"

Jeff made no response.

Yolanda clapped her hands: "Come on, Chef. What needs doing? Tell me."

Easing out from his cloud of woe, the chef spoke softly. "Well, first off, three haddock and chips: one breaded and two battered."

Dekker pointed to the cartons. "Breaded have got the cross on and battered have the circle on."

"Do you want them garnished, Chef?" Yolanda asked.

"Sure. Do you know what to do?" queried Jeff.

"I trained in the Weever Plaza, New York. Is that good enough?"

"Aw God, she's better than I am. I'm redundant," wailed Jeff.

"No, you're not redundant," Yolanda assured him, "You're Chef. Now come on. Let's go! We're on it!"

Dekker opened the cartons, and Yolanda decanted them carefully onto warmed plates. Everyone watched as Yolanda set about presenting the dishes speedily and artfully with a variety of trimmings. Nobody said anything; it seemed that any intervention would only slow her down. Then she offered the dishes for inspection, to which Jeff simply nodded each time, seemingly overwhelmed. She called service, and Lena – the head waitress – with what looked like a smile of relief, took the dishes away along with sauces.

She wasn't the only one who was relieved; Chizzie couldn't help but applaud. The others joined him, and even

Jeff managed to get his hands together. Then, he got up, shook Yolanda's hand and thanked her before turning to Dekker and gratefully thanking him. Chizzie, seizing his opportunity, strode over to Yolanda and kissed her cheek: it was a big chance, which was too good to miss. He also thanked Dekker; there was no kiss for the big man, though, just a high five, but it was well meant for all that.

"It looks like you've lost some weight, Denis," Chizzie commented.

"Twenty pounds," confirmed Denis. "I'm working out with Sven now – just helpin' him stay off the booze really. I'm gettin' him hooked on end… end… them hormones that sounds like 'dolphins.'"

"Endorphins."

"That's it!"

"Well, it's doing wonders for you, Denis; it really is."

"Talking about weight loss, I'm fading to weightless here!" cried Yolanda. "I need something to eat, even if it's just cheese on toast, so everybody just stand back, please!"

"No, no, allow me," insisted Jeff, leaping to his feet. "My treat!"

But, in seconds, his enthusiasm evaporated and self-doubt seized him once again. "No. No. You'll do it better than I ever could," he whined. "I'd probably poison you. I poison food; I poison the air."

But Yolanda turned on him. "No, Chef, no," she insisted. "I would like you to—"

The service bell rang, and Lena called out: "One steak au poivre and one beef wellington! Compliments to the chef on the haddock and chips!"

It hit Jeff like a wet haddock. "The only thing complimented and it's somebody else's. I'm hopeless," he blurted as he sagged.

The door swung open and Johnny stepped into the kitchen. "What's going on?" he blared.

"Chef phoned in sick, so we're all pitching in," answered Chizzie.

"What's *he* doing in here?" Johnny demanded, pointing to Dekker.

Chizzie explained.

Yolanda held up her hand, and stepped between Chizzie and Johnny. "Look, I need to tell you something. Your chef is not sick: he's working for my father. My father offered him a contract last night, paying more than you're paying, and your man took it."

"What?" exclaimed Johnny. "He's gone? He can't do that!"

"He's done it," replied Yolanda. "It's a fait accompli."

Johnny could barely take it in. "He... he... what're we going to do?" he whined. He clearly did not share Chizzie's confidence in Jeff. For Johnny, a chef should advertise the quality of his work by his girth – chefs should be small, round, cheery fellows. There was something slightly troubling about a thin chef. Johnny eyed the man cautiously.

Chizzie broke the silence. "Jeff's stepping up to the plate," he replied, feigning complete confidence.

"No. No. I can't," insisted Jeff.

"He's nobbled you too?" asked Johnny in disbelief.

"No, no, I'm just not cut out for head chef."

"One steak au poivre and one beef wellington!" cried Lena returning and adding, "Compliments to the chef on the coq au vin!"

"Uh? Eh?" blurted Jeff. "But that was mine! All mine!"

"See! There you are. You're the man!" cried Yolanda. "Let's go; let's go, Chef. Direct me! Come on! And Chizzie make me a sandwich please! Let's go!"

Johnny, still stunned, turned to Yolanda; "Why on earth would your father steal my chef?"

"I don't know. You'd best keep your wits about you, though, Mr Bryson. He's probably up to something: probably some kind of stinker. My mother didn't call him 'Gordonzola' for nothing."

CHAPTER 15

Charlie Fairfoull looked very pleased. "It's looking good," he said. "We've got the provost of Millburgh coming and most of the councillors, and Lord Tulloh is very likely."

"Very likely?" queried Weever. "What's that mean?"

"Not sober, most probably; his lordship has got something of a reputation in that regard."

"Well, we can't have a drunk falling over in the middle of our party, lord or no lord. If he gets here, tell him he can get as drunk as a lord when he's done, but not before."

"His valet will keep him right; I've met the guy, and he knows how to handle the old boy."

"Okay. Now, I've thought about the trees – the West Wood ones – at the eighth hole. I want them down – this morning. The politicians have to see how we need that route through the woods. It's the jewel in the crown. They've got to know that, and seeing is believing. So, get our guys on to it and cut through. And get security – there must be no interlopers."

"There'll be one helluva row."

"So what? I don't care. I didn't come here shelling out good money to have tree huggers calling the shots. So, these trees will be gone, right? They'll be gone by noon today. The councillors have never seen these trees, so what's it to them? But we'll keep 'em sweet anyhow: they'll get gift packs on arrival."

"They'll have to declare them, which could be seen as bribery."

"Okay, the gift packs go to the wives."

"Not all the councillors are men; there's two women."

"Then it's gift packs for all: wives, husbands, partners, children, hamsters, parrots, the lot. Weever perfumes for the ladies and Weever sports products for the men – unless they're gay, in which case they'll get Weever health products. Oh, what the hell – just let 'em all choose. If the gays want perfume, they get perfume. That's how they went gay in the first place: they were exposed to perfume far too young."

"Really?"

"Think about it. What is perfume? It's chemicals, right? And half the drugs we use come from plants, right? And what does perfume actually do?"

"It makes you smell nice?"

"More than that. It goes in the nose, through the veins, into the blood and into the brain. That's how it works: it affects the brain. With an adult brain, that's okay, but a young child's brain is very different: it's developing and it's vulnerable. And ask yourself this: what is perfume actually based on?"

"Chemicals?"

"Plants – female plant parts. The female plant puts out perfume to attract insects that carry pollen, right? And what's pollen?"

"It's yellow powder?"

"It's the male plant part – the sperm or the essence of the male. With its perfume, the female plant's begging for the male. Expose a young boy to too much perfume, and what's that going to do? It's going to make his brain want a male partner, that's what."

Fairfoull hesitated for a moment before sounding thoughtful. "Well, I've never thought of it like that, Gordon. What about lesbians, though?"

"Well, it's the opposite of course – not enough perfume in their early life. Or too much male company early on. You've heard of phenomonones?"

"Pheromones?"

"Yeah. They're hormones, right? They float in the air. We've all got them; we all produce them: humans, bears, insects, everybody. They're going out all the time. Now, a young girl spending too much time with males is gonna soak up lots and lots of male pheromones, right? Into the blood it goes, then into the brain, and, hey presto, you have yourself a lesbian. Yolanda's okay; I made sure of that, despite her mother. In any case, her mother's so darn cussed she's probably half male hormones."

"Interesting theories, Gordon."

"More than theories, Charlie. That's just how it is, no doubt about it. The male–female balance is delicate; it's very, very delicate, especially in kids. You know not everybody's a perfect male or perfect female, don't you? Except very few, that is, and you're looking at one right now."

"Really? I didn't know that. Okay, right; I'll need to be off now and get things organised."

"Are you smirking?"

"Not at all."

"Don't patronise me, Charlie. I know that tone."

Unable to hold back any longer, Fairfoull burst out laughing.

"Oh, you laugh, Charlie; you laugh. You go right ahead, but there's something out there that's making people gay. As sure as hell, something's got to these people."

Fairfoull laughed even louder.

"Are you gay? No. No. You can't be: you and Yolanda hit it on. Or maybe it's off now; maybe you are one."

Fairfoull's laughter, no longer stifled, swelled in volume, and soared into a state of helpless cackling and falsetto trills as his shoulders shook uncontrollably.

Undaunted, Weever fastened on to another possibility. "Or maybe you're one of those bicyclists – bisexuals – pedalling two wheels."

Fairfoull was laughing so much that he was running out of breath; he reached weakly for a chair and plonked himself down, clutching his sides, his eyes watering, so utterly consumed with laughter that even Weever couldn't help laughing – laughing at Fairfoull laughing at him.

"They laughed at Columbus, you know," said Weever.

"He thought he was in India," gasped Fairfoull.

But this was one too far for Weever: he was no laughing stock. He stopped laughing suddenly, and, turning deadly serious, advised Fairfoull that he do the same. "Enough, Charlie. It's over!" he snapped. "You've had your laugh, now get out of here and get to work."

Breathing heavily and moaning, Fairfoull rose from the chair and rubbed his ribs. "Oh dear. Whew. Right. I'll get the trees down right away and I'll see to the gift packs. The caterers'll be here soon with the marquee and food."

"What about the booze? Is there enough for the press?"

"There's enough for the press and the councillors too. We've a whole load of stuff."

"Even so, get some more. Some of these people sound like bottomless pits. And Lord Tulloh, he'll take some filling by the sound of things."

There was no reply, for Fairfoull suddenly burst out laughing again and was making for the door when his mobile phone rang. "It's Barrington," he said, turning to Weever.

Weever nodded.

Charlie took the call. "Hello, Mr Barrington. How are you on such a gay day?"

For a moment, there was silence.

Then, sounding a little wary, Barrington replied: "Well, nearly as happy as you are, possibly."

Charlie burst out laughing again. "Good for you, Robert; it's good to get the old happy muscles going now and again. Now, what may I do for you?"

"It's just a brief call to let you know that our opponents are in disarray. It seems all the objectors to Mr Weever's development have lost heart and they're in no mood to mount any kind of organised protest. So, now would seem to be an eminently propitious time to pursue any initiative that Mr Weever and your good self might have in mind. Strike while the iron's hot, as they say – though that's perhaps not the most appropriate metaphor, but you know what I—"

"Yes, yes, Robert, that's very good; it's excellent news – and very timely too. We're about to exercise our initiative, as you say, and there might be some kind of reaction tomorrow. So, keep your head down and your ear to the ground. Then let us know what we need to know. It's great to have you on the team, Robert. Thank you for your help; it's valued as always. Take care now."

"Anytime I can be of service just let—"

"Yes, Robert, excellent; I have your number, and we'll be in touch when we need you. It's good to talk again. You take care now. Bye."

Smiling, Fairfoull turned to Weever. "It looks like the objectors have buckled," he said, "The heart's gone out of them, and they've given up. We can push on."

"What'd I say? I knew they were gutless. They all are. Lots of noise like a wounded bear, then they roll over and we skin 'em."

Chizzie, Yolanda, Dekker and Sven were not quite ready to be skinned. Acting on Yolanda's hunch, they had anticipated Weever's move on the woods and were waiting as the woodcutters arrived to do their work. A Landcruiser came up quickly behind the woodcutters and drew to a halt. Fairfoull stepped out of the vehicle.

Yolanda greeted him cheerily, "Good morning, Charlie. Come to join us on our nature ramble?"

"You're on private property, I'm afraid, lady and gentlemen," declared Fairfoull, striding towards the party of four. "And I have to ask you to leave."

"We're exercising our right to roam, sir," replied Yolanda. "Perhaps you're not familiar with that piece of legislation?"

"I am very familiar with it, madam; familiar enough to know that you are not at liberty to interfere with the legitimate working of land. So, I repeat: you must leave the property immediately."

"Exactly what work would that be, sir?" enquired Yolanda.

"That's commercially sensitive information, madam. Now please leave."

"It wouldn't be the felling of protected trees, would it?"

Fairfoull looked about for a few seconds, then turned and fixed his gaze on Yolanda. He held it there for a few moments as if to indicate that he had much to say but would not voice it.

"Oh, look, a little star!" cried Sven, picking up a flower and holding it against his chest, "I'm the sheriff now. I say what goes."

"No, Sven, that's Arctic starflower; don't pull that!" Chizzie exclaimed.

Chastened, Sven apologised.

"It seems that you people aren't quite so holy after all,"

quipped Fairfoull before walking away, taking out his walkie-talkie and contacting Weever.

On the other end of the transmission, Weever took up his walkie-talkie in his office. "Yolanda? A tree hugger?" he barked. "What the hell next? Tell her I want to see her or she's outta here! I've just about had it with her!" Weever rarely exploded, for the simple reason that he rarely encountered anything he couldn't shift. Consequently, in meeting an obstruction, he would usually vent his seething anger in a very controlled manner, which manifested itself through coolly delivered abuse. But now, in the privacy of his office, he could cut loose. Surrounded by thick stone walls, Weever yelled, "*I don't care how you do it, but get these fucking bums outta there! Fuck 'em!*"

"But Yolanda's one of them," cautioned Fairfoull.

"Get her outta there, but be careful. I don't want her harmed. It's not Yolanda I'm fighting; it's her mother. But the other fuckers – you kick their ass any way you like! Only remember this: I didn't tell you. Whatever you do, it's your fucking show! I know nothing. Just get it done before the celebs get here."

"But—"

"Get on and get it done! Do it!"

"I-I can't do that."

"Can't do what?"

"Attack these people. I'm calling the police."

"You can't get the police if the trees are protected! The police'll protect them!"

"I just need these people to get out of the way long enough for me to get the trees cut. Confusion'll do the trick."

"Fuck up, Charlie, and you're outta here! It's your fucking ass on the line now. Got it?"

"Got it. But Yolanda won't budge; I know her well enough to know that."

"Right, leave her to me. Get her!"

Fairfoull walked towards Yolanda, held up his walkie-talkie and explained, "Yolanda, your father sends his love and asks kindly to speak with you."

Yolanda laughed. "Tell him I'm not speaking to him till he stops cutting the trees here. Tell him that."

Fairfoull told him, and, as expected, Weever took it badly.

"What the fuck!" Weever ranted, "Tell her I want to see her or she's fucking outta here too. I've just about had it with her! Tell her! Fuck it!"

Fairfoull called to Yolanda, "Your father understands how passionately you feel, and is certain your concerns and his interests can be reconciled amicably over coffee."

"Tell him no. I need a guarantee on the trees or it's no deal."

Fairfoull told Weever.

Weever exploded again with a volley of even more expletives.

Fairfoull called to Yolanda, "He says there's meringues!"

Yolanda smiled.

"Best you speak with him, Yolanda," said Chizzie quietly. "Maybe you can talk him round."

When Yolanda and her father met in the drawing room of McShellach House, they embraced. Weever threw his arms round her and squeezed her tightly. He kissed Yolanda's cheeks, and, for a moment, she seemed overwhelmed, as she looked like some limp body fished out of a river, but she pushed with her forearms and eased herself free gently.

"Sweetheart! How are you?" Weever trilled.

"I'm good, thank you. And you?" she responded.

"I'm good too."

"Two goods."

Weever laughed nervously. "Now, two coffees?"

"You know I don't take coffee."

"Of course. I'm sorry. Tea, right?"

"Herbal infusion."

"Shit! Argh! Excuse me! Look… look, I know how this could play out. Let's just get the tough stuff over with first. You're mad at me, right? You want to tee me up and hit me clean out the park. Only, the thing is, Yolanda, I'm your dad. Never forget that. It's just not right for us to be strangers – or enemies even. It burns me up. Every day I ask myself the same question over and over: your mother aside, where did we go wrong, Yolanda?"

"We?"

"We used to get along so well."

"I grew up."

"Aw, come on, Yolanda, throw me a line here; you know I care. What do I have to do?"

"You know what you have to do."

"The trees, right?"

"We can start there."

"Oh, a list. There's a list."

"As long as my arm."

"Yolanda, please. Please don't treat me like shit. I'm your dad, right?"

"Yes, Father."

"Dad – call me Dad. Whatever happens, I'll always be your daddy."

"I have no choice. You're on my birth certificate."

"Aw, Yolanda. Yolanda, please, it breaks me up to hear you talk like this. D'you know something? Let me tell you, the sweetest memories I have ever had – that I've ever had in my whole life – they're of you. Nothing can ever beat the pleasure of hearing you call me Daddy. Nothing."

"And I used to be so proud of you."

"Thank you, that means so much."

"You're more than a father to me."

"I'm your daddy."

"You're a nightmare. I want to embrace the good in you, but, frankly, I'm repelled by the brute in you."

"Nightmare? Brute? *What…?*"

"I know there's people out there who think you're God, but most people hate your guts, and, believe me, it's not great for a girl to see her daddy reviled like that. It's awful!"

"Pah! Losers! That's all they are. Business is winners and losers, mostly losers, and they get sore. So what? I am what I am, Yolanda, I'm a winner and I don't hide it. People respect me for that. They may not like me, but they sure do respect me."

"No, Father, they don't; they don't. You go too far. You don't care who you stand on."

"I put bread on tables, Yolanda. I—"

"I've heard it! I've heard it!"

"Well, will you get it into your head that I'm in business? I take care of business, Yolanda. I'm not a priest; I'm not a nurse. We all have our destiny. Mine, God help me, is putting food on tables. I was made to make this world a better place. I do that, and it's the great legacy I pass on to you."

"The West Wood was a far better place before you cut into it."

"No, no, no. It was not, Yolanda! We've created a firebreak up there; it's absolutely essential! It'll save the place!"

"You created a fairway."

"The important thing is the firebreak. Yes, I want that fairway – of course I do – but think, if fire had broken out there last week, what would the woods be now? Ash! I have irrigation coupling points going in there. Now, if fire hits the woods, we've got water to throw at it. You've paid a small price, Yolanda, and you've got a whole heap of insurance!"

Yolanda pursed her lips before replying. "There's a logic to what you say, and if that had been your main reason for destroying valuable trees, I perhaps would thank you, but you're a manipulative liar, dear father."

"What? You call me liar? I'm not a liar! I'm no worse than anyone else. I'm a businessman. And, yes, I go at it like a hunter. They get in my cross hairs, and I take 'em out. I don't hide from that. It's in my nature. It's me! I'm not a jobsworth; I'm not a time-server."

Yolanda rose from her chair. "This is pointless. I knew it would happen. It's your way or no way. There's just no point in talking to you."

"No, wait, Yolanda, wait!"

"You take me for a dummy. You take everyone for a dummy. Well, you're the fool – a blustering, deceitful, pretentious, conniving fool of a brute – so you can just get lost!" With that, she got up and left.

"No, Yolanda, come back! Come back! Listen! Listen, Yolanda. Come back!"

But Yolanda was not listening, and she was not coming back.

Weever returned to his office. After he'd punched his desk several times, he kicked the waste-paper bin round the room, and then paced up and down several times issuing every expletive in his arsenal. Next, angrily, he phoned Fairfoull and demanded, "You get those trees down tonight – no ifs, no buts. By dawn, they're gone. No excuses!"

After lunch, the sun came out. It cheered Weever up, fortified by the righteousness he felt about his actions. *The sunlight* isn't exactly upon the golf course, but it is fairly close by, and that's just as it should be, thought Weever, *because the work is incomplete, and it would not be right to shine a light on a work that was not yet ready to receive it*; although shining a light on a work-in-progress was exactly what he was about to do. The contradiction, however, did not trouble him.

When he got the call telling him the guests and the press had begun to arrive for the seed-sowing ceremony, Weever's adrenalin began to flow, and, instinctively, he checked his hairpiece for adhesion and his teeth for greenery. Then he retired upstairs to observe the arrivals from his dressing-room window.

His heart sank. He wasn't expecting much, but the tawdry bunch that met his gaze failed to meet even his lowest expectations. They seemed like a mere rabble – anorak people mostly, and not a waxed coat among them. It was of no matter, though; the important thing was that they would get him what he wanted, so he called Fairfoull to confirm that they were now ready to receive him. The numbers intrigued Weever.

"There are a few more of them than I expected," he said. "You said there would be about a dozen or so. There's at least twice that number. Are we getting national coverage?"

Fairfoull confirmed, "Regrettably not. It's simply that word gets round very quickly in a place like this, especially the word 'booze'. But not to worry, we've enough booze to see every one of them laid out and pickled. Though what we do with them after that is anybody's guess."

"That's their problem, Charlie. Get the dumpsters standing by. As long as all the stiffs are off the premises by nightfall, who cares?"

"Except our noble gentlemen of the press, of course; we need them fit enough to get their stuff away."

"Well, make sure every reporter gets a copy of your release before he or she passes out. Shove one in every pocket, and if their lights are out, staple one to their shirts, their ears or anything showing. And be sure that our photographer's on soda and he gets his stuff to the editors before five o'clock."

"No problem."

"Okay, I'm on my way." Weever checked himself in the full-length mirror once again, then went off to greet his guests.

For most people, a traditional toast would be quite sufficient to celebrate the first sowing of seed on a new golf course, but it could never be enough for Weever. He had to arrive in his McShellach tartan trews behind a piper who was clad in full Highland regalia and playing 'Hail To The Chief'.

First off, Weever greeted the VIPs – Lord Tulloh, Sir Reggie Tallboys and the provost of Millburgh. Then, forgetting them almost immediately, he took up the gold-plated tray himself and was mounting the first tee, until Fairfoull reminded him that it would look much better if Lord Tulloh were to cast the first seed.

His lordship, Lord Tulloh, thus received the tray of seed, which he accepted graciously and eyed very carefully for a moment or two. Then he took a pinch of seed, raised it to his lips, and shoved it in his mouth before munching away thoughtfully. On the verge of giving it his approval, or so it seemed, he was seized abruptly by the elbow and ushered away by his valet, who got him to spit out the seed. It was an incident that evoked mixed emotions among his audience, drawing cries of hilarity amid gasps of concern. The fears were misplaced, however, for – minutes later – Lord Tulloh was back, seedless and now fully conversant with correct procedure. Helped by his valet and Charlie Fairfoull, he mounted the first tee and accepted the tray of seed again while the piper played 'Cock o' the North'. Spirits rose, people

clapped in time and began to rejoice. But not Lord Tulloh –
he developed vertigo and lurched forwards suddenly, spilling
his seed. A face-to-face meeting with the ground was on its
way for the hapless lord until the doughty arms of his valet
interceded again and delivered him from ignominy. Happily,
the seed was now technically sown.

So, as his lordship was helped away to gather his wits in
the refreshment tent, Fairfoull cued the two female dancers,
and off they went dancing round the tee while the piper played
'Highland Cathedral'. Fairfoull cast his eyes to the heavens,
as if now expecting rain to fall on his wretched parade, but
nothing seemed imminent, so a wry smile crossed his face.
The dancing was applauded enthusiastically, not least because
it was now time for everyone to hit the refreshment tent.

Weever had other ideas, though. He wanted the
councillors to see his pride and joy, the eighth hole, and to
get them to applaud his vision and everything he was about
to do. So, instead of refreshments, Weever hit them with a
speech. "Lords, distinguished guests, ladies and gentlemen,"
he began. "Here you see a masterpiece in the making! A
wonderful piece of work is happening on this land. Already,
we've opened up a whole new vista – a wonderful thing
never seen since the time of Christ. And, on top of that,
we've saved a national treasure – we have saved your West
Wood. These woods were in deadly danger – terrible danger
– but we have created a firebreak that will save them for all
time! For your children and their children. They are our gift
to Scotland."

Fairfoull started the applause and the others followed.

"I've had thousands of environmentalists thanking me on
Twitter and Facebook for this and for all the other great work
we're doing here," continued Weever, receiving more applause.
"When you see what we've created, you'll agree it's very, very

special. In fact, it's miraculous; there's no doubt about it. And it's not just me saying that – that's from people all over the world. So, good folks, we go to the eighth green! And you'll see the magic for yourselves."

A muffled groan passed through the ranks. Fortunately, it was possible to interpret this as a purr of delight, and off they went briskly towards the eighth hole; the quicker this was over, the quicker they'd get to the refreshment tent. The fact that Lord Tulloh was already in there, and very likely draining the place of all its best stuff, was evidently a worry to many.

Halfway along the fairway leading to the eighth green lay Paw's house and the large earthen mound round it. And who should be on that mound, arms folded, legs apart, but Paw, looking very grim-faced and silent as the party approached. Weever bit his lip, but seemed set to ignore the old man.

Paw, though, wasn't ignoring Weever. He shouted for all to hear: "Don't be taken in, you folks! Weever doesn't care about any of you any more than he cares about me. And look what he's done to me." He pointed to the mounded earth. "Is that any way to treat a human bein'? Look at it! How am I supposed to live wi' this round my house?"

Weever stopped and held up his hand, bringing the party to a halt.

Fairfoull whispered tersely into Weever's ear, "Ignore him, there's nothing to be gained here. Move on."

But Weever struck a defiant air. "No," he hissed, "I won't let this go."

"*He's a lyin' thievin' snake!*" shouted Paw.

"Ladies and gentlemen," replied Weever in expansive style, "allow me to present Mr Paw known to us on the site as 'Toil and Trouble'!"

Laughter trickled through the party.

"Toil's the word," replied Paw, "I've toiled on these hills all my life, an' now I'm a laughing-stock and bein' driven out of my own home!"

Weever moved closer to the mound and pointed at Paw. "Ladies and gentlemen, we have bent over backwards to help this man – I say 'man' because he is no gentleman. We have offered him three times the worth of that hovel he calls a home and yet—"

"Liar! That's sheer lies. You lying bastard!" roared Paw.

"You see! Foul-mouthed and drunk – that's the kind he is! That's what we're up against."

"I am not drunk!"

"Then you're a savage!" replied Weever.

"You're a womanising pimp!"

Fairfoull clapped his hands in the air. "Right, ladies and gentlemen, we need to move on. Come along!"

"No, no," insisted Weever. "People can't leave without knowing that we're doing our very best here. We're doing great things, wonderful things."

"If this is yer best, you're the savage! No wonder ye've been married three times. Who would want tae keep the likes o' you?" declared Paw.

"You see this man?" declared Weever pointing at Paw. "He tries to blacken my name, as he blackens everything he touches. He's suggesting now that my three marriages somehow make me tacky – you'll agree that's pretty stinky coming from someone who lives in a hovel. I have two sons and a daughter from my marriages, and I'm proud of all of them. Come to your senses if you have any, Mr Paw, and get out of that pigsty you call a home. It's insanitary. It's disgusting!"

"This house has been my home for over forty years, and I won't be leaving it for you, you bastard!"

"Mind your manners, if you have any!"

170

"It's the truth! You push people around! You're a fucking bastard! That's what you are – a fucking bastard!"

"Terrible! Disgusting! Clean your mouth out!"

"I'll call you what you are, you bastard! You shit!"

Weever assumed a sad expression and sighed, before he turned to look appealingly at the party.

Then, suddenly, like a big puppet, up popped Sven from behind Paw. He clambered up onto the rim of earth and stood next to Paw. "Leave him alone!" he shouted through cupped hands. But the words had hardly left his mouth when he began to wobble. He waved his arms about in a desperate effort to recover his balance, but then, losing it, he fell forwards and somersaulted to the bottom of the mound. With difficulty and looking a little dazed, he got to his feet and was standing, albeit unsteadily, before Paw reached him. Sven staggered a few steps backwards and pointed a wayward finger at Weever. "You… you…" he began, "you should be in jail! That's where you belong. You're a bloody criminal! You… you—"

"You're drunk!" Weever broke in, emphatically and triumphantly.

"You see? This is another one we're up against, ladies and gentlemen; that's who we're up against here – tramps and drunks! We provide great quality jobs for Tannadee, and they provide what? A spectacle to frighten nearly every investor on the planet. But not the Weever Organisation; we won't let you down. We're gonna help these people; we're gonna help them in spite of themselves. We're gonna help Tannadee to a bigger and a better future. We're up for it! The thing is, are you? Are you up for it?"

A resounding roar went up. "Yes! Yes!" they cried.

And, triumphantly, Weever turned and led his party to the eighth green, where he presented the great view to the great admiration of his party.

Even Weever was amazed at his luck. If he had paid Paw

and Sven, they couldn't have performed better – the one foul-mouthed and out of control, the other a mindless drunk. This was the opportunity he'd craved – the giant step onto the moral high-ground, the shadow of which could mask many a shady manoeuvre.

CHAPTER 16

They were in the pergola when Chizzie found them. Winding down from his ten-kilometre run, he'd jogged past the pergola, and there they were – Paw and Sven – looking dazed and exhausted. Paw actually looked ill, with his normally pink face drained to white.

Though reluctant to talk, they explained to Chizzie that they had come to the hotel to let Billy know, ahead of all the gossip, what had happened between them and Weever. But, on reaching the hotel gate, Paw had felt too weak to face Billy, and Sven had begun to fear that the merest whiff of alcohol could send him off on one of his binges. So, to the pergola they had gone, to gather their wits and strength, but these had proved slow in coming, and now Paw had a headache, and Sven had a pounding hangover.

"Effing and blinding I was," confessed Paw quietly. "I never knew I had such anger in me. Awful... awful it was. Oh God, just awful."

"It's in all of us, you can be sure!" replied a voice from behind Chizzie. It was Johnny. "Effing and blinding's in all of us. I should know: I did it professionally, as a football manager. And I was good at it, but I wasn't half as good as the voices behind me in the best seats, believe me. Anyway, you're here now. Councillor Maddox phoned and told me about you and Weever. You're feeling ill now, right? Sore head. Your boiling blood's scorched your brain?"

Paw nodded.

"What happened?" asked Chizzie.

Sven tried to explain, "We... we... we—"

"We disgraced ourselves," Paw broke in. "I was roaring my face off, all foul-mouthed like a drunk – sorry Sven."

"It's okay. I was drunk, probably still am. So drunk I don't even know how drunk I am. I don't know anything anymore. Who am I really? Why do I do these things?" Sven shook his head.

Paw recounted their clash with Weever and, in reliving it, fell into even deeper gloom.

Sven looked at him, focussing hard. "You're crying!" he yelped.

Paw wiped his cheeks with his hand. "I'm sorry," he gasped. "The... the only time I ever cried in fifty years was when Morag died... and now this. Agh!"

Sven lurched towards Paw and slapped his arm around him. A lifetime of quiet dignity that commanded affection and respect from all who knew Paw had been wrenched from him and torn to shreds on the Weever lands.

Paw wiped his cheeks with his sleeve. "The one thing a man should be able to do is defend his family home," he said with a sniffle. "A man driven from his home is not a man. But I... I can't fight him. The law's in my way. I can't win. Morag's picture's at the door; she's goin' to see her man done in and crawlin' away like a beaten dog. And what's Billy goin' to think?" He took a huge breath suddenly, shook his head wildly and shot to his feet, with fists clenched. "*No! No! I won't be beaten!*" he yelled. "*I bloody well won't!*" He stamped one of his feet and, with fierce determination, he growled, "If they want me out, they'll have to carry me in a box! I'm not goin'! Not for Weever! Not for anybody! They can cover the whole bloody house in muck. I am not going anywhere!"

"*Good man, Paw!*" Johnny yelled, slapping Paw on the back, "We're with you. You won't be driven out. All for one and one for all! He's tried to buy us out, and he wants Paw out. Well, you won't be driven out, Paw – we'll see to that."

"So what do we do?" asked Chizzie.

"Eh… I don't know," replied Johnny, stroking his chin. "But we'll think of something. We need to speak to Weever first and sort things out. I'm thinking there's more to his game than meets the eye."

"I need to speak to Billy first," said Paw, taking a deep breath.

"He'll be in the kitchen," said Chizzie, "I'll take you there."

"I'm here," called a voice from behind the pergola. It was Billy.

Paw swung round. "What're you doin' here, Billy?"

"Chef sent me out to get some roses for the tables," Billy confirmed.

"And what did you hear?" asked Paw tentatively.

"Everythin'," replied Billy, who stepped backwards and disappeared behind the tall cotoneaster bush that grew behind the pergola.

"*Where're you going?*" shouted Paw. "*Billy, come back!* He's run off!"

But Billy hadn't run off. He came round to the front of the pergola and, looking mostly at the ground, went quickly over to Paw, threw his arms around him and hugged him. "I'm going to move that fucking earth," he said over Paw's shoulder.

"No, Billy, no," insisted Paw. "You stay out of it, and don't swear. Johnny and Chizzie'll sort this out."

Billy said nothing, he just kept on hugging, until – seemingly clearer in his mind – he released his grip. Avoiding eye contact again, he whacked Sven on the shoulder, and then he turned away and left.

Appealing to Weever's better nature would probably be as productive as trying to grow coconuts in the Cairngorms, so Chizzie decided to approach Charlie Fairfoull. He went to the Weever site office and was informed that Mr Fairfoull was on the twelfth fairway of the golf course, beyond the river.

"What river?" asked Chizzie, confused.

"The river that was in the school grounds," replied the clerk of works.

"Was? What d'you mean *was?*"

"We've bought the ground beyond the river, and Mr Fairfoull's up there marking it out now."

"He can't be! That ground is school property!"

The man simply shrugged.

Angrily, Chizzie walked quickly to the river and, sure enough, there was Charlie Fairfoull supervising the staking out of a new tee. Also there was Jim, who was taking photos on his mobile phone.

Chizzie went over to them. "What's going on?" he asked.

"Pure bedlam!" replied Jim tersely, "They've marched in here and just taken over. Can you believe it? It's a land grab. This is school property. We don't actually own it, Lord Tulloh owns it, but we have an understanding. Weever's outfit claim they've bought it, but I haven't been notified; I've not heard a dickybird. I phoned Lord Tulloh earlier. His valet says I can meet him at seven o'clock, but God knows what condition he'll be in. I wanted our solicitor there, but he can't make it. I need to speak to Tulloh before the bulldozers move in. This… this is… it's an attack on civil society, that's what it is! They've no title deed and they've no planning permission, but it doesn't seem to bother them; they just don't care. They've got men and bulldozers, and they're just taking us over! It's like a war – an invasion." Jim held out his arms and wheeled round slowly, dazed. "They've just taken what they want. It's like bloody Russia!"

"If they've no planning permission, they'll be thrown out," Chizzie replied.

Jim shook his head. "No, no they won't; they'll get retrospective approval." He looked hard at Fairfoull. "Because they'll shout about jobs and economic development, and – while that might be true – it won't be our jobs and our Tannadee, will it, Mr Fairfoull?"

Charlie Fairfoull said nothing; he merely raised his eyebrows and shrugged his shoulders, affecting an air of innocent helplessness.

Jim turned away. "Come on, Chizzie, we've got work to do." Jim walked away, with Chizzie following.

When they were far enough away, Chizzie turned to Jim and took out his mobile phone. "Hang on, Jim; I get a signal here sometimes. I want to speak to Yolanda about this. She can knock them back."

But it was Chizzie who took the knock-back when she answered. "You're in Edinburgh?" he exclaimed in astonishment. "How... how long are you away for?"

"I don't know, Chizzie," answered Yolanda.

Through the wavering connection, Chizzie listened, his ear pressed hard against the phone.

"I... I just feel a bit rundown right now," continued Yolanda, "which is not like me. I don't know why I'm like this – maybe it's just too many things crowding in. I need a bit of space right now. I know my father will be giving you trouble, but is it my fight? He's my father. I'm so tied in knots about everything going on that I just need some space right now, which I know is kinda kooky – people who need space go to places like Tannadee, they don't go to cities. But, right now, I need to be anonymous; I need to lose myself in the crowd. Then I'll sort myself out and I'll be in touch, I promise."

Chizzie hardly knew what to think, he felt as lost as Yolanda. There was nothing much he could say. All he could think of was to wish her well. "Well, I hope you feel better real soon, Yolanda. We'll all miss you here and can't wait to see you again – me especially."

"That's very kind of you, Chizzie. But—"

"And a special evening awaits you. A very special evening."

"Chizzie, what I'm trying to say is that I might not be back."

"Eh?" Chizzie spluttered as a shower of ice seemed to shoot through his body. "You might not be back?" he whined. "Not at all? How? Why?"

"I can't say. I just need to think, Chizzie. I need to sort things out. Sorry about just upping and leaving, but it's… it's what's right for me right now, that's all I can say. Whatever happens, I'll call you. I promise. Love you." With that she ended the call.

Chizzie blinked like a man who'd been whacked over the head. Slowly, he put away his phone.

"What'd she say?" asked Jim.

Chizzie paused for a moment in bewilderment: she'd said, "Love you". Did that mean she was really in love with him or was it just a casual, platonic kind of remark from a friend?

It baffled Chizzie and consumed him for a moment until Jim asked again, "What did she say, Chizzie?"

Chizzie burst out of his daydream. "Eh, oh, nothing. She can't help. She's in Edinburgh."

Just before seven o'clock, at Jim's request, Chizzie drove Jim to Tulloh House and accompanied him into the drawing room of the great baronial house. There, the valet introduced them to Lord Tulloh, the laird, who wore a thick, dark-blue, woollen dressing-gown and was seated in a large, olive-coloured leather chair by the roaring log fire. Three large, black cushions held him upright. His face was almost as red as the fire. Sleepily, he welcomed the two visitors and asked them to be seated on the large settee, then he rubbed his hands together and invited them to join him in a drink. Chizzie accepted a brandy in the belief that here, in Lord Tulloh's house, it might be thought rude not to accept. Jim took a malt whisky. The measures were large, in keeping with his lordship's portion. The valet helped himself to a small sherry and sat down in the other chair by the fire, opposite Lord Tulloh. When Jim explained what had happened in the school grounds, Lord Tulloh seemed genuinely perturbed.

"I… I've signed no papers," he said uncertainly. "Have I, Donald?"

"No, Patrick," replied the valet. "You've sold no land. You discussed the matter with Mr Weever and indicated a willingness to sell, but there was never any commitment of any kind. Clearly, Mr Weever has overstepped the mark."

"Mr Weever very kindly cleared all the scrub from the gardens, though," acknowledged Lord Tulloh.

"That's true," replied the valet.

"And the money from a land sale would put a new roof on the east wing of the house," continued Lord Tulloh in a tinny, high-pitched tone.

"Yes, I dread to think what another winter would do to that wing," added the valet, holding on to his sherry, but taking no sip.

"Well, I'm sorry to hear that your roof is in such need of repair," said Jim, "but I have to point out that we always understood from your late father that the grounds we occupy on your estate would be available to the school for as long as the school had fifty pupils. We have more than that, Lord Tulloh."

"Patrick, please. Call me Patrick. And this is Donald," Lord Tulloh offered.

Donald, the valet, nodded. It was clearly an unusual relationship, with the valet soaking up the heat of the fire along with his master. Several people in the village speculated on the nature of their relationship, but most preferred to mind their own business.

"Without these grounds," Jim went on, "the school will be less attractive to prospective pupils and the school's future will be seriously jeopardised, possibly fatally. And who's to say what Weever will do next. If he wins this ground, he'll want more; it's in the nature of the man. We have to stand our ground or the entire school will be gone. And if the school goes, Tannadee as we know it is dead!" He turned and placed a hand on Chizzie's shoulder. "This young man here is the future! Here is a young man dedicating his life to Tannadee. His whole working life in front of him."

Jim had earlier instructed Chizzie to look into Lord Tulloh's face with big, doleful eyes at this point, but he couldn't do it. Instead he tried to look aggrieved.

"We need all our young people," Jim went on. "We need to hold our ground, Lord Tulloh. For Tannadee, for decency and for democracy even."

"I'm all for democracy," replied Lord Tulloh. "But I do so need filthy lucre to get the east wing roofed. It's my family's heritage. I have no choice: I'm dutybound. I wish I wasn't, but I am."

Jim took a deep breath. "I always knew we could lose your land at any time, but I also know we have first refusal if the land goes up for sale."

"That's true," conceded Donald.

"Is it?" chirped Lord Tulloh anxiously.

"Indeed," said Donald. "And the sum required to buy the

180

land is set at the current market value as determined by three independent land agents. I can inform you that the value is one hundred and twenty thousand pounds."

"But Mr Weever offered a hundred and fifty thousand pounds!" exclaimed Lord Tulloh.

"Can you find a hundred and twenty, Jim?" Donald asked.

Jim shook his head, and looked at Donald as if to say, "Silly question."

"Thank God!" blurted Lord Tulloh. "No, no, I do apologise; actually, I am really deeply sorry if that means the school suffers, but what can I do? I don't want to go down as the laird that lost the lot here. The burden of ancestry hangs over me, with all these portraits looking down and accusing me. I get nightmares. I'll have them in my grave. I have to save this place if it's the last thing I do. I'm sorry, Jim, but I can't refuse Mr Weever's generous offer. I have liabilities. You understand. We must sell to Mr Weever. I'm terribly sorry."

"Can you really not raise a hundred and twenty thousand?" asked Donald.

"I can't get that figure; I could maybe get halfway, but no more," said Jim weakly, "Our funding is stretched to the very limit; we have borrowings. I have borrowings personally, and every avenue we have is cleaned out. But an investment in the school will turn the corner for us. We'll be state of the art, and we break even in four years, then we go from strength to strength. I have to… I have to beseech you quite frankly, Lord Tulloh, not to let us down. I have to appeal to your sense of honour. I know that sounds like moral blackmail, but please do not let us down."

Chizzie winced. To see a proud man like Jim begging was awful. It was clear that Lord Tulloh was also affected.

He sighed, glanced at Jim, then looked away towards the fire. "We are but flotsam on a sea of troubles, dear Jim," he said. "Many a time I have wanted desperately to be free of all this, to be gone, to be far away and to give it all over to my nephew. I never wanted it, never. I only ever wanted to be a ballet dancer. I do so love the dance – the grace, the strength, the fluid movement. Unfortunately, my fluid movements took a very different direction, and you see the result. But, oh it's so ghastly boring here if you're not the hunting-and-shooting type, and that's not me; it's not me at all. So, I fell in with the demon drink, as it keeps my dreams afloat. I would've so loved to have danced on stage. But there we are – it was not to be… not to be." He winced slightly, but found a brave smile to follow. "So there we have it: I'm a closet dancer. Silly of me, you'll think, coming from a man who can barely stand up much of the time."

"No, no, I quite understand," replied Chizzie. "We can all too easily find ourselves closeted. All too easily."

"My brother could help me," Lord Tulloh went on, "but he won't. He despises me, you see. He thinks I'll drink every penny I get, but I wouldn't, would I, Donald?"

"You most certainly wouldn't, Patrick. You certainly would not," declared the valet.

"Donald would see that things were done properly, but he doesn't approve of Donald either," continued Lord Tulloh.

"So there we are, Jim," Donald cut in sharply. "You see our position. You need to pay one hundred and twenty thousand pounds. We're most terribly sorry, but we have no alternative."

Jim puffed out his cheeks, groaned and placed his head in his hands.

Suddenly, it all got too much for Chizzie, and anger and bravado welled up in him. "We'll get that money!" he exclaimed. "We'll get it! Count on it! Don't sell to Weever. We'll get the money."

Jim responded with another groan and shook his head. A rush of youthful blood to the head was not going to convince him of salvation. "We haven't a cat in hell's chance," he muttered. Then dolefully, almost ashamedly, he looked up at Lord Tulloh and looked him straight in the eye. "I appeal to you, Lord Tulloh. I appeal to your honour as a gentleman, for the sake of Tannadee, if not for the school or for this young man or for me," he pleaded.

Lord Tulloh's lips twitched; he glanced at Donald. Chizzie sensed the man was weakening, but seconds later Lord Tulloh seemed to recover his resolve and furrowed his brow. His lips twitched again and his brow furrowed again, the lord was clearly in turmoil. He spoke slowly and deliberately. "I know I'm what they call a petrolhead," he said.

"'Pisshead' is the word they use," said Donald.

"Oh, pisshead. Right. Thank you, Donald," said Patrick.

"One has instructions to tell it like it is," said Donald, turning to Jim.

"And he does," confirmed his lordship.

Donald turned to his lordship and smiled reassuringly. "It's the best way."

His lordship returned the smile and nodded. "Of course. So, I am what they call a pisshead. But I am an honourable pisshead and I will respect the arrangements made by my late father. I'll give you four months to find the hundred and twenty thousand pounds."

"Two months," insisted Donald. "Mr Weever's made it very clear he can't wait. We can't risk more than two months."

Jim let out a sigh. "Two months, six months, twelve months: it might as well be a million years. We'll never get it. We haven't a cat in hell's chance."

"We'll get it!" insisted Chizzie. "We'll get it!" He was sincere. He was determined, for – like his father – he was no quitter.

However, when he got back to his own fireside, that determination had already begun to ebb. Jim's words and, more emphatically, his face had told the stark truth. Slumped in his easy chair as the darkness of the night drew in, Chizzie continued gazing at the fire. The logs had lost all their brightness; by then they were ashen and all but doused, like his spirits. He had no school, no woman and no future. For the first time in his life, he felt thoroughly beaten. He could almost feel his very soul dissolving away into the gloom and the chill of night.

CHAPTER 17

Next morning, Charlie Fairfoull brought the news of the delayed land deal to Weever and found him in a thoughtful mood. The great man had just been speaking to Yolanda on the phone and was convinced he'd all but persuaded her to fly back to Texas with him. But the bad news swung his mood. "They've what? They've gone back on the deal?" he roared, throwing himself backwards in his chair. "They can't, we shook hands on it!"

"Not quite," replied Fairfoull, taking the chair on the other side of Weever's desk. "We shook hands, but not on a deal. Tulloh – or, more exactly, Tulloh's man – said they accepted the figure in principle but they'd consult the school before finalising."

"We need that ground. I want a lake there. I want a lake!"

"And his lordship needs the money. It's a formality, but there is one tiny little snag. Tulloh's given the school two months to find the money to buy the land outright."

"He's what? Our figure?"

"A hundred and twenty thou."

"They told us one fifty! The bastards!"

"It's a legal clause in the lease; apparently, they get priority. But the good thing is that they'll never find the money. Our man Barrington assures me the school's fundraising is bottomed-out completely; they're over their heads. We'll get that ground. We just have to wait two months, that's all."

"Two months!"

"It's not a problem. And we could find a piece of ground to give to the school, as a goodwill gesture that keeps us in with the natives. We'll need them at some point."

"Are you kidding? I hate these goddamn natives! They piss me off! They're foul-mouthed and they're drunk. Who do they think they are? God's chosen people? They need to learn life is tough, life is mean, and it can knock you down and down and down – if you let it. But you can't let that happen to you. You can't go gettin' bum lazy. If you sit still, you rot, you stink and you get stinkin' drunk. We saw that yesterday. You don't want to see that in your mirror. It's not in my mirror! I'll fight those humpties—"

"Numpties."

"Numpties… and I'll shake the goddamn shit clean outta them. Things're gonna be different round here."

"I wouldn't rock the boat too much, Gordon. They have their own rules and they get by. It's best we just keep out their way."

"No way, Charlie boy, no way. I won't accept their rules!"

"Rules are for fools, right?" asked Fairfoull quietly, raising an eyebrow.

Weever hesitated, then screwed up his eyes. "No. No. Rules are good. They're good. Freedom is a set of rules. Without rules, where are you? You're in the jungle, right? I don't want to be in the jungle."

"You might get eaten."

"Sure. I'm not Tarzan. I don't break rules, I bend them; I bend them till they squeal. If rigid rules are all you've got, you're dust. They gotta bend sometimes, so somebody can break out and go for it."

"To live or die on the roll of the dice. Death or Glory!"

"No, Charlie boy, no – any fool can get himself killed. That's not my game. The calculated gamble, that's my game:

ninety per cent calculated and ten per cent gamble. And I've been around long enough to know the odds here. We could start building that green tomorrow and we'd get it done, no problem."

"The natives might get restless."

"The cops can handle that."

"PC Tunnock?"

"It'll go over his head."

"We don't need to lock horns, though, Gordon. Anything can happen with that. We could get hurt. It's an outside chance, of course, but it's more than ten per cent. A couple of months is no problem to us; I strongly suggest we wait."

Weever thought for a moment, then smiled. "Okay. You're right, Charlie. I'd love to kick ass. Boy oh boy, how I'd just love to kick ass. Oh boy. But yeah, yeah, sure; we'll sit back and we'll let the rules work for us."

"That's real classy, if I may say so, Gordon."

"It's what nice people do, ain't it, Charlie?"

The two men laughed.

"And that's what we're going to do," continued Weever. "We're going to be very nice. We're going to give Lord Tulloh the time of his life; he's a boozer and gambler, right?"

"He's still a boozer, but no longer a gambler, I believe."

"Once a gambler always a gambler; inside him and all the rest there's a flame that never dies. We simply need to throw some firewater on the flame and up he'll go – boom!"

"It won't win us the deal, though, Gordon."

"Oh, but it will, Charlie boy, it will; when he's on fire and spinning like a roulette wheel, he'll sign any deal."

"Not with his manservant Donald by his side, he won't."

"Then we'll have to get rid of him, Charlie boy."

While Weever's multi-million-pound golf course rose steadily from the ground, fresh and perfectly formed, darker days descended on Chizzie, Jim and Johnny. Johnny, though, maintained a semblance of optimism based on the simple notion that bad luck has to run out sometime. If bad luck was all there was, nobody would get out of bed in the morning, so there has to be good luck somewhere; all you have to do is find it.

And Johnny found it, or rather it found him. After sending out heaps of begging letters, making appeals and arranging sponsored events, the 'Save Our Sports Field' campaign had gathered just over seventy thousand pounds, which was a tremendous achievement in the normal course of events, but still not enough. Then came the call that brought a ray of hope. It came from Mr McLogan, a solicitor in Millburgh and a partner in the firm that Johnny had entrusted with his affairs.

"I have been informed that Tannadee is in dire need of a substantial sum of money and I think I might be able to help you there," explained the lawyer.

"How much?" asked Johnny.

"Thirty thousand pounds."

"You want thirty thousand pounds!"

"No, I'm helping you to get thirty thousand pounds. I'm directing you to a bequest that is in a position to offer you that sum. You see, I have the honour of being retained by the Colonel Mungo McBraid Bequest to provide the trustees with legal advice and representation. The bequest is an unusual one," the lawyer explained. "It seeks to reward physical prowess rather than the more commonly lauded academic prowess. In the course of discharging my responsibilities on behalf of the bequest, it has come to my notice that Tannadee falls within the boundary of privilege; that is to say that Tannadee is in a position to petition the bequest for funds. Now, it so happens that the bequest is required to make a substantial tranche of money available every ten years, and this is the first year of award."

"Thirty thousand pounds?"

"You are ahead of me, Mr Bryson."

Thirty thousand pounds on top of seventy made a nice round landmark figure that pleased Johnny greatly and struck a note of excitement in his voice. He knew that a hundred thousand pounds would give the fund weight and make it likely to attract more funds.

"We get thirty thousand pounds?"

"You have to win it, Mr Bryson."

"How... how d'you mean 'win it'?"

"The bequest sponsors a competition in the Bonnlarig Highland Games in which towns and villages in the Bonnlarig area enter teams and compete against each other for the prize. You see, Colonel McBraid was hugely devoted to the old traditional sports of the Highlands. He believed these sports nurtured the Highland spirit and would keep it alive in the Bonnlarig district. With that in mind, he devised the competition – to be reckoned in traditional units, namely yards, pounds, gallons and the like."

"Good man," broke in Johnny, delighted to hear of tradition respected.

"Priority this year is given to education," continued the lawyer, "especially to a school if there is one. It's admirably suited to your purposes, you will agree. Now, the competition is quite straightforward really – there are ten events in all, points are allocated according to finishing order in each event, and the village with the most points gets the money. As I say, this is the first time the competition is being held, so expect a few rough edges."

"When's it take place?"

"Next month, on Saturday the eighteenth."

"*The eighteenth of next month?* That's only six weeks away! We don't have any Highland Games people! Nobody who could win anything. Where are we going to get them?"

"You'll need to find them, and they must have either been resident in your village for at least one calendar year by the first of next month or be able to provide written proof of an ancestor born within three miles of the village."

"I smell a rat. How come we get only one month to prepare?"

"Well, strictly speaking, you're not eligible at all, Mr Bryson. You see, Tannadee is not actually in the Bonnlarig district according to the most recent district map, which dates back to 1851. But Bonnlarig, like many other Highland districts, is a somewhat shapeless, notional territory that has swelled and shrunk over time with the fortunes of the clans that dwelt within it. That being the case, there are other maps, older ones, and – lo and behold – we see Tannadee within the Bonnlarig boundary, so you have a case; it's a good one, bearing in mind that Highland history was a particular passion of Colonel McBraid. What you must do right away is petition the board of trustees for a special dispensation that will permit you to compete."

"How do we do that?"

"I'll arrange it for you."

"How much?"

"Gratis and pro bono."

"How much is that in pounds?"

"It means no charge, Mr Bryson."

"What's the catch?"

"No catch and no charge, Mr Bryson. I appreciate that, in the sad and rapacious times in which we find ourselves, something for nothing may attract an element of suspicion, but I assure you most sincerely that no fee is attached to the information I am providing here and now."

"Eh? Oh. Well... well, thank you; that's unusually kind of you – er, I mean kind of you—"

"These are unusual times, Mr Bryson," broke in the lawyer. "In these straitened times, we in the old guard must stick together. I need hardly point out that if you go under, I lose a valued client. Weever, for sure, will not be using my firm. So, there we have it: bound as we are by an element of self-interest, I want you to succeed. And if I can be of further help in any way, please do not hesitate to get in touch."

"Free?" asked Johnny, involuntarily hitting a note of incredulity.

"If necessary," replied the lawyer, involuntarily gravely.

Given such a concession, there was no way that Johnny would fail to find it necessary. The lawyer knew this, of course, but they faced a common enemy together, and – as the old saying goes – my enemy's enemy is my friend. Furthermore, hate most assuredly drives even harder than love, so the relationship between lawyer and client, on this occasion, was set to be very positive.

"Between you and me," continued the lawyer, lowering his voice, "the board are a feckless bunch, mostly the colonel's old friends and some family members. McBraid might have been a fine judge of stocks and shares, but he was no judge of character if these people are anything to reckon by. Then again, he always did have a rather wicked sense of humour and, frankly, he was a bit gaga by the end. So, be careful. I recommend flattery and a cool head. Oh, and there's one thing in your favour: the Tannadee school bursar, Mr Barrington, is clerk to the trustees; he doesn't have any voting rights, but he undoubtedly will have influence. You'll want to flatter him generously."

"Well, thank you, Mr McLogan; many thanks indeed. I'll be in touch – definitely."

"Geoffrey," insisted the lawyer.

"Geoffrey," echoed Johnny, squirming. Intimacy, of any kind, with a lawyer was like chewing a lemon for Johnny, but that, of course, was what he had to do in his line of business from time to time. As he often said, "If you can't chomp a lemon and smile at the same time, hospitality is not for you."

CHAPTER 18

The news of the bequest injected new life into the campaigners, particularly Jim and Johnny. Jim felt sure he could muster and train a band of locals who would put Tannadee in with a good chance – especially since the other towns and villages in the district were unlikely to have any great athletes on their books. Chizzie felt his earlier optimism was now vindicated, possibly even rewarded; the bequest was a wonderful opportunity. It was hard for him to dismiss entirely the notion that aliens, who were much smarter than humans, were manipulating events on earth for their own amusement and, currently, he was in their favour.

Whatever the case may be – God, aliens or nothing at all – it was with great hope and gratitude that Chizzie, Johnny and Jim went to meet the trustees. Only one thing weighed heavily on Chizzie's mind: it was the silence of Yolanda. He thought to phone her and got as far as placing his thumb on her name, but he didn't press the key – pushing Yolanda almost certainly would not be a good move. She had said she would be in touch, and Chizzie felt he had no option but simply to wait, however difficult that wait might be.

Two days later, on a fine, sunny evening, Chizzie, Johnny and Jim arrived – as arranged – at the Fairfield church hall in Millburgh, where they were to present themselves to the bequest committee. They were slightly late on account of

Johnny's intimate knowledge of Millburgh turning out to be less than intimate, but ten minutes is neither here nor there in parts of the Highlands – particularly in those parts – so Chizzie was not too perturbed, especially since each of the three of them were attired magnificently in kilt, tweed jacket, waistcoat and brogues. The traditional Highland approach, they had agreed, was likely to make the best impression on the committee.

Up the church path Jim strode confidently, leading the way, his brogues crunching on the pink gravel; being six feet four, lithe and broad-shouldered, he could have been a sergeant major at the head of the Scots Guards. But Chizzie wondered if he was really as confident as he looked. On the plus side, they say people make up their minds about you in the first ten seconds of seeing you, and no one could fail to be impressed by the sixty-two-year-old Jim looking more like a forty-two-year-old. Arguably less impressive was Johnny marching behind Jim, with his little legs advancing at twice the cadence of Jim's. In his hands, he clutched a briefcase containing a copy of the district map sent to him by Mr McLogan, the lawyer, and he wore a grim determination on his face that few could match.

For Chizzie, it was a perfect evening for the kilt – cool and calm – and his spirits were high, having been liberated by the sense of freedom that a kilt brings on a cool evening. He was all the more heartened by the assured singing of a carefree blackbird in the rowan tree by the sunny side of the church hall.

As soon as he placed one foot inside the hall doorway, though, all pleasure fled. It was like another world, a world of sour and musty air, dank and colourless. However, it struck Chizzie quickly that this would play to their advantage. In this dingy environment, the three gentlemen

– small, medium and large, and looking resplendent in Highland dress – were certain to make a powerful impact. They clumped down the brown corridor and marched into the hall to find six committee members plus Barrington, the Tannadee school's bursar, seated behind a long table at the far end, and they looked every bit as enervated as the musty air. Barrington, not noted for his *joie de vivre*, looked the brightest of the bunch.

Smiling as best they could, the Tannadee men approached the table. No one moved to greet them. Murmuring took place behind the table. Then a man – who introduced himself as Mr Warrender, the committee chairman – rose and asked Jim brusquely to introduce himself and his colleagues. Jim complied, and the chairman introduced his committee members and Barrington. The atmosphere was as brittle as the creaking floorboards. There was an otherworldliness about the place. Chizzie began to think he might be at the wrong meeting, and on the point of joining the freemasons or some similar outfit.

Three red, plastic chairs had been laid out in front of the committee, a couple of metres away from the table. Smiling uncertainly at the committee members, Chizzie seated himself on one of the plastic chairs. Johnny sat to his right, while Jim took the chair on Chizzie's left. Johnny stared at the chairman and seemed to be wondering whether he had an enemy before him or a friend. Chizzie had seen Mr Warrender before, but couldn't quite place him. Then it struck him: they'd met a few years earlier at an athletics meeting where the man had been a very punctilious official. According to one of the other officials, Warrender had served in the navy, where he was in charge of the panic button on a minesweeper, and was retired early on account of repetitive strain injury.

The meeting seemed about to get underway when the door burst open suddenly and in swept a well-built woman in her late fifties wearing a tartan two-piece and sensible, buff-coloured shoes. Her flowing russet locks were handsome, but her make-up was lavish.

"Ah, Doris! Er, Mrs Beaumont," cried chairman Warrender, checking himself quickly and greeting her with a broad smile.

"Sorry I'm late, gentlemen!" declared Mrs Beaumont, finding a seat at the table. "I was in Perth when the elastic snapped in my car seat with a crack so loud I thought I'd been shot at. I zoomed down St John Street before I knew where I was and… Phew! Do excuse me, I'm out of breath." She fanned herself with her notebook. "Bear with me." She fanned herself some more while the others looked on as if watching some kind of exotic show. "Now where was I?"

"Shot and breathless," moaned Barrington.

"Ah, yes. In St John Street. Then up galloped a career-crazed young copper, smelling of sweat and pickled onions – and d'you know what? He accused me of speeding the wrong way down a one-way street. Huh! 'Not on your nellie,' I said, and produced my Scottish Women's Institute card. He fled. So here I am – pooped but unbowed. Apologies for perspiring, but you do understand."

Mr Warrender was quick to put her at ease as she fanned herself vigorously. "Well, actually, it's all right, Mrs Beaumont," he said, with a cautious smile. "You see, we're still waiting for Mr Grossett and Mr Waddell."

Mrs Beaumont smiled back with a wink.

Jim glanced at Chizzie and raised his eyebrows.

Barrington shifted uneasily in his chair and looked pointedly at his watch. Then, as if on cue, the door swung open and in came Mr Grossett, who was a thin, nervous-looking man wearing a beige anorak, steel-framed glasses, a brown corduroy bargeman's cap and brown Hush Puppies.

If ever a man needs a laxative, it's this man, thought Chizzie.

"Ah, Mr Grossett, good evening and welcome!" said the chairman.

"Evening," returned Grossett curtly, before moving swiftly to a chair behind the table to join the other committee members.

Warrender addressed the newcomer in a stiff but friendly manner, "We're just waiting for Mr Waddell now, Mr Grossett. Didn't see him out there, did you?"

Grossett, looking very tense, and sitting with his knees together and his hands clamped on his thighs, replied tersely in the negative.

Warrender, evidently seeing a fellow sufferer, attempted to loosen the man up by offering warm words. "It's a fine evening," he said, "with a fine, big moon rising in the east. Glorious, eh?"

Grossett replied curtly in the affirmative.

Everyone looked at their watches.

Warrender, on a roll seemingly, broke the uneasy silence: "Mr Waddell will be along shortly. He always turns up."

"That's not difficult; there's only one meeting a year," sighed Mrs Beaumont, with a furtive glance at Warrender, who bit his lip.

Finally, the door flew open and in came Mr Waddell: a cheery soul in his mid-sixties, with a big, ruddy face; a slight stoop; and bushy, white hair; and wearing an old, grey raincoat, unbuttoned.

"Ah, good evening, Mr Waddell!" cried Warrender, obviously relieved.

"Good evening, everyone!" returned Waddell as he clattered in, carrying an old suitcase, before plonking himself next to Mrs Beaumont, who leaned away from him.

"Going somewhere nice?" she asked cheekily, eyeing the suitcase.

"Yes," replied Waddell. "Oh yes. I'm going round to Mother's – I've a big load of washing, you see. I've big things on this weekend: it's the National Budgerigar Show and I'm in two classes."

"And the budgies?" enquired Mrs Beaumont.

"Yes, all budgies; oh yes. I dabbled with cockatoos for a while, but – dear, oh dear – they're far too much bother; it's all budgies now, yes. Do you have a budgie?"

Mrs Beaumont shuddered and replied in the negative. The others waited for Waddell to settle. He shook his head and tidied his bushy, white hair. Dust and some tiny fine feathers flew out. Mrs Beaumont leaned further away.

"It's been one of those days," confided Waddell.

"Evidently," replied Mrs Beaumont, with more than a hint of sarcasm.

"You've a feather on you, you know, Mrs Beaumont?" observed Waddell, eyeing her shoulder. "Are you sure you don't have a budgie?"

"I think you'll find it's one of yours, actually. From your head."

Inspecting closely the tiny feather between forefinger and thumb, Waddell confirmed its origin: "You're right, you're right; yes, it's one of Royston's that," he said. "Do you want one?"

"What?" squeaked Mrs Beaumont recoiling.

"A budgie. Do you want a budgie?" replied Waddell.

At this, Barrington's composure cracked. "Right!" he yelped. "Let's get this started or we'll be here all night!"

Warrender sprang into action. This, evidently, was his fifteen minutes in the limelight. Fifteen minutes of public platform would be his before the nerves set in. "Right. Meeting called to order," he announced. "Mr Barrington, are you ready to minute?"

"Yes!" replied Barrington peevishly.

"Doris, er, Mrs Beaumont, are you quite ready?" Warrender enquired.

"Aye, aye, skipper; I'm fully recovered," she replied, with a wink.

"Right," said Warrender, clearing his throat. "We are quorate, so let's get straight to it. It's a one item EGM, and we all know what it's about. So, Mr Bryson, without further ado, please would you kindly tell us why you think Tannadee qualifies for the Colonel Mungo McBraid Bequest? The floor is yours."

Johnny stood up, threw back his shoulders, then took out his copy of the old map. Jim, without standing up, took one top corner and Chizzie likewise took the other top corner. Johnny pointed out that every map known to exist before 1851 had included Tannadee in the Bonnlarig district. They could verify this for themselves at the Millburgh Central Library, where the archivist was very helpful. He then went on to emphasise the benefits for the entire Tannadee community in such a calm and organised way that it prompted Chizzie and Jim to exchange a glance with eyebrows raised in pleasant surprise. Arguably, some of the committee members looked interested, though dazed would have been a more apt description in Mr Waddell's case.

Thanking Johnny politely, skipper Warrender then opened the meeting to questions and comments. Mr Waddell was first in: he let off a mighty snore as his head lurched onto Mrs Beaumont's right shoulder. So loud was the snore that it could almost be felt. It occurred to Chizzie that Richter of the famous earthquake scale would likely have been very impressed.

"Was that six r's or seven r's?" Mrs Beaumont enquired, pretending to minute Mr Waddell's contribution.

"Anyone else?" asked Warrender, glancing quickly left and right, but the company remained tight-lipped. "Any comments?"

Only Mr Waddell was forthcoming, as he rent the air once again with a rasping roof-rattler. It put Chizzie in mind of a vintage air display he'd once witnessed at RAF Leuchars. Mrs Beaumont moved to safer ground by easing her chair sideways as far as she could.

"No questions?" repeated Warrender.

Barrington drew forwards. "The school is part-funded by the local authority," he said. "As such, the local authority could take part ownership of the school grounds in the event of the very unfortunate demise of the school. Purchase of the land in question might therefore not be an appropriate purpose to which bequest funds can be put."

Looking only slightly aggrieved, Jim pointed out that the land would be held in a community trust and would not be part of any settlement with the local authority.

A reddish sunbeam streamed through a gap in the curtains and grew bright on Barrington's face. It caused him to screw up his eyes and he seemed, to Chizzie's mind, like an interrogator cross-examining himself as he continued to raise concerns: questioning, for example, why Tannadee had not opted for a community buyout before now.

Jim acknowledged that this could have been a way forward for the school, but the need for it was never a priority until Mr Weever arrived. Throughout Barrington's seemingly hostile questioning, Jim remained calm, but Johnny was clearly reaching boiling point: his face had reddened markedly and beads of sweat had appeared on his brow, like little troops going over the top. Fortunately, the hostilities stopped before Johnny blew up, and Warrender called for the vote.

But Mrs Muskett had a question.

"It's too late, we're going to the vote," declared chairman Warrender.

"We should hear her question," said Barrington.

"I have asked for the vote and that is how it stands," replied Warrender. "We now vote."

"She has a right to be heard," insisted Barrington.

"Who says?" snapped Grossett.

"Through the chair, please. Through the chair," chairman Warrender reminded everyone.

"Will the land be open to the general public?" asked Mrs Muskett.

"Yes, it will," replied Johnny.

"Through the chair!" insisted Warrender.

"What about health and safety, then?" cried another committee member.

"It's not a problem," said Johnny.

"*Through the chair!*" bawled the increasingly exasperated Warrender.

"Mr Chairman," said Captain Crispin Dokiss, late of the Lowland Buffs, also known as 'The Dumpers' on account of their provisioning role in the army – food, ammo, etc. – but widely attributed to their response whenever a call to combat came their way. "We need a complete appraisal of the historical maps."

"You can't expect that to be done here and now!" answered Johnny angrily. "A vote's been called!"

"Through the chair! Speak through the chair!" remonstrated Warrender.

"What's Weever saying about this?" asked Mr Bonally.

"It's not about Weever," yelled Johnny.

"Why not?" asked Captain Truss.

"Because it's not," insisted Johnny, tersely, getting redder.

"Through the chair or I'm leaving!" yelled Warrender.

"Exercise your authority!" someone advised.

"We've answered all your questions," continued Johnny, "so we need a decision."

"What if they want the land for fracking?" asked Truss.

"They will not come fracking in Tannadee!" Johnny insisted.

"Right! That's it! I quit!" declared Warrender, and he picked up his notebook and walked off towards the door.

The committee members watched him go.

Then someone coughed, prompting Warrender to turn sharply and look over his shoulder. "Eh?" he uttered, in hope it seemed. But there was no one down on their knees begging him to return, and so, half-peevishly and half-forlornly, he turned and walked out, clasping to his heavy heart the notebook and pen that were now surplus to requirements, rather like himself.

"We are not a cattle market, Mr Bryson," cried committee member Sandy Dunkie, the local head gamekeeper, "You can't just come in here and herd us about, you know."

Suddenly, Chizzie heard a pipe band in the distance and it seemed to be getting closer. Then he realised it was no pipe band: it was his father's nose hairs buzzing.

With his eyes fixed to the heavens, Johnny appeared to be counting to himself. Then, solemnly, he drew a deep breath and with measured calmness, he declared, "I am not herding; I am explaining."

At this point, Warrender, seemingly concerned that he'd left a power vacuum behind, strode back into the hall. And, without the slightest acknowledgement from anyone, he took up the chair again.

"You're a Johnny-cum-lately wanting us to stump up to save your skins," continued Dunkie, cockily. "You've got a cheek, so you have."

Dunkie was on extremely dangerous ground here. If he thought time was a great healer, he was wrong. Johnny was not healed. Three years earlier, a gamekeeper had killed Bobby, Johnny's collie, in a snare. The dog was in the snare for four days before it was discovered. Dunkie wasn't the culprit, but he was a gamekeeper, and that was enough for Johnny. He detested them all and barred them from his hotel. The colour rose in Johnny's cheeks. Jim saw the warning signs and was about to suggest a break – but it was too late.

"I've just explained to you!" roared Johnny. *"Don't you bloody well listen? All the banging done your ears in, has it? Listen! I showed you our credentials. You saw the map. That's what matters! You glorified rat-catcher!"*

"Steady on now, Johnny, steady on now," muttered Jim.

Johnny ranted on, "He calls himself a head gamekeeper. Head banger, that's what he is. Bang! Bang! Bang! No wonder his bloody head's done in. Gamekeepers are made for only one thing – and that's to make village idiots look good!"

"I resent that! That's outrageous!" cried Dunkie. "I am a highly trained professional."

"You're a disgrace to the human race, that's what you are!" roared Johnny.

"Right, it's time to vote!" declared Warrender quickly.

"All those in favour of admitting Tannadee to the McBraid Bequest's Highland Games, please show your hands."

Four hands went up, including Warrender's.

"All those against?" Warrender enquired.

Again, there were four hands.

"It's a tie!" declared Warrender. "It's up to Mr Waddell now; he hasn't voted."

Mrs Beaumont tapped his shoulder.

Mr Waddell registered his state of readiness by letting off another thunderous rasper.

"He can't vote," said Barrington.

"Why not?" asked Grossett.

"He's fast asleep, and he has been for the last ten minutes!" Barrington declared.

"Maybe he's thinking," said Mrs Pullar, who always saw the good in people.

"He's snoring!" barked Barrington.

"Maybe he's just a heavy thinker," remarked Grossett.

Then Waddell appeared to mutter something. Everyone stopped. They waited. There was nothing, but then Wadell's lips began moving. Everyone leaned in, and, sure enough, he muttered again. It sounded like "Who's a pretty boy?" His straining audience waited for something more coherent. It did not arrive; that was it. The oracle had fallen silent.

Warrender requested that someone wake Mr Waddell, and Mrs Beaumont obliged.

"*Oi! You!*" she bawled into the slumbering non-voter's left ear, causing an involuntary spasm and yelp from him.

"Mr Waddell, would you kindly cast your vote, please?" asked Warrender.

"Objection!" yelled Barrington angrily. "That man does not know what he is voting for. To all intents and purposes, he is a dodo!"

"He'll be a big hit in the budgie show then," observed Mrs Beaumont.

"It's not often you get something previously extinct walking through your doors," remarked Mrs Pullar.

"You haven't been in the men's locker room at Millburgh golf club," declared Grossett.

Waddell, clearly in the groove, let fly another gurgling rasper.

"He's off again!" cried Barrington. "He's a complete and utter dodo!"

"Mr Waddell is no more a dodo than any other British voter," opined Grossett.

"What?" asked Barrington, bristling. "What d'you mean?"

The committee members turned towards Grossett.

"Well, he may not be conscious of what he's voting for, but then who is these days?" said Grossett.

The committee members turned towards Barrington, who gaped, speechless with indignation. The heads swung back to Grossett. It was like a tennis match with big hitters winding up.

"In a general election," continued Grossett, "who actually knows what they're voting for?"

"Well, most people apparently," replied Barrington, "seeing as they take the trouble to turn up wide awake. Unlike him there!"

All heads swung in the direction of Mr Waddell, who – with his head back and mouth agape – remained totally unaware of his immense significance.

"Awake or out for the count," insisted Grossett, "most people haven't a clue what they're voting for. I mean, who knows what the national debt is? Eh? Or who the shadow foreign secretary is? Eh?"

Everyone looked to Barrington, then back to Grossett, who pointed at Barrington suddenly.

"You!" he said. "Name your local housing convener!"

"Me?" gulped Barrington.

"Yes, you," confirmed Grossett.

Barrington struggled. "Er... er..."

"Exactly!" cried Grossett, folding his arms triumphantly. "Not knowing what the hell you're voting for is one of our greatest traditions. And that man there," indicating Waddell, "is one of its finest examples. Ladies and gentlemen, I give you Mr Waddell – the very model of modern British democracy!"

Barrington looked aghast. "You... you're an anarchist!" he gasped.

"I'm a realist," replied the now feisty Mr Grossett.

"Subversion, that's what you're talking," cried Barrington. "Yes, subversion! That's what you're actually talking. Not content with insulting the great British public, you insult the very concept of democracy!"

"I insult no one; I merely tell it like it is!" continued Grossett, now pointing to the quietly dormant Mr Waddell. "There you have it; there's the true voice of democracy: slumbering ignorance. And, what's more, by remaining unconscious, that man can actually lay claim to being the only head among us free of all propaganda; it could, in fact, be that he – Mr Waddell, the erstwhile dodo – is in prime position to come up with the right decision. Unconscious he may be, but he's as pure as the driven snow! I say he votes!"

"Yes, let him vote!" called Mrs Pullar.

Warrender, drawing strength from Grossett's fire, now seemed more confident than ever and made a firm decision: "Nothing in the rules says he actually has to be conscious during the meeting, so he votes."

Mr Waddell learned of his enfranchisement through Mrs Beaumont, who exclaimed, "Wake up, pal! You're on!"

This time, Waddell jerked and responded with another mighty rasper that seemed to vibrate the table and chairs. Then, his head bucked into wakefulness.

Seizing the opportunity, Warrender invited the sleepy giant of democracy to vote.

Looking as if unsure of his whereabouts, Mr Waddell shook his head vigorously, emitting dust and another little feather. He looked around and, as things seemed to become clearer, he spoke. "I… I thought I'd voted," he said.

"No," said the chairman, shaking his head. "No."

"Oh. Ah… er, right… right then," replied Waddell, now very confused but nevertheless cheery. "I'm… I'm easy, really," he confided with a shrug.

Barrington swooped in like a hawk. "Easy? That's not a vote! Easy? What on earth's that mean?"

"Eh, well, you know, either way – whatever – I'm happy," floundered Waddell, now less cheery.

"Happy?" cried Barrington. "That's not a vote either; what's happy got to do with it?"

Warrender stepped in bravely. "We need a yes or a no, please, Mr Waddell."

"Ah, well… er… ah… right…" replied Waddell, looking about. "Who's got the most votes?"

"Nobody. It's a tie," said Warrender.

"Ah. Oh. Well… in that case…" muttered Waddell, fingering his lips.

"Yes?" barked Barrington.

"In that case, I vote with Mr Grossett," said Waddell.

"What?" exploded Barrington.

"Thank you, Mr Waddell. That's most kind," said Grossett

"In the name of God, what for?" cried Barrington fiercely.

"Mind your own business," interceded Grossett. "Who d'you think you are – the Spanish Inquisition?"

"We're a free country," observed Mrs Pullar.

"Free to be as daft as a brush, obviously," snarled Barrington, staring hard at the erstwhile snorer. "Stop being obtuse, Mr Waddell; elucidate and state your own position clearly! It's your decision we want, not anyone else's!"

Waddell looked confused.

"Your own position and no one else's!" barked Barrington.

"Er, sitting," Waddell replied, perplexed.

"For or against!" cried Barrington. "Are you for the motion or against it?"

Waddell froze for a moment, before turning again to Grossett. "How did you vote?" he asked.

"For," said Grossett.

"For," said Waddell, turning towards Barrington.

"For what?" asked Barrington.

"For for," replied Waddell, instinctively, before turning to Grossett again. "For?" he asked.

"For," affirmed Grossett.

"For," affirmed Waddell.

"Six fors!" yelled Johnny. "It's a landslide!"

Warrender leaped at the chance. "Right! There we have it! A decision! It's for! We admit Tannadee to the Colonel McBraid Bequest Highland Games. Thank you all for your attendance, ladies and gentlemen." Turning to his right, he asked politely, "Mrs Beaumont, would you mind giving me a lift, please?" Then a second thought apparently struck him, something to do with car elastic perhaps. "Actually, I think I'll walk; it's such a fine evening." And, with that, Mr Warrender gathered up his things and strode decisively out of the room.

The rest of the attendees disbanded quickly.

As soon as they were away from the church, Johnny stopped walking and, facing Jim, he let loose: "How dare Barrington attack us like that? He was a bloody disgrace in there! He nearly scuppered us, the bloody fool! You need to put him straight on a few things!"

Jim seemed to agree. "Yes, yes, it was very strange. I've never seen him like that before."

"He looked almost demented," said Chizzie.

Johnny went further. "It wouldn't surprise me if he's got rabies. He was almost eating poor old Waddell there."

"Something's bitten Robert, that's for sure," Jim answered quietly.

Chizzie wondered, "Maybe he's having second thoughts? He certainly hasn't been very active lately…"

"He's obviously stressed about something," said Jim, "and stress can do strange things to people, especially someone with principles as old-fashioned as Robert's."

Johnny exploded: "Stress? Stress? What can he know about stress? He doesn't know the meaning of the word."

"You'd be surprised," said Jim calmly. "He can be a very sensitive man, can Robert. Maybe the strain of the school's funding problems has got to him; he's worked very hard on that. I'll have a word with him to see what's up. I'm not sure he's very well."

"It might be that he's the victim of practical jokers," Chizzie suggested to Jim.

"Really?" Jim quizzed.

"It's just a thought," confirmed Chizzie.

Jim stroked his chin. "Looking at Robert's actions in another way, he's possibly been very shrewd, you know. Because of him, the record will show that the committee was no pushover. Shambolic it might've been, but that is not on the record. The record that Weever and his lawyers will see shows that we were scrutinised very thoroughly and we came through by the narrowest of margins. Weever can accuse no one of a stitch-up. We won fair and square. Perhaps there's more to Robert Barrington than we think."

"Piffle!" exclaimed Johnny.

But there was indeed more: Robert Barrington, the sensitive man of principle, was off to report to his controller.

CHAPTER 19

"*Nil desperandum*, Robert," said Charlie Fairfoull, airily on the phone. "Despair not. It's early days yet."

"Early days? Ugh!" came the surly reply from Barrington. "Really, I don't think I can keep it up much longer. I never was any good at acting. I'm too honest. If I'm found to be devious and plotting, I'll be driven out of town like a rat. I think people are suspicious already. I need to come in from the cold, Charlie. I really do."

"No, no, Robert; no, you hang in there just a little longer. We'll soon get the land we need, and then it's all systems go for a bigger and better resort. I need hardly tell you that means more responsibility for you. A word to the wise, though, Robert: show no weakness. Mr Weever does not like weakness. So hang in there and play it cool. There's not much more we need you to do."

"I'm just very concerned that the village will turn ugly very soon, and I'll be the principal target. The tide's moving against us, and—"

"Robert, Robert, stop there – stop. Take it from me, Mr Weever is not in the habit of letting a bunch of villagers put one over on him."

"Well, he needs to know there's talk of a protest march of some kind and some hotheads are talking about storming the golf course. That could be very nasty."

"Oh? When is this happening?"

"I don't know yet; it's only a rumour, but it could be soon. I don't want to seem alarmist, but—"

"I get the picture; that's very interesting, Robert. We'll follow that up. Do you have any idea how many might be involved?"

"Well, there was talk of a hundred."

"Do you think they'll get that?"

"No, more like thirty, I would say. But some people are extremely irate about losing so much of the school playing field, and they're sounding off about getting reporters and TV-news crews in."

"Right, leave it with me, Robert; you've been extremely helpful. Let me know as soon as you get firm details."

"You will make sure that Mr Weever knows I supplied the vital information, won't you?"

"Of course... of course, Robert. He'll be very grateful, believe me."

"And you will remind him of my precarious position? Security could be overwhelmed; it's like sitting on a powder keg here."

"Mr Weever will be very appreciative, Robert, have no fear. He's a powerful man and he won't let you down. Believe me."

"Of course, of course," replied Barrington, sounding no jollier than before.

"Keep smiling, Robert. We'll speak soon."

He put the phone down, then phoned Weever in Texas to give him the news about Barrington's failure to block Tannadee's bequest application. Weever, like Charlie, was disappointed but not down.

"We'll get that land; we'll get the bastards, no question," came the voice over the phone. "The question is whether our guy Barrington can hold it together. He needs to step up. His morale's hit the deck, you say?"

"He's a bit down, yeah."

"It's lucky he's not a major player. One little nip from a flea circus and he's taking a count of nine."

"He'll bounce back, though, Gordon. He will. He prides himself on getting results. He thinks he's let you down, that's all. He'll get over it. He'll find a way to win Donald over."

"As they're both gay, it shouldn't be that difficult."

"I'm not so sure they are gay."

"Oh, they are. There's no doubt about it; I can sniff 'em out a mile off. That Barrington, he can be very cocky; it's a sure sign."

"He's a cocky one all right. He's feeling down right now, but, when he's up, he is very up. In a good wind, he'll soar like a pterodactyl. We just have to be the wind beneath his flimsy wings, that's all."

"Let's just hope he doesn't crap on us."

"He won't, Gordon, but it looks like there might be some flak on the way. Barrington tells me there's some kind of protest afoot. Some of the natives are very unhappy about us buying the playing field at the school."

"Oh, are they now?"

"But it's no problem. I'll get the cops on it and get it tied up."

"You'll do no such thing. I want this."

"What? You want protesters?"

"I sure do. I've a score to settle. It's time to push back. We hit these bastards and punch their juicy faces all over the fucking field. Especially the guy who hit me with the fruit cake. I'm taking him out. I'm taking my gun too. You never know how these things will go; they can really kick off big time."

"Whoa! Whoa there, Gordon; this isn't the Alamo. You can't go hitting people here, let alone shooting them. Let the cops handle it."

"The lonesome PC? Are you kidding? I want this fight, Charlie. I want it. The gun's for emergencies, but I want to win this. Money isn't everything. Happiness is what counts, and I won't be happy till I've kicked the shit clean outta these hillbillies. When you're top of the heap, you're due respect, and I ain't getting any from these sons of bitches. I want to whip 'em. I want their guts, Charlie!"

"Okay, I hear you, Gordon. We'll match them. We'll have our own little counter-demonstration."

"Not little! Bigger! Bigger! Anything they've got, we get bigger. They've got clubs, we get bigger clubs—"

"They won't have clubs, Gordon. They'll have placards on poles, and banners. That's the way they do things here."

"Poles? What size of poles?"

"Oh... 'bout four feet, I'd say."

"Right, we'll get six feet – and thicker too. How many troops have they got?"

"Troops?"

"How many've they got?"

"Well, thirty, I'm told."

"Right, we'll get fifty."

"Where? Where from? Security firms?"

"Anywhere, but only solid types. No weedy floppers. See to it."

"One more thing, Gordon: there's someone actually trying to hurt us right now. There's a banner in a tree on the eighth fairway and it isn't exactly complimentary to us."

"What's it say?"

"Well, it... it says 'Weever's signature hole.'"

"No problem, I'm fine with that. That's someone very omniscient."

"Omniscient! I say, where'd that big beauty come from?"

"I'm filling up on killer words, Charlie. People are gonna see I can hit big words too. I'm learning a new word every week. It was one a day, but... well, it got too much: every time I learned a new one, another went out the window. D'you find that?"

"Well… yes… yes, sometimes."

"Don't patronise me, Charlie. I know that tone."

"Well, don't ask leading questions, Gordon." Fairfoull ignored the growl that came his way: "Look, what I was trying to say, Gordon, is this: the person who put up the banner wasn't entirely omniscient. You see there's a logo-like thing up there too."

"Like what?"

"Well… it looks kinda like a bull's ass with the letters 'BS' hanging between its legs."

"*What?* You mean… The bastards! The shits! Get that *down*! You get somebody up there and get that ripped off right now."

"I can't put any of our guys up there right now, Gordon; it's too dangerous, it's getting dark here. Health and safety would crucify us if anything went wrong."

"Well, somebody's got up there no problem or that trash wouldn't be up there, would it?"

"Monkey Boy, I was told."

"Who? Who's Monkey Boy?"

"Paw's boy. He's the one most likely to have put it there. The other thing is that it's not actually on our land, so it's not straightforward. The tree's on Paw's land: you know, the old guy behind the mound. I'll speak to him about it tomorrow."

"No, you'll tear it down right now, Charlie. Right now, you hear?"

"I can't do that, Gordon; I'd be trespassing. That could spell trouble. Things are a bit fragile right now. I'll speak to him."

"I want it down. How high is that shit?"

"Too high, Gordon. Too high."

"Then shoot it. I don't want the press seeing that! No pictures!"

"Well... shooting would be tricky, Gordon. How's plan A coming along?"

"That's none of your business right now. It's top secret. Look, when the wind blows does the sign with the BS enter our air space?"

"Well... yeah, you could say that. It billows over the fence line sometimes, a little bit."

"Right, shoot it! No question. As soon as that shit trespasses, you shoot it. In fact, you know what? Don't even wait; who the hell cares? Go out and hit the fucking thing right now. Take that crap out! It's disgusting, it's filthy, it's horrible!"

"Uh, well..."

"Now, Charlie! The word is 'now'! Do it now! I don't want that filth up there a minute longer! Now, Charlie! Understand? Now!"

And with that he ended the call.

As darkness fell, in the Tannadee Hotel lounge bar, Chizzie, Johnny and Jim were celebrating their success with the Colonel McBraid Bequest committee. Sipping their drinks, they speculated on who could represent them at the Highland Games. Tannadee's best asset was the school; being a school that emphasised the benefits of physical activity, it had several staff members who were experienced athletes, some with experience of amateur Highland Games. Three of the selections were easy to make: Sven, the reforming drunkard, would be the thrower; Dekker, the erstwhile chip fryer, would be the wrestler; and Billy would be the sprinter. The other events would require a selection contest, including the half-mile, Chizzie's event. Jim hadn't made Chizzie the automatic choice, but Chizzie knew it was the right decision: there

216

could be no favouritism. If he was in the team, he would have to be there on merit, not simply because he'd helped secure Tannadee's entry to the games.

Jamie Taylor – the young, singing protester – sauntered up to them, clutching his glass of lager. "Terrible what Weever's doing, isn't it?" he said cheerily, rocking backwards and forwards slightly as he spoke. "My mum's organising a protest march against Weever's land grab. It's going to be at the school grounds. She reckons she'll get about fifty people and some TV-news crews by Thursday. She asked Mr Barrington to help out, but he's not feeling too well at the moment. Does anybody here want to help set things up?"

"Good idea, Jamie; that's excellent. I'll help," enthused Chizzie.

But Jim shook his head adamantly. "No, no, no. I don't want anything like that. Apart from the fact that it could turn nasty, it would be counter-productive: if word gets out that we're about to lose a part of our playing field, parents might look elsewhere. We need to keep a lid on things until we've explored every avenue."

"Mum won't be pleased," said Jamie, grim-faced. "I think she'll go ahead, anyway."

"I won't allow it on the school grounds," insisted Jim. "It could all get very messy."

Chizzie looked for a compromise: "How about you allow fifteen protesters, Jim, with no TV crews and no big publicity. Just enough action to let Weever know we won't roll over and make him think again. We can't do nothing."

Jim thought for a moment. "All right," he agreed, "Fifteen protesters, but that's it, no more. Any more and I halt the march."

Jamie sniffed, then drained his glass. "I'll tell Mother, but she won't be pleased," he said turning away and burping. "Excuse me. See ya."

"You're not marching, Chizzie," said Johnny, "and neither am I. If there're TV crews there and it all goes pear-shaped I don't want our business taking a hit."

Looking outraged, Chizzie replied defiantly, "I'm joining the march, Father. I might even lead it."

Two days later, it was on. Fifteen protesters carrying banners and placards set off from the village square and marched behind a piper through the streets towards the school. Everyone they passed applauded. Not one person booed or jeered. As they entered the school grounds, Weever arrived in a helicopter on his side of the stream. He got out, wearing the old fighter pilot's helmet that he now wore on these trips to keep his hairpiece in place. He was in fighting mood.

"*Fucking flight delays!*" he bawled over the noise of the helicopter as it flew away. Weever had seen the protesters arrive and immediately quizzed Fairfoull on the preparedness of his own troops. He removed the helmet and handed it to one of the bodyguards. "Right this is it!" he said. "Are our guys all set?"

"Absolutely, Gordon," confirmed Fairfoull.

"Are our poles bigger than theirs?"

"Yes, indeed."

"Have we got more troops than them?"

"Indeed."

"Are they solid and sturdy?"

"Absolutely."

"Are they fired up and ready?"

"They're all fired up and ready."

"Where are they? Are they here?"

"They are. Follow me."

"Have you got my gun?"

"It's on standby. Derek Henderson's looking after it. He'll be close by."

They strode across the stream and watched the approaching protesters.

"Where are our guys?" Weever asked anxiously, looking around. "I don't see them. I see only six guys with aprons; is this a disguise? Have they got weapons concealed?"

Fairfoull merely smiled, walked over to one of four tables and pulled off a large, white cloth. "Here they are! Our troops!" he declared revealing stacks of cups, saucers, mugs and plates; and a coffee machine and an urn, both running off a generator. Then, moving swiftly to the next table, he revealed a large variety of luscious-looking sandwiches made from French bread, wholemeal bread, white bread, ryebread and organic bread, all generously filled with a variety of meats and veggies. Weever stood agape as Fairfoull proceeded to the next table and revealed a large selection of fruits and cakes.

"Look, don't mess about, Charlie," Weever said hurriedly, eyeing the advancing enemy, "Where the hell are our troops?"

"These are our troops, Gordon," he said pointing to the mugs and cups. "Rock-solid, sturdy types as promised, and here are the poles," he said pointing to his signboards bidding welcome and offering teas, coffee, sandwiches, fruit, cakes and scones – all free!

Weever stood frozen, managing only to whine.

"We kill 'em dead with kindness, Gordon," smiled Fairfoull.

"Wha? Ugh. Kill 'em with kindness?" replied Weever. "Are you nuts? They'll shove it up our asses."

"No, they won't. Ian's over there filming it for our YouTube channel; they can see that. If they try to throw us off, they're going to look like ungrateful retards, and they can't afford

219

that. We've got 'em, Gordon. And here they come. Smile! Let 'em have it!"

The protesters arrived at the tables chanting, "Weever out! Weever out!"

"Smile, Gordon, smile; burn 'em up!" insisted Fairfoull through a gritted grin. Then he threw his arms wide and, smiling, played the perfect host. "Welcome! Welcome everyone! Thrice welcome! You are, of course, perfectly within your legal rights to voice your concerns peacefully – we respect that. But we are neighbours after all, so let us agree to differ and enjoy a lovely afternoon together. Help yourself to whatever you wish. There's plenty of food for everyone; we were expecting a bigger turnout, but, *hey*, that's all the more for us. Come on, folks! Come away!"

"You're on school property!" shouted one of the protesters.

"That is not our understanding," replied Fairfoull.

As the protesters eyed the laden tables, their intensity dropped and a look of puzzlement took over. It was clearly difficult to protest against cups and saucers, mugs and sandwiches, just as Fairfoull had calculated.

"Welcome; welcome, everyone!" repeated a smiling Fairfoull, spreading his arms out wide again. "Help yourselves! Tuck in!"

For a moment, there was only a wary silence, then Jessie Taylor cried, "Where are the news crews?"

"They're not here," came a reply.

"It looks like Weever TV is here, though," observed Johnny pointing to a man with a large camera.

Jessie Taylor pointed angrily at Weever and shouted, *"You've nobbled them, haven't you? You've nobbled the media."*

"We haven't nobbled anybody," pleaded Weever with an acid smile and a shrug.

"And where's PC Tunnock?" enquired a protester.

"He's been called to a road accident on the Beef Tub Road," Jim answered.

"It stinks! The whole thing. Let's throw it all in the burn!" roared a protester.

But Chizzie stepped forwards hurriedly, then wheeled round to face the protesters, with his arms aloft: "Hold it! Hold it! This is a stunt to make us look like Luddites and numpties and we mustn't fall for it! We're being filmed, but we're also filming." Chizzie pointed to Johnny, who was holding a camera, and Jim, who was holding a camcorder. "We'll ensure there's no shenanigans and no fancy editing."

The protesters cheered again.

Chizzie clapped his hands. "So let's shift these tables!"

The protesters roared in agreement.

"And here's how we do it," continued Chizzie. "We carry the tables – crockery, food and all – very, very carefully over to their side of the burn."

This got the protesters really excited and they cheered and waved their placards.

Chizzie beckoned to Dekker, who was wearing an improvised white armband with the word "Steward" scrawled on it in black felt tip. "The key word is 'carefully'," Chizzie emphasised. "We get four strong guys on each table, and we carry them across nice and gently."

But Weever strode angrily towards them, wagging a finger. "No, no! No, you don't!" he yelled. "You keep your—"

Fairfoull cut him off. "No, Gordon, no! We're being filmed; we're being filmed," he whispered tersely, and gestured towards Johnny and Jim. "We can still come out on top. We can still beat 'em with kindness and generosity. Believe me, it's hard to beat."

"You and your goddamned kindness shit," hissed Weever. "We're the ones looking like numpties now."

"Not if we smile, Gordon; it's a winner, so – for God's sake – smile. Look like a daddy at a picnic." Fairfoull turned towards the protesters; "Wherever you're most comfortable, ladies and gentlemen, wherever you're most comfortable; you go right ahead."

This invitation stopped the protesters in their tracks, and a cloud of suspicion seemed to come over them as if maybe the tables were booby trapped. Some looked under the tables, like remote jungle dwellers who'd never seen a table before. They tested the table legs and found nothing wanting. Chizzie, satisfied that the tables held no nasty surprises, ordered the advance.

But Weever had seen his chance to avenge his fruit bun humiliation. Sven, with his back to Weever, was close enough to hit with a cupcake. Weever snatched one from the table and threw it. It missed Sven, but not Mrs Taylor. It thudded into her shoulder, and she let out a scream before shouting, "What d'you think you're doing you great big oaf?"

Sven knew instantly what he was doing: he returned the doughty cupcake, but it missed Weever by an inch or so.

"They hit my mum!" cried Jamie Taylor. "Let's throw the stuff in the burn!" The protesters roared in approval. Chizzie turned to them, appealing for calm. Weever beckoned to his employee with the shotgun. Fairfoull joined Chizzie in an appeal for calm, but, behind him, the situation had deepened.

Weever took hold of the shotgun and, staring venomously at the protesters, snapped it shut and fired it into the air. The protesters froze, some screamed, and a puff of feathers burst across the sky as a gull, which had been circling above the sandwiches previously, plummeted posthumously towards the jostling protesters, chiefly Mr McTurk, the old forester, who had decorated his placard very neatly with the words "Weever, Ya Bawbag". Seeing the bird in the nick of time, he swung his placard at it and whacked it straight into the beard of the minister of The Free Kirk of United Brethren. This was not a church noted for its unity, and it was immediately clear why. The minister retaliated with a wild swing of his own, whacking the wild man of the woods on the side of the head. The woodsman whacked back, but, before he was able to admire the fruit of his labours, a thin-faced protester of the United Brethren, in a rare exhibition of their proclaimed unity, joined with his minister and whacked the woodsman with his placard that read boldly "Weever, You Scumbag". The minister retired from the fray and left it to the ardent member of his flock to see justice done.

Neither 'Bawbag' nor 'Scumbag' was up for surrender, and blow for blow they went, while the others looked on in disbelief, until Jessie Taylor yelled, "Somebody, for God's sake, stop them!"

"I'll stop 'em," chirped Sven, dashing towards the warring gentlemen. First, he jabbed Scumbag in the crotch with his pole, then swinging round he jabbed Bawbag likewise. This took the wind out of the two and they froze, bent over in what looked like more than just mild agony. Calm returned.

Johnny, though, had lost it. He scurried over to the warriors and bawled, "You idiots! Now we're done for. Weever's got it all on film, and the world's going to see what morons we are!"

"No, Dad. No. Look over there!" Chizzie pointed to Weever, who was being assailed by an irate woman. She was slapping a retreating Weever about the chest as security men ran to his rescue.

"It's Mary McLean of the Hedgehog Sanitorium!" exclaimed Chizzie.

"And she's beating the hell out of Weever!" exclaimed Johnny.

Chizzie swung round to see if Jim was filming it. He was. "We're safe!" cried Chizzie. "Jim's recorded it. Weever can't show us up without us showing him being beaten up by a woman. Thank God for animal welfare!"

Mary McLean was not done, though; with a shout of, "You vile brute!" she threw an egg sandwich straight at the man, and it splattered over his chest. "You think you can do just what you want, Mr Weever. Well, you can't! You lousy creep!"

Weever, not one for satisfying critics, replied, "You bitch!" and he threw a lettuce-and-tomato sandwich at Mary's face.

Her scream hit the charged air like a fuse, and many of the demonstrators, cursing and yelling outrage, rushed towards Weever, who backed off warily, pointing his gun at his would-be assailants.

"*Back off or I shoot,*" he roared. "I'm allowed to in self-defence! And, let me tell you, I shoot straight. I don't miss. I'm a hunter."

"You're an idiot!" shouted one of the protesters.

"How many shells have you got in that gun?" asked Sven, walking briskly but slightly unsteadily up to Weever. "Let me tell you: none!" he declared.

"Oh, really?" chuckled Weever. "Do you think so? Do you want to find out, big boy? Are you feeling lucky?" He snorted sarcastically and pointed the gun straight at Sven.

Sven took another step towards Weever, who raised the gun to point at Sven's head.

Fairfoull came fretfully up behind his boss. "Okay, okay," he said raising his arms, "everybody just calm down, please."

"He hit a lady," said a protester.

Fairfoull held his hands up in peace. "On behalf of us all, we're sorry about that. Very sorry, but things kinda got out of hand and, when that happens, no one's a winner."

"I'm sorry too," said Mary, "I shouldn't have thrown anything, but what he did was just so vile and so wanton." She burst into tears and was led away sobbing.

"I'll write her an official apology," promised Fairfoull.

But this was not enough for one protester, she shouted angrily, "It shouldn't be you; it should be him! The cowboy!"

Sven took another step towards Weever and giggled cheekily. He was now only a few yards away from the gun. "You don't scare me, Weever. You've no ammunition in that gun," he said cockily.

"Oh, haven't I now?" queried Weever.

"No, you haven't."

"Oh, yes I have."

"Oh, no, you haven't."

"Oh, yes, I have."

Sven turned to the demonstrators and sweeping his arms upwards like a concert conductor, exclaimed, "Okay everybody!"

Most of the protesters responded with, "Oh, no, you haven't!"

This bemused Weever for a second. He'd heard this kind of thing before somewhere, then it struck him: a pantomime. He was being taken for a pantomime fool. He steadied himself, clinging to his gun, and, with exaggerated poise, he again raised it level with Sven's head and uttered tersely, "Okay, big boy, you want to find out? You step right this way."

Fairfoull tried to intervene again, but Weever barked angrily, "Stay out of this!"

Sven took a few more steps towards the gun, then he stopped and turned towards his fellow demonstrators. "If he shoots me, I want to be cremated," he declared. "And I want Weever hanged."

Shouts went up: "Don't be stupid, Sven."; "He's a maniac!"; and "Crazy!"

Chizzie joined the calls. "Back off, Sven! Back off!"

"You heard him, numpty, back off!" yelled Weever. "Get the hell away from me!"

Sven smiled cockily. "I'm not backing off. I know you're bluffing."

"No, sonny, I'm not. I warn you; I am not bluffing!"

With a cheeky grin, Sven turned to his audience, then took a small step towards Weever.

Weever appealed to the others, "You see, you see, he's coming at me. I've got no choice!"

Fairfoull marched towards Weever, "Gordon, put the gun down for Chrissake."

"Get back. I've every right!" insisted Weever. "I'm under attack on my own property." Sven took another small step closer to Weever and smiled.

"Get back, sonny boy!" Weever warned. "Get back."

But Sven continued grinning and edged forwards.

"One more step," said Weever, "and it's curtains, numpty. Just one more."

Aghast, Chizzie tried again, "Get back, Sven!"

There came a shout, "He's crazy enough to do it; back off, Sven!"

Fairfoull leaned towards Weever and said, "Gordon—"

"Shut up!" said the boss.

The protesters called for sanity: "Come to your senses, both of you!"; "Back off, Weever!"; and "Back off, Sven; he's not worth it!"

Chizzie, dry-mouthed, couldn't just stand by; he swallowed hard, and taking a deep breath, began walking slowly towards the eyeballing pair. The protesters went eerily silent. The closer Chizzie got to the pair, the more the pulse in his ears pounded like someone trying frantically to hammer sense into his head. A feeling of mortal danger came over him, which was so overwhelming that he began to feel dizzy and very hot. Neither Sven nor Weever acknowledged his arrival until he cleared his throat, which felt like sandpaper. Chizzie gazed at the gun. It had an animal presence, like it was alive: like a spitting cobra about to strike.

"*Get back!*" roared Weever, staring wildly at Chizzie.

Sven, a picture of calm, turned his head casually towards Chizzie and bade him go.

Chizzie hesitated for a moment; he'd said nothing, but it was clear he'd done all he could. So he turned and walked slowly away, wondering all the time whether he'd simply chickened out, or had been thoroughly sensible and done the right thing, possibly saving lives.

Sven, almost laughing, eyed Weever and announced, "I'm taking that step, Gordon; I'm taking that step."

"It's up to you," Weever replied sternly.

Sven took the ultimate step.

Without a word, in complete silence, Weever raised his gun straight at Sven's forehead, put his finger to the trigger and "*Bang!*" he shouted. Then he burst out laughing. "You fools! You really thought I'd do it; ha, ha, ha. You're the ones who are crazy! Look and see, it's empty!" He held the gun skywards, squeezed the trigger, and a volley of shot blasted into the air. Weever lurched backwards, almost losing his balance. Then, ashen-faced and looking bewildered, he swallowed hard, rubbed his shoulder and stared at Sven.

"You… you could've killed him!" shouted Chizzie.

"I didn't; I wouldn't. I aimed past him," Weever replied vacantly. Then suddenly recovering his composure, like he was under new management, he grabbed a slice of carrot cake from the table beside him and yelled, "*But this won't miss!*" and he threw the slice at Sven.

Sven ducked and it flew over him. But Sven's cream-tea scone did not miss; skimming off Weever's forehead, it left a streak of jam just below the artificial hairline.

Weever wiped the stuff off angrily, examined it and then exclaimed pitifully, "I'm cut! Jeezus. I'm cut! He's cut my head!"

"It's raspberry jam!" Fairfoull informed him and beckoned to the bodyguards, who rushed forwards and began to usher him away.

"He's jet-lagged and stressed. He gets disorientated sometimes," Fairfoull explained.

"Oh, yeah, yeah, of course; he's really a pussycat," commented a protester.

"No. He's not a pussycat, but he's no killer either."

Jessie Taylor joined in. "Oh, yes, he is; he said he's a hunter."

Chizzie, feeling drained, intervened. "Okay, okay, folks; that's it. Let's just call it a day and go home, eh? We've made our point, and I, for one, haven't the stomach for a picnic right now. So let's go, eh?"

The appeal was met with a murmur of agreement and then – quietly, as if dazed – the demonstrators turned and moved away towards the school.

The only protester left was Weever himself; he was still protesting his innocence and desperate for a scapegoat. Halting his minders, he approached Derek Henderson, the assistant who'd handed him the gun. "I said one shot, you idiot!"

"I'm really sorry, sir; I just forgot," said Henderson. "But it's double-barrelled and you didn't examine it. I didn't know—"

"You... you're fired! You fucker! You absolute fucker! Fuck off!" Then he turned on Fairfoull and ranted, "And you! Cups and saucers! Pah! What a foolish shit idea! What a dumb—"

"It would've worked given half a chance," insisted Fairfoull. "We could've had them eating out of our hands – literally. And they would've quietened down; you can't eat and yell at the same time."

"They were about to shove your tables over the creek, you idiot!"

"Fine. Excellent. They take them over and now they're in our debt – we've made a concession. They'd be minded to make a concession too. You don't rage against a man when you're eating his lovely food. It's human nature. And look at the weather: this day was made for us – it was a blessing. We'd have given them a picnic they'd remember for the rest of their lives. Now, they'll remember it for all the wrong reasons. What a disaster!"

"I... I could've been jailed, you mutt!"

"Oh yeah, yeah. Never mind the stiff with no head."

"That loser? Who cares? I mean, really, who cares? I feed thousands of families all around the—"

"Yeah, yeah, we know; we know all that. My problem is that I cared enough about you to put my neck on the line. But guess what? Surprise, surprise, you couldn't see it. I could've just stood back and watched you launch in, then watch you get run out of town – and maybe even strung up."

"Run out of town? Me?"

"You! If you'd got your way, there'd be carnage, and you'd be the biggest casualty. But hey-ho, there we go, and off I go. *Hasta la vista*, baby."

"You're fired!"

"Too late; I quit."

"I fired you first; you're fired."

"Seems like you're firing all over the place today, Gordon. Anyway, whatever, I'm outta here."

CHAPTER 20

Over in the school pavilion, Sven, still smelling faintly of booze, sat staring at the floor dejectedly as he poured out his feelings of shame and self-loathing. Most of the protesters sat silently, witnessing his agony. Seated around him were Chizzie, Johnny and Jim. They listened, hoping that the near-death experience would prove cathartic, and rid Sven of his drink-fuelled antics once and for all. The omens were good; never before had Sven been so introspective and rigorous with himself.

"My life hung on the flick of a finger," he murmured. "And for what?" He put his head in his hands and shook his head. "I know nothing about guns. I just assumed he'd fired and that was it."

"That's one helluva assumption," said Jim. "Never assumpt when you're looking down the barrel of a gun."

Sven lifted his head and managed a wan smile. "Well, it's done it for me. This time I'm off the booze for good. This time's for real, honest to God it is. It has to be. I could've been blown to bits; there'd have been blood all over the place and over all these people. Yeah. I felt the heat of that thing when it fired; it was like the fires of hell. I get chills just thinking about it. Lord Almighty, if a man can't take that for a lesson, he doesn't deserve to live. And I got a lotta livin' to do. Clean livin'. Good livin.'"

"I'll chum ye, Sven," said a rotund man with a red nose and a white beard, who looked like an off-duty Santa Claus.

"You'll what?" asked Sven.

"I'll go teetotal wi' ye."

"And so will I," said another.

"Me too," added one more.

"And me, Sven," came another, "we're on your bandwagon."

Johnny looked alarmed. "Steady on, guys, steady. You'll put me out of business!"

"There're plenty of non-alcoholic drinks on the go these days," advised Santa Claus.

"Get plenty in," advised another.

"Yeah, we're not coming to lose our heads anymore, we're coming for each other; isn't that right, guys?"

"Aye, good company an' all that. It's better than drink," agreed one.

One of the tougher-looking men appeared to be a little embarrassed, but nodded in agreement, nonetheless. Team Clear Head was hitting town.

When night came, and Chizzie lay abed, the ghostly faces of Sven and Weever played on his mind. Both men's faces had briefly turned white after the gun went off in the stand-off. Their spectral faces, if nothing else, suggested that neither man was beyond sensibility. Both possessed, albeit deep inside them, a common humanity that could be brought to common purpose. On the other hand, these ghostly faces held no grace, and they gave way to visions of the cake fight. The man from the gutter and the man of a dozen mansions had joined the battle without so much as a thought fired. Sven, though, was clearly and profoundly affected, and, according to Billy Pung later on, he'd been unable to eat anything at teatime and had talked about going to church on Sunday. The ethereal faces had disappeared, but sleep proved elusive.

That Jim hadn't made him an automatic choice still stung. But he would prove his worth in the selection race. By one o' clock, he'd run the selection race seven times – winning every time – before moving on to the big day itself, which saw him win three times in spectacular fashion. It was a beautiful day. And Yolanda was there, smiling admiringly and cheering him on. Contented, he began drifting off. Then, suddenly, cold reality struck like a blunt instrument: would she really be there? Would she ever return? These sobering questions kept him awake. For over forty minutes, he tossed and turned. Finally, looking straight at the ceiling, he managed to convince himself that no good would come of thinking about Yolanda right now. So, very determinedly, he directed his mind to a new training schedule, and mulling it over, he eventually fell asleep.

Next day, Fairfoull entered Weever's office and declared, "You rang, milord."

"Cut the crap and sit down. I'm unfiring you. You're back on the payroll," said Weever, irritably.

"I don't recall being consulted in the matter."

"Shut up. Sit down and listen. I'm getting that land; I'm not being railroaded by a bunch of nutcases. Look, we both got it wrong: without me, your tables would've hit the water, and that's a fact; and, without you, somebody could've got killed. I'm big enough to admit that." Weever looked up, searching for a sarcastic smile, but Fairfoull had it under control. "And, let's be honest, who could've known so many booze-crazy nutters live in any one place; they're pure nutcases – the real McCoy. But no problem; we're going to sort them out. My plan to get Donald away from Lord Tulloh has worked."

"Your plan worked?" exclaimed Fairfoull with undisguised surprise.

Weever cast him a stern look: "Of course it worked. My plan was so damn good that, even with Digger's Spanish knuckleheads fucking it up, it worked."

"Some plan."

"You bet. Some plan, and mine, all mine."

"What happened?"

"Whatever the Spanish is for 'numpty' is what happened. Digger found that Donald's mother lives in Spain; she's got a villa there, on the Costa del Sol. Donald's a devoted son: he'll do anything for his dear, old mama. So, my great plan was to kidnap the mother's Yorkshire terrier and hold it to ransom. She's devoted to the mutt. When she fell to pieces, Donald would go over to comfort her; we would go to town with his lordship, Lord Tulloh; and we would get what we wanted before Donald got back. So, Digger got in touch with his associates in Spain; it turns out they're an old guy and his two sons, but the two sons are laid up with injuries they got in a supermarket. It seems they went to the express checkout, for ten items or less, and they saw the guy in front had eleven items, so they went crazy. All their lives, they've broken all the rules – it's their living – but they went nuts because the guy in front had eleven items. They couldn't let the little guy bend the rules just a tiny bit. Their luck was out, though; the other guy's a blackbelt in karate and he laid them out with more than ten bruises each. They were waiting for the sons to heal, but it was taking too long, so the old boss man decided he'd do it himself; he thought it was a nice easy job. This is a man with angina, shaky knees and a hip replacement."

"The cream of the crop."

"But he made it; he got the dog in a bag, but she attacked him."

"The dog?"

"No, the mother – she's a feisty, old bitch."

234

"He was shuffling down the drive with the dog, and the mother was after him, though she's got two hip replacements; she fell over and knocked herself out. He ran back to see if she was okay – he didn't want a homicide on his books. He checked her breathing, but she came to and pulled up his balaclava, then his crummy dentures fell out and bit her face, and she fainted. He called an ambulance and took off. He was going like a wonky bat out of hell, then his trousers fell down – he's lost weight recently, and over he went. He got up and—"

"A meteorite hit him on the head?"

"No, surprisingly. His phone was gone; it had fallen out his trousers. He scrambled around looking for it and found it eventually. Then he heard an ambulance in the distance and saw the mother sitting up. He covered his face with the dog in the bag, and it farted in his face; he dropped the bag, and the dog howled, but it was only a scrape. He got to the car in the nick of time and drove off. Job done."

"Miraculous!"

"Never again. We've had to ship him to Florida in case his face hits the papers."

"So Donald is over in Spain?"

"Yes, he's over in sunny Spain. And now we go to town with his lordship."

"What's that mean, exactly?"

"We've found one of Tulloh's old gambling pals from his old gambling circle. Panton's his name, but – unlike our noble friend – Panton's an unreconstructed, hooked-line-and-sinker gambler. He owes me twenty-three thousand pounds. The trouble is, I'm not the only one he owes and he can't pay up, so I'm employing him, and he's going to get me the playing field for sure."

"How's he doing that?"

"Easy. We give him a chauffeur-driven car, and he calls in on the lord and makes out he's a big success. He tells the lord he's looking for a stretch of land to build a summer house on and he's seen the ideal spot. And, lo and behold, it turns out the ideal spot is owned by none other than his old friend Lord Tulloh. He offers thirty thousand pounds, and Tulloh jumps at it."

"The playing field?"

"No, no. The offer's for West Forgie, that's the official name of Panton's ideal spot, but the playing field is officially East Forgie. Now, when Panton gets his lordship legless, he presents him with the letter of sale which has East Forgie written on it in a very rough hand so that 'east' looks like 'west.'"

"What if he sees the difference?"

"He won't. I've tried it. But just to help things along, Panton will clean his lordship's reading glasses with a light oil."

"You mean Panton'll smear his glasses?"

"He'll smear them with initiative. When the plan succeeds, Panton will clear his debt, and we'll clear the playing field."

"Oh, you swine."

"Oink, oink."

With breakfast over, Chizzie lay back in his chair and gazed at the ceiling. "I could hardly sleep a wink last night for thinking about yesterday."

Johnny put down his newspaper and poured himself another cup of tea. "The stuff of nightmares, eh?"

"Yeah, but, as they say, every cloud has a silver lining: if Sven can keep off the booze, at least some good might come of it."

"If he doesn't learn this time, he never will. He's had more comebacks than Lazarus. It's up to him. My worry is for the hotel. Do you think we're safe? If the news gets out, it'll be splashed across all the media."

"Weever'll see that off. He needs a blackout as much as we do. We've both got nuclear options: mutually assured destruction."

"The balance of terror – yeah, great. We just carry on as if everything's hunky-dory."

"Nothing else for it, Father."

"Except that I'm giving the two board-whacking idiots a three-course meal on the house. They're going to sit together, and I'm going to take loads of pictures of them smiling, all best of friends."

"A portrait of country pursuits: a wee bit of fun in the countryside as two country bumpkins beat each other senseless in fine, old rustic style."

"That's the idea."

CHAPTER 21

Up in his bedroom, while getting his kit together for the first Tannadee team training session, Chizzie stood for a moment at the window and cast his eyes over the field where Weever and Sven had so nearly come to grief. Weever's people had done a good job of cleaning up, even the dead gull's feathers seemed all but gone. Cleaning up, of course, was something Weever was good at, and the playing field would probably be in Weever's hands very soon, possibly even in just a few days. How different it might be if Yolanda were here. Chizzie envisaged running with her on the rim of Dennan Hill. What a boost to morale that would be, not just for him but for the whole community. The stark reality, though, was that she wasn't there, and a daydream might be all there would ever be. Then it struck him: Yolanda, far from being an ally, might actually be part of a sophisticated ploy to outwit the good people of Tannadee. Maybe she had come to win their confidence, only to lead them up the garden path? *Like father, like daughter,* Chizzie thought. She had Weever genes and far more to gain from a ruthless commercial career than from compassion and care spent on a bunch of nobodies in the back of beyond.

After his run, Chizzie went to the hotel kitchen to bring Billy the good news of his selection for the Highland Games, but Billy wasn't there. This was unusual since he was always punctual and had proved very reliable recently. Now it seemed that the unpredictable young man might have had second thoughts about kitchen life and had taken himself off into the hills again. If so, the repercussions could be serious, not just for Billy but also for the hotel – the situation in the kitchen in particular had become very fragile lately. With Yolanda's sudden departure, chef Jeff Proudfoot's confidence had taken a steep dive, and it looked as if the man might crumble. But, as Billy had rapidly acquired some kitchen skills and become more than a porter, the chef's confidence had returned gradually. Now, though, with Billy failing to appear, a look of ominous gloom had overtaken the chef's face.

Seeing this, Chizzie offered his services, but Proudfoot declined, reiterating that he'd find it impossible to work alongside a manager. "I won't be far away if you need me," Chizzie assured him warmly, with no hint of the alarm he felt inside. "And please… let me know as soon as Billy gets here."

No sooner had the words left Chizzie's mouth than the door burst open and in walked Billy. Without a word he went straight past Chizzie. Proudfoot greeted him, but there was no response.

"Did you sleep in or something, Billy?" Chizzie enquired tactfully.

Billy barely responded, he merely grunted and looked at Proudfoot, who seemed about to say something.

But Chizzie raised a hand to stop him and asked, "Is something up, Billy?"

Billy stood motionless for a moment, then he spoke. "Sort of," he said, looking away.

"Do you want to tell me?"

Billy compressed his lips, then took a deep breath. "Yeah," he said, his head bowed. Then he took another deep breath and looked up. "They called me Monkey Boy an' Wolf Boy."

"Who? Who's 'they', Billy?"

"The workmen at the golf course."

"Why'd they do that, Billy?" asked Chizzie.

Proudfoot put down his dishcloth and went quickly over to Billy and hugged him. To Chizzie's surprise, Billy hugged him back. Delighted though he was to see Billy's show of affection, Chizzie was livid about the name-calling. Whatever Billy might have done to provoke the workmen, there was no excuse for their gross insults.

"I'll speak to them, Billy," Chizzie said tersely. "We'll get an apology." Then, with a change of tone, he tried to sound cheerful. "Right now, though, Billy, I've great news: you've been picked to represent Tannadee at running. That's a great honour. You're the automatic choice. I wish I was an automatic choice. It'll be a great day."

"I'm not runnin' – not for nobody!" Billy barked angrily, releasing Proudfoot.

Chizzie blinked at the outburst, and wondered if maybe he should have waited. But the deed was done, and now he needed to repair the damage. "Really? Why Billy? Like I said, it's... it's a really great honour. And it's for Tannadee and—"

"I ain't runnin'; I ain't runnin' like a dog. They'll call me names again. Dog Boy. Woof, woof. I'm not havin' it. I'm not runnin' for nobody."

"I'll run," said Proudfoot.

Chizzie smiled wryly. "Thanks Jeff, but Billy's the man we need; he's the fastest. Besides, you're down for the cycling." Hoping that a quiet appeal would change Billy's mind, Chizzie moved nearer to the troubled young man: "Billy, we need you. We really do."

"I ain't runnin'. An' that's it! Finished! Okay?" declared Billy.

Chizzie nodded; this was obviously not a good time to be pressing Billy. The really important thing was that Billy had come on in leaps and bounds. If he liked a task, he did it with great commitment and care. Chizzie smiled reassuringly at Billy, and, with a glance at Jeff, he left.

After lunch the next day, Chizzie drew up his training schedule, then walked to the school, where he found Jim at his desk: a red-eyed, drained-looking figure with two empty coffee mugs on the desk and a pile of filled A4 envelopes at his left elbow. Seemingly, he'd been up all night preparing the pile, which, as Jim explained, contained the full training schedules and dietary plans for the competitors in each event featured in the games. With a weary smile, Jim presented Chizzie with his envelope.

Chizzie opened it and was relieved to find that Jim's schedule was very similar to his own; basically, it was a mixture of speed training, leg strengthening and stamina work – nothing that was unfamiliar to him and none of the extremely punishing stuff he'd half-expected from a man renowned in earlier times for his fiercely competitive nature.

The first squad-training session began on the track at Tannadee School on a fine evening. In reality, it proved more of a social occasion than a serious workout. Thirty-two men, including half a dozen youths, had answered the call and most were treating it like a rallying of the clan. There was laughter and back-slapping and jokes about their physical conditions. Jim welcomed everyone and introduced his coaching team, comprising Chizzie as his assistant, and John McDee in charge of strength and conditioning. Jim emphasised how important the games were to the future of Tannadee, at which point the hilarity fell away.

"The cause is important, and each one of us is important to that cause," Jim insisted. "Things happen. People will be forced to pull out for all sorts of reasons, so everyone is needed, we need reserves. We need every man jack. Now, clearly, we have a wide range of fitness levels here today, so we'll spend this first session simply loosening up followed by some light circuit training. John McDee, our head of PE, will take the session. Afterwards, I want the throwers and cyclists to get a training pack from Chizzie, while the runners and jumpers get a pack from me."

A note of alarm crossed a few faces. Clearly, the notion of a training pack was not something anticipated by all.

Two of those present were a big surprise to Chizzie – they were Barrington and Devine. They caught Chizzie's eye before he could dodge them as they made to approach. Each arrived with a personal cloud of midges about him. Barrington, wearing a khaki cap fitted with a face net, was instantly recognisable by his complaining voice. Apparently, he was here to offer his services as timekeeper and recorder.

Devine, in a commodious dark-blue tracksuit that smelled like it was barely out of its wrappings, was keen to explain his recent conversion to physical activity. He had recently had an epiphany-type moment: "Every damn person that saw my daughter's wedding photograph took me for her grandad. They couldn't all be wrong, so this is the new me – getting out and shakin' it all about."

"Hair dye too, I see," observed Chizzie.

"I had to do something."

"It suits you; you look ten years younger."

"Only ten?" asked Devine with a hint of genuine anxiety, as he fended off his own squadron of midges, plus those repelled by Barrington's defences.

242

Chizzie felt pity. "When you're fitter and tightened up, you'll look almost like your son."

"I hope not; he's a balloon. But I get the drift, thanks. Billy Pung not here?"

"No."

"That's a pity. I thought he would be. I tell you, that lad could win the bloody prize money all on his own. Get him in your team. I saw him chase a rabbit once; talk about fast – what a bloody speed. Absolutely phenomenal!"

"Unfortunately, they don't allow rabbits or hares in athletics," quipped Barrington. "Perhaps he'd be more at home on a dog track."

Chizzie ignored the jibe. "We've tried to get Billy on board, but he won't have it."

"Why not?" asked Devine, building up a sweat from swatting midges.

Chizzie sighed. "Billy insists that running's strictly for animals."

"Hah! And he should know," quipped Barrington, the ready wit.

"What's that mean?" asked Chizzie sharply.

"Well, come on, face it," answered Barrington, "the last thing this school needs is a Billy Pung scuttling about like something prehistoric. It's imperative that the school attracts more affluent, well-connected people. What parent in their right mind is going to subject their child to the ordeal of rubbing shoulders with the likes of Billy Pung? It's a harsh view, I know – very harsh, you may even say – but it's a pragmatic one and an honest one. Far from saving the school, Pung could bankrupt the place. The best thing you can do is keep him away from any public display whatsoever."

Struggling to keep a lid on things, in spite of knowing that an emotional response was exactly what Barrington wanted, Chizzie held himself together and, inwardly seething, excused himself with a sardonic smile and jogged away to join the warm-up.

Two days later, Weever summoned Fairfoull to his office. "Hallelujah! We are go!" he cried. "Panton's delivered! So we move in, fast. I want my tanks on their lawn – now!"

"Tanks?" asked Fairfoull.

"Machines. Bulldozers. I want them up and running before the numpties make their next move."

"They don't have any moves; they don't have the money and they'll never get enough."

"There might be more wacky do-gooders out there or more crummy bequests, who knows? I'm not waiting to find out. We knock the stuffing clean out of them now. We cut the place up and shape it like I want it, and it's game over. There's no way back for them."

"You really hate these people, don't you? They've got to you. It's like an obsession."

"I hate everything they stand for. This community talk, what is it? It's bullshit; it's communism, that's what it is. Community, communism, it all leads to the same thing. Community plus cancer equals communism, and these people are diseased. Just look at what they did to me: they attacked me and tried to humiliate me; they hit me with fruit cakes and showered me with sultanas; and they drew me into a shooting gallery. Aaagh. I can't stand the thought of my life being sold for the sake of that worthless pondlife. A life for a life. What's his life compared to mine. I shit better'n him, most days."

"They're not communists, Gordon. They're just—"

"They're communists! I see it. I smell it. It's in the air. I know it. I know when it's around. You'll learn. You'll see. You've got to be looking out for it. Believe me, it's the end of

244

freedom when that happens. We're fighting for the American dream here."

An hour later, Fairfoull entered Weever's office as summoned again, and he found the great master planner in a state of even greater emotion this time: Weever was pacing up and down, with files scattered across the carpet in front of the big desk.

"My plan worked so well – so, so well; it was beautiful," he muttered in a pitch that was almost a squeak. "It was perfect," he croaked, now thumping the air with his fist. So successful had been the plan that, evidently, it had swept him clean past elation and into sublime tears of joy. But there was no joy. The tears were of anguish. Weever kicked the waste-paper bin and yelled as his bunion stung. He grabbed a piece of paper, crumpled it and threw it wildly at the window.

"The plan worked you say?" asked Fairfoull, "So why are you angry?"

"Damn right I'm angry – damn right I am! My beautiful plan. Aaagh! Why? Why am I surrounded by the numptiest of numpties in this world! The actual bucket-bottom slime of life. That shit Panton – he had it. He had it. He had the letter of sale in his hand for the field, the east field, and do you know what he did? He got himself a conscience! All the hard work was done; it was all signed up, sealed and delivered. And then, instead of payoff, what's he do? He goes fluffy. That man, that shit, he tore up the letter and… I mean, Jeezus, what kind of man does that? After all we went through. How could he? I gave him such a wonderful deal. Not only that but he's suckered the chauffeur and cleared off with the Bentley. He'll sell it to some Glasgow scum and walk off with a few thou. But I'll catch him, I'll catch him; once a gambler, always a gambler. He won't be hard to find. I'll get the bastard. I'll get him."

"So what now?"

Weever took a deep breath and exhaled powerfully. "Plan B," he said. "It's plan B."

"And what's that?"

Weever exhaled powerfully again, clearing the hurt from his chest, then he took in a gentle breath through his nose. "When Tulloh's funny buddy Donald goes away, we'll strike. We'll invite his lordship to dinner. We'll wine him, we'll dine him and we'll treat him like the toff he is, or at least thinks he is. He will enjoy himself very immensely and very wonderfully. We'll lay on the kind of entertainment that gets him going – you'll have to find out what that is – and we'll sucker him into a poker game. He'll get in way too deep – and we'll skin the creep. When he owes us big time, we'll settle with the land purchase. It's beautifully simple, wouldn't you agree?"

"That could destroy the man."

Weever shrugged in mock apology. "That's life. That's life, Charlie. And, let's face it, if he does go pop, he'll go out having the bestest time of his life. He'll go out like a winner!"

"Some winner."

"And, for good measure, we'll sabotage Team Tannadee. Buckingham can help."

"Buckingham? Who's Buckingham?"

"The wimpy guy with the pervert uncles."

"Barrington, you mean?"

"Whatever. I want him on the case. He needs to step up. I want him to groom his lordship and be his buddy."

"Barrington? Buddy? You think that's possible?"

"It's an order. Tell him that if he can't do it, we'll get someone who can."

246

CHAPTER 22

Over the next two weeks, excitement grew steadily in Tannadee. Highland Games fever had caught just about everyone. Even supporters of Weever's golf complex were behind the team. Blood, it seems, runs thick in Highland villages; that and a desperate desire to put one over on your neighbours. These powerful drivers of blood and pride saw the would-be athletes of Tannadee, like those in the other villages of the district, working hard to get higher, further and faster. And Chizzie was one of them. He was feeling fitter than he'd been for years.

Gradually, though, he became aware of something like an insidious plague that was bringing down the finest and fittest of the athletes in Tannadee. They were hurting, they were limping and they were groaning. Muscles, ligaments and tendons beyond their prime were now being stretched beyond their natural limits by brains that thought they were ten years younger. The mid-thirties is a dangerous age, being neither young nor old; it is a time when things snap, and the waiting room at Dr Rash's surgery was gradually seeing more and more male faces, which is a rare sight in a place where men are men. Not even Chizzie was spared.

When Chizzie entered the waiting room of the surgery, it was almost empty, which was pleasing since it meant he was avoiding most of the coughers and sneezers. That was the advantage of a late appointment. The disadvantage was that the elderly Dr Rush would not be at his sharpest by this time in the evening – 'knackered' being the expression he often employed.

Among other things at this hour, the unsteady doctor had the unnerving habit of stepping into the waiting room and calling the unfortunate patients by the affliction they had last presented. Chizzie kept his ears primed for 'Mr Earwax', which would doubtless be him. And, indeed, it was Mr Earwax who was called, following the hurried but ungainly departure of the pretty 'Miss Verruca'.

Chizzie explained that he was troubled with a niggling pain in his lower back, which was curtailing his training schedule.

"Get onto the couch then, face down, and raise your shirt, if you would, please," said Dr Rush.

Chizzie obliged.

The elderly doctor felt about a bit, hummed a bit and then, applying some kind of massage, he asked quietly, "Are you sure you're telling me everything, Mr Bryson?"

"Er… yes, I think so," replied Chizzie, earnestly trying to think of anything that could possibly have a bearing on his condition.

Then, Dr Rush took a step back and, lowering his head gravely, he fixed his gaze on Chizzie, eyeball to eyeball. "Getting plenty of the big vitamin, are we, eh? The big, big vitamin?"

"Well, I take a vitamin pill every day, Doctor Rush," confirmed Chizzie.

"I'm talking about vitamin X," the doctor replied with a wink.

"Vitamin X?" enquired Chizzie.

"Sex, man! Sex!" explained the doctor, his head jerking suddenly and his right arm twitching. "Sex, m'boy, sex; the primordial bash: the cure for all ills, especially the lower-back stuff. Oh yes. Nothing like it. Nothing at all. Take my advice, get yourself off to the dancing and find yourself a young lady wife. You'll never look back. Oh yes. Thirty-six glorious years I had of it; thirty-six wonderful years with no regrets, no not for a moment. And, oh, how it haunts me still," he sighed, biting his fingernails desperately.

Chizzie hardly knew what to say.

"Miss it?" continued the doctor unprompted. "Oh yes, oh gosh yes, but – oh no, no, no, no, no – I couldn't marry another. Never, no, no; not after Dorothy. A one-off was Dorothy! They broke the mould after Dorothy; broke the mould, they did. Broke the mould," whined the old doctor, and he took out a large, white handkerchief and blew hard into it.

Having come to the surgery in the reasonable expectation that his role was that of the patient, Chizzie now found himself, bewilderingly, in the healing position. Here he was, by his mere presence, now counselling a poor, worn-out healer in the gloom of his self-imposed chastity. How do you sort out a seventy-three-year-old man's sex-life when you haven't even had one of your own? Clearly, neither man could do much for the other. Chizzie's thoughts turned to horse liniment. Tucking his shirt in, he excused himself and slipped away quietly.

A few minutes down the road, as a light drizzle chilled his face and the niggling, little back pain made its presence felt again, it occurred to Chizzie that he was unlikely to be the only athlete in Tannadee without a remedy for his ills, and, consequently, the prospects for Tannadee's Highland Games team were probably getting grimmer by the day.

And he was right.

Over the next few days, Chizzie's phone rang with gloomy news so often that it began to sound like a tolling bell.

Tannadee's best men were falling apart. Flesh and blood were proving unequal to the pains and strains of athletic competition.

It was not all bad news, though, for Tannadee was not alone in its predicament: the plague of aches and injuries that had swept through Tannadee had also swept through the other competing villages, for here – in this little corner of the world – there were no fancy sports clinics, no osteopaths, no remedial gymnasts and not even a physiotherapist. In every village there was but one prescription for all muscular strains and pains: it was, quite simply, "Rest! And plenty of it!"

Eventually, though, there came another remedy. This entailed trawling through the family histories to find new blood, and high-performance blood in particular. Mostly, they found it. The village of Altnaclog, for example, found an ex-pro cyclist whose only connection with the place was a hill-farming relative born in 1769; Garthbay found a miler with a connection from the nineteenth century; and Findandie found a sprinter with comparatively recent credentials, namely a great-great-grandfather born near Findandie in 1921. The search was on. Soon, every village in the district was hauling in talent, all except Tannadee.

Here, a moral dilemma reared its tormented head. On the one side, Johnny Bryson, with his competitive streak impelling him, couldn't accept being left behind in the scramble for talent, and he was all for hiring a genealogist and getting level with the other villages, but Jim found the whole rat race demeaning and appealed to the other villages to prohibit the import of strangers. He also appealed to the bequest committee, but they declined to get involved – they'd already done Tannadee one favour, and if they conceded anything more to Tannadee, the good people of the other villages would be up in arms and clamouring at the committee's ears

250

with cries of favouritism, bias, bribery and worse. In any case, the bequest's lawyer, Mr McLogan, couldn't find any reason to prohibit the import, though he did say it was something they should look at for the future.

Chizzie, meanwhile, didn't know which way to turn – if Tannadee didn't acquire new men, their chances were diminishing rapidly. On the other hand, if Tannadee did accept new athletes in the form of strangers – people who'd possibly never even heard of Tannadee, let alone set foot in the village – what would that say about the integrity of their community? They would, in effect, be selling out, and Weever would have an argument for rampant commercial exploitation. Although Tannadee might get its hands on the money with outside help, other hands would be on it too – for there was talk of athletes' coaches demanding a share of any winnings. Tannadee couldn't afford to shed a penny, and so, weighing it all up, Chizzie and Jim came to the conclusion that a team of complete strangers was a lose-lose situation for Tannadee. Tannadee would have to put its faith in its own, and they would win or lose, possibly even live or die, by their very own blood, sweat, toil and tears.

With three weeks to go before the games, on a humid, cool and cloudy Saturday afternoon, which was thronging with midges, the Tannadee athletes presented themselves for selection at the school playing fields. There was no need for selection, though. Natural selection had already done the work. Survival of the fittest never saw a better day. It had weeded out candidates to the extent that barely enough men remained standing. In all but one event – the cycling – there was just one candidate. The only selection criterion for the runners had therefore become: can the candidate make it to the finish before he drops? Fortunately, none was likely to fail that test.

In spite of the low-key nature of the selection event, Jim honoured the occasion with an appearance fit for any Olympiad, with his shiny, grey hair brushed back, and his lightly tanned face gleaming above his white shirt, red bow tie and blue blazer with paisley-pattern handkerchief perched in the top pocket. Grey flannels and dark brogues completed the ensemble. The man looked so impressive that he seemed to command even the respect of the midges, for they left him alone.

Chizzie, on the other hand, in his maroon tracksuit, had no such luck and slapped on more repellent before starting his warm-up. He had a race to run, which was a formality perhaps, but it nevertheless seemed essential for team morale that each athlete should see his teammates perform at competition level – except for the hill runner, of course. Jim had arranged a team of school pupils and former pupils to compete against the Tannadee team, all of them useful competitors, so it wasn't going to be a dawdle.

By late afternoon, Tannadee was able to confirm that it had the right quantity of athletes. Quality, though, was another matter. As expected, half the team looked like good prospects compared to the athletes in the other villages, but the other half looked like certain losers – the man in the sprinting event, for example, was actually a schoolboy, a well-developed young lad for his age but no match for what was zooming around in the other villages now that professional and semi-pro athletes were being acquired there. And a half-good team probably had no more than a fifty-fifty chance of getting enough points to win the prize outright. For Tannadee to come away with the prize, much would depend on how evenly or unevenly the victories were spread across the events on the big day. The key to victory overall could lie in winning half the events and scoring reasonably well in the others. Proudfoot the chef, for example, could conceivably get third place in the cycling event. He looked surprisingly impressive in the selection trial. As a former time-trial racer with his own carbon-framed bicycle, he easily beat the other cyclists, lapping every one of them.

At four-forty, Jim gathered all the athletes together in the changing room for the formality of reading out the team sheet. A glance round the room did nothing to boost Chizzie's morale – there were just too many faces that looked like losers.

But hope there must be, he thought to himself, *An indomitable spirit sometimes lurks behind even the least heroic face.* No hope was not an option.

CHAPTER 23

The Tannadee team, created more by natural selection than design, was now ready to meet whatever might come its way. But Jim wanted more. When the next school day ended, Jim met Chizzie outside his office and handed over a double-wrapped brown envelope.

"Take this and let no one else see it," whispered Jim. "We need to know the strengths, weaknesses and backgrounds of our guys so we bring out the best in them, especially when the going gets tough, as it will. So, I got Andy Grant to compile profiles on all of them. If anybody knows our guys inside out, it's him: he's trained them all at Millburgh Athletics Club. He pulls no punches. Let no one else see it."

A short while later, up in his bedroom and feeling like some international spy with top secret documents, Chizzie perused the profiles he'd been given, which read thus:

HILL RACE

'Honest' Bob McDee: *A PE teacher and hill runner. Five feet eight inches tall, slim from the waist up, but surprisingly muscular downstairs, featuring sturdy thighs and bulbous calves. After a trampolining accident put him in a coma for six months, Bob developed an infatuation with the truth. He's no philosopher; his notion of truth means tell no lies. He paid a heavy price. When the wife asks, "How do I look?" and you reply, "Dowdy," you're in trouble. And 'Honest' Bob McDee* certainly got trouble, until psychotherapy put him right. Now he is 'normal': he's happily married with two kids and as accommodating as the next man.

ONE-MILE RACE

Dave Dalrymple: *Six feet five inches tall, he's a powered skeleton, who's known on the athletics clubs' circuit as 'Have Bones Will Rattle'. He's a former marathon runner who couldn't hack the distance any more – he kept hitting 'the wall', he says; other times he 'just blew up' for no apparent reason. He looks like an intellectual, but he hasn't got the time to do much thinking because he's a hypochondriac with a mind full of pills. He has pills for every ailment under the sun – everything and anything imaginable – but his particular concern at the moment is 'water balance'. This, he believes fervently, is the key to his current state of underperformance. But doctors, or 'quacks' as he prefers to call them, insist that if there is one thing that is not out of balance, it is his water. The anxiety over this is giving him blackouts, and when he's running he can't pace himself properly. His mind is about as secure as a one-legged hippo with trapped wind, but he battles on with a new-found determination born of anger at his second-class treatment under the National Health Service. In races, he has taken to going off very fast early on, galloping round the first lap like he's going for a world record, and people go "Ooh" and "Aah" as he streaks away. Then, in the final lap, they go "Aaargh" and "Aww" as, with all stamina spent, he comes home a floundering, flailing wreck, straining every sinew and stretching for the line, but getting almost nowhere, like some mime artist against an imaginary plate-glass window. All this stretching and straining has given him a squeak in his left knee, but he won't go near the quacks in case* they section him under the Mental Health Act. He's self-prescribing fish oils currently. He teaches mathematics in Tannadee. Fortunately, his maths is more solid than his health.

HAMMER THROWING

Sven Johansen (aka the Tundra Tinker and the Viking Hitman): *A hammer thrower, sheaf hurler and caber tosser; he's six feet two inches tall, Danish, well-built, fair-haired and good-looking in a puppet kind of way. From the day that a professional athletics coach ironed him out, Sven's only fault in the arena had been an occasional inclination to throw himself instead of the hammer. Admiring ladies loved that, though, and they loved his good looks, his bulging muscles and his ever-ready willingness to share himself. Also loved is the fact that, through all his trials and tribulations, he's done it his way; he is his own man – a one-off. In the entire history of the Highland Games in the Bonnlarig district, no one has ever been so popular in his heyday, not even the Greek contortionist known locally as Andreas Oomagoolis, who – in the 1960s – swayed the ladies into ecstasy with his elastic gymnastics and low sperm count. Free of the drink now, Sven is determined to atone for his earlier waywardness.*

CYCLING

Jeff Proudfoot: *A cyclist. All the stress and repression bottled up in the hotel kitchen is discharged in the fury of cycling through the buffeting winds and driving rain that so often sweep the winding, hilly roads above Tannadee. On these roads, the recharged Jeff Proudfoot, all demons exorcised, regains enough sanity to continue cooking for 'intolerant, impatient bastards' once again.*

WRESTLING

Denis Dekker: *A wrestler, five feet eleven inches tall and forty-two-year-old fish fryer, born to fry like his father and grandfather before him – "Cradled at birth in a chip pan and swathed in batter," as he likes to say. He learned to 'handle' himself early on, when school chums took to calling him 'Fatso', 'Fish-face', 'Oil Slick' and other less flattering epithets, alluding to his fish-frying heritage. Finally, he snapped when the school bully circulated a rumour that 'Fat Boy' dipped his hair in the chip fat every morning to save on hair-cream, which, of course, was a scurrilous lie, only the comb got dipped. He took up boxing after that and enjoyed it – especially the hitting bit. He lost enthusiasm for boxing when he progressed through the grades and found himself in the company of fighters who were able to punch through his shield of protective blubber. The consequent bruising not only dulled his enthusiasm for boxing but, more alarmingly, put him off fish and chips. Thankfully, this was only a phase. He took up judo for a while – nearly two years. Then, taking in a Highland Games one day, he was to meet the third love in his own personal trinity of romance: first and foremost, there was fish and chips of course; then the girl (his wife and mother of two); and, now, the wrestling. The wrestling was right up his street, and he was a regular on the games circuit for several years until that awful day of shame when he was disqualified and banned sine die for biting his opponent's leg. He was reinstated when the opponent, years later, found God and confessed that he had bitten his own leg by mistake. Now happily vindicated, Dekker is setting out to restore his reputation with a vengeance – or at least as much vengeance as a genial, fish-happy cuisinier can muster.*

ONE HUNDRED YARDS

Damien Ferry: *A sprinter. He appeared suddenly on the scene to offer his services, as he probably thought there was* *money to be had. Like many a fast man, he's neurotic. He keeps himself under tight control with cigarettes. He's the one who can be seen blowing smoke out of open windows. He competes on the amateur Highland Games circuit. One day this guy is a winner, but the next day he's an abject loser; he's as fickle and unpredictable as the Scottish weather. On sunny days, his usual attire of a bright, paisley-patterned shirt above faded jeans and grey patent-leather shoes is as incongruous as his sprinting–smoking lifestyle. He lives in Perth, but qualifies to represent Tannadee through a grandfather who resided in the hills near the village. He's one of those marginals who could be the difference between victory and defeat.*

These, then, were the men on whom destiny had bestowed the future of Tannadee. Supporting these leading lights in their quest, to some extent, were the following:

Lawrence Cramonde: *A high-jumper who's very tall, very thin and very quiet. He's almost invisible. He teaches English.*

Gavin Foskett: *A long jumper; he was missing at the selection trial due to arriving early and thinking he'd turned up on the wrong day. A no-hoper.*

The mildly optimistic view of their team's chances that Chizzie and Jim shared was not shared by everyone. From the reports received from Barrington and their private detective, Weever and Fairfoull estimated that Tannadee would most likely finish in third place at the games. This was confirmed by the bookies in Millburgh. For Weever, the important thing was that two teams were better placed than Tannadee. These two teams, nevertheless, could not be left to their own devices.

"How're we doin'?" asked Weever, who was sipping iced tea by his Texas pool while he phoned. "Our coaches are pushing them hard, I hope, in… where was it? Oxdale and…?"

"Findandie," replied Fairfoull, his feet on his desk in Tannadee while he was sipping hot tea. "Well, actually, Gordon, both turned down the offer of coaching. It seems they've got their own programmes and didn't take too kindly to out-of-towners muscling in on their act, so to speak. You know what they're like round here."

Weever shook his head, then took another sip of iced tea and worked it round his mouth. "Fools! Trying to help hillbillies is like trying to push water uphill. I've met a few – too many. One's too many. But I want no slip-ups, Charlie; no slip-ups. I have to know these villages are going to beat Tannadee. They took the equipment, right?"

"They sure did! We have lift-off. They loved the stuff; they all absolutely loved it. If they lose, it won't be for lack of input from us, you can be sure."

"They ain't gonna lose, Charlie."

"No. 'Course not."

"You have to see to it."

"No problem, Gordon. It's in the bag," replied Charlie with less than complete assurance. He might have been even less assured if he had consulted eBay, where he could have seen most of his donated gym equipment up for sale by enterprising Highlanders.

In reality, Weever's offers were little more than a futile gesture from a man who knew little about physical fitness; with only a few weeks to go, he'd left it too late. The pro and semi-pro athletes had their own training regimes and all the equipment they needed. So, if these teams' chances were to be secured or further enhanced, Weever would have to find another way to do it. For the moment, though, he was satisfied with the way things were. The bookies are rarely wrong. They don't, after all, set up shop and employ people to lose money. But if the odds should move against him perversely for any reason, one thing was certain: Weever would not hesitate to meet the challenge. In fact, the challenge would not only be met, it would be pre-empted. And moves in that direction were already afoot, as Jim now found out.

With just one week to go to the big day, Jim received an email message that was brief and as sharp as a needle. It hit its mark, for Jim's tone was flat and sombre when he phoned Chizzie, waking him from his post-lunch nap. "Ferry's quit," he groaned. "He's not running. He's walked away. We have no sprinter."

Chizzie froze at the news. Though not entirely unexpected given Ferry's unpredictable nature, it came as a shock all the same, and he sat speechless for a moment unable to arrange his thoughts. No sprinter, no win. "I knew Ferry was taciturn and awkward," Chizzie replied sleepily, fanning away fumes from the embrocation he'd applied to his back earlier, "but to just walk out and leave us high and dry, that's… that's strange. He knows how much we need him. That's bad, even for Ferry."

"Well, good or bad, 'personal reasons' covers a multitude of things; we just have to accept he's left us. So, who else can sprint for us?"

Chizzie thought hard for a moment: "One of the pupils," he suggested. "Jamie Lindsay's pretty quick."

"He's away on holiday, I think to a camp in France somewhere. Anyway, I'm not recalling him just to see him get fifth place; he's not that fast."

Silence ensued for nearly half a minute as both men thought deep and hard, with just the faint hiss of the phone in their ears.

Wildly, Chizzie's mind raced, as he tried desperately to think of a replacement. A crazy thought flashed across his mind. "How about you, Jim?" he said quietly. His next thought was, *How stupid.* "Sorry, Jim", he added swiftly. "I'm… I'm not thinking straight."

"No, no, Chizzie, you're right. I'd thought of it myself. I might be sixty-four, but I'm still fit. I could do a very good sprint over fifty… maybe even sixty yards, I have the power, but a hundred yards? That takes more than power: it needs stamina that I don't have. Truly, nothing would give me greater pleasure than to run, believe me… but to come last…"

"Of course, of course. You have your pride, Jim, no question. No, we can't have—"

"I was thinking more of the points, Chizzie. I wouldn't get what's needed."

With that, Chizzie decided not to press. Jim deserved better than to be humiliated in front of his own people, but it was clear that the suggestion had flung open the doors on some long-treasured dream in Jim. Jim mumbled for a few moments, seemingly mulling over the matter with great seriousness; he was a man with a desperate dream who was unable to break free from the shackles of reality.

Chizzie put him out of his misery hurriedly. "I'll have a word with Billy. Billy's our man. It has to be Billy."

But Jim held on to the other possibility. "When dusk falls," Jim replied, almost whispering, "I'll get on the track and see what I can do."

"No, no, Jim. No. Not at your age. Don't even think about it!"

"If the worst is to happen, Chizzie, I'd rather die on the track than die among the derelict remains of the school."

Such morbid talk was strange coming from Jim, and, for a moment, it left Chizzie chilled and speechless again. Then it galvanised him. "I'll get Billy on board," he insisted, "All that talent right here in our midst and he's squandering it. He's got to see sense. He must!"

"If he doesn't want to, he won't, Chizzie; he's got to want to and he doesn't want to, so we're stuck. Now, I've told you about Ferry's quitting, but I don't want anyone else to know just yet. It's best we say nothing till after the dinner; I want the guys to enjoy themselves and to build up a good team spirit; camaraderie's important and worth a few points in itself. Ferry's absence could go unnoticed for a while, and, fingers crossed, maybe the whole night. He doesn't exactly shine in company: most of the time he's looking for a quiet corner on his own to puff his rank cigarettes. When they do notice, we know nothing. We sit on it till breakfast time. Now, I'm away to check my health insurance policy. See you at the dinner."

"Jim, I don't want you to run. It's not my place to stop you or select you, but I know that desperation has got the better of you. You mustn't put yourself in harm's way. Think of all the people that need you. I'm one of them, and I'm saying please don't do it. Please do not run, Jim; it's dangerous. You're in no condition for an all-out sprint."

Silence hung on the line for a moment.

Then came, "Thank you, Chizzie, I appreciate your concern."

Finally, the phone was put down.

CHAPTER 24

Later that evening, the Tannadee athletes gathered for the grand dinner. Laid on by Johnny Bryson at the Tannadee Hotel, the grand dinner was a new venture for the hotelier; he was a man who believed there was no such thing as a free lunch, yet here he was providing a free dinner for sixteen people, some of whom, privately, he could not abide. But the stakes were high – he was facing a threat to his very existence, for it was now obvious to him that Weever was a rolling monster who ate little people like him as much for the fun of it as for any commercial reason. Eliminating people was in Weever's blood, it seemed, and Johnny knew he had to fight him or quit. Like Weever, Johnny was no quitter, but there was little he could actually do in the face of Weever's millions. The grand dinner was one of the few things he could do. According to Jim, the dinner would do much to create a strong team spirit: a spirit strong enough to inspire the Tannadee team when their guys did well and bolster them when they were down.

Smart but casual was the dress code for the evening. Johnny and Jim, though, went the extra mile, with both appearing in full Highland dress. Chizzie chose to appear in his Flower of Scotland tartan trews and Jacobite shirt. Only one other athlete had chosen to defy the casual look and was dressed to impress: it was the long jumper, and he wore a royal-blue blazer, purple bow tie and light-grey trousers. The rest had taken the invitation at face value and arrived in a wide spectrum of casualness, ranging from Dekker's outfit – which seemed to consist of green gardening trousers and a red-plaid lumberjack shirt – to the miler, who looked like he might just dash off a play before the night was out, attired as he was in black cashmere sweater, black shirt, grey cravat, black trousers and black suede shoes. He was either a man of some style or someone who'd failed to wash his dark colours separately.

Everyone was in good spirits, bar one: the chef, Jeff Proudfoot. Here was a bag of nerves. So much rested on him getting it right – or, rather, not getting it wrong – and it was proving a heavy load. Under stress, the memory of the great food-poisoning outbreak of which he'd been a part evoked frightening images of angry bacteria. The thought of these things decimating his teammates all but numbed him. He'd confided this to Chizzie. And, though it frightened Chizzie that his chef was so frightened, he sought to reassure him by offering to taste all the food before it was plated up. But Jeff would not accept this. He was old-school. He would do the tasting personally. If the ship was to go down, like a good captain, he would go down with it. All Chizzie's protestations were in vain. The chef was a proud man, even if he was slightly unbalanced.

Some would have it that one of the athletes should have been seated at the head of the table – they, after all, were the people carrying the honour of Tannadee into the arena. But Johnny saw it differently. Firstly, he was mine host and master of his own house, so no Johnny, no big dinner. It was his food they'd all be tucking in to without paying, though, secretly, he hoped to recoup some of his outlay through the bar: some of the athletes might not be up to much in track and field, but they looked like they could shift a few pints. Also, he was convinced that an MBE or some higher honour would be finding its way to him shortly, as due reward for all he had done to secure the local economy. Thus, he was the closest thing to a VIP on the premises. He also thought it appropriate to seat himself as far away as possible from the district council's representative – an elderly councillor who, seated at the low end of the table, was glancing obsessively at his watch every few minutes.

On Johnny's right sat a pale-looking Jim, and next to Jim sat Barrington, who was representing the bequest. There was no mention of Ferry's absence. Then, suddenly, it surfaced.

"Where's Ferry?" shouted the long jumper, well ahead of any schedule imagined by Jim.

Jim and Chizzie froze. They faced a dilemma: the truth or strategic misinformation? The truth it was; it had to be. Without trust, the team could fall apart.

Jim got to his feet. "Damien, for personal reasons, has withdrawn for the meantime, but we very much hope to see him back very shortly." It was the truth coated with a bit of fudge that Jim hoped would see them through the dinner at least.

For a moment, the men looked stunned, then they turned their heads this way and that, looking at each other and questioning each other silently.

Johnny Bryson shot to his feet. "If anybody else's thinking of leaving, now's the time to say!"

It was more of an outburst than an invitation. A deathly silence followed. Johnny scanned the company with a searing look. The athletes scanned each other. No one said a word.

Then, "Right," said Johnny, "we're all in this together! Chins up! We stay strong. We'll win yet. The key thing is loyalty – loyalty to one another. We fight for each other. A strong team will beat a bunch of prima donnas any day."

"Johnny's right!" Dekker yelled, rising to his feet while desperately trying to swallow the bread roll he'd already embarked upon. "Yeah! Yeah!" he cried, waving his right hand above his head, as if playing for time until he either thought of something useful or until he got all the bread roll down the hatch. The bread roll decided it, for – after a big gulp – he piped up, "We have every chance! We do. We still have a great chance if only we believe in each other. Together we're a force. As a bunch of individuals, we're... well, not nothing; I was going to say nothing, but we're never nothing. The point is that we're better as a team, we're good for each other, and that kind of thing brings out the best in people. I know that because it happened to me personally. I owe my livelihood to loyalty. I have two fish restaurants, as some of you know, but what you probably don't know is that the Millburgh one nearly went bust when a supermarket opened their own cafe at prices I couldn't match. I was done for. I was washed up. I was finished. I was out of it. But you know what? Loyalty! Loyalty saved me. Half my customers stuck by me. And, not long after, the supermarket contracted out the cafe, the contracting company closed the doors at five o'clock every day, and I was back in business again. And now my loyal customers get the rewards they rightly deserve. They get subsidised chips."

"Subsidised chips?" asked the long jumper, mystified at such a thing.

"Yes," continued Dekker. "The disloyal customers – the defectors – get smaller portions, and the chips they would've got go to the loyals; the loyals also get bigger fish. So, I say one for all and all for one! We are the Companions! We are together. And together we will win!"

This inspirational example of sharp-end survival had an instant effect: mostly of mystification, but after a few moments, there came positive murmurings. There was substance in what the fish-frying wrestler had said, albeit somewhat oblique, and he was, after all, an experienced athlete.

But, inevitably, there came a downer. "You're overlooking one thing," said the long jumper, "we're a companion short: we have no sprinter."

"Leave that to me!" yelled Chizzie on instinct, getting to his feet and regretting the recklessness of his outburst instantly. He had nothing to offer.

"See," said the wrestler, "seek and ye shall find."

If only it were true, thought Chizzie, smiling through the anguish of deceit. Desperately, he wanted to add, "But if anyone knows anyone out there who could possibly fit the bill, then for God's sake bring him in. I've an old man about to kill himself!"

The reassurances, however unfounded, settled the company, and they relaxed once again. They liked the look of the menu; most of them did, at any rate: only Dalrymple and the long jumper looked uneasy.

Dalrymple touched nothing. He declined the soup, which was probably too salty. He declined the melon, which was probably too sugary. After staring at the Yorkshire pudding, he declined that too, probably on account of it sucking up his juices and throwing his water balance into mayhem. Denis Dekker on the other hand had no inhibitions whatsoever and he laid into his meal like a starved lion. Only too happy to help out, thoughtfully, he hoovered up Dalrymple's soup, his bread roll, and his entire portion of roast beef with Yorkshire pudding and garden peas.

Dalrymple, though, was not the only malcontent.

The long jumper expressed his dissatisfaction. "You call that Yorkshire pudding?" he bleated. "I can get this kind of pap at home!"

"No, you couldn't," interjected Dekker, "not this quality. This is extremely good food. If you don't want it, I'll eat it."

"And what do I eat?"

"Well, here's the chef, ask him."

"Is everything all right?" asked Proudfoot coming up to the table cheerily, expecting compliments for his great efforts.

"No, as a matter of fact, it isn't!" exclaimed the surly long jumper. "Everything is not all right."

Struck with horror, Proudfoot swung his head towards Johnny. Was it food poisoning? Surely not! But the little hotelier remained silent – silent and looking very red, possibly poisoned! But no, Johnny was in a deep sulk, his mind now focussed again on the cost of feeding the ungrateful numpties sharing his table. It was especially hard to bear knowing that these numpties would not be winning any prize money despite his rallying call.

"No," said the long jumper, whining even louder, "I expected a handsome meal, a meal fit for the occasion, and what do I get? I get lentil soup and Yorkshire pud. I could get that anywhere; I could get that at home for heaven's sake, and my wife can't even cook properly!"

"No, you couldn't," repeated Dekker. "You couldn't get that at home, not this quality."

"Hear, hear!" cried Sven, "and Denis should know, he's tested more of it than anyone."

Seeking a seconder, the long jumper turned to his neighbour, Dalrymple. "What d'you think?" he asked.

But Dalrymple's thoughts remained a mystery. He made no reply.

"He's had nothing!" cried the long jumper pointing to Dalrymple. "Look! Nothing at all!"

"In no position to judge then, is he?" quipped Sven. "It could be that he's vegetarian."

"Oh God, not another one," whimpered Proudfoot.

"He's not a vegetarian. He's a finicky feeder that's all," replied the long jumper.

"You make me sound like a horse," Dalrymple whined.

"All I want to do," protested Proudfoot, "is provide you with a meal fit for your needs – a meal fit for a gladiator!"

"Gladiators were vegetarians," advised the lonesome councillor, betraying his history-teacher background.

This did not appease the long jumper, and he appealed to the others. "Who's not happy with this stuff?" he cried.

Trouble was brewing. Pointing to a man passing the dining-room window, Proudfoot saw his chance to escape suddenly. "Here's Ferry!" he shouted.

Jim and Chizzie jolted and exchanged a fearful glance, then their eyes widened with hope. It could be great news! Chizzie got quickly to his feet, dumped his napkin and hurried to meet the newcomer.

Proudfoot, too, tried to leave, but the long jumper had other ideas.

"Hold it, chef! Hold it! What's Dalrymple going to eat?" the long jumper demanded.

"It's okay," said Dalrymple, "It's no problem, I have my own stuff."

"That's not good enough!" insisted the long jumper.

"What exactly is wrong with the meal?" Proudfoot asked, with a pained smile. He was clearly hurting. Such invective! And directed at a man who'd quite literally been prepared to put his life on the line for these people. Had he not sampled every portion personally so that, in the event of it proving toxic, he himself would go down with the dish before serving? Being prepared to die rather than kill, he had taken the bizarre step of presenting Chizzie with a signed affidavit absolving him and any other staff member of blame, and testifying that he took the food of his own free will and without coercion from any quarter. He'd even got a lawyer to draw the thing up. The man was serious. The signature was even smudged, as if from tear drops. The injustice of it all!

Ferry looked very drawn and worried when Chizzie approached him outside the hotel entrance. His head bowed, pacing around in a small circle and smoking rapidly, he hardly noticed Chizzie until he was almost within touching distance.

Chizzie greeted him warmly, hoping against hope that the man had changed his mind and was now back in the team. Realistically, though, Chizzie knew that if he were back in the team, he wouldn't be pacing about and smoking like a bush fire. "Damien, it's good to see you," he said, "How are you? Rejoining us?"

Ferry threw the butt of his cigarette away and, throwing his hands in the air, he unloaded: "Chizzie… man, I'm sorry; I really am. I never wanted to quit, but… ugh…" He shook his head. "I had to. I've got a job. It's in Edinburgh, an' I'm havin' to start right away. I have a family to feed, an' I couldn't turn it down, could I? I mean…" He looked appealingly at Chizzie for approval.

Chizzie smiled bravely. "'Course not," he said. "I understand."

"I'm really sorry, honest to God. I've let you down, and all the guys."

"No, you haven't; you've done the right thing, Damien. Don't apologise for that."

"I came to apologise personally to the guys – they deserve that much… but… you…you know… I can't; I can't do it. I can't face them."

He seemed on the point of breaking down, so Chizzie took him by the hand and squeezed it. "I understand completely, Damien. Don't you worry. You've done the right thing, no question. I'll let them know you came. You cared enough to come, and they'll appreciate that. And I know I speak for all of us when I wish you all the very best in your new job."

Ferry looked up tearfully. "You're a gent, Chizzie; a real gent," he said. "You're stuck now, I know and I wish I could help. Maybe I can, though, in a way. You see, Billy Pung asked me to help him run faster a little while back and we've been having some personal training sessions together at the back of his house. Get him on board an' you've got yourself a sprinter; an', really, he's better than I am. I'm not just saying that. It's true."

Chizzie smiled and thanked him for the tip, though he knew Billy was not going to relent. On the other hand, why was Billy training if he didn't want to run? Maybe he just wanted to catch more rabbits. They shook hands and Ferry turned to leave.

"Oh, an' one more thing," he said, calling over his shoulder, "the job's with the Palatine Country Club Group, a Weever company. I'll be driving a delivery truck. I thought that maybe you should know that."

"Thanks," Chizzie replied quietly, lifting his eyebrows in surprise.

So, the jobless Ferry suddenly got a job just when Tannadee needed him most, and not just any job: a job with a Weever company. Quite a coincidence. Chizzie rubbed his chin and watched Ferry go. He felt no animosity towards the man – Ferry was a mere pawn struggling to make a living, and he had the decency to try and be honourable. Others, it seemed, might not be quite so honourable. He pondered the possibilities for a moment. Then, recalling suddenly the animosity that was welling up in the dining room before he left, he turned and hurried back, fearing the worst, and hoping to arrive in time to prevent poor Proudfoot being thrown out of the window or possibly even strung up on the light fittings. He hurried into the hotel and headed for the dining room. But he was too late! There, through the open doors, he met with a terrible, fearful din and the awful sight of poor Proudfoot being hoisted into the air.

"It's a lynch mob! God save us!" Chizzie gasped. He raced into the room. Dekker and McDee were the main culprits. Undaunted, but conscious that he might not be conscious for much longer, Chizzie rushed at Dekker and grabbed his shoulder. "Let him go! Let go!" he cried.

"Yo!" bawled Dekker in his face. "Here we go! Here we go! Here we go!"

McDee joined in the chant, and Proudfoot joined them too; he was the happiest of them all. Shoulder-high, he was carried round the table by Dekker and McDee. Nearly everyone was chanting, clapping and cheering, until, finally, they lowered the overwhelmed chef to the floor by the door.

Next, Dekker walloped Chizzie exultantly on the back with one hand while raising Proudfoot's right arm with the other, almost wrenching the poor chef's limb from its socket. "Yo, Chizzie! Yo Jeff!" Dekker bawled, before shaking Proudfoot's aching arm. "Our talisman!" he yelled. "What a man! Inspirational! Best fish and chips I've tasted in a very long time! And I speak as a man commended in the UK Fish and Chip Shop of the Year competition! And, *wow*, that Yorkshire pudding! Wowee! Puddin' to die for! *Yes, siree!*"

A chorus of cheers rent the air. "Supreme! Superb! A dream!" came the calls.

Clearly, even if quality hadn't played a major part in Dekker's appraisal of the food, quantity definitely had. Proudfoot, flushed and embarrassed, thanked everyone for their kind appreciation of all the hard work he'd put in on their behalf and he gave his utmost assurance that he would continue to ensure that Team Tannadee, this band of brothers, the Companions, would dine like the champions they were. They deserved the best, and the best is what they would get!

And, with that, the chef removed his hat and, taking a bow before throwing his hat in the air, he walked away proudly to his kitchen. Thoughts of Ferry seemed to have vanished. But only for a moment.

"Why'd Ferry leave?" cried the long jumper, bringing things back down to earth with a sting. "Is he still with us?"

The jollity ended, and, in the quiet that followed, all eyes swung towards Jim and Chizzie.

Chizzie piped up gamely, "As some of you may have seen, I have just spoken to Damien. Sadly, it is the case that Damien will not be joining us on Saturday after all. He's been offered a job in Edinburgh and has to start right away. He came to tell us personally, which I think you will agree was very brave of him, but he was so upset that he was in no condition to make a speech, so I thanked him and told him to go. I'm sure that, despite our loss, you'll join me in wishing him well. He's waited quite a while for a chance like this, and it's just very unfortunate that he's had to go at this time." Chizzie made no mention of the Weever connection.

"I heard Weever offered him a job!" someone shouted. "Is that where he's going?"

"Weever?" cried several people, before all eyes swung back to Chizzie again.

"So I'm told," Chizzie replied as flatly as possible.

Some people groaned, while others became angry.

"The bastard!" someone shouted.

"Everybody stay calm!" Dekker yelled, waving his hands. "Stay calm. If Weever's muckin' us about, then we have to turn that into a positive. Maybe he wants us to crack up, but maybe not; we don't know for sure. We don't know, so—"

"Yeah, we do; it stinks!" said the long jumper, who was eager to pounce.

"Maybe," continued Dekker. "But if so, we have to rise above it. As a team. The more we're hit, the stronger we'll get. This band of brothers won't be beaten. We won't be beaten!"

"The Companions!" someone shouted.

"The Companions!" echoed most of the other athletes.

Only two athletes were not quite so companionable: one of these, the long jumper, got to his feet and asked sombrely, "Do we have a replacement for Ferry?"

Once again all eyes swung in Chizzie's direction. Chizzie gulped and, nodding his head, replied softly, "Er, we're working on it. We're very hopeful of a replacement very soon. I can't say any more than that at this stage."

"Billy Pung?" enquired someone.

"I can't say at this stage," repeated Chizzie.

"It's Billy Pung!" declared someone emphatically.

The athletes cheered, at least most of them did, and the high spirits returned.

Only Barrington looked glum and deep in thought.

After the meal, most of the company retired to the residents' lounge for coffee, fruit juice and mineral water, depending on one's views on luxury, water balance and human rights. Chizzie left quickly to congratulate Proudfoot and bring him into the company. Given the old saying that you can't please everybody all of the time, the evening had gone spectacularly well and that was due almost entirely to Jeff Proudfoot. He'd put everything he had into the task and had come up trumps; a result that probably surprised everybody, and none more than Jeff himself. He deserved a personal thank you from the management, and when Chizzie went to deliver it he found the chef in his tiny office at the back of the kitchen. There was no denying that Jeff deserved to be smiling from ear to ear. But Jeff was far from smiling – he was slumped over his desk, his head in his hands.

Anxiously, Chizzie hurried over to him. "What's up, Jeff?" he asked quietly, laying a hand on the chef's shoulder and anticipating grim news – a bereavement possibly.

Jeff sat upright slowly, grunted, then inhaled deeply, and, with a shake of his head, sighed. "I can't race, Chizzie. I can't race; I'm so sorry."

Chizzie's jaw dropped. "What?" he spluttered, feeling almost electrocuted.

"It's my knee," continued the chef. "It's got worse. The swellin' won't go down."

"I didn't know you had swelling," Chizzie replied slowly.

"I thought I could work it off. It clears up usually, but this time it's just got worse."

"Have you seen the doctor?"

"He just says rest it."

Chizzie blew out his cheeks in despair.

"Honest to God, I'm so sorry. An' after the guys cheerin' me, an' saying I was their talisman an' I was inspirational. I thought, *Goddammit, knee or no knee, I'm battlin' on.* But, argh, it's gone purple, and there's a rash in my crotch – not sexual you understand, it's friction burns – but a chef with a rash on the crotch, that's dynamite. You can't have that, so I'm... I'm just knackered, completely knackered. I can't go on. I couldn't face another turbo session." His chin began to wobble and his voice faltered. "If I could help these guys, God, I would; I would. I'd die on the bike out there for these guys, so I would!"

Yet another man prepared to die for the cause. Chizzie was beginning to feel like the angel of death. He placed a reassuring hand on Jeff's shoulder. "I understand, Jeff. It's okay," he said. "You've done all you can – more in fact. It is what it is. It's our fate; we just have to work with it."

"There's one thing, though," Jeff added, "with my knee getting worse and worse, I put an ad in a cycling mag last week asking for someone with a Tannadee area connection to come and race for us, and…"

"Yes?"

"Nothing."

Great, thought Chizzie. *No sprinter, no cyclist, no Tannadee, and, frankly, no hope.*

Just then, Billy barged through the fly screen at the back door of the kitchen. "That's the rubbish bins full," he reported, rubbing his hands.

Not quite, thought Chizzie, *make room for one more thing: me.*

CHAPTER 25

Taking the same route as before, Robert Barrington again made it safely to Charlie Fairfoull's office without being noticed.

With the pleasantries over, Fairfoull excused himself and fetched Weever, who threw the door open with a show of strength that clearly defined the pecking order. Barrington leaped to his feet and offered his hand, which was duly crushed. The greeting was minimalist. Weever took the chair behind the desk and sat tight-lipped, with his arms folded.

Fairfoull began by passing on Barrington's false information that Billy Pung, the fastest man in the hills, was going to run for Tannadee. Having laid the lie, Barrington now had his chance to shine by ensuring Billy Pung would not actually be running. A task even Barrington couldn't fail at, since no one was more adamant about not running than Billy Pung himself.

"So, what's the plan?" Weever asked brusquely.

"Well, sir, like most great plans, it's beautifully simple," Barrington began, "We get Pung to disappear by calling him the names he so ardently hates."

"Like what? Like Monkey Boy?"

"Exactly. We get people on his tail relentlessly, calling and calling, and he will simply head for the hills."

"Are you sure about that?"

"Absolutely, sir. I'd bet my entire skin on it."

"Your skin?" Weever queried in a tone run through with the word 'oddball'.

"Indeed, everything," replied Barrington.

Weever was not so sure. The prospect of Tannadee winning was now worrying him out of all proportion. Image counted for so much with Weever, both in his personal world and in the world of business. In his personal world, it kept him confident among his friends, his lady friends in particular. In business, image was a vital tool in clinching deals. It was hugely important, arguably more important even than money to a man loaded with the stuff. To be humiliated by a bunch of hillbillies was unthinkable: there was no telling how deadly that could prove on social media.

Of course, if he knew the truth about Tannadee's position, he would actually be laughing. Billy Pung had steadfastly resisted all attempts to join the team; even Paw couldn't persuade him. In desperation, Jim had gone into training for the sprint race, despite no insurer being willing to cover him for the event. A cyclist was lined up – Jamie Taylor – who, like nearly everyone else in Tannadee, had turned against Weever in order to defend their village against a person who was now perceived to be a rapacious land-grabber. In reality, though, Taylor was no more than a makeweight: he was a keen mountain-bike enthusiast, but no match for semi-pros on the flat.

Fairfoull reminded Weever of the threat: "He's very fast is Billy boy, according to folk who should know."

"What's 'very fast'?" asked Weever.

"Fast enough to run down rabbits, we're told," replied Fairfoull.

"How fast are rabbits over here?"

"I don't know."

"That's a big help then. Are the other sprinters faster than rabbits?"

"With respect, Gordon, the big question is whether Billy Pung can beat Gribben and Muirhead."

"And the answer?"

"No one knows."

"Well, what's the point of asking, for Christ's sake?"

"Well, we know what we don't know and that's the first step to knowing, but we have to find out before Saturday. I keep being told that Pung is very fast, and possibly faster than Ferry. So it looks like we might've shot ourselves in the foot by removing Ferry. The Garthbay team and Oxdale team are pretty sure their men, that's Gribben and Muirhead, could beat Ferry."

"So why the hell'd we take out Ferry then?"

"Because Ferry's unpredictable; at his best, he could certainly match Muirhead and maybe even Gribben too, if Gribben wasn't quite up for it. They're all temperamental, these guys. You never know what they'll do. They're nutters or very close to it."

"So what's the solution? We offer Billy boy a job?"

"No chance. He's never taking a job with us."

Barrington intervened. "But I can send him packing – that I can assure you, sir. He's an unstable creature, as I say, and keenly sensitive to insults, particularly anything with an animal reference."

"That sounds a bit thin to me," scoffed Weever.

"With respect, Mr Weever," continued Barrington, "I know Pung and I know his—"

Weever held up his hand. "Can the other guys be made faster? Gribben and Muirhead – those guys?"

"How d'you mean?" asked Fairfoull.

"Can we get more speed out of them? What else would I mean?"

"Well, we're not talking dragsters here, Gordon. We can't

just shove a turbo in their shorts and watch them burn up the track."

"What're they getting paid?"

"I have no idea."

"You don't know?"

"They're paid enough, apparently, or they wouldn't have signed up, Gordon."

"Maybe more would help."

"They've got all they need, Gordon; pride will do the rest. If they're found taking our money, they'll get disqualified and we'll look shit."

"Nobody will know it's our money."

"Round here, everyone will know."

"I want to be there, Charlie. I want like hell to attend these games – I deserve to be there – but there's no way I'll be there if I'm looking like a loser. Do you understand what I'm saying, Charlie?"

"Yes, I do. Loud and clear, Gordon."

"So we fix Monkey Boy and we fix Lord Tulloh – without delay."

"By hook or by crook, we'll get Donald away from here and get Lord Tulloh all to ourselves."

"Oh, Donald's away," broke in Barrington. "He left for Spain this morning."

"He's gone?" exclaimed Fairfoull.

"Yes, his mother's having panic attacks. Apparently, some crazy, old man bit her in the face when he ran off with her dog, and now she's seeing vampires biting her every night. She's in therapy. Donald's gone to help her."

"Why didn't you say this earlier?"

"Well… I didn't think it important."

"It's extremely important," said Fairfoull. "Action stations! Plan Overture! Right, Robert, thank you very much. You've been a great help, but now I need to say goodbye. I have much to do."

"Perhaps I can be of help."

"Not with this one, Robert; another time I'm sure, but not now. I'll let you know. You've been a great help. For now, though, it's thank you and goodbye."

Looking somewhat stunned, Barrington got the message, rose to his feet and headed for the door like a reprimanded servant.

But Weever had another idea. "Hang on! Wait a minute! Maybe you can help."

Turning like an eager puppy, Barrington brightened.

"I want you to get information on Tannadee's three biggest hitters," continued Weever. "You know who they are?"

"Sven, Dekker and Chizzie Bryson?" replied Barrington nervously.

"Exactly. Without them I'm told Tannadee is down the tubes. So, I want to know what these three are planning to do over the next two days."

"You mean their training schedule?"

"That and more: I want to know where they will be at any given time."

"Well, with all due respect, sir, I have to say that I doubt if even they themselves would know that."

"Are you telling me you can't do this task?"

"No, no, not at all. If there's anything to know, I can assure you I'll get it. I can certainly get their training plans."

"That would be a start. Be as quick as you can."

Barrington looked at Fairfoull as if begging for support, but none came.

Fairfoull simply smiled. "See you later, then, Robert. I know you won't let us down."

Barrington pursed his lips and left.

Weever shuffled in his chair. "That guy gives me the creeps. He'd better get results."

"I think he might surprise you, Gordon; he's a cute little operator in his own way."

"He looks constipated if you ask me."

"Well, let's just see."

"That sucker Sven's another bastard who gives me the creeps. I'd like to take him out with my bare hands."

"Well, we'll need something more subtle than that, I'm afraid."

"Poison the bastard."

"We'll hold that in reserve. I've spoken to Carl Crawford our—"

"Security chief?"

"Yeah, and he's ahead of the game. He's come up with some ideas for the hits. First off, he recommends Whiplash Jenny for Dekker, she'll shunt him off his motorbike and he'll be out for weeks with neck and back pain. Then, for Sven, it needs to be a bit more subtle: we'll get him back on the booze. Apparently, he still goes into bars in the belief that testing his willpower will cure him for good. Some psychologist told him that repetition will form a new pathway in his brain, and he'll be a new man."

"He'd be a new man if he had a brain."

"Carl has guys who will approach Sven in the pub and get him boozing again. And, lastly, Chizzie Bryson, he's a bit more difficult – he has a brain. But Carl's working on it."

"And Plan Overture?" asked Weever, putting his feet up on the desk. "Is it all set?"

"It's all set, Gordon, and good to go."

"Then get the invitation out right away. This is gonna be the best goddamn dinner Lord Tulloh has ever seen. I want everything!"

"I know, I know—"

"Music, drinks and – most important of all – the poker game."

"We're all set, Gordon. All set and ready to roll. We've got a string quartet to play his favourite music, we've got excerpts from *Swan Lake*, we've got *Romeo and Juliet*'s 'Dance of the Knight', then we've got Schubert's 'Lieder' and then we have 'The Trout'—"

"Trout? No trout for me. I don't like trout. I'm having salmon."

"'The Trout' I refer to is a piece of music by Schubert."

"Aw, not that singing fish you hang on the wall?"

"No, but now you mention it, we do have a great menu."

"'The Trout'? Fish music? Jeezus. I want a call to get me the hell out of there when that happens!"

"No problem, Gordon. As I said, it's a great menu with all Lord Tulloh's favourites, especially sherry trifle."

"Lots of sherry."

"Indeed, and we have his favourite whisky. Plus, of course, my very friendly friends will come and play a little poker."

"Excellent."

"Actually, though, Gordon… some of the guys… they might not… you know… be too comfortable with fleecing the old boy."

"You mean they want more money?"

"No, they might just think it's a teeny-weeny bit cruel. I mean, let's face it, it could destroy the guy."

"They're not backing out are they? If they—"

"No, no, nobody's backing out, Gordon. I'm just saying… maybe we need to feel our way a little bit when the time comes."

"What the hell's that mean?"

"Well… it means… we know when to stop, sort of thing; know when enough's enough."

"You know when to stop, Charlie. We stop when we get what we want. Don't go weak on me, Charlie boy! I want that damn field!"

"Gordon, I have to say this – I owe it to you to say it straight – let the damn field go. It's not worth it. Just let it go."

"And I'm telling you straight that we had a deal, Tulloh and me, and that creep backed out. He cheated. He cheated me, and I won't be cheated. No one cheats me. This is not about the field – this is about Gordon B. Weever. This is about who I am, for Christ's sake!"

Fairfoull paused for a moment, then nodded. "Understood. It will be done."

"Look, Charlie, you need to learn something very fast: life is cruel. It's more than a game. It's get real or get bust. Believe me, I am one of the kindest people. I am the kindest person I've ever met. Some think only fools are kind, but I am no fool. Lord Tulloh is a fool. He's an utter fool. If he goes down and can't get up, then, you know what? That's just too bad; it's just too bad, because that's where he's meant to be. There's no point in holding him up like a rag doll – that's no favour to anybody. In the end, you don't help the sucker, you only prolong the agony. And, what's more important, you destroy human progress. We're doing mankind a favour. It's survival of the fittest out there. I mean, keeping that guy alive is a kick in the balls for humanity. You allow these guys to breed and you go backwards; that's not progress."

"Well, who knows? Sometimes even the weak prove strong. Look at that guy Stephen Hawking."

"Who?"

"Stephen Hawking. The great scientist; the one who lived in a wheelchair and had an electronic voice."

"Oh, that guy. Well, you said it, the guy proved strong; he proved himself – he proved good. And I don't care if he's a lump of meat paste, if he proves good – right on, no problem. I mean, even a horse would be good if it came up with a great idea."

"That's a bit difficult, though, if all he can do is say 'neigh' and go clippity-clop."

"Charlie, believe me, that's two more things than I get from some would-be employees. And these losers and Lord Tulloh should give up for the sake of humanity, or at least should stop breeding. This planet is going to blow up sometime. We've got to get off. We've got to get to other stars. You can't do that carrying retards. You need the best, and, right now, the best are losing. It's all the thickos and losers that are breeding fastest and watering down human brain power. We're going backwards out of kindness. It's no good. It's no good breeding the weak. We need the strong, and if that means having no heart, then so be it. You gotta get real; you gotta ask yourself, do you want a future? Or do you want a caring, nicey-nicey swamp that's gonna blow? Bang! Wheee!" He illustrated with a swing of his arms. "You get shit all over the universe. And, as the shit flies by, some smart heap of meat paste up there says, 'There they go; there goes humanity. That's what happens when you don't stay strong.' Tulloh is really, really pathetically weak and he's got it coming. So do it, Charlie, and do it now! Blow him away!"

"Yessir!"

"Oh, and take away the mound at the old son-of-a-bitch's house. Put some trees in."

"What? You mean Paw's place?"

"Yep."

For a moment, Fairfoull gazed at Weever in disbelief. "Are you serious?"

"Just do it, Charlie."

"What kind of trees? Big ones? Evergreens?"

"Just wait till you hear from Yolanda."

"She's with us?"

Weever said nothing, he merely laughed and waved Fairfoull away.

CHAPTER 26

With only two days to go until the big day, the Highland Games loomed very large in Chizzie's mind. All the hard work was behind him. It was now time to focus simply on keeping toned and injury free. A nice, airy jog round Dennan Hill was ideal. So, after some biscuits and fruit juice, off he went into the woods.

Only a couple of hundred yards in, out leaped Billy Pung from behind a holly bush. "Stop!" he cried, blocking the path. "Danger! There's men after you. That man in the car there," he said, pointing to the car park, "he's one."

Chizzie looked over his shoulder. "Where?"

"The one in the black car: he's one of them. He's watching you."

Chizzie squinted his eyes. "He's reading a paper, Billy."

"He's pretending; he's watching. His friend's on the hill and he's watching. They're both watching. They're talking on these radio things."

"Walkie-talkies?"

"Aye. They've made a trap – them two and the young gamekeeper from Rawdor Estate. They want to break your leg."

Knowing that Billy's mind wasn't exactly what could be called 'mainstream', Chizzie was unsure what to make of Billy's excitement. "How'd you know all this, Billy?"

"I've seen them. I've heard them. You can see. I'll take you."

"Where?"

"You know the squeaky tree?"

"No."

"The big tree with a dead one leaning on it? It squeaks when the wind blows?"

Chizzie was none the wiser.

"It's on the top path. Follow me," commanded Billy as he set off.

Chizzie felt he had no option but to follow.

Approaching the end of the woods and the start of the top path, Billy suddenly stopped. "I've an idea," he declared. "Don't go to the trap. We get the man up there first."

"What d'you mean 'get the man', Billy?" Chizzie asked, fearing that Billy's imagination had wandered too far off the scale even by Billy's wild standards. But there was a playfulness in Billy's voice and a face that was reassuring. "Okay, we'll have a look at this man first," Chizzie agreed.

Billy turned to the left. "Follow me," he said and took a narrow, bracken-fringed path off to the side, "We'll get behind him." Billy led Chizzie round the back of the hill and up to the peat hags, where a large man, wearing a camo jacket and trousers and holding binoculars in one hand, lay on the ground, looking down to the top path.

"That's him," said Billy, pointing.

Chizzie and Billy squatted behind a peat hag and watched. Then Billy leaped up and whispered, "I'll get him."

"No, Billy, no. Stay here," whispered Chizzie.

But Billy was off, crouching low and following the contours of the hags until Chizzie could see him about five yards away from the man. Billy moved forwards stealthily and disappeared behind a peat hag. Listening intently, Chizzie wondered whether to intervene or remain where he was; the man might be entirely innocent, a birdwatcher perhaps. A gust of wind shook the emerging heather flowers in front of

Chizzie's eyes. He pondered for a minute, then decided he needed to catch up with Billy to prevent any trouble. He moved forwards at a crouch and began to follow Billy's footprints, but – only a few yards along – a roar exploded from where the man had been. Then came another roar, followed by a torrent of expletives. Chizzie peered above the hags and saw the burly man was now chasing Billy, who was laughing and seemingly in no hurry. They disappeared from view. Within seconds, though, new sounds came: a squelching, gluey sucking with an accompaniment of roaring and groaning. Strangely, there was a kind of rhythm and narrative to it. It put Chizzie in mind of an offering entitled 'Vox Humana and Mother Earth' he'd once sat through at the Edinburgh Music Festival.

With the time for diplomacy now clearly gone, Chizzie dared to put his head above the heather again. The man was pulling himself out of the pool of sticky peat into which he'd evidently fallen. He hauled himself onto the heather, with gloop pouring out of his sleeves, all the while issuing a wide range of expletives. He sat down and rubbed his trousers and hands on clumps of heather, smearing his head inadvertently as he wiped away the sweat.

Chizzie watched then ducked as the man looked round before getting to his feet with a final round of expletives. Lying low, Chizzie was able to discern that Mr Unhappy was now making his departure in the opposite direction. He peered over the heather at eye level and saw the man heading down the hill, with a squadron of blow flies keeping him busy.

A few minutes later Billy appeared, smiling and clearly rather pleased with his work. "I got him for you!" he said, clapping his hands.

Chizzie, in two minds as to whether to scold or congratulate, replied, "The poor devil. I'm just glad it was him and not me. What a mess. When he hits the car park, he's going to look an absolute fool. Never do anything like that again, please, Billy, but thanks anyway. What exactly did you do to him?"

"Well, first he got the mud bombs, then he got the rabbit."

"Rabbit? What rabbit?"

"The dead rabbit in the mud. He got that in the mush, right under the hooter, yah beauty!"

"D'you know who he was?"

"No, but I've seen him at Weever's place. I'll show you the trap."

They got back on the path, and Billy pointed at the squeaky tree, which, since the wind had dropped, was not actually squeaking now. Then he stopped and pointed to a tree root that crossed the path and lay partially submerged in the ground. Chizzie recognised it as an obstacle he always hopped over. Without a word, Billy stamped on the ground in front of the tree root, and the surface fell away instantly, revealing a hole. He stamped further until the full extent of the hole was revealed. By Chizzie's reckoning, it measured about a foot square and eight inches deep, excluding the sharp stones at the bottom. It had been burrowed just below the surface to make it look like an animal trap laid by a naive poacher after a roe deer. A rather obvious snare nearby confirmed the pretence.

Feeling slightly unnerved by the very look of the trap, Chizzie took a deep breath and sighed. "It's a nasty piece of work that. Clearly, whoever made it meant business,."

"Somebody don't like you," said Billy.

"You're right there," agreed Chizzie, taking another deep breath. "Are there any more of these, d'you know?"

"There's no more."

"They could've seriously hurt other people, not just me."

"No, just you; they put planks on it till they saw you coming. The planks are over in the bushes."

Chizzie shook his head. "Right. Let's take out the rocks and fill this in."

As they gathered loose soil and small stones, Chizzie's sense of fragility and powerlessness in the face of evil turned to anger. He was determined to find out who was behind all this, and if Billy was right, it shouldn't take long to find the culprit. On the other hand, Chizzie knew that confronting the culprit would result in nothing more than a barefaced denial, and might even give the culprit some perverse sort of pleasure in seeing his would-be victim worried and upset. Far better, perhaps, to be quietly wary and ignore the vile brutes.

Later that evening as Chizzie and Johnny sat reading their papers in the living room, the phone rang. It was Dekker with shattering news. He'd sustained whiplash and multiple bruises following a hit-and-run accident when he was on his motorbike in Millburgh. For all his bulk and bravado, he was an emotional man and, almost sobbing, the wrestler explained he was left with no choice but to admit defeat and withdraw from the team he had come to love.

The news hit like a wrecking ball. Half-stunned, Chizzie put the phone down with a clatter, causing Johnny to peer over his newspaper and enquire if something was up. Chizzie explained in a dry, funereal tone and moved over to the settee, where he flopped onto his back and put his hands to his head.

Johnny sought to offer comfort; he leaned over Chizzie with Rocky the budgie nibbling the few hairs on the top of his head. "Dekker is no big deal," he said dismissively. "He'd probably lose every bout."

"Not so. Not so," Chizzie replied adamantly. "With a bit of luck, he might actually have won maximum points – he's in good condition again."

"Again?"

"Well, as good as he's ever been. He's a lot better than he looks. And he's up for it – or he was up for it until this."

"Who's our reserve?"

"Nobody. There is no reserve."

"How about Sven? He did a bit of wrestling in the past. How about we move him to the wrestling and Stevie Johnson to the hammer?"

"That's a lose-lose situation. Sven won't win big points and neither will Stevie. Sven can at least get a decent point or two from the hammer, and possibly a lot more. We just have to accept we don't have a wrestler."

"Well, don't look at me like that – I'm not wrestling."

"God forbid! No. I'm just looking to see if there are white flags in your eyes."

"No white flags. We soldier on. I say we take the fight to Weever; we go over to his place and we—"

"No, Dad, no. No. Weever would just love that; he'd laugh in your face. You can't prove anything."

"We go to Tunnock then and we get the police on it."

"What can Tunny do? We've no proof."

"We've been attacked, for God's sake. We're entitled to justice!"

"Justice? Are you kidding? We're up against Weever here. If justice went into action right now, the only one to suffer would be Billy. He and I would tell the truth, and he'd get charged with assault."

"You wouldn't testify against him."

"Not if I could help it, but sometimes justice bites the hand that feeds it. What matters is that Billy was in the right."

"Bugger justice!"

"Exactly. It's a sad and dangerous thing to say, but, sometimes, you've just got to walk on the wild side, and that's definitely where Billy is. He did right."

"And wrong."

"He's only human."

"That's debatable."

Chizzie shot a withering look at Johnny, treating the remark with the contempt he felt it deserved. "Justice or no justice, we soldier on," he said. "We stay positive. As long as there are no more call-offs, we can still win through."

At that, the phone rang. Coming on the back of what he'd just said, the ringing sounded terribly ominous to Chizzie, eerie even and possibly contaminated by the very mention of call-offs. Without moving, father and son gazed at one another. The budgie flew off and perched on a picture frame above the fireplace. The phone rang on. Seized with the irrational thought that the longer he delayed, the less likely it was that he would have contaminated the phone with the word 'call-off', Chizzie made no move. Then Johnny put down his paper.

With the spell broken, Chizzie jumped to his feet and went bravely to the phone. He steadied himself for bad news. And it came. PC Tunnock was on the line. In a brittle, formal tone, the PC informed Chizzie that Sven was currently in the custody suite at Millburgh police station, detained as much for his own safety as that of the public. Apparently, in an alcohol-fuelled frenzy, he'd run amok in a bar in Millburgh, where a friend was holding a birthday celebration. He'd thrown chairs, attacked two strangers, and leaped over the bar and served drinks freely until restrained by four police officers. This was much like the former self he'd vowed to leave behind. This time, the news hit Chizzie so hard he almost heard the bang and felt the flesh rip from his bones.

With barely enough energy to thank the PC for the call, he put the phone down slowly.

"Who was it?" Johnny asked.

Without reply, Chizzie slumped onto the sofa, put his head in his hands again and stared at the ceiling. Even with Dekker and Sven in the team, Tannadee's prospects were at best uncertain, but, now, Tannadee's prospects were very certain: they were goners. All the effort they'd put in, all the community spirit that had flourished, and all the hope that had been kindled, all were gone to nothing, vanquished in less than a day.

How could it possibly be? the devastated Chizzie asked himself. It was no mere coincidence, surely: a poacher's trap, a hit-and-run motorbike accident and a bout of barroom madness. It all pointed to a cruel, concerted attack. Or was he putting two and two together and making five?

Johnny, now looking rather peeved, asked again who it was. With a throaty, despairing sigh, Chizzie recounted the call.

"I knew it! Knew it!" cried Johnny. "He's totally untrustworthy. I knew he'd let us down."

"Leave off, will you?" responded Chizzie, "You don't know anything! I need to see him – I need to get the facts. There's skulduggery going on left, right and centre, and we need to straighten it out."

Sometime later, as Chizzie arrived at Sven's cell, the police doctor was just leaving. He explained that Sven had responded well to simple rehydration treatment, and was now reasonably fit and well, though – inevitably – feeling exhausted and sore. The custody sergeant added that a reliable witness had seen two men slip something into Sven's drink, so no charges were being brought. Sven was free to go.

Chizzie collected Sven, got him settled in the car and drove him home.

On the way, Sven lay snoring on the back seat of the car until, about a mile short of Tannadee, he woke suddenly and sat upright, rubbing his forehead: "Aw, man, I am so tired; so, so tired."

"And I'm not surprised," replied Chizzie, "It sounds like you spent a week's worth of energy all in one evening. Why in the name of God did you go into that bar? I can't understand it."

"To beat my demons, Chizzie. I knew I could do it. I didn't want to just kick the booze, I wanted to thrash it and show it who's boss now. Alcohol would be everywhere, but I would defy it. I would take everything it could throw at me and I would still be standing, unbowed and unbeaten."

"It's a bloody dangerous thing to do, if you don't mind me saying."

"It had to be; it had to be right on the edge, so I know I can be there and still win. Then I get my life back."

"You didn't think about failing?"

"Never. Not for a second. I knew I had it in me. I'm a passionate guy. When I love, I love; when I hate, I hate. I hate booze and what it's done to me. I don't hate often, it's not my way, but I do hate booze. I hate, hate, hate it. No way did I give in to it. Somebody hit my ginger beer with something. That's what put me out." And, with that, he sank back onto the seat and was snoring within seconds.

As they drew up outside the hotel, Chizzie met Jim and asked, "Have you decided on what to tell the others?"

"Yes. We give them the truth," declared Jim.

"Which is?"

"They needn't worry."

"Needn't worry?" asked Chizzie incredulously.

"No. Because one accident is unfortunate, two is remarkable and three is suspicious; it's on the edge. Weever will know that. Any more and he gets the police at his door – for general enquiries only, but Weever can't afford the official suspicion implied in such a visit."

"You're sure it's Weever?"

"There's no doubt about it; the other teams might be up for a bit of gamesmanship, but they wouldn't stoop so low as to endanger life. These incidents are in a different league."

"He's certainly more than just a bully. I think he's capable of pushing it too far."

"I'd be surprised if he did, but who knows?"

"You say Weever's on the edge, but so are we. I don't want anyone to know about the trap set for me. Morale's going to be near rock-bottom already in our camp with two key men out of action."

"One and a half. If we can get that sad heap of humanity in your back seat up on its feet, something might yet be made of it. And if we can get Billy on board, we still have a chance."

"If, if, if. We're running out of ifs, Jim. If we lose just one more, we're out. Guys like Dalrymple are teetering on the edge, even without Weever's assault. We need to assure the guys that Dekker and Sven were just unfortunate; no one will be entirely surprised about Sven, more's the pity."

Jim thought for a moment. "Agreed," he said at last, "I'll see to it. I'll just tell them to relax, stay at home and take things easy."

CHAPTER 27

Secure in the knowledge of certain victory, Weever arrived by helicopter in good spirits and met Fairfoull for refreshments in his drawing room.

"Yes, our prospects have improved quite remarkably all of a sudden," quipped Fairfoull, bringing a sarcastic laugh from Weever. "Two down and out, and the rest down in the mouth."

With another chuckle, Weever held up his champagne glass and gave a toast, "Here's to Digger and his merry men."

"To Digger and his merry men," chimed Fairfoull.

They drained their glasses, then Weever wiped his lips with his hand. "Now, I want you to turn your head to the right and look above the fireplace," he said.

Fairfoull's gaze alighted on a large portrait painting in a gold frame. The subject was something vaguely resembling Weever naked from the waist up and wearing a kilt, while clutching a golden caber. "*Chieftain of the Glen*, I call it," enthused Weever. "What d'you think?"

Fairfoull knew exactly what to think, but not what to say. *Monarch of the Glen* it was not, though if it was, it would probably be in the rutting season. The head was about twenty years out of date and the rest of the body belonged to someone else. Even in his prime, Weever could never have looked so impressive. "Impressive!" declared Fairfoull. It was not entirely a lie. The painting certainly made an impression

– not a great one – but one delivering an impression likely to haunt the viewer for some time.

"I had to rush the guy, so a few tweaks are still needed here and there; he wasn't happy, but I think it's pretty good, even if I say so myself."

The tweak that Fairfoull had in mind involved turning the painting round and starting again, but the client was clearly delighted, and if that made him a nicer person, Fairfoull was all for it. "Congratulations, Gordon," he said, nodding approvingly, safe in the knowledge that few would encounter the thing. He was wrong.

"I want you to get a top-line photographer and get my portrait out there in the press, maybe even on TV, but definitely in the local press. I need some really good PR, and this is a great start."

Almost numb, Fairfoull responded, "I'll get on to it right away."

"And put some words together to go with the photo."

"Will do."

"Before you do that, though, there's the seating arrangements at the Highland Games. I want my rightful place – the place of honour."

Fairfoull blew out his cheeks. "It's a bit late in the day for that," he said.

"Who's the big guy? Who's the biggest guest there? Any royals? I'm going to be seated next to them."

"No royals, Gordon. The big cheese will be the Lord Lieutenant."

"A lieutenant! That's the best they can do?"

"He's no ordinary lieutenant, Gordon. He's the Queen's representative in these parts. I think he was a major at one time."

"Okay. Whatever. I'm sitting next to him."

"Well, I don't know quite—"

"I know, I know absolutely. It's me; I'm sitting next to the guy. Digger and the boys will arrange things. Now go get 'em on to it."

The following day, Chizzie remained in the hotel, immersing himself in paper work. It was the safest place to be, the work needed to be done, and it took his mind off his biggest worry.

But being bottled up got to be more difficult than he'd thought. After watching the early evening news on TV, he became restless and decided to take a walk. He took to the path along the south shore of the loch; it was an unconventional route for him and one that was likely to foil any further attempt to put him out of the running.

As he stood for a moment and looked out over the loch, the wide expanse of fresh, clean water seemed to embrace him and draw all clutter from his head. And the great, limpid body infused him with its calmness, so that Chizzie too became calm and his troubles eased.

Moving on, he passed Paw's place and thought of calling in. Sven and Billy would be there with the answers to most of his problems, but the thoughts of mustering his powers of persuasion and the likelihood of bitter disappointment were too much for him and he walked on until – finding a dry, mossy rock that was almost designed for the purpose, under a low-hanging birch – he sat down to have a good think. The silvery-grey water provided the perfect screen while he endeavoured to find the form of words that would get Billy into the Tannadee team. After losing himself in thought for a while and failing to come up with anything that he'd never tried before, he raised his head and looked out across the water. To his surprise, a small rowing boat had appeared about two hundred yards out, just beyond a little headland. But the boat was not moving. There appeared to be no one in it, or if they were in it, they were hiding beneath what could be a blanket. A cold shiver ran suddenly through Chizzie. Someone might have fallen overboard. Certainly, there was no sign of life, no sign of splashing, and he'd heard nothing. On a flat, calm evening like this, the boat couldn't simply have drifted there. Someone put it there. But who? He called out.

There was no response. There seemed to be a rumpled blanket spread across the seats of the boat. Someone could be under there, injured maybe. He called again. This time he saw something move. A few seconds later, a torso swung bolt upright in the middle of the boat as if emerging from a deck below. It put on a wide-brimmed hat, peered through binoculars in Chizzie's direction, then swung a pair of oars into the water and began pulling towards Chizzie. The rower, though slight, pulled strongly and urgently, like a man on a mission.

As he watched, it slowly dawned on Chizzie that there might, in fact, be more to this than he'd first thought. This could be sinister. There was purpose in the rower's actions. Whoever it was pulled strongly like a man hellbent on some kind of business. Chizzie and the rower were alone. There were no witnesses. He could be found hanging from a tree. The thought of discretion being the better part of valour crossed Chizzie's mind, and yet the rower was seemingly no heavyweight. The rower was the wiry type, though they are often the worst and the meanest of all, as they use weapons. Chizzie would have nothing to hand but a small branch at best. It was time to retire. But no, he wasn't going to let Weever make him a coward. He would stand his ground. If need be, he could always run; there weren't many who could match him. He looked around for an escape route, one with plenty of blind twists to confound a gunman.

The boat approached the shore about eighty yards away, behind a rocky outcrop, where Chizzie knew there was a small, sandy beach. He waited, concealing himself partly behind a big silver birch tree. It should take the rower no more than a couple of minutes to arrive. Chizzie waited, but no one came. There was no sign of anyone.

A few minutes passed. He decided to take the initiative and move closer, which was a move that might take the rower by surprise. Cautiously, he approached the rocky outcrop and peered round it. The boat was there, beached on the little sand strip, but there was no sign of the rower. He looked around and listened intently. Evidently, the rower had gone. He hesitated for a moment, then stepped forwards to examine the boat.

But the rower had not gone. The dark figure emerging from a swathe of tall bracken, slipped out behind the unsuspecting Chizzie and grunted, "Hey you!"

Chizzie swung round and then gasped, hardly believing his eyes. "Yolanda!" he cried.

"Chizzie! Hey! I knew curiosity would get the better of you!" She laughed, holding out her arms to embrace him.

Speechless, Chizzie could only hug her. With so much to say, he hardly knew where to start. "Aw, it's great to see you back, Yolanda!" he whispered warmly. "Welcome back. You're so very, very welcome here."

"I'm glad to be back," Yolanda replied.

"Where've you been? It seems like ages since you were here. We've been very concerned. We think about you a lot round here, you know."

"I was in Canada. I'll explain later."

"You're all right? You were flat out in the boat."

Yolanda laughed. "I'm very all right, thank you. I just couldn't sleep. I'm a little jet-lagged, so I came out onto the water, and this might sound a bit silly, but I just wanted to imbibe the place, really feel it. And what better place than out on the loch? So I lay back, and then it happened: I knew I wanted to be here more than any other place. I felt at one with here, like I was one of the clouds floating in the sky."

Coming from a Scottish person this would have sounded strange, but Chizzie had met Americans before and was not at all surprised.

"And how about you? Are you all right?" she asked.

"Oh, I'm perfectly all right, thank you. But, frankly... to be brutally honest... I have to say that if your father had his way I would not be all right."

"Oh?"

"He's waging war against us."

"How so?"

Chizzie explained.

Looking very apologetic, Yolanda replied, "I'll try, Chizzie; I will try to call him off, but I can't promise. There are things I've been able to do, like getting the mound removed from Paw's place. On the land issue, though, I've had no success, I'm afraid. I thought I'd got there one day, but he's such a cussed old guy at times. Only my mother can turn him over. She's married again, to a lawyer who thinks she's been palmed off with a mere pittance, and he wants her to go after dear old dad."

"I thought you said it was all settled?"

"It's settled formally, but Mother knows a thing or two about Daddy, and she and her new hubby are turning the screws. I'm the only thing that stands between the warring parties. I moderate things – provided dear old daddy swings a few favours my way. But it sounds like he's reached the pit-bull stage here, and even I can't reach him now."

"The pit-bull stage?"

"Yes. Blind aggression. Numb to the pain, he'll fight to the death. I've seen it before; he'll fight on, no matter what. He'll just fight for the hell of it. It's crazy. Would it really be such a great loss to you?"

Chizzie explained the significance of the land.

Yolanda lost herself in thought for a few moments, then she brightened suddenly. "I want to be out on the water again," she said, "just a little dabble in the middle of the loch. There's room for two. Care to join me?"

"I'd love to," Chizzie replied, nodding. "There's enough light for a couple of hours yet, so it should be very pleasant out there."

The air on the loch was humid, but the light, southerly breeze kept it cool and refreshing. The only other craft on the water was a small dinghy that was floating well away on the far side, so they effectively had the whole glistening loch to themselves. Yolanda took the oars for the first fifteen minutes, and not much was said other than polite talk about the sights and sounds of the loch. She would need to stop rowing if they were to talk more seriously. And she did.

Carefully, she stowed the oars along the floor of the boat, then closed her eyes and drank in the air. The evening sun glowed amber-gold on the water. A curlew called far off, and the fragrance of the air on the loch mingling with the faint smell of wood smoke from some distant cottage enveloped Chizzie like a magic spell. He knew this was an evening he'd never forget, whatever happened.

"You asked where I'd been," Yolanda began.

Chizzie nodded almost drunk with pleasure. He could've been in a dream; afloat on a dream with this mesmerising lady of the lake, he felt weightless and, to some extent, witless as the boat bobbed gently and rhythmically to the slow pulse of evening on the water. It was hard to concentrate, but the serious business had begun. He blinked rapidly and slowly, hauled himself upright and leaned forwards. "I'm listening," he said.

"I explained before I left that I needed to work certain things out."

Chizzie nodded.

"Well, in a nutshell," she continued, "I couldn't settle and couldn't think things out as easily as I'd hoped. I moved around, hoping new places would help me clear my head. I went to Edinburgh for a while, then some other places, then finally to Canada, to be part of a hotel project big Daddy is developing there. But always in my mind was Tannadee. Wherever I went, I never shook off Tannadee. Eventually, I took the hint, and so here I am. I don't know where the future lies; I only know that here is where I want to be right now. So, there's not much to tell really: no great adventures, just some hard working and some plain thinking."

Chizzie hesitated for a moment as he digested the information. "Well, I'm so glad you feel that way, Yolanda," he replied finally. "It's great to have you here. Truly, the place is never brighter than when you're around, and it desperately needs brightening. Dark clouds have descended on us."

"Dad's kicked you in the teeth."

"More than just the teeth."

"I really wish I could help."

"All I need to know is that there'll be no more attacks."

"I could get him to promise."

"Thank you."

"But it wouldn't mean a thing. You're nothing and you're in his way."

"I see."

"Perhaps if I speak to Mother; she's my sledgehammer, if she's in the mood. I can get brownie points for calling her off."

"Any help is greatly appreciated."

"Well, we'll see. Have you had enough fresh air?"

Chizzie nodded and, taking the oars gently, headed for shore. For two very sociable people, they were strangely silent. With too much to say seemingly and being too concerned with avoiding saying the wrong thing, they found themselves unable to say anything. Chizzie contented himself with a change of pace, demonstrating what a strong lad he was by shifting the boat along at an impressive speed, until a slight niggle in his back warned him not to get carried away. As Yolanda gazed at the sky, having seemingly taken over Chizzie's dream, he eased off and took on a dolorous demeanour, which he hoped would win at least a sympathetic hug and possibly a very concerted effort from Yolanda to get her father to call off his attack on the school.

As they stepped off the Weever jetty onto the grassy shore, both remarked on how much they'd enjoyed the little boat trip. Chizzie searched Yolanda's face for some sign that kissing her would not be unwelcome. She appeared to be searching his face. A kiss seemed appropriate, but what kind of kiss? With half of Yolanda's genes donated by her mother, a knee in the crotch could greet any wrong move. He needed to be careful. He was heavily invested in Tannadee, as a teacher, hotelier and downright decent bloke. The last thing he needed was for word to go about that he was some kind of lizard. His private kissing scale flashed through his mind. It was a scale of one to five where number one, barely a touch with the lips, was appropriate for distant relatives and the like; number five, by contrast, was a liquid, fiery, Latin thing, which was rarely used. A number two, or perhaps a three, seemed about right. He began to lean forwards still not quite decided on a two or a three. Then, suddenly, she just grabbed him by the chest, and hit him with a number four, possibly even a four point five. Caution was a goner, his arms wrapped around her and he squeezed her tight. She squeezed too. Lips locked long and firm, hitting five on the scale, then they unlocked for air, then locked again with another five. Locked there on the shore, so enveloped in love, their future was forged; and if the rocks should melt with the sun, and all the seas gang dry, as Robert Burns would have it, they would never have known. As they paused for air again, Chizzie all but wept with joy.

Hand in hand now, they walked towards the gate of the Weever estate, and – on passing Paw's place – it struck Chizzie that Yolanda might be the one to persuade Billy to do the right thing and run for Tannadee. He knew for sure that Billy admired Yolanda, so perhaps, in this gilded hour, she could pull off a conversion. But the jet lag had kicked in and she declined, postponing her attempt until the following day.

At the gate, they arranged that Yolanda would provide lunch tomorrow, and Chizzie would see to dinner. Then they hugged and kissed again, and bade each other goodnight.

Chizzie walked into the ruby sunset feeling like a film star. It was a day that had made him rich beyond all coin, and he felt nothing could dent him now.

CHAPTER 28

One day to go. Though all the excitement of the previous day with Yolanda had kept him awake into the wee small hours, Chizzie awoke at nine o'clock, surprisingly energised, and his head abuzz and churning with thoughts of Yolanda and the Tannadee team. Jim's phone message asked to see him in his office, so, after a hurried breakfast, he went straight there. The smile that greeted him was almost as wide as the door Jim opened.

"We're in the running, Chizzie! We're in the running literally! Billy Pung is going to run!" Jim declared, fist-pumping the air.

"Wow! Fantastic! Brilliant!" cried Chizzie.

"He's doing it for Sven, he said. He's really pumped up about what happened to him."

"That's good to hear. And what about Sven himself?"

"He reckons he'll be fit enough by tomorrow. Right now, he's doing light exercises. He knows his body, he says, and he'll be ready. With the mood he's in, he'll be ready even if he isn't. We'll check him out tomorrow."

"With Billy and Sven on board, we're up there with the best."

"Not quite, but it's not impossible. Here, take a look at this," Jim dropped a blue folder on the desk. "Our spies' reports."

Chizzie sat down and opened the folder.

Jim continued, "It's very inconclusive, but the general feeling is that we'll come third or fourth overall. But, with Billy running, we're probably up to third or second. Personally,

I think we can do it. I really believe we can win if we get every ounce out of our guys. What d'you think?" There seemed to be more hope in Jim's voice than confidence.

"How reliable are these reports?" Chizzie asked.

Jim blew through his lips and shrugged his shoulders. Chizzie attached little importance to these so-called reports privately. He knew they were little more than gossip brought in by farmers who liked nothing better than meeting other farmers in order to put one over on them, and they were all at it, in all the villages. So, in fact, nobody really knew anything about anybody. And, even if they did know something, that something would depend on other factors such as weather, training schedule and state of health. Any reckoning was, at best, a rough guess.

Chizzie flipped through a couple of other reports in the folder and was no better impressed.

Then the phone rang and, within seconds of picking it up, Jim's face fell. "Aw no! Oh no!" he moaned. "What on earth possessed you to prune trees on the day before the games? Aw, Jamie, Jamie, man... Yeah, I'm sure it hurts... Well, of course I'm very sorry for your injury, but... Well, you know what it means for the team... Yes, yes, I will. Okay, thanks for letting me know right away. Mend soon." Jim put the phone down with an agonised sigh and shook his head.

"Jamie Taylor?" asked Chizzie quietly, fearing the news.

Jim sighed heavily again and nodded. "Ach! What a silly, silly man. He's just gone and wrenched his bloody ankle pruning trees. And now we've no cyclist! Aaargh!"

"He wasn't exactly a big winner, though, was he?" said Chizzie, as much reassuring himself as Jim.

"No. He knew himself he wasn't a winner, but he was probably worth a couple of crucial points all the same. Now

308

we're looking at zero points in the cycling. God knows, I might even have to cycle myself now."

"Is there a reserve?"

"You mean a reserve reserve? Bob Christie."

"Bob Christie? He'll be lapped on the first lap."

"He's a point."

The phone rang again. Jim looked to the ceiling, crossed his fingers, picked up the phone and muttered, "Please, oh God, not another one."

The caller was excited; so much so that Chizzie could clearly hear the voice; it sounded like, "Great news! Great news!"

Jim pressed a button and put the phone on speaker. Chizzie knew instantly it was Jeff Proudfoot calling.

Excitedly, Jeff delivered his great news, "His name's Eddie Wibble and he's on his way. He's a better cyclist than I could ever be. He'll be here, at the hotel, at about one o'clock. D'you want to meet him here?"

"Of course, of course," roared Jim. "I'll meet him anywhere! See you at one o'clock. Good on you, Jeff! Good man! Well done! Fantastic!" Jim's eyes were wide and shining as he put the phone down before he sprang to his feet. Chizzie remained firmly seated, smiling, while Jim stomped round the room punching the air and declaring, "What a day! What an absolute bloody day! A roller-coaster day! First, we're up in the air; next, we're down and out; then, we're back in the air again; and all before it's even lunchtime!"

With lunchtime looming, Chizzie hurried back to the hotel. Mindful of Yolanda's jet lag and the late night she had kept, he thought it best to phone the estate's executive assistant to see whether she was actually up and about.

He was informed that not only was Yolanda up and about, she was out on the golf course supervising the removal of the mound and the planting of trees. Amazed and delighted at the news, Chizzie went to his flat, at the top of the hotel, to rub more embrocation into the small of his back. Then he headed eagerly for lunch with Yolanda.

Tofu was new to Chizzie and, despite some of it looking rather like the putty he used in his shed windows, the marinade and crispy batter together with the herb-infused rice made a delicious meal. With Chizzie's forthcoming race in mind, grape juice rather than wine complemented the meal, and it did just enough to wash away the faint inhibitions Chizzie felt at being on the Weever estate.

After the meal, they lay down on the large sofa, arm in arm, and indulged their affections. Now was the time to raise the burning question.

"What did your father say when you told him about the attacks on us?" Chizzie asked.

"He knows nothing," replied Yolanda.

"Really?"

"No. He knows all right. I can read him like a billboard. I know his tones of voice. For what it's worth, though, he did say that, in his opinion, it's very likely that the culprits have cleared off."

"Well, that's good."

"It's not worth two pennies. What it means is he's got something else cooking. He aches to hurt you. He's fixed on vengeance. He wants to stop you getting what you want. I can't stop him right now, but if you could throw him a piece of meat, maybe I'd have a better chance."

"What kind of meat?"

"Well, maybe half the land he's after?"

"Impossible. It's all or nothing. There's no halfway on that. Besides, he strikes me as the kind of man who regards kindness as weakness. Give him an inch, and he'll take a mile."

Yolanda hummed quietly.

"You know he would, Yolanda. Did you speak to your mother?"

"Mother can't intervene; she's on a trans-Siberian rally right now and is 'up to her fanny in mammoth shit' to quote her directly."

"We're all in it one way or another."

"Then we dig ourselves out."

Chizzie thought for a moment. "How's your father feel about you and me being together?"

"He doesn't; he knows it'll all blow over soon enough."

Chizzie looked agog, robbed of speech.

"He's wrong, of course… unless you know different?"

"He couldn't be more wrong."

Spontaneously, they hugged affectionately and kissed. Then they both fell asleep, with his arm across her shoulders, and her head resting on his shoulder.

Nearly an hour later, Chizzie awoke and knew instantly there was something he should have remembered, but he couldn't remember what it was. Carefully, he slid his shoulder away from Yolanda's cheek and removed his numb left arm from under her shoulders. Then, the thing he should have remembered hit him: the new cyclist was arriving at one o'clock, up at the hotel. He glanced at his watch; it was twelve-fifty. There was no time to lose. Yolanda lay undisturbed. Spying a notepad on the coffee table, he wrote down quickly the time to dine that evening and beneath it added very carefully some favourite lines from Robert Burns:

Not vernal show'rs to budding flow'rs,
Not August to the farmer,
So dear can be, as thou to me,
My fair, my lovely charmer.

He placed the note on a cushion next to where he'd lain, then he kissed his fair and lovely charmer gently on the cheek and quietly took his leave.

In spite of his plan to do no running whatsoever on this day, the day before his big race, he had no choice and ran all the way to the hotel. At exactly one o'clock, just as he was walking up the hotel's driveway, hoping to catch his breath, an old camper van overtook him and shrouded him in a cloud of oily, blue smoke. Two bicycles were strapped to the roof of the vehicle, and at the wheel was a cheery-looking chap wearing glasses and a red woollen hat. Though the man was at the wheel, it was fairly obvious that the animated woman passenger was doing all the driving. Was this the much sought after Eddie Wibble? Certainly, these new arrivals were not the hotel's typical clientele.

Chizzie walked quickly up the drive and met the camper-van man just as he approached the hotel door. "Mr Wibble?" Chizzie called cheerily.

"Yeah... Jeff?" came the reply.

"No, I'm Jeff," interrupted Proudfoot as he and Jim advanced quickly from the doorway.

Eddie greeted them with a big smile, which was big enough to lift his glasses. Though first impressions can be false, it seemed very clear to Chizzie that Mr Wibble was not quite what had been hoped for. Here was a man with an innocent face – a face that was too innocent and lacking the hungry eyes of the predator; a good thing in the common man, undoubtedly, but not in a cyclist carrying the hopes, and perhaps the fate, of Tannadee.

It had been a particularly long drive for the Wibbles, Eddie explained, and it was actually time for his wife's afternoon nap. This, apparently, was why she had not left the camper van.

So, without any further delay, they all piled into the camper van and drove off to the school grounds, where Eddie was keen to demonstrate his worth. It wasn't difficult to see why it had been a particularly long journey – the camper van whined gratingly even at thirty miles an hour. Mrs Wibble said not a word beyond a cursory, "Hello."

Chizzie formed the impression that she had taken on all the troubles of the world and was blaming every one of them on the three gentlemen crushed together in the back seat.

But, whatever Mrs Wibble might lack in *joie de vivre* and social graces, Eddie more than made up for in class on the track. Not only did he complete two laps that were quicker than anything seen before in Tannadee, but he accomplished them without any sign of strain or heavy breathing. The Tannadee men were delighted, indeed thrilled, and they applauded Eddie heartily as he came over to them for appraisal. There was no doubt about it, Tannadee's prospects had just taken a big leap forward. Mrs Wibble might have remained sullenly in the camper van, but Tannadee had its man for the cycle track.

Here was a valuable asset to be handled with care, and, immediately, Chizzie offered the Wibbles two nights' bed and board at the hotel for free. The offer was politely declined, however, as Eddie explained that he and his wife preferred to stick to their tried and tested routine and would happily sleep in their beloved camper van. The word 'happily' was not one that struck Chizzie as being entirely appropriate, but the Wibbles would surely know what suited them best. Apparently this was a vital part of his plan for big events, or did it have more to do with other big plans. Who knew? So the camper van it would be for the Wibbles, which would be parked in the school grounds where they reckoned they would get all the privacy they evidently desired. A desire that became all the clearer when Jim handed Chizzie a copy of Andy Grant's profile of Eddie, hurriedly compiled from several sources. It read:

Eddie Wibble: *five feet eleven inches tall, slim build, big glasses and a smallish head with a large mop-type hairstyle, which his wife requires him to wear as a kind of safety device, so that, when Eddie overreaches himself, he blacks out with the heat. Originally riding out of Skinflats, Stirlingshire, Eddie is now riding out of Greenock, Renfrewshire.*

Eddie's attack on life is two-pronged: one, to become a daddy; and, two, to become a professional cyclist, though not necessarily in that order. Not unless you're his wife, Lizzie, that is – she definitely puts the daddy bit as top priority and regards the two prongs as almost mutually exclusive, since bashing one's testicles regularly on a bicycle saddle does a man's prospects of daddyhood no good whatsoever apparently and is most probably the reason why she is currently not the hub of the very large family she so fervently desires. But she knows, too, that if Eddie is not cycling, Eddie is not Eddie, he is somebody else, a stranger to the natural affability of the man she loves and a man even further removed from daddyhood than Eddie Wibble the cyclist. So, Lizzie, devoted wife that she is, has struck a deal with her man that sees Eddie going hell-for-leather in the daddy stakes and going hard at the cycling on the track with a unique high-buttocked style that keeps his most vital organs well clear of the nefarious saddle, which, coincidentally, brings him a whole new fan base among the ladies, members of the gay community and adventurous horse flies. Now completely dedicated to both prongs, Eddie is making progress on all fronts.

CHAPTER 29

Chizzie's joy turned to rapture when Yolanda arrived for dinner, looking very refreshed and pleased with herself in a 1960s-style, floral summer frock, with her glistening hair brushed and loose. As she pressed herself against Chizzie, uttering the words that he'd left on the note, the fragrance of lavender and fresh air about her melted all Chizzie's usual inhibitions and they kissed lovingly, completely oblivious to passers-by.

But the mood changed halfway through the meal.

"You're not hungry?" Yolanda asked, watching Chizzie pick at his breaded haddock.

"Strangely, I'm not," replied Chizzie. "Normally, I'm ravenous before a big race, but... I don't know what it is; I just seem to have lost my appetite."

Yolanda looked him in the eye, "Don't tell me you're ill."

"I don't know. Maybe it's just nerves, but nerves don't affect me too much usually. Tomorrow's so very different, though: it's not just about me; it's about all of us. On top of that, I'm in love with a wonderful woman and it's very distracting. I can hardly think straight. A voice in the back of my head keeps firing questions and casting doubts: *Have I done too little speed work? Have I done too much speed work? Have I overdone the carbohydrate loading? Have I done too little? Is that the niggle in my back again?* Even utterly weird things come up..." He hesitated, then cast a furtive glance at Yolanda and looked away.

"Like what?" Yolanda asked solemnly.

Chizzie looked troubled. "Well… just weird things really."

"Involving me?" Yolanda asked, again looking him straight in the eye.

Chizzie now wished he'd never mentioned it, but he had, and she deserved an answer. So, taking a deep breath, he began, "This is all from the back of my mind, you understand – stream of consciousness sort of thing, where everything and anything goes…"

"Okay, like what?"

"Well, like… like are you a plant working for your father, sent to undermine us?"

Yolanda hesitated for a moment and put down her fork before saying quietly, "Good question, Mr Bryson."

"Yes."

"And what do you think yourself?"

"Well… personally, I think never in a million years, Miss Weever."

Yolanda broke into a broad smile. "And you, Mr Bryson, are so damn right!"

More than the words, the tone seemed just right. An animal feeling of absolute trust overwhelmed Chizzie. The smile sent a bolt of exhilaration through him. Maybe he was just feeling what he wanted to feel. He fixed his eyes on hers for a moment, then, spontaneously, they both reached across the table and squeezed the other's hand.

"I just wish I could cast off this feeling of unease," continued Chizzie shaking his head. "I'm not usually gloomy like this. I really do fear I'm getting more like my dad with every passing day."

"Isn't it natural for a Scotsman to be gloomy? We're doomed, ah tell ye, doomed, and all that."

Chizzie, stifling a smile, feigned a look of reproach. "Not necessarily, my lady. Some of us like a laugh now and again. It's just that I've got this uneasy feeling for some odd reason and I can't shake it off." Chizzie felt he knew enough about life to understand that things don't normally go as smoothly as they'd gone today: "Things have gone too well, Yolanda. It's not natural. We're due a knock-back. Success is two steps forwards and one step back."

"Bryson's first law of fundynamics?"

Chizzie smiled. "Second law, actually."

"And the first?"

"Hurt nobody."

"Laudable, but a bit negative, isn't it, for a fun law?"

"It's a positive attitude. Tell me, is your father attending the games?"

"He sure would be if he thought he was certain to win, but he's made no mention of it, so I'd take that as a confidence booster. He's rarely wrong."

"Only because he flattens the opposition when he is wrong."

"Well, he won't turn up to get egg on his face, that's for sure, so take it as a positive and cheer up, Mr Bryson. And eat up too."

Chizzie pondered, staring directly at Yolanda. The sunlight shone on her face, her hair held a radiant glow, and she smiled the smile that got him every time. Suddenly, he leaned over to her: "You know, you are very, very good for me, Miss Weever; very, very, very good indeed. And you know what? I'm going to finish this haddock, and, when I've done that, I'm ordering dessert! I'm bloody ravenous!"

After dinner, Chizzie and Yolanda ambled, hand in hand, towards the south shore of the loch. They didn't expect it to be entirely trouble-free, since the breeze had dropped

317

slightly and some midges were out, but midges weren't the only trouble – earthworks were underway on the golf course near the Wibbles' camper van. Looking out for hostile moves and sensing something sinister about the works, Chizzie and Yolanda quickly agreed that she would handle this, and they headed towards the workmen.

Standing on a small grassy knoll, Yolanda beckoned to the foreman, who jumped off his digger and came over. "What's going on?" she asked.

"Mr Fairfoull wants this green reshaped for tomorrow," came the reply. "We could be working till dark."

"Leave it and go home!" Yolanda told him.

"Well, we can't do that, Miss Weever; you see, it's not up to us. It's up to Mr Fairfoull."

"It's up to me, and I'm saying leave it and go home."

The foreman blinked and puffed his cheeks. "We'll get fired, Miss Weever."

"No, you won't. I'll see to it."

The foreman thought for a moment. "Hang on," he said, beckoning to the man on the dumper truck, "Willie, have you got that phone of yours?"

"It doesn't work here," Willie answered.

"I know," said the foreman, "but it records, doesn't it?"

"Aye, it does."

"Right, Miss Weever, I need to get this on camera for Mr Fairfoull."

"Is Mr Fairfoull around?"

"No, he's gone off to one of the other villages."

"D'you know why he went?" Yolanda asked.

"A romantic evening, maybe," quipped the dumper man, with a lascivious grin.

The foreman frowned at him then turned his attention to Yolanda again. "I don't know why Mr Fairfoull went, Miss

Weever," he continued, "but if you don't mind repeating what you said, we'll finish up here now an' go home."

Yolanda happily agreed and did so, and the men – true to their word – finished up and left.

Ambling on, Chizzie and Yolanda encountered similar work being carried out next to Paw's house. This was summarily dealt with.

"Your daddy sure is a tryer," said Chizzie before they took the path to Paw's door to enquire about Sven's fitness. He knocked three times, but there was no answer.

They carried on until they arrived at the loch shore, where Chizzie and Yolanda watched an osprey try unsuccessfully to grab a fish. Then, casting their gaze along the shore, they spied three men lying on the sand next to a smouldering fire, which no doubt was keeping the midges away; each man appeared to have a very still fishing rod. As Chizzie and Yolanda approached them, two of the men sat up – they were Sven and Billy. They exchanged greetings. The third man had a tweed cap over his face, but was clearly Paw; he remained flat out.

"Conserving energy, Paw, I see," said Chizzie, smiling.

"Well, sort of," muttered Paw, moving the cap slightly from his face. "I couldn't sleep last night with all the upset in my head, then, just when I get forty winks, along comes work outside the house. Here's nice and peaceful." After removing the cap fully from his face and struggling to raise himself onto his elbows, he added, "Thanks again, Miss Weever, for getting rid of that awful earth mound."

Yolanda smiled. "No problem. It should never have happened in the first place.

"Much appreciated," Paw gasped, before falling flat on his back again. "Excuse me," he whispered, placing the tweed cap over his face.

Chizzie turned to Sven. "How're you feeling, Sven?"

"I'm good, Chizzie, real good. I've been doin' some throwin' up in the top field. I'm a bit sore now, but it's nothin' to bother me. I'm ready. I can't wait. I'm up for it. I'm feelin' like a volcano: I'm keepin' quiet and keepin' a lid on things, then – *boom* – tomorrow I explode. I'm gonna get my own back on Weever big time."

Billy nodded. "Yeah. I'm goin' with Sven. If he's restin', I'm restin'. I'm ready and I'm explodin' too. You bet your sweet ass, I am."

"Language, Billy!" came weakly through Paw's tweed cap.

"He's fired up all right," said Sven. "Good on you, Billy. We'll bloody show them!"

"Language, both of you," reiterated Paw.

"It's only locker room talk, Paw," said Sven, "We're getting psyched up."

"Keep it for tomorrow," grumbled Paw.

"You're right. You're right, Paw. We'll bottle it up, and let it build and build. That's the best way."

Billy agreed, "Yeah, buildin' it up, buildin' it up. Then booom! Boomtime!"

As the sun set behind the northern hills, Chizzie and Yolanda lingered at the estate gate before parting reluctantly. A fiery, red glow burgeoned on the rim of the northern hills, matching the glow that filled Chizzie's heart. If everything could just hold together now, he vowed he would become an eternal optimist and never again be cynical about fickle fate. It was a bit like the feeling he got when he once hit a beautiful golf shot. Though he'd never hit a shot like it again, the fact that he knew he could do it kept that particular dream alive.

By the time he arrived at the hotel steps, however, the Calvinistic guilt that clawed at his Scottish conscience began to gain the upper hand again and a feeling of unease overtook him. Things had gone too well this day, and he knew it; he just knew there would be a price to pay. There had to be. It could not be other. Perhaps the fiery glow on the northern hills was an omen telling him all that he'd won this day would go up in flames tomorrow. As sure as the astringent scent of winter hangs forever in the Scottish air, there would be a price to pay. He felt it. And it came.

Knowing that he wouldn't sleep until he felt really tired, Chizzie got himself a cocoa and sauntered through to the living room, closing the door behind him very deliberately and calmly to shut out all thoughts of the roller-coaster day and tomorrow looming. Only new and very different thoughts were allowed in this room for now – thoughts on a holiday maybe. He switched on the TV; there were many recorded programmes he'd yet to see. But, no sooner had he sat down in his comfy armchair and taken a sip, when the door opened and his father entered. Chizzie's greeting drew but a grunt from his father who, with solemn-face, handed him a sheet of paper. This was clearly not good news, and Chizzie's stomach sank. He looked at the paper, it was an email message from Lord Tulloh forwarded by Jim. It read:

Dear Jim,

I am so ashamed writing this. My first instinct was not to tell you, but, on reflection, it seemed only right to let you know.

I write from my bed in cardiology at Ninewells Hospital in Dundee. I collapsed from a mini-stroke at Dundee Airport en route to Spain. Whatever you do, though, spare no pity for me. I deserve every punishment that comes my way. My shame and sorrow are infinite, for I have gambled away your chance to own the playing field. I indulged myself, like a spoiled, gluttonous child; got drunk and played poker with that terrible man, Weever, and his people; and I lost heavily. Who would have thought it? Me, lose heavily? What an idiot! What a moron! I'm ghastly! A worthless fool! I deserve to die. Why don't they just pull the plugs? I would do it myself, but I am under constant observation here. A suicide risk, I heard them say, but enough of my despicable self-indulgence. You should know that, finally, I've wagered everything on Tannadee winning the Colonel McBraid Bequest at the Highland Games. So utterly foolish though I have been, there is yet a chance to recover the situation from my appalling blunder. If you can win the bequest, you will have the ground. I know the significance of the playing ground for everyone – it is no mere ground to our people – so I hope with all my heart that you and your wonderful team, who are so spirited and so heroic, can right the terrible wrong I have done to our community.

I am so sorry to place this heavy burden upon you. I have let you down grievously and I deserve no mercy, but if you can find it in your heart to forgive me, I can perhaps, in time, show my face in Tannadee again and do something good for once, though I assure you nothing can erase the shame that haunts me and will forever haunt me. I have been a fool nearly all of my miserable, worthless life – and worst of all is my weakness for gambling. I crave the winning high! I'm a plunger. I rush in. It's like the wind just takes me and carries me off. But I will stop. I will beat it.

With the help of Donald and good people like you, I will muster resolve and conquer the awful demon.

In boundless shame and overwhelming remorse, I wish you God speed and the strength to right my appalling wrong.

Your pitiful, weak and heart-broken friend,
Patrick

Half-stunned, Chizzie stared at the message for a moment, groaned weakly, and, putting a hand to his forehead, gasped. Words failed him, and he felt crushed by the numbness that seized him.

But Johnny had words, and he vented them: "That's it. We're stuffed. That... that... blitherin' fool has done for us. He's—"

"Hold it, Dad. Hold it," Chizzie interrupted, holding up a hand and moving towards the sofa. "We don't know the full circumstances; the poor man's devastated and he's contemplated suicide."

"And a good thing too! It's about the only thing he's ever got right! That good-for-nothing fool!"

"The poor man, Dad. For God's sake, have some pity!"

"What d'you mean 'the poor man'? It's poor us: he's sold us out! We're dead and buried, like he should be."

"He's suicidal and he's had some kind of stroke; he could've died, for God's sake."

"Frankly, I wish he would die! And quick, before Weever can call in his bet. What a pillock! What a traitor!"

"What a thing to say."

"He said himself that he deserves to die; he said it himself."

"Well, you're both wrong. His successor would likely sell to the highest bidder, and guess who that would be?"

"Well, that's sealed it then; Weever's hands are on the deeds, and we're finished. The team's wrecked. The town's wrecked. We're beat. We die!"

"We have a chance."

"Fat chance."

"As Patrick says, we can win the bequest."

"We won't win. I hate to say it, but we're beat – we won't win."

"Well, we certainly won't win if we don't believe in ourselves. I believe in us!"

"Nobody else will, that's for sure."

"What I can't believe is that you've surrendered, Dad, and without a fight."

"I'm facing the facts, that's all."

Chizzie eyed his father with a burning stare and Johnny relented finally.

"Okay, okay, you're right, you're right," he growled. "I just had to get all the burning anger out of my system. Of course I'm up for it. There's no way I'm going to let Weever walk all over us. And I'm certainly not going to let myself be sold down the river by Lord Tulloh. He's a poor man – yes, you're right – and he needs help; boy does he need help. But, God, I would so like to kick him up the effin' arse."

The next day, just after noon, Tannadee rolled out of town, heading for the McBraid Memorial Park in Oxdale where the games were to be held. Three coaches and numerous cars carried the supporters, while Jim drove a minibus to keep the team together, except for the Wibbles who travelled in their camper van. Johnny, as Tannadee's representative on the liaison committee, went ahead by car, taking Yolanda with him.

On arriving at the McBraid Memorial Park, the team found the place thronging with people.

"It's all to do with the cheap beer", opined Gavin Foskett, the long jumper, who was never a man to overestimate the human condition. It was an opinion not entirely fanciful, though, for as Chizzie stepped down from the minibus his nostrils met the faint smell of beer on the light breeze, and it was surprisingly refreshing; it seemed actually to enhance the

Highland air and the smell of the new-mown grass. And the sound of bagpipes in the air lifted his spirits as ever. Chizzie Bryson was a man firmly of the belief that Highland air was made for the pipes, just as surely as lowland air was made for chips.

It was a tight squeeze in the small changing room allocated to Tannadee, and it became all the tighter when the door flew open and in burst Denis Dekker.

"Hi there, Companions!" He bawled. "Up and at 'em!"

"Denis!" cried Chizzie, peering round the door having nearly been knocked off his feet by Dekker's dramatic arrival. "Thought you were laid low!"

"Not me! No! It was all a ruse. I've never felt better. First, let me apologise, though. I'm sorry to have deceived you all. But, you see, when I was bashed off my motorbike, I saw the culprit running away around the corner, and one of my loyal customers saw the rat – a woman, actually – get into a car and go speeding off. So, it was deliberate. Somebody was out to get me, in a stolen car. I didn't know who: it could've been anybody: another village; a bookie; even one of you guys – sorry for even thinking that, but you never know; or it could even have been another chip-shop owner, God forbid."

"It was Weever, that's who," said Chizzie.

"Maybe. Who knows? But, the thing is, I had to let them think they'd got me or who knows what might've happened. In reality, though, I've never felt better – the rest's done me a power of good. So, onwards and upwards, Companions! Onwards and upwards to victory!"

The talisman was back. Morale hit the roof. Chizzie felt glorious suddenly – like a winner in waiting.

The cheers were almost deafening: "Yahoo!"; "Right on!"; and "Bravo Denisimo!"

A very relieved-looking Ron Gillespie tossed his new wrestling kit aside and hugged Dekker like the man had just saved him from certain death.

CHAPTER 30

As team captain, Chizzie went into action as soon as his team were kitted out and in their tracksuits. He led them off to the warm-up field for some light loosening exercises. Yolanda, who had offered to be Chizzie's gofer, was already there to meet them and she greeted Chizzie with a big, wavering smile that looked like it could burst into laughter any second. And erupt it did as soon as Chizzie came up to her; she started laughing so hard she couldn't speak, every time she tried to speak she just squealed and giggled, clutching her sides. The sight of her in such paroxysms, though bewildering, was very infectious and Chizzie began to laugh too.

"What are we laughing at?" he asked.

It took nearly a minute for Yolanda to pull herself together. With a deep breath and fragile composure, she blurted out, "Wait till you see your father," and then she burst into more raucous laughter.

"How d'you mean? Is he okay?" asked Chizzie, tempering his laugh.

"Judge for yourself; here he comes. See the ancient warriors over there?"

"Yes."

"Your dad's one of them."

"What?"

"It's true," she squealed and covered her mouth to gag her laughter.

"What's he doing there?"

Yolanda, wiping her eyes with her handkerchief, steadied herself and took a deep breath. "He's in the battle re-enactment. The McFassills were a man short so your dad volunteered."

"Oh my God! What's he thinking? For heaven's sake! I have to talk him out of it before it's too late."

"I think it's already too late."

And it was. When Chizzie hailed his dad and ran over to him, Johnny was smiling broadly and looking supremely satisfied with himself. On his head he wore a large, purple Highland bonnet with an eagle feather clasped to it, and the rest of him, except for one bare shoulder, was covered by a large plaid held by a broad leather belt round his waist. On his legs were thick, grey socks, each fitted with a skein dhu, and on his feet were things that looked like moccasins.

For a moment, Chizzie was speechless. Wide-eyed, he exclaimed, "Wha... what on earth do you think you're doing? You look absolutely ridiculous."

Johnny's smile dropped indignantly. "I'm having fun, that's what I'm doing. I thought you were all for more fun. I thought you'd be pleased to see me joining in the battle re-enactment. You said I needed to get more fun, and that's exactly what I'm doing. The McFassills were a man short, so I volunteered for them. Yolanda thought I looked the part. She even took my picture and said I looked very special."

"What battle re-enactment are you talking about?"

"The Battle of the Tooth. It's in the programme. Didn't you look? It's a bit of local culture before the games start. The Olympic Games has its opening ceremony, and we've got ours: 'Highlanders Through The Ages.'"

"I knew that was happening, but I didn't know there was a battle re-enactment and that you'd be in it."

"We're the action – the local heritage. You don't know the Battle of the Tooth?"

"Of course I know it. I just didn't expect to see you up to the neck in it!"

"Well, now, you're going to see it happen before your very eyes, and you're in for a treat. It's going to be great."

"I hope you're not wielding weapons?"

"Just a rubber thing. I'm a rookie. Other guys have steel swords, but they're all blunt. We just make it look real with our enthusiasm."

"Oh my God; no, no, no, you don't, Dad, not you. I know you. I know your enthusiasm. Rubber or not, you're not losing to anybody."

"I knew it, I knew it; as soon as I try to have a bit of harmless fun, you're down on me. It's all right you having fun – yes, fine, good thing that – but when it comes to the old man it's, 'Stop! What d'you think you're doing, you daft old bugger?' Well hear this: everybody – including people of my age, surprising as it might seem to you – needs to let off steam now and again, and that's just what we're doing. Basically, we're just swinging till we're knackered, and, let's face it, that won't take long, they're mostly all couch potatoes. They need the exercise, and if this gets them off their backsides, it can only be a good thing. And the beauty of it is that it's completely natural. It's the old hunter-clobberer thing. Everybody wants to be Rob Roy at some time or other. It's going to be great. It's the dream workout! And it's fun, fun, fun!"

"Slaughtering each other is fun?"

"You know, for a fun-loving guy you're sounding awfully pc these days," Johnny complained.

"You say it's life-enhancing; it's actually life-threatening! That's what it is," insisted Chizzie.

"Geoff McLogan thinks it's a great thing, and he's a lawyer."

Chizzie shook his head. "'Course he thinks it's a great thing. He gets all the lawsuits for bust teeth, broken jaws, double vision, hernias, and all the other things that meet the walloped and counted out. It's a goldmine for him!"

"We're all insured, for God's sake!" moaned an exasperated Johnny. "It's no more than you get playing rugby or American football. This is what people want. Everybody's dying to clout somebody out there. It's in the blood, it's human and it's perfectly natural! Look at the MacDonalds and the Campbells, for starters – get them together and you'd get a real ding-dong! Burgers versus soups! And, the fact is, our show is all stage-managed. It's very authentic, and I've been shown what to do."

"Authentic? I didn't know Celtic football club was around in the sixteenth century."

"How d'you mean?"

"That guy there, he's wearing Celtic football socks, and shin pads. That doesn't augur well for authenticity or safety."

"He's probably just got varicose veins or something. Authentic as possible is what it is. Stop nit-picking, will you?"

"Are you wearing anything underneath?"

"None of your business."

"Father, you're a hotelier. Hoteliers do not go around whacking customers and exposing themselves."

"I've got shorts on!"

"You could paint your face blue, then nobody'd know who you are."

"Right, that's it!" Johnny retorted. "We're moving off. See you later."

And off Johnny went, shaking his head.

"Remember, keep the heid, Father," shouted Chizzie. *"You're not Rob Roy, you're a hotelier! No customers, no hotel!"*

A rousing medley of pipe tunes entertained the crowd until the games chairman, Frank Tosh, got to his feet and bade them all welcome, and then he prattled on and on and on, clearly in love with the sound of his own voice booming out over the packed showground. When his speech finally finished, and the VIPs had been introduced, the official opening ceremony was announced, and 'Highlanders Through The Ages' began.

Rams' horns blared and the Picts began walking about and painting each other blue. Next, the Romans appeared, carrying bricks and drainage pipes – signs of civilisation. Then it was the turn of the Gaels, who were hairy and punchy, noisy and bewigged. They departed, and in came the Vikings, who bounced about and were all very lively, mean-looking devils, growling like chain smokers deprived of their ciggies; then they cleared off for a smoke. Finally, the sound of a harp rent the air, clean and wholesome; Saint Columba entered carrying a big cross; monks sang; and folk were converted. The crowd applauded.

And then it was the big one: the Battle of the Tooth. The warriors entered cockily and took up their positions. Johnny was indistinguishable from the others of his troupe, for which Chizzie gave much thanks privately.

The crowd was hushed and the re-enactment got underway. It was a night-time scene, and the McFassills were seen sleeping peacefully beside some calves tethered in the middle of the arena. Then on came the McGooles, a gust of wind confirmed they were in authentic costume – no underpants. They sneaked up to reclaim their cattle, as they saw it, or steal the things as the McFassills saw it. In truth, so much rustling went on in the sixteenth century that it was almost like pass the parcel, and the cattle were almost permanently dizzy with all the travelling. So, there were the McGooles, sneaking up to reclaim their cattle with hardly a sound, and they were almost away with the livestock when, suddenly, an insomniac McFassill leaped to his feet and went berserk on the clanger. The clansmen lay into each other with enthusiasm. There was a script, but it was very soon out the window, and nobody was going down – everybody was a hero. The pace got faster and faster, and they were going at each other like their lives depended on it. Johnny was lost in the melee. It was almost as good as the original. Very soon the participants were red, bruised and lashing out like madmen.

The crowd loved it. "Fabulous entertainment!" opined one blue-rinse near to Chizzie.

But Chizzie was thinking somebody had got to do something there.

And, at last, in came Sergeant Mackay and PC Tunnock. They strode onto the battleground, blowing their whistles and informing the panting participants it was all over. Enough was enough. The participants objected vehemently. The policemen took out their notebooks and pencils, they were having none of it. The crowd whistled, booed and shouted things. It was ugly. Mackay and Tunnock consulted each other quickly and decided to let everyone off with a stern finger-wagging. A semblance of pride and dignity was thus maintained, even if some of the participants had clearly left most of their share on the turf. The clansmen took their leave, many limping and some requiring support from colleagues, and all, to a man, trading insults and trying to look proud even as the bruises swelled and turned horrible colours. It's not about how much damage you inflict, it's about how much you can thole: that's the mark of a man in these parts.

While Weever's security team covered the stairway and stood ready to ply him with his favourite popcorn, a steward in full Highland outfit conducted Weever and Fairfoull to their seats in the VIP section of the grandstand.

An elderly man in a dark uniform and military cap rose stiffly from the seat next to Weever's and offered his hand: "Ah, Mr Weever I presume," he said, "we meet at last. Welcome. So good of you to step in at the last minute."

"My pleasure, Lord Lieutenant. Glad to help out," replied Weever.

"That's Lord Leftenant," returned the man, correcting Weever's American pronunciation.

"Whatever. It's a great honour to be with you today, sir."

They shook hands heartily and sat down.

"The name's Sir Hew Hawkshaw," said the Lord Lieutenant. "Do call me Hew," and, pointing to the woman on his right, he added, "and this is my wife, Lady Hawkshaw."

The lady nodded and smiled towards Weever. She looked about ten years younger than her husband, and seemed to consolidate his position by exuding an air of quiet refinement and self-imposed discipline. Her beige jacket and skirt, and her wide-brimmed bonnet, portrayed a confident yet practical nature.

After exchanging pleasantries, Weever introduced Fairfoull.

"Now, we have a sort of table service here," said Sir Hew, "so if you'd like a refreshment or some nibbles, do let me know and I'll call over the valet-type chappie. That's him over there. Oh, he's coming over. Fancy a G&T, a gin and tonic?"

"Well, it's a bit early really, but we are in the Highlands, so what the hell; I'll have a scotch, a single malt," requested Weever.

The steward took the order and retreated to get their drinks.

Ten minutes later, with three G&Ts inside him, Sir Hew was chattering away relentlessly while Weever affected an air of pleasant abandon, until, suddenly, a loud boom on the tannoy brought the games to life.

Frank Tosh on the mic introduced Weever as the honorary deputy Chieftain of the Games. The announcement received a mixed reception: some cheering and some booing.

"It's the price of fame," Weever explained. "Losers, they don't like me. People who know me, they like me. They really like me, and they'll like me even more when I become a clan chief real soon."

"Oh, jolly good. Which clan, if I might ask?"

"Clan McShellach."

"And where do they hold out?"

"Here. They're local."

"Oh. How very handy for you. Here's my card," said the Lord Lieutenant, presenting an ornately embossed example in flowing copperplate.

Weever scanned the card. "Hawkshaw – that's a fine name," he said politely, without offering his own card.

"It's not the real spelling, I have to say," said Sir Hew, reaching into his breast pocket and taking out another card. "Here, look – here's an older card with the real spelling. I had to change it, it was causing too much confusion. I keep the older ones for people who can handle it."

Weever examined the older card, then read out the name Hardwicksaughton letter by letter. "That's Hawkshaw?" he asked.

"Yes, that's it – Hawkshaw; that's the true spelling."

"It's nothing like it."

"It's not meant to be. That's how it is in the countryside. It keeps the wrong people at bay, so to speak. You see, if a stranger pronounces one's name correctly, one knows they're one of us and they're not just any old hoi polloi off the street, so to speak." At which, he laughed in a brittle, defensive tone. "Townies don't understand the countryside, you see. We have a community unlike theirs. We're in it together, but apart. We keep to ourselves, yet we are one. It is we who shaped the land."

"I see," said Weever, not seeing.

The crowd was buzzing by then; it was whipped up and ready for the next humdinger. But Chizzie was anxious. His father had been in the thick of the melee and it looked like he was one of the walking wounded. So, as the public address system announced the parade of the athletes, Chizzie was caught in two minds: should he lead out his team as planned or go looking for his father? Quickly, he decided to lead out the team and get Jim to find out if Johnny was okay. Putting Johnny's condition to the back of his mind, he focussed on the job at hand and got his team to line up behind the Ardnavale team, which was a proud moment for Chizzie.

Then came a terrible turn of events: just as the Ardnavale team stepped away into the arena and were introduced to the crowd, Bob McDee broke ranks suddenly and ran towards the changing rooms.

"What's up with Bob?" Chizzie asked anxiously.

"He's got the shits!" replied Dekker. "He tried like hell to hold it in, but he just couldn't. I think... I think we're one down, Chizzie."

Chizzie froze; pride drained from him like he was a gutter. But Tannadee were summoned, the public address called their name, and their supporters and their fellow villagers cheered and applauded to greet their proud men. Their proud men, sickened and saddened to the core suddenly, had to rally there and then.

Chizzie bit his lip, then – pushing a smile across his face – he reached for the pole with Tannadee's banner on it and held it high. "Companions, forward!" he cried. "We can win yet! Forward Tannadee!"

And out they marched, smiling bravely and waving to their people – nine men ready for action and one in the toilet.

With the parade completed, Chizzie rushed immediately to the changing room to find out what condition Bob McDee was in. It was just possible, to Chizzie's mind, that he could swap events with him; Bob would run the half-mile and Chizzie would tackle the hill race; this situation was far from ideal, but probably the best option available. The news, however, was dire.

Through the toilet door, Bob confided, "Fifty yards, that's it! That's all I could manage. The half-mile is completely out, unless they halt the race for comfort breaks. I'm really sorry, Chizzie. I'm crushed and gutted. I can't understand it. I just followed my normal routine, doing nothing out of the ordinary. I ate what I normally eat... oh, except for one thing – I had an energy bar. I got it from Barrington. I was peckish and feeling a wee bit drained, sort of, you know. But not half as drained as I feel now. It was nerves, really. You'll need to excuse me, Chizzie. I think... I think I'm off again. Yep! Here we go!"

Chizzie left hurriedly, and headed back to the team to convey the grim news and make sure everybody avoided Barrington's energy bars, or – for that matter – anything else from Barrington. Before he got there, though, a hand pulled at his shoulder: it was Yolanda.

"I hear you need a runner, captain," she said, smiling with a determined look on her face.

"You?" Chizzie queried.

"Me."

"No, Yolanda," Chizzie replied with a firm but apologetic smile.

"No, no, not the hill race."

"I'm a woman, is that it?"

"Well... sort of... yeah... well, no, actually; that was just my reflex reaction, but it's wrong – of course it is. But there is a good reason: that hill can be dangerous, not everyone that goes up there comes down a happy bunny; you have to know your way around. And this is Scotland – sunny one minute and stormy the next."

"Then you do the hill race, as you're wearing your trail-running shoes, and I'll do your race, the half-mile. I'm fit for anything. You know I am. I've done it all: strength work, endurance, the lot. I'm the fittest person you've got."

Chizzie blinked and thought for a moment. Yolanda wouldn't lie about her ability or risk personal embarrassment through losing badly in front of thousands. Eyeing her again, Chizzie asked quietly, "Have you got your kit?"

"I sure have," she replied. "I thought I might have a run round the track when it's all over, to see what it feels like, so I've come prepared. I can change in the dancers' changing room."

Without a further word, Chizzie grabbed her in his arms and kissed her. "You beauty, Yolanda," he whispered. "You absolute beauty. We'll get you registered."

As they approached the officials' tent, two familiar figures appeared out of the milling throng; they were Johnny and Jim. To Chizzie's great relief and surprise, his father looked none the worse for his battle experience – a little red in the cheeks, and complaining about the itchiness of the plaid he'd worn, but otherwise quite unaffected.

"Hail the great warrior, fresh from the field of battle!" cried Jim, smiling and clapping Johnny on the back.

"It's good to see you in one piece, Father!" said Chizzie. "I thought for one desperate minute you were one of the walking wounded."

"No fear," replied Johnny. "I got cornered once, but I just let fly with my war cry and they scattered pronto."

"Your war cry?" asked Chizzie.

"Smallpox!" One yell and they took off as fast as their hairy legs could take them.

Chizzie explained how they'd lost their hill runner and that Yolanda would run in the half-mile.

Johnny fastened on to the Barrington energy bar right away. "He's laced it – I bet you; he's put syrup of figs or something in it."

Jim responded immediately. "Whoa there, Johnny, not so fast. There's no proof the energy bar had anything to do with it. It could be a hundred things. Nobody at the school would stoop that low. I'll vouch for him."

Johnny clearly wasn't satisfied, but his respect for Jim kept him quiet. Together, they went into the officials' tent to register their new runner. The officials were a traditional bunch who were used to being absolute rulers on the local Highland Games circuit, and Chizzie knew the likely reaction to Yolanda's application, so it was heartening to have Jim and Johnny with him.

The official – a weather-beaten, white-haired man – was seated behind a kitchen table. At first, he ignored them, reading the contents of a note before handing it to the man standing beside him. As expected, when Chizzie explained the Tannadee team's position to the official, his first reaction was complete silence and a look of puzzlement; it was as though he'd just been asked the exchange rate between the pound sterling and the Mongolian tögrög. Then, following a glance at the man standing beside him, the official moved his lips. "You're a woman," he observed with a frown.

Yolanda flushed slightly and flashed a look that told Chizzie she was struggling to restrain herself from giving a reply the official would never forget. "I am indeed," she replied stiffly but politely.

"Of the female gender," quipped Johnny.

The official looked uncertain for a moment, seemingly unsure as to whether he was receiving extra information or contempt. "We can't have a woman," he replied frostily. "The events are strictly for gentlemen."

Johnny leaned forwards. "If the events are strictly for gentlemen, half the bloody competitors would be out on their ear – half of them don't even know what a gentlemen looks like."

Chizzie knew he had only seconds to deal with the official before either Yolanda blew, Johnny blew or, possibly, both blew. "Nowhere does it say the competitor has to be a man," Chizzie insisted.

"In that case," broke in the man beside the official, "my team's entering a horse."

Jim was quick to reason. "If your horse can sign his name and outline his family connection with the area, fine, he's in. Other than that, he's out."

"And he'll need shorts," added Johnny. "We're not having competitors running about bare arsed, even if it's a habit in your neck of the woods."

"I have shorts," said Yolanda, "and I have a direct connection with the area, apart from having a house here." She reached into the inner pocket of her jacket and handed a copy of her family tree to the official: "All verified by a reputable genealogist, you'll find."

The official took the copy and examined it carefully. Then, finally, with undisguised reluctance, he pushed a form across the table to Yolanda and mumbled, "Fill that in."

While Yolanda hurried off to get changed, Chizzie made his way quickly back to the warm-up field and arrived in time to hear the athletes being called for the first event on the programme – it was the one-mile race. The fateful hour had arrived. The vital contest was suddenly underway. Nervousness shot through Chizzie like an electrical storm.

CHAPTER 31

At the one-mile race starting line, the runners assembled and were introduced over the public address system. But, as soon as the introductions were over, out of the blue, there was an altercation. The Garthbay runner, who was clearly unhappy about something, was seen arguing with his team manager. The runner had stepped back from the line and was seemingly refusing to run. The starter simply ignored him, though – there was no pussyfooting – and he called the runners to the line. Then the Garthbay team manager whipped out some banknotes, which his runner snatched ungratefully and shoved inside his shorts, and he joined the others poised on the line.

Bang! Off went the gun, and away they went. Dave Dalrymple, the Tannadee man, raced into the lead. Quickly, though, he seemed to have second thoughts. Chizzie, an experienced middle-distance man himself, knew exactly what Dave was thinking: *There's no way I'm going out there to be the hare, I'm not leading all the way and dying in the home straight. No more of that for me! I'm staying with the pack; I'm going to bide my time and then go flat out in the last lap, the others ain't so hot.*

So, round they went, in a bunch. The ground was uneven and cattle-trodden, and the grass was quite long and produced a faint swishing sound as the runners went by. Dalrymple was clearly trying to focus and trying to save himself for the final lap, but he was agitated. He frequently looked behind him at the Garthbay man, who seemed to be muttering.

341

Chizzie listened in as they went by and caught snippets from the Garthbay runner: "Forty quid! A measly forty quid!" he muttered judderingly. "They promised a hundred! The bastards! The bastards!"

It wasn't difficult to see why Dalrymple was agitated. It must have been like he was being followed by a radio broadcasting a phone-in show. Dalrymple moved to the front of the pack, getting away from the "Forty quid! Forty measly quid!" And he was looking good. Until, suddenly, he looked alarmed.

Chizzie, in turn, looked alarmed: it was looking like one of Dalrymple's dreaded afflictions had struck. Which one was it? Most likely, the squeaking knee. "What's up?" Chizzie asked as Dalrymple went by the next time.

"Nothing," replied Dalrymple tautly. He was no fool: he wasn't giving away information likely to be useful to an enemy. He shook his arms, trying to relax and to pretend the squeak wasn't there, but the intermittent outbursts of "Forty measly quid!" and "Bastards" were clearly getting to him. He increased his pace a little, but his look of alarm got worse: the squeaking was seemingly getting louder.

As they took the bend at the end of the third lap, Dalrymple lengthened his stride while maintaining the same cadence. He sailed into the back straight – with the squeaking not so pronounced by then apparently, or maybe starting to come and go a bit – he was beginning to look quite comfortable; he even treated himself to a good look round. The crowd were excited and clearly up for it, he could see them gesticulating, though he probably couldn't hear them for the sound of his own juddering breath, and the heavy pattering and panting behind him.

Then suddenly his expression changed: it looked like goodbye to alarm and hullo to feeling tremendous. He'd cracked it finally, he'd found the elusive formula! He began winding up, preparing to make the big move off the next bend. He was going to stretch them out and burn them all off.

Then, whack! A spiked shoe struck his heel. He stumbled, staggered and fell. Sprawling in a crazy jumble, he looked like a heap of failed scaffolding. His mouth bit the turf and took a soil sample. It was a taste of Scotland no one wants, but it sprung Dalrymple into a frenzy, he leaped back onto his feet and galloped off after the pack muttering, "Bastards! Bastards!"

His great hurtling strides brought gasps from the crowd. The crowd was going wild; he could hear them and probably even feel them, as they were yelling out loud and pointing. The pointing didn't help, though; it could've meant something had popped out of his shorts. He eyed his crotch. But there was only one thing on his mind by then, and that was, *Bastards!* He was really going after them and soaring round the final bend, with his huge ground-gobbling strides eating space like it was manna for legs.

It was the other runners who were glancing round by then, and when they saw what was coming, they panicked like sheep before a wolf. They jostled and elbowed each other as Dalrymple came up close on their tails.

As he came upon them, he took a big breath and bawled, "Bastards!"

The others jolted, the one at the front stumbled and collided with the man behind him, and down they went. The next man clipped those two, staggered a bit, lost his balance and down he went. By then, they were all down bar Dalrymple.

By the time they got to their feet, Dalrymple was fifteen yards out in front, and there's just fifty yards to go. The sudden realisation of it seemed to hit him as he looked round, it checked his stride for a second and he jolted clumsily.

By then, the crowd were in a frenzy – only one thing could excite them more, and that was blood. And they could get it – the blood vessels on Dalrymple's temples were just about popping out.

With thirty yards to go, a mere thirty yards, it happened: he hit the dreaded 'wall', and away went his energy like it was sucked out by a vacuum cleaner. It was all in the mind by then; his heart was screaming, "Get me out of here!"; his ears were ringing like alarm bells; his arms were tingling like they were wired to the electricity grid; and his legs were buckling like they were made of chains. There was nothing left but what was in his head, and even that was threatening to say goodnight; everything was a blur.

He looked round, and there was a shape right behind him: the Garthbay man! The Tannadee man groaned. Desperately, he threw his head back and flailed every sinew; his limbs were going up and down, and in and out; his head was going from side to side; and he was staggering. But the line loomed nearer, ever so near, so to be robbed now would be so cruel. He hung on desperately and somehow his feet got him there. He was over the line! He was first! He'd done it! He'd won! Victory was his, all his.

Completely and utterly shattered, Dalrymple fell over like a man shot with a blunderbuss. The St Andrew's Ambulance people were on him right away, and they caught him halfway down. For a moment, he was hanging like a suspension bridge collapsed in a hurricane. Then, very, very gently, they lifted his remains upright, and he was walked up and down to ease his aching muscles and scalded lungs. A path was cleared for him as the stewards pushed back the hundreds of spectators craving his picture and autograph.

A press crew bawled questions at him, but all he seemed fit for was fainting, until in bounced Johnny Bryson, blowing cigar smoke everywhere, and the stricken Dalrymple went from white to green as he groaned for air. But Johnny's insistence that everything be channelled through him took the focus off Dalrymple, and the athlete staggered away in the confusion.

Heading for the changing rooms beneath the stand, he was ambushed again by the ambulance people, who hauled him off to their casualty tent, and they went to work on him with ice packs, while the good ladies of the RVS tried to get some tea down him. But it wasn't his kind of tea, and he was trying desperately to fend everybody off when Chizzie arrived and got the hounds off him.

After a brief discussion, Dalrymple agreed to remain under supervision for a while, provided his only attendant was the gentle, young ambulance lady who seemed to enjoy taking his temperature and pulse as much as he was enjoying her taking it. Perhaps Dalrymple's racing pulse had won him something greater than he could ever have expected from racing a country mile. He was both a winner today and for evermore.

CHAPTER 32

"I know you'll fit in very nicely here," Sir Hew went on. "We're very accommodating. We've all kinds here. We've even got an anti-monarchist."

Weever raised his eyebrows in polite surprise.

"And he's gay," Sir Hew confided.

Weever smiled mechanically.

"And proud of it," came a voice very near.

"See what I mean?" declared Sir Hew. "All kinds. On top of that, he's my son."

"Oh dear. Where is he?" asked Weever.

"Right behind you," confirmed Sir Hew's son.

A look of 'oh my God' crossed Weever's face and he smiled bravely, until a hand thrust itself over his shoulder and nearly whacked his face.

"Crispin Hawkshaw," said the owner of the hand, "pleased to meet you."

Weever turned slightly, feigning stiffness in the neck, and gave the hand more of a rattle than a shake. "Do you have other sons?" Weever asked Sir Hew.

"No, three daughters and just the one... sort of... boy," explained Sir Hew.

"He's not a 'sort of' boy," hissed Lady Hawkshaw.

"He's not a boy. He's a man," insisted Crispin.

"He's in films, you know, Mr Weever," added Lady Hawkshaw proudly. "He's a movie actor."

"Sort of," counselled Sir Hew.

"What d'you mean 'sort of' again?" asked his wife.

"Well, look at his parts," Sir Hew answered.

"No, thank you," whispered Weever cheekily to Fairfoull.

"He never gets lines," continued Sir Hew. "As Sleepy Homo Erectus, all he did was grunt. As Mincing Menswear Assistant, all he did was mince. As Obstreperous Dinosaur, he—"

"I've had lines!" Crispin cried.

"Yes, he did," affirmed Lady Hawkshaw. "He had lines as Talking Gall Bladder."

"Government information films don't count," replied Sir Hew. "In any case, the other organs got all the limelight. Even Large Intestine got more words."

Weever, munching popcorn, grimaced, "Please, I've just had my lunch, if you don't mind."

"I do beg your pardon," said Sir Hew. "We're not normally like this."

"Yes, we are," bawled a child sitting behind Lady Hawkshaw, who agreed with a sigh.

Indicating the two boys behind him, Sir Hew introduced them: "My nephews – Ludo and Archie. Actually, I call them Vesuvius and Etna, you never know when they'll blow and what'll shoot out. Talking of shooting, I hear you're organising shooting parties. We'll fit in very nicely, there are only six of us. We'll see to your crows, buzzards and that sort of thing, of course." He tapped his nose.

Weever and Fairfoull exchanged a sidelong look of alarm.

CHAPTER 33

Next, it was muscle time. Into the arena came the heavy men – the hammer throwers – among them Sven Johansen for Tannadee. Displaying their big biceps and swinging their kilts, they swaggered along to the sound of Tina Turner's 'Simply the Best' on the public address speakers. Some of the womenfolk screamed. Their husbands and boyfriends smiled meekly and self-consciously, but then someone mentioned Dalrymple and they perked up again. The 'heavies' were introduced one by one. The biggest cheer was for Sven, Tannadee's own Viking Hitman. After the introductions, the big boys loosened up, each with his own old-style Highland hammer, which is essentially a pickaxe handle with a small cannonball on the end, like a big lollipop.

The first to throw is the Tottiepans beefcake or, more accurately, the Tottiepans pork scratchings, since he was a bit paler than the others. He stepped towards the throwing circle, lifting his feet carefully to avoid stabbing the ground with the traditional spike jutting like a knife from the toe of each shoe. In the circle, he stubbed his toe-spikes into the turf, got the firm grip he wanted, lifted up the hammer, whirled it with all his might and threw it a respectable seventy feet – respectable for pork scratchings, that is.

Then on came the Findandie man, who was something of a frankfurter. He took the lead with a throw of eighty-four feet, which brought a murmur of approval from the crowd.

348

Sven, the prime steak of the afternoon, entered the circle after that and began clapping rhythmically to the crowd; he wanted them clapping too. They responded immediately, clapping faster and faster towards a crescendo; even the grandstand began jumping, as its ageing timbers, substantially lightened by woodworm, took up the rhythm. Sven swung and swung, the pace quickened, the volume rose, and Sven released the hammer. Up it went, sailing through the air – it carried for a sizzling ninety-two feet. The crowd roared and applauded. A sporadic chant of, "Sven! Sven!" went up from the crowd. Delighted, Sven skipped a step or two, and applauded the crowd before making way for the next man.

Up next it was the Garthbay man, a guy looking rather like a rissole, who entered the circle quickly. He whirled the hammer rapidly and sent it swiftly high into the air, soaring past every other throw to over one hundred feet – one hundred and six feet to be exact. The crowd gasped; the people were stunned. Sven couldn't believe it; he himself had never thrown that distance in his life. It had been a cherished dream all his adult life to get over the magic one hundred, but only the very best ever get there. And here, here was a rissole bursting through the barrier before his very eyes.

The other throwers couldn't believe it either; they looked at each other, their eyebrows raised and their expressions saying, "Dope test?" or "Light hammer?". However, who would dare be so foolhardy or so crass as to approach the guy and voice those doubts? The answer to that was no one, so they smiled politely and joined in the applause of the crowd. To the Highland heavy there is only one thing worse than cheating, and that is impugning a man's honour without iron-clad proof – you only ever do that once. The guys knew this, so no one said a word.

Nevertheless, the Garthbay guy was nursing his hammer awfully close and keeping well away from everyone.

In the second throw, the two guys before Sven – the pork scratchings and the frankfurter – threw even shorter than their earlier attempts, no doubt demoralised by the suspicion they felt but couldn't reveal.

But Sven was fired up, he has no doubts: he knows clearly that the Garthbay man was cheating. He was fired up more than ever. He got the crowd clapping again, and they took up the rhythm fervently and they drove him on. He stomped up and down the circle, then he took up his throwing position, dug his toes in firmly, looked at the one-hundred-feet distance marker, glared at it, spat on his hands, took up his hammer, and whirled it and whirled it and whirled it, as the crowd reached a crescendo. Sven released the hammer into the air with a mighty throw and a yell like a rutting stag, the crowd roared and some screamed as the hammer soared. It was a big one, and the crowd knew it. High the hammer sailed, higher than his previous throw, and when it descended in a graceful arc then hit the ground – it was past one hundred feet! The crowd cheered wildly, and some women screamed. Sven jumped in the air: he was delirious – he'd done it! He was a one-hundred-feet man! It was one hundred feet and nine inches to be exact, a tremendous personal best. But, of course, it still wasn't enough to win. When the realisation of this dawned on the crowd, an eerie silence fell over the place, the sound went down like a sigh from a dying beast.

Then it was announced that the Garthbay man had declined a second throw; apparently, he'd strained his shoulder. Murmurs went up, and a cloud of suspicion hung in the air. The Garthbay thrower's coach remonstrated with his man and, finally, persuaded him to throw again. So, the big guy got back in the circle amid a hum of excitement. He rubbed his shoulder so that everyone knew what a martyr he was, and brave as they come, but he couldn't resist a little dig at Sven. He copied Sven's routine: he fixed his eyes on the one-hundred-feet mark, spat on his hands and thumped his toes into the ground.

His coach appealed for clapping from the crowd, but he got almost nothing, so he shouted, "Garthbay! Garthbay!"

The Garthbay people responded immediately and worked up some clapping for their man.

The big man swung his hammer as swiftly as before, and as swiftly as before it flew through the air, roared on by the Garthbay fans. It was a big one, for sure: it went over the one-hundred-feet mark again! The Garthbay fans roared even louder when the distance was announced: one hundred feet and eleven inches! Again, it was further than Sven's best. The big man took the plaudits from his people and, thanking the crowd like Sven did, he tried a little skip, but he stumbled over his toe-spikes and nearly came a cropper. Then, he walked off, waving, but remembered just in time to rub his shoulder and produce a grimace to hide his obvious pain.

The crowd soon cut the chatter and settled themselves for the reappearance of Sven. The Tannadee people, the women especially, are primed and ready, but there's no Sven. A murmur of bewilderment rose and it grew louder.

Chizzie was as puzzled as anybody, and rushed over to the throwers' area and looked about. There was no sign of Sven. Chizzie called his name, but there was no response. The word 'booze' crossed his mind: Had the worst happened? Had his man despaired and hit the bottle?

A chant went up: "Sven! Sven!"

Then, at the far end, just as the Garthbay coach stepped forwards to collect his man's hammer, Sven got in before him and whipped the hammer away. The coach tried to grab it, but Sven made off with it and ran over to the one-hundred-and-ten-feet marker. He yelled for people at the far end, the throwing circle end, to get out of the way. Chizzie, sensing a drunken disaster, was the first to respond and ushered people away from the throwing-circle area. Sven looked at the throwing circle in the distance, dug his feet in, swung the hammer rapidly round his ears three times, then – with a furious swish – it leaped away, high into the air. The crowd gasped, and the hammer flew. It was going, going and going; further and further it flew. People scattered from the throwing area and beyond. Then, gradually, down the hammer came, and, when it hit the ground finally, it was a mighty distance: it was ten feet past the throwing circle!

The Tannadee people roared and applauded; some started chanting, "Sven! Sven!" Others, knowing the significance of the throw, started chanting, "Cheat! Cheat!"

The significance had not escaped Chizzie; he stepped in quickly to take the hammer, and walked off with it, taking it to old Arthur Shillinglaw – the chief official for throwing events – and demanding to see it weighed again. As the crowd buzzed like a bee hive, the hammer was duly weighed – and, yes, it was light!

The Garthbay man's throws were declared null and void immediately, but no official called the man a cheat, that would taint the whole event and – even worse – bring in the lawyers.

However, the good folk of Tannadee were not ducking it: the word 'cheat' hit the air all around the ground.

Ushered by his skulking coach, the Garthbay man slunk off to a waiting Land Rover full of green wellies and two gundogs, and they drove off quickly out of the ground.

The chants of, "Sven! Sven!" were now all over the ground, but not for long, for then it was announced that Sven's throws also had been ruled invalid on account of his dangerous and ungentlemanly conduct.

Chizzie, unusually excited by the superhuman efforts of his men, yelled to Shillinglaw, "Is there no justice? That man's hammer was light and my man's just exposed him!"

But Shillinglaw and his team were adamant; they're hill farmers and they've had their fill of townie types – they won't budge. But, importantly, Sven is not actually disqualified and he still has one throw left.

After the other throwers had given their all to no improvement, Sven stepped into the circle, dug his toes firmly into the turf, looked up and glared at the one-hundred-feet marker.

The Tannadee people and the tourists are roaring and clapping like demons, though the Garthbay people are stubbornly silent and willing him to fail.

Sven spat on his hands and took up the hammer. He started to swing, and the hammer swirled round and round and round; gathering up all his anger, all his pride and all his lifelong dreams, he combined them into one mighty vortex. He was whirling like a propeller, spinning and spinning; then, bursting free, the hammer shot from his hands and it zipped away into the air. Up, up and up it went, accompanied by the gasps of the crowd; higher and higher it hurtled, like a comet towards the brilliant sun. Sven shaded his eyes and roared it on. The yelling supporters urged it on too. It seemed right at home in the air. Then it began to descend majestically in a long, beautiful arc, until – near the ground – it wiggled and waggled, then dipped finally and hit the ground with a thump. There was a moment's hush, and then a mighty roar – it was over the one-hundred-feet mark! There was no doubt about it.

"One hundred and one feet two inches!" declared the judge excitedly over his megaphone, his heart clearly keen on justice.

The crowd were delirious – and all for five pounds gate money, with children under sixteen getting in free and youths paying two pounds.

But Sven was in tears; he was applauding his public, many of whom were also in tears. Some excited young women spilled onto the track, and started dancing up and down. Sven covered his eyes, then wiped his face with both hands.

Chizzie, with the hairs on the back of his neck still standing, rushed up to his man and threw a towel over him, as much to hide his own tears as Sven's. They knew the hand of posterity had touched that humble field that day – this day of days, a day set to glow forever, not just in the mind of one athlete, but also in the minds of all those who witnessed the great event and saw with their very own eyes the extraordinary power of an ordinary man with a wound in his heart, passion in his soul and right in his head.

CHAPTER 34

Sir Hew squinted his eyes. "I say, isn't the muscly chap who won the hammer the lad you just about shot?"

Weever grunted.

"I'm rather glad you didn't, actually. I've a small wager on Tannadee – I drew them in our little sweepstake. I thought I'd got a real bummer, frankly, but turns out they're looking jolly good value, don't you think?"

Weever gave another grunt.

"Do you have a small wager on?"

"Er... no."

Fairfoull changed the subject quickly, "Quite a dancer, that one in red."

"Yeah," replied Weever, "strong thighs, very firm and very fit. Nice. There might be a place for her with us, Charlie."

"PR maybe?" suggested Fairfoull.

Weever nodded. "Yeah, note that."

"Hayley McTaggart, that is," said Sir Hew. "She used to be even livelier before the bought-in udders."

"Udders?" queried Weever.

"Boob job," Sir Hew stated.

"She had breast implants," explained Lady Hawkshaw, shaking her head.

"It slows her down; it must do, all that on her chest. It's like a week's shopping," said Sir Hew.

"She was in the newspaper again recently," said Lady Hawkshaw.

"I remember that," replied Sir Hew. "Very open about her boobs, she was."

"What? She showed her boobs?" asked Weever.

"No, no. She said the big boobs gave her new confidence following her terrible experience on holiday," said Sir Hew.

"Her mother collapsed in Poundland," explained Lady Hawkshaw.

"Mortified, absolutely mortified the old dear would've been if anyone knew she'd been in Poundland."

"Let alone died in it."

"So, Hayley hauled her mother along to Waitrose, where she could die with dignity, apparently."

"She didn't expire, though; the air in Waitrose brought her round."

"As I say, we're a mixed bunch in the countryside," concluded Sir Hew.

While the huge tumult caused by the hammer throwing gradually subsided, on came the sheep dogs. No show in these parts could be considered complete without a sheep dog demonstration. Being well practised, they quickly got going: the sheep, the dogs and the whistling shepherds. Unfortunately for them, most of the spectators went off to find the toilets or refreshments.

CHAPTER 35

Chizzie, buoyed by the great success of his team so far, went to the warm-up field to fire up his cyclist, Eddie Wibble, who was next in the arena. But Eddie, along with the other cyclists, was making his way to the farthest corner of the field, where they all dismounted. Chizzie thought this rather strange. Competitors usually warmed up by themselves; they certainly didn't warm up with an exchange of chat and gossip.

As Chizzie watched them, Billy came running up very quickly. "Sir, Mr Bryson, Chizzie," he called, clearly unsure what to call his former teacher, present boss and teammate.

"Take it easy, Billy. It's a bit early for you to be working up a sweat. You're last on, remember; you've got over an hour yet," replied Chizzie.

"Eddie Wibble sent me; he says to get you, and you've to go and hide over there in the bushes, where the cyclists are. There's some kinda deal goin' on, he says. Hurry!"

This chimed with Chizzie's concerns. Cycling had a reputation for doping and performance-enhancing drugs. If any dealing was going on, he had to stop it.

"Stay here, Billy," he said, and then he ran over to one of the golf buggies used for ferrying kit around. He climbed into it and sped off to where the cyclists were gathered, taking a longer but more secluded route outside the ground. Cycle racing had been a particular passion of the late McBraid's wife, so, unlike any of the other events, he had put up a little trophy and some extra prize money in her memory – a thousand pounds to be precise, so the cycling was expected to be particularly keenly fought. But, here, perversely, the cyclists were in a bunch, chatting away like they were on a Sunday picnic.

Chizzie parked the buggy behind the bushes and crept stealthily along to where he could crouch among the foliage and listen to what was being said.

"Right, lads," said McCrann, the tough-looking rider for Findandie. "Yez know the score. This isnae aboot glory nor nuthin'; this is aboot bread an' butter. Me an' Andy Torburt here, we're aw' the wey up fae Glesca the day—"

"Milngavie, ectually, not quite Glasgow. And it's Andrew Torbet," clarified the cyclist, with a withering and superior look at McCrann.

But McCrann hardly missed a breath: "Ah mean, if we wis tae tek a tumble or sumpin', an' come awa' wi nuthin'; we'd be seriously oot o' pocket, yez ken whut ah mean? Ah mean, ah'm on appearance money, but the performance bonus is pitiful. It's a disgrace!"

"You mean you want to win," said the Oxdale man.

"Nit nicessirily," chimed Torbet, looking enigmatic enough to be the brains behind the proposition.

"This is a piddlin' wee tournament," continued McCrann, "Let's face it, it's nuthin really, is it? Ah mean, eh? There's only the four o' us in it really. The others are dunderheids. So there's nae glory nor nuthin' fur enybody here; it's aboot the lolly an' nuthin' else, that's aw' there is tae it. Yez see what ah'm sayin'?"

"If we're sinsible, we're all winnahs," said Torbet by way of translation.

"Wan fur all, an' all fur wan," declared McCrann, going for the grand gesture, but losing his authority to midges as he waved them away.

"Equal shayahs," said Torbet, translating again.

"Equal whut?" asked McCrann.

"Shayahs. Equal shayahs," repeated Torbet as if the man were an idiot.

"Aye, right; shares — equal shares," announced McCrann translating for the benefit of the others. "Wan fur all, an' all fur wan," he repeated, completely ignoring the midges this time.

But there was no ignoring the midges, and the meeting was becoming like a bookies' convention, with hands flying everywhere.

"Right, let's wrap it up before we're eaten alive," said the Oxdale man.

"Are yez furrit, then? Whut's the score, lads?" asked McCrann, with just a hint of aggression.

Eddie seemed at a loss what to think. As he'd explained to Chizzie earlier, the Wibbles had paid out handsomely for his new bike, and, rightly, Mrs Wibble expected him to win. If he didn't win, his career on wheels might just come to a very abrupt end. On the other hand, McCrann looked like the type that might just reorganise your body in such a way that your career would come to an abrupt end from a different direction.

"So whut's the story, lads? Ye've hud time tae think noo," said McCrann, clearly expecting a positive outcome.

The Oxdale man didn't disappoint him and threw in his lot with the proposition. "It makes sense when you think about it," he said. "This way, we all get a bite at the cherry, and we all stay in business. All for one, and one for all — that's for me."

Three pairs of eyes now fastened on to the swithering Wibble.

"Well," said Wibble, swallowing hard, "I don't mind—"

"Champion!" exclaimed McCrann.

"As long as I get to win," continued Eddie, bravely.

The negotiations faltered suddenly. All eyes trained on McCrann, who looked ready to pounce.

But, seconds later, a smile broke across his craggy face. "Nae bother," he said pleasantly, to Eddie's great relief. "The Wibble man's hot right now – ah saw 'um at Crieff th'uther week. Well done, ma man."

Eddie smiled humbly.

"Yew heven't seen me lately. Eh've been in Frence," advised Torbet in a manner that suggested the word 'France' came with automatic assurance of 'hot' performance.

"Next time, Andy, next time," said McCrann dismissively.

"We ken trust yew, eh take it?" said Torbet, fixing his gaze quickly on Wibble.

"'Course we can trust 'um," replied McCrann, clapping Eddie's non-fleshy left shoulder with a very firm hand, "Nae problems there, eh, ma man?"

"No. No problems," affirmed Eddie.

"Ye'll be wantin' second place, ah suppose?" said McCrann turning to McLatchey, the Oxdale man.

McLatchey shrugged his shoulders: "I need the cash. I haven't been too well lately. I've another kid on the way."

"Ye can manage a guid second though?" McCrann questioned.

"I'll give it everything. Yeah. I can do it. Yep," confirmed McLatchey.

"Right, yer second," said McCrann.

"You can have first if it helps," said Eddie to McLatchey.

"No, no," McLatchey insisted, "You'll look more convincing than me on the last lap. Second's fine for me."

"Eh went thiid, then," said Torbet, peevishly.

"Fine," said McCrann, "ye kin huv thurd. Ah had a black puddin' supper three hours ago, an' it's takin' time tae settle in – so an easy day's fine by me. Everybody happy, then? A thousan' quid split four ways – that's whut now? Uhm, two-fifty each. An' we keep oor appearance money oorsels."

"Appearance money?" asked Eddie sheepishly. He wasn't getting any.

"Sure. So, hauns taegither everybody," shouted McCrann, stretching out the palm of his mighty right hand.

The Oxdale man laid his hand on McCrann's, Torbet followed suit, and Eddie followed him. Then McCrann put his left hand on Eddie's hand, and the other left hands piled in like a freemasons' jamboree.

As they shook their hands up and down, McCrann reaffirmed the order: "The Wibble man furst, the McLatchey man second, Wullie thurd—"

"Andrew!" corrected Torbet.

"Aw, right – Andrew. An' me fur the early bath. Wan fur all, an' all fur wan!"

"Wan fur all, an' all fur wan!" chorused the others as best they could.

It was a done deal and Eddie Wibble was clearly very pleased. A win would delight his wife and restore her faith in him, and, moreover, he'd make some money. He glanced furtively at the bushes and winked. Chizzie blushed and thought for a moment – he'd just heard a race being fixed, and he'd sat there and done absolutely nothing about it. He had to step in. He got to his feet and pushed through the bushes. But the cyclists were away quickly – fanning out over the field in a crude attempt to make it look like they were all warming up on their own. Chizzie could only watch them go. He thought about shouting, but it was all too late. He went back to the golf buggy, climbed in and sped round the ground to confront Eddie. But was it right to tell Eddie that there could be no deal with McCrann and the others? Eddie was going to win, and Tannadee needed the points. Nobody would get hurt. By the time he got out of the buggy, he still couldn't decide what to say to Eddie.

He didn't get the chance to say anything.

Yolanda came running up to him and said, "Jim's in the casualty tent!"

"What? What's up?" demanded Chizzie.

"He felt giddy suddenly and fell onto your father, who caught him. It's not serious; he's just a bit drunk really – a victim of his own popularity. Seemingly, everybody's been buying him drinks, and he's just too polite to refuse."

"Bloody hell! Are you sure he's okay?"

"That's what they're saying."

"I'd better go and see."

"No, no, Chizzie, you need to relax; you've a race to run, remember?"

"Tell me about it, but who's going to cover for Jim? There's only me. I need to be at every event and get everybody ready now."

"Your dad said not to worry; he'll cover the jumping events. You can't be everywhere."

Chizzie lifted his head to hear the public address announcement. "Is that the cyclists they're calling?"

"Yes. Yes, it is."

"But I haven't spoken to Eddie yet."

"He knows what to do I'm sure."

"I'm not so sure he does," mumbled Chizzie.

The cyclists gathered near the starting line for their five-lap race; this was a traditional knockout race called 'De'il Tak the Hin'most' in which the hindmost competitor at the end of each lap has to drop out of the race, as if snatched away by the pursuing Devil. What the public didn't know, of course, was that the Devil in these parts had just been made redundant and been replaced by another red revolutionary in the shape of Glasgow man Alex McCrann.

It was difficult for Eddie Wibble – the heir apparent to the winner's laurels – to not look unusually complacent and smug, but he worked at it and conjured up a mean, hungry, nervous look. "Thank God for socialism," he was heard to say to himself, as he drummed his fingers on the handlebars while humming a few lines of 'The Internationale'.

The track was rougher than most, but at least it was mown shorter than the running track inside it and cinders had been scattered over it to firm it up.

"To the line gentlemen!" called the starter. The racers moved forwards to be held upright by their assistants: the wives in the cases of McCrann and Wibble; a man with a wide-brimmed hat held up Torbet; and village coaches held up the others.

"Get set!" cried the starter.

Then the gun banged, and off they went.

With all the drama preceding this event, the crowd were in the mood for a battle royal and looking forward to seeing riders hurtling into the crowd or getting flattened. Little did they know, of course, that it was all cut and dried; not even the bookies knew, though a little wisp of suspicion had arisen when a couple of unusually heavy bets came in late on.

McCrann, safe in the knowledge that he wouldn't be around for very long, shot off like a rocket and lapped up the adoration. Frank Tosh reading out, over the public address system, recounted the highlights of McCrann's once illustrious career as an Olympic competitor and time-trials champion. The crowd hummed approvingly, preparing themselves for a treat. The other riders responded as best they could, bearing in mind they had farther to go. As they approached the line for the first time, the crowd cheered McCrann on.

"Go Jack! Go!" cried Mrs McCrann, who was standing at the trackside and waving her umbrella.

Mrs Wibble, who was standing nearby, had a word for her man too. "*Gonads! Off yer gonads!*" she yelled, in the sure knowledge that country bumpkins didn't know a gonad from a bicycle pump. She repeated the injunction, and Eddie flashed her a look that said emphatically: "I am not on my gonads; I am at least two inches off the bloomin' saddle!"

The Tottiepans man, who had already fallen well behind the pack, went out after one lap. After two laps, the Altnaclog man departed. Only the conspirators remained and the plan kicked into gear.

Halfway through the third lap, a look of anguish seized the face of McCrann, and everyone could see a terrible affliction had suddenly struck the man and his race was over. McCrann, old trooper that he was, dropped out shaking his head in mock despair, pointing to his knee and limping. His wife consoled him with her arms around him.

The crowd sighed heavily, the class act had gone, so what could the others offer? The others continued in a bunch, exchanging the lead several times to look authentic.

The riders came round for the end of the fourth lap and Torbet prepared to drop out. Then, suddenly, out of the blue and only twenty yards before the line, a terrible conversion from radical socialism to free-market capitalism took place in the head of Torbet. Putting his head down, he accelerated past Eddie, who fell back on his seat in surprise, causing Mrs Wibble to scream. But Eddie was off his crotch in a flash and he accelerated after the traitor, Torbet, who had shot past McLatchey by then. With ten yards to go, McLatchey hadn't enough time to respond and Wibble got to the line before him by half a length. McLatchey was out, but Torbet was still very much in the race and going for the win.

Suddenly, the crowd became heated again, ice creams started melting and dribbling over hands, and cherry sauce slid over tightening fingers.

"*Come on, Tannadee!*" roared some.

"*Come on, Garthbay!*" roared others.

The reckoning was at hand. Eddie dug in hard, but, try as he might, he just couldn't gain on Torbet, who was by then five yards ahead. Into the back straight, Eddie was still five yards down, but, on the bend, Torbet began to show signs of tiring. Eddie, seeing his chance, got his backside in the air.

"Yeehoo!" cried Mrs Wibble.

The gap began closing. But Torbet gritted his teeth and stopped the rot. Eddie gritted his teeth too and began making inroads again as he found yet more speed. The riders fizzed over the cinders, and the crowd was buzzing. As they went into the home straight, McCrann was there at the trackside, bawling at Torbet's face with a barrage of expletives fit to bring down a bullock, but Torbet barely wobbled.

As Eddie came by, McCrann roared him on: "*He's wobblin', Wibble! Get 'um, son! Get 'um! For Christ's sake!*"

And, sure enough, Torbet was fading fast again. With only twenty yards to go, Wibble was right on Torbet's tail, and then, with only ten yards to go, Eddie was just half a length down. But Torbet gave it everything. He just wouldn't yield – he just wouldn't – and Eddie, still gaining though he was, was clean out of track. With only yards to go, victory was surely Torbet's and Wibble was second.

Just then, onto the trackside came a woman; it was Mrs McCrann. She stumbled and fell, her arms outstretched. The crowd howled in horror. Mercifully, she fell short of the whizzing bicycles and the only casualty was her rolled-up umbrella, which went straight through Torbet's front spokes, bringing his bike to a sudden halt a yard before the line.

However, Torbet didn't halt, he hurtled through the air and he was over the line. He was first!

But, no. In a bicycle race you need a bicycle – the clue's in the title – and Torbet didn't have a bicycle; he'd crossed the line as a pedestrian! It was instant disqualification. It was Eddie who'd won!

Torbet and Garthbay protested vehemently, but the incident was declared an act of God, and the verdict stood. When Torbet then whispered his threat to spill the beans about the compact made earlier, down by the bushes, alpha male McCrann whispered something along the lines of, "I know where you live," and everything quietened down.

Not a happy man, Torbet departed immediately, leaving the others with an even bigger haul.

Mrs McCrann, of course, was all apologies and deep compassion. "What a travesty, and a fella Glesca man, tae," she observed for the press. "It's particularly gallin', ah kin tell ye, when wan o' yer ain goes doon. Ah knew ah shouldnae ha' pit ma flatties oan; ah said tae masel' goin oe'r that mud, 'Helen,' ah says, 'wan slip an' yer mince, doll.' But wud ah listen? Naw, naw, no' me. Ah've got tae bash oan; ah'm that pig-heidit at times – ma ain worst enemy, ah tell ye. Look at ma new tracksuit! The dry-cleaners'll tak a hairy fit when they see me comin'! An' look at ma brolly tae – that coulda been ma heid!"

And Torbet of course, had he been present, would have wished that it had been.

Later, down at the far end of the warm-up field, three riders divided up the loot and parted very amicably.

CHAPTER 36

"Fix!" cried Weever, no longer able to keep a lid on things.

"Shhh, not so loud," pleaded Sir Hew. "We're doing very well here – we've got maximum points."

"There's no way a creep like that could've won; he's got legs like a spider!"

"Legs are funny things," observed Sir Hew. "It's amazing what you can do with only one. We had a chap, a gamekeeper, with an astonishing pair of legs; well, not really a pair – two very different legs on the one man actually. A fine chap he was, but not the brightest gamekeeper ever. Though you don't exactly need to be a genius to be a gamekeeper, do you? Two brain cells would do it – one for each leg. There was a most extraordinary set on that gamekeeper: his left leg was shorter than the right on account of his walking round the hills anticlockwise for nearly fifty-odd years. Very odd, wouldn't you say?"

"What?"

"Odd."

"Yes."

"You can imagine his problems on the flat; in high winds, it was all he could do to avoid going round in circles. It was God's will, he said. He couldn't be persuaded to even things up. He was a God-fearing man, you see, with very firm beliefs. He claims he met an alien from outer space on the moors last year, and he's never been the same since. He breaks out in tongues at times. You know, tongues?"

"Oh yes," replied Weever.

"Boolawoolatanga wanga panga prrrrrp peep peep poop poop doko najja dinko," erupted Ludo.

"Thank you, Ludo, a demonstration was not required," observed Sir Hew. "Out of respect for the man, though, we'll say no more. Suffice it to say that his head went funny. Then it spread to his legs, which lost all power. He retired to his bed and kept to himself. He's a vegetable now."

CHAPTER 37

Going into the long jump, Tannadee had the lead, being five points ahead of second-placed Oxdale and eighteen points ahead of bookies' favourite Garthbay. With tension mounting and partisan loyalties aflame, a quiver of excitement swept round the arena every time commentator Frank Tosh got on the tannoy with an announcement.

Right then, he was about to announce the long-jump event, but, just as his lips met the microphone, Johnny Bryson and PC Tunnock, who were both sipping tea by Tosh's side, pointed out the important fact that only two people were at the jumping area. Frank – who was growing to like the sound of his own voice more and more, and, consequently, getting more commanding by the minute – took the situation in hand immediately. Grabbing his walkie-talkie, he got in touch with the long-jump judge, while Johnny got on his walkie-talkie to Chizzie.

"Where is our long jumper?" Johnny asked. "He should be jumping now."

"There's sort of a problem," answered Chizzie with some reluctance.

"What sort of a problem?"

"Well, it's… it's…"

"It's what?"

"Sort of technical."

"Technical?"

"Yeah, a technicality."

"What sort of technicality?"

"Well – a mutiny exactly."

"A what?"

"A mutin—"

"A peaceful protest!" broke in another voice on Chizzie's walkie-talkie.

"Yes," said Chizzie eagerly. "A protest. I'm... I'm in discussions right now. I'll get back to you."

"How long will you be?" demanded Johnny.

"I don't know. Over and out."

Taking stock for a second, Johnny looked bewildered, then he turned to those next to him. They'd heard everything, but, while PC Tunnock and Frank merely exchanged a quizzical look, the look from Johnny was very different and very red, and – within seconds – he'd leaped out of his seat and was shouting, "Leave it to me!" in the kind of commanding tone that Frank could only dream of.

The catalyst for the mutiny proved to be location, location, location – that and ice cream. The long-jump pit had been allocated to the far side of the arena by someone in the organising committee who thought that the long-jumping spectacle would be so boring that its only hope of capturing interest was to put it right beside the ice-cream vans and burger vans. The jumpers clearly had other opinions: they were mad – hopping mad.

"How can we concentrate with all that bloody chiming going on! You can't even hear yourself think!" declared Rodney McScroon, the spokesperson for the jumping men.

"Ees okay for you boys; ees only malarkin,'" replied Toni Fantoni from the lead ice-cream van. "We gotta make a livin' here. And ees like I ain't got enough goin' on here with all these smelly burgers ees gettin' in everythin'. How can I serve prize-winnin' chocolate chip, with onions and mad cow

370

disease crawlin' all over! Eh?" And he wasn't finished. "I got a son at university; ees studyin' the medical physics. You want I can't pay his fees? You want deaths?"

With that, the jumping men quit the sand and went looking. They were no longer hopping mad: they were absolutely livid. They homed in on the first big cheese they could find, and that was Chizzie, who happened to think of himself as more of a cheese slice than a big, weighty Stilton.

The jumpers nevertheless came down very heavy, descending on Chizzie like foodies who'd been denied cheese for a week. Restraint hadn't a look in; they pushed and they shoved, and they yelled and they prodded: it was ugly. Chizzie felt like a cork in a whirlpool. Then Johnny arrived, and it all stopped instantly. No wages, not even expenses, would they get if they didn't buckle down and get on with it.

"It's up to you!" boomed Johnny, like he owned the place, "You've got ten seconds!"

"We'd... we'd like to discuss it," replied McScroon.

"No discussion; eight seconds," returned Johnny.

The jumping men looked at each other and muttered darkly. Chizzie didn't know what to do. The Tannadee jumper was unlikely to bring home big points, so it was no skin off his nose if the event didn't go ahead. On the other hand, it could look like a stunt contrived to help Tannadee.

"Two seconds!" announced Johnny.

"Okay! Okay, we'll do it!" yelped McScroon, in a high-pitched tone, "but we're not happy."

"Boohoo," commiserated Johnny. "You're ten minutes late, so get on with it."

But then a tall, paunchy man in a blue blazer stepped forwards. "You have absolutely no right to speak to these lads like that," he declared in resonating, oratorical fashion.

"And just who are you?" asked Johnny, "Vladimir Putin?"

"No, Ronald Patullo, I was an official at the Commonwealth Games in Edinburgh."

"So what?"

"So I know what I'm talking about. These lads train hard all year for events like this, and then what happens? They get chucked over to the far side and treated like dirt. It's just not on, you know. It's just not on."

"Right then, that's no problem; we'll sort it out, right here this minute," replied Johnny cockily.

"Eh?"

"Yeah, it's no problem: there'll be no more long jump, not this year, not any year and never again; this is the very last long jump ever seen in this district. So, goodbye, moanin' minnies. *Hasta la vista!*"

"Hang on, hang on," exclaimed the complainant, glancing round at the anxious faces and feeling the eyes of mutiny now directed at him. "That was a negotiating position. I was merely making observations."

"Well, get this, Mr…"

"Patullo."

"Any more observations from you, Patullo, and it's curtains for these creeps. Get it?"

"Er…"

"Get on with it or go! Which is it?"

To Chizzie's mind, the mutiny might be over, but an even bigger problem was now looming. "Hold it a minute," he broke in, holding up his hands, like a man of peace. "Let's just calm down here. We can't simply wipe out the long jump."

"Certainly not," agreed Patullo, brightening. "Without a long jump, these games will lose all credibility."

"Oh really?" enquired Johnny with menace.

"Oh, yes, they would," asserted Patullo, "I know what I'm talking about, I was an official—"

"At the Commonwealth Games," Johnny intercepted. "Well, this isn't the—"

"We take your point," interrupted Chizzie, turning to Patullo. "You have a right to the same treatment as everyone else."

"Yes, indeed," replied blazer-man Patullo, "we could take legal action."

"Yeah, the European Court of Human Rights," commented one ambitious soul.

Johnny laughed. "Join the queue," he quipped. "It starts at Thurso and is four hundred miles long, with every whining sod and demented loser in the country in it demanding freedom for this, that and the other: freedom to burgle, freedom from dandruff, freedom to be an idiot and freedom to stick a bog brush in your ear. Well, I've got news for you lot: I am an official here; I am the judge, the jury and the hangman. And if you don't like it, mister, you can lump it. Jump it or lump it! That's your choice, matey!"

Chizzie, as embarrassed as much as he was anxious, raised his hands in peace again, then placed one on Johnny's back and one on Patullo's back, forming a sort of bridge between the warring factions. "Now, let's just simmer down here, please," he pleaded. "We'll do better cooperating than fighting." Then, turning to Patullo, he added, "We can't do anything about it this year, but I give you my word that we'll do our very best to get the long jump right in front of the grandstand for you next time. That's all I can do for you in the circumstances. In the meantime, please make the best of it."

"You're a gentleman, sir, and a scholar," said Patullo, turning with hand outstretched.

He and Chizzie shook hands, and the recalcitrant jumpers turned and left, with a sneering glance at the seething Johnny Bryson.

"They'll take you for a lummock now, you'll see," insisted Johnny, barely able to contain himself.

"You overreached yourself there," replied Chizzie. "You've no authority to speak to them like that. It was embarrassing."

"It's nothing of the kind; I only did what any person with common sense would do."

"A little consideration goes a long way, you know. A little humility and humanity does no harm. Put yourself in their position. They've all trained hard for this."

"You're marked as a sucker now. You'll see. However, it's your funeral." And off Johnny went.

With the mutiny resolved, everything settled down nicely. Until they found rabbit droppings in the sand pit. Then all hell broke loose again. The Oxdale jumper had just thudded into the sand on his second jump when his keen eye, ever on the lookout for stools of one kind or another, caught sight of the offending pellets. "You get them all in the long jump: dog, cat, rabbit, fox, deer, rodent and even ones from children," he informed Chizzie.

And that was it. The jumping boys were out of there like it was about to blow.

"Absolutely sick we are! Sick, sick, sick of it! Everywhere we go, we're jumping into dung heaps!" explained spokesman McScroon. "Get that sand replaced immediately, or we're out of here and off to Environmental Health to report you," he informed the official who had now turned up and was standing next to Chizzie. "We'll close you down!"

"Where am I going to find sand on a Saturday afternoon?" pleaded the official.

"At a builders' merchants, a golf club or a bowling green," replied McScroon, "And not just any sand, mind you – the particles must be sub-angular or rounded in shape, and with a particle size ranging from nought point one two five millimetres to one point two millimetres, so as not to cause injury."

The official looked aghast and stunned for a moment, as if the jumper was speaking in tongues. Then, with raised eyebrows, he enquired sarcastically, "Any particular colour?"

"Mid to dark brown," came the reply.

The official gaped again.

But McScroon added helpfully, "Tay sand's the best. That's the one to get."

Half an hour later, the Tay sand duly arrived in a big truck, the sand pit was refilled and the long jump resumed, and it quickly became so boring that the only people who made the effort to stay with it were the official and Chizzie.

"Was it worth it?" yelled Toni Fantoni, who – taking the law into his own hands – was moving his ice-cream van away to seek a better site closer to the action.

"Frankly, no," grumbled the official.

But it was worth something to Tannadee: one point. It was enough to keep them ahead overall, by the narrowest of margins.

CHAPTER 38

"Our man kept landing on his bottom," complained Sir Hew. "Someone needs to tell him one lands on one's feet. Come on, Tannadee – buck up! Rip, spit or bust!"

"Quiet, Hew – you're supposed to be neutral!" remonstrated Lady Hawkshaw.

"Whoops!"

Lady Hawkshaw leaned towards Weever. "He has these turns."

"I get a bit excited," admitted Sir Hew.

"It's his head," said Lady Hawkshaw. "You see he—"

"There's no need for details, dear," said Sir Hew.

"Did you take your pill?"

"I did, but the sun reacts with it."

"Then find a seat in the shade."

"I can't. It's my duty – I've got to be here."

"Why's your bum called your bottom?" bawled Ludo, the older nephew. "It's nowhere near the bottom; it's halfway up!"

Weever cast an ominous glance at Sir Hew, who closed his eyes and groaned.

"Your feet, that should be your bottom," continued the lad, "and your bottom, that could be your feet. But then how would we measure things?" he mused.

"In bums!" replied Crispin. "Twelve inches equals one bum! Three feet becomes three bums. Four feet six is four bums six. Ben Nevis? It's over four thousand bums. Mt Everest—"

"That's enough!" insisted Lady Hawkshaw.

"Twenty-nine thousand bums," reported Crispin.

"Thank you," said the nephew.

"And Bigfoot becomes Bigbum," chirped Sir Hew with a big laugh.

"Are you sure you took that pill?" asked his wife.

"Positive."

"Well, get into the shade somewhere."

"I can't; it's my duty! I told you."

Seeing his chance to get shot of Sir Hew, Weever broke in. "I can take care of that. I've enough presence for both of us, believe me. Nothing's more important than your health. You go up back now and relax."

"Thank you, Mr Weever," said Lady Hawkshaw with a smile.

But Sir Hew was adamant. "No, no, duty calls; I remain steadfast – I will not desert my post. I'd rather die."

"What? In this place?" asked Weever.

"Wherever I make my stand and however many arrows it takes," declared Sir Hew.

"You sound like General Custer," said Lady Hawkshaw. "And look what happened to him."

"Did he have ADHD too?" asked Ludo.

"Nobody's got ADHD," insisted Lady Hawkshaw.

"I have," said the boy.

"Who told you that?" asked Lady Hawkshaw.

"Sandy Bruce-Thompson – he's got it," confirmed Ludo.

The steward approached Sir Hew. "Begging your pardon, sir, but the Duke of Buckie sends his regards and requests that you meet him in the VIP lounge downstairs."

"Ah, wonderful! Good old Buckie! Good-oh! Superb! Buckie's here. He said he would be. Right, everybody, we're on the move downstairs to say hello to dear old Buckie."

Lady Hawkshaw grimaced. "I'll stay here and maintain a presence. Someone has to."

"No, no, no," said Sir Hew excitedly. "Mr Weever has enough presence for us all, he said it himself; he doesn't mind."

Weever waved away all doubt. "No. Absolutely. Not at all. No problem. You all go now and meet your great friend."

Lady Hawkshaw grimaced again, "He's not my—"

"He's a very dear friend," chirped Sir Hew, "and he'll want to see everyone. Come along, dear."

"Yes, you enjoy yourselves; have a great time," Weever declared. Then, as the Hawkshaws moved out of earshot, he uttered, "God, I thought they'd never go. Aaagh, my head; it's spinning with that endless prattle. Does he never shut up? I can't even think straight. I nearly blew my top a while back. Now I can't even do that. My brain's gone numb. If I ever get him on a shooting party, he'll be the first thing I shoot, believe me. How are we doing?"

"Well, it's touch and go, Gordon. It's between Tannadee and Oxdale. Tannadee is in front," explained Fairfoull.

"And Garthbay?"

"Nowhere."

"*What?*"

CHAPTER 39

Into the arena came the men in leotards, acknowledging the applause with waving arms, like gladiators of yore. Traditional Highland wrestling was always popular in these parts. Frank Tosh introduced the gallant grapplers, then explained the rules of Grampian wrestling for the sake of the uninitiated. Not that there was much to explain really: each bout, held in a circle six yards wide, lasts a maximum of five minutes and the aim is to get your opponent out of the ring by any reasonable means, without leaving the ring yourself. If you're unable to evict your opponent, you try to win by pinning your opponent's shoulders to the ground for five seconds. Not mentioned by Frank, but known to all combatants privately, were the supplementary rules: namely, no biting, no nipping, no gouging, no scratching, no spitting, no grabbing of the privates and no interfering with orifices. It's common sense really, but desperation can do terrible things to a man whose morality is adrift on a sea of hormones.

In his public address, Frank also drew attention to the three marked rings: one in the middle, and one at either end of the ground. The bouts would take place simultaneously, with a five-minute interval between each set. By the end of the competition, all the wrestlers would have grappled each other and the points been totalled up. During the intervals, the traditional dancing competition would be underway. Each competitor was allowed a ringman, who would patrol the perimeter of the ring and ensure that his grappler got a fair deal. With Jim out of action, Chizzie was the Tannadee ringman.

Denis Dekker was the man grappling for Tannadee. His first opponent was the Tottiepans man. He appeared to find Dekker vaguely familiar, but, seemingly, couldn't quite place his face – not surprising really in view of Dekker's lengthy absence from the ring.

The bout got under way. They grabbed each other's shoulders. Instantly, there came a startled look from the Tottiepans man as the old calling card hit him suddenly – that smell! Like a smack on the nose! A smell that only the born-and-bred fish fryer with his own fish and chip shop that was prone to the occasional fire could acquire through the years. Though it completely escaped Dekker, it was his best weapon.

To avoid the insistent odour that hung in Dekker's beard and wafted from his every pore, the poor Tottiepans man turned his head to the side desperately, but, even here, there was no respite – not with Dekker's armpits, which were full of reinforcements. The fetid fug of the fusty armpits infected the Tottiepans man's every breath, and his tortured eyes seemed to beg for oxygen, but the next thing he knew was that Dekker had spun round, so they were back to back, and Dekker was carrying him off to the edge of the ring. They were like Siamese twins joined at the buttocks. With his feet in the air, there was nothing the Tottiepans man could do. However, being of surprisingly philosophical bent, he relaxed visibly, sucked up the oxygen he needed and left Dekker to it. In some ways, he could be regarded as the lucky one, as he was the one getting the lift. When the time came for the big heave-ho, he, not Dekker, would have the greater reserves.

Thus, seemingly raised in spirit as well as in body, the Tottiepans grappler appeared impervious to the baying

380

of the crowd and merely eyed the passing of a wispy cloud before the song of a rising skylark caught his attention. For a moment or two, he appeared mesmerised by the flying fleck soaring so free. "Kinda puts it all in perspective," said the look on his face before he turned his head to watch a meadow pipit swoop by. The man was a regular birdwatcher, and not just a birdwatcher: he was a plane spotter too, and a jumbo jet high in the sky now caught his eye and brought a wistful smile.

Chizzie caught the bug too and watched wistfully as the cruising craft trailed its steaming breath across the wide, blue sky. Where had it come from? And where was it going to? From gay Paris, perhaps, to the Golden Gate Bridge of San Francisco, linking with its lengthy sweep the edge of Europe, the Atlantic Ocean, the Canadian tundra, the wide rolling prairies, the towering Rockies and, at this very minute, the Tottiepans man's gaping crotch. What a world: so vast, yet so small.

Then suddenly, a development. Dekker had come to a halt, and panting and sweating, he began flexing at the knees. The Tottiepans grappler, seeing his chance, snapped out of his reverie and made his move. He took a deep breath, swung his legs in the air and heaved. And then he cried, "Waaah!" as, catapulted by the heaving Dekker, he flew clean out the ring, head over heels. Clearly, philosophy and wrestling are not a good mix.

Dekker, the unphilosophical and down-to-earth fish fryer, was now one bout to the good. And the birdwatching, philosophical wrestler was no doubt a much wiser man.

Next into the ring with Dekker came a sallow, downy youth wearing a black leotard and sporting a large head surmounted by erect, lurid, red hair. Below the hair lay a face with a smattering of lurid, red, fluffy beard – an ensemble that, in modish circles, was doubtless something of a fashion

381

statement. However, to Dekker, a mere fish fryer, it bore all the horrors of a chip-pan fire and accounted for his unusually nervous disposition. For a minute or two he paced up and down, wringing his hands.

And who could blame him? For the professional fryer, there can be no greater fear than the fat going up, the walls blowing out and the roof hitting the floor. But Dekker was no ordinary fish fryer, he was a highly experienced, if somewhat unfit, athlete. By pursing his lips, he banished the nervous look and focussed on the job in hand. Secure in his ring-craft and in the knowledge that every chip-pan fire that ever burst about him had safely been capped and snuffed, he was ready to do exactly the same to this young whipper-snapper in the fancy gear.

When they came together and locked arms, Dekker seemed taken immediately by a whiff of something, most probably the white talcum powder visible in the young lad's armpits. A benign, avuncular look suffused Dekker's face. He looked almost sorry for the lad and all his youthful innocence. He might have felt even sorrier had he known the poor lad was not only giving out whiffs, but was also receiving them – and those were nowhere near as sweet as baby powder. Quickly, the young lad – the powdered sapling – broke free and quit the fug.

The two danced around for a bit; round and round they went for over a minute, each making occasional gestures as if to grab the other, but the respective whiffs were proving just too much and too inhibiting. The two men were more huff and puff than meat slammer, which clearly suited Dekker very nicely, thank you, since you can never have too many breathers in his condition.

Eventually, as his strength checked in again, Dekker got cocky – cocky enough for him to give his rumpled version of the Muhammad Ali Shuffle. In reality, it was more of a Michelin Man Shuffle or like somebody shaking a duvet. But it had the desired effect, and the young lad, looking insulted, seemingly made his mind up to take Dekker on, fug or no fug.

The young man's steely gaze unnerved Dekker for he ceased his shuffling, squared up to the lad and squatted low. Then, suddenly, Dekker pointed over the young lad's shoulder. "Look! Your mum!" he cried.

The young lad turned and looked, Dekker pounced, and – seizing him by the arm – he spun the sapling round and round, spinning him faster and faster. It was like the hammer throwing event all over again, until he let go finally and threw the lad clean out of the ring.

"Kids," Dekker muttered, shaking his head at the reeling youngster. "What on earth do they teach them these days?"

His third opponent, Alex Walker, was not going to be so easy. Here was one of those dour sheep-farmers with a moan tattooed permanently on his face – the kind of face that makes even rhubarb seem sweet by comparison.

As they locked on for the start, Dekker screwed up his face as if aware of an unusual smell wafting off his opponent. Even Chizzie smelled it; it was sheep dip! This was shaping up to be the contest of the afternoon: chip fat versus sheep dip, or the Battle of the Body Odours, as legend would no doubt have it.

With both men being squat and reasonably strong, it was clear to both that victory in this bout lay in points rather than an outright win, so – feeling for the slight shift in balance that would be enough to get them a fall – they remained locked together. Like a pair of giant crabs doing the tango, they wheeled round and round the ring, flicking their legs under each other. The sheep man was slightly the stronger, but Dekker the greasier and more able to slide out of trouble.

Locked in this impasse, time went by slowly – very, very slowly – but conversation was, of course, pointless. Gradually, Dekker looked more and more uneasy, and more and more self-conscious, doubtless aware that, here he was, in front of a paying public, hugging and holding a half-naked man – and him a complete stranger at that. What thoughts weigh on a man in these circumstances? Possibly, *Here I am with a big, burly bloke and handling him just like I do the missus when she's up for it – and for much longer too. Ugh!*

Clearly fearful that people should think he was enjoying himself, Dekker kept his puffing and grunting to a minimum, and seemed keen to break free. But the sheep man had other ideas.

They must get awful lonely up in these hills, thought Chizzie. Then on further reflection, he thought, *Maybe I'm reading too much into this. It's just good, clean fun.*

But Dekker looked unsure.

"Relax, Denis; relax!" Chizzie shouted.

And, Dekker, appreciating the support, relaxed a bit. Then the slapping started: the sheep man started slapping Dekker.

Dekker looked troubled again, clearly thinking along the lines of, *When a sheep man turns slapper, it's time to worry.* Understandably, Dekker began sweating profusely. First, it was a slap on the left, then a right, then just about everywhere and anywhere; nothing too harsh but nevertheless very unnerving to a man unused to this kind of thing outside the marital bedchamber.

Chizzie tried to look on the bright side: *Perhaps it's a sign of affection,* he mused.

Then, Dekker, possibly fearing some kind of proposal, burst free with a mighty effort and backed clean away.

The sheep-farmer's expression, though noticeably redder, remained unchanged. For one reason or another, though, he clearly had a passion for Dekker and right away came after him. Going into the final minute, Dekker was a desperate man. There was no time for any Muhammad Ali Shuffle here; there was barely enough time to think as he divided his time frantically between looking at the clock and keeping the relentless sheep man at bay. Finally, the ref called time, declared the contest a draw, and Dekker got the hell out of there.

From a man who evidently wanted his body, Dekker went on to one who seemed hellbent on avoiding it. Word about Dekker's odour had apparently got round, and no one was less willing to indulge in it than Dekker's new opponent. And it wasn't difficult to see why: when you're tanned, with a great physique and long, flowing, blond hair like a lion's mane, you don't want to be slumming it with a chip-frying greaseball.

So, no sooner had they locked on than the dandy broke free; a second's contact with Dekker was clearly a second too long for this man. But Dekker looked relaxed; to have space once again was clearly invigorating after the claustrophobic bout with the sheep man, and, anyway, the long stand-off with the dour devil of the hills had no doubt burned up a fair amount of his stamina. On top of which, some of the dandy man's tan was coming off and was now decorating Dekker's shoulders, so he, too, wasn't all that keen on bodily contact.

"I could end up lookin' like a zebra – or even a bumble bee," Dekker quipped to Chizzie as the dandy backed away for air.

The choice of insect was prophetic – a self-fulfilling prophecy even – for, next, with sheer bravado, Dekker went into his Muhammad Ali Shuffle, and demonstrated for all to see how to dance like a bumble bee and sting like a noodle.

Unfortunately, even that modest effort took its toll, and he quickly gave it up. The dandy, meanwhile, seemed to be expending most of his energy on his hair, as he was stroking it incessantly and tossing his head back every few seconds.

"Maybe it's a wig," quipped Dekker in another sharp aside to Chizzie, "If I could just grab it accidentally, who knows?"

Then the referee broke in and told them to quit pussyfooting and get on with it, or they'd both be disqualified.

They stepped forwards with what looked convincingly like vigour, and Dekker swung his arm to clout the dandy man's hair accidentally. It was a mistake. As quick as a snake, the dandy man grabbed Dekker by the wrist, and, catching him off balance, proceeded to swing him round and round just like Dekker had done with the powdery, young lad. Dekker was in trouble and he knew it. Once your momentum's all bound up with centrifugal force, it's very difficult to extricate yourself, hence the First Law of Grampian Wrestling: first, dizzy your opponent. Having succeeded in that, the dandy man was about to demonstrate the Second Law of Grampian Wrestling: next, chuck him out of the ring. There was no time to lose. Dekker had to think of something quickly, but what could he do? He was spinning so fast his feet were barely on the ground.

But every cloud, as they say, has a silver lining, even greasy ones. It's not all pimples and pong; no, greasiness can actually pay off at times, and this was looking like one of those times. Just when Dekker was about to be hurled into space, his greasiness and the transferring tan combined to undermine the dandy man's grip, and Dekker found himself ejaculated prematurely. Thudding across the ground, he came to a halt just inside the ring. Staggering, he got to his feet, but the rampant dandy man prepared for the *coup de grace*.

With his victim only inches inside the line, the dandy man rushed forwards in a shoulder charge that would punt the ponging fish fryer, not just out of the ring but clean out of the showground. Dekker saw them all coming, for it was obvious from the shake of his head that Dekker's vision was blurry; there must have been at least three of them in Dekker's vision, and he made to dodge them all. But alas, his legs simply wobbled, and all he could do was crouch to defend himself, like a hedgehog. Then, in a flash, he thought better of it and sought to leap out the way, but he slipped in the process and hit the ground so fast that he didn't even have time to look up and say cheerio as the charging dandy man, fooled completely by Dekker's incompetence, shot past him and zoomed clean out the ring.

When Dekker looked up eventually, it was to see a dazed dandy man extricating himself stickily from a face-down encounter with a cow pat that had been left behind by a four-legged participant in the Battle of the Tooth.

Dekker had won the contest, and the dandy man had a deeper tan than ever before. Everyone was a winner!

Well, almost everyone: the surly dandy man, who was a hard man to please evidently, put in an official protest immediately, citing the smell and the unnatural greasiness of his opponent as unsporting conduct, but the officials proved reluctant to penalise a man on the grounds of his livelihood – especially when some of the officials were themselves chicken farmers and knew only too well the bitter sting of ostracism. The dandy man stormed off, sulking and promising to take the matter to an ombudsman of some kind.

Dekker's thoughts were focussed more modestly on his throbbing bunions and aching knees.

Being a little worse for wear but having done very well by his own reckoning, Dekker approached his final bout with a kind of cheery fatalism. He knew full well that 'Gentleman' Bob Waterman, the Garthbay man, was the toughest opponent on the programme, and he was fortunate to be meeting him in his last bout when, presumably, the man wouldn't be quite so strong or determined.

How wrong can you be? As soon as they locked on, Waterman was on him like an octopus, slipping Dekker's grip and grabbing his legs before he'd even taken two breaths. He clasped Dekker's calves near his ankles and lifted him clean off the ground. But he was just a little too low with the hold, and the fish fryer took full advantage of the only option open to him: he clambered aboard and got his legs over Waterman's shoulders. In seconds, he was sitting with his crotch right in Waterman's face – a state of affairs not exactly charming for either man. Whether it is better to have your nether regions nibbled or your nibblers nobbled is a moot question, and probably a matter only for the medical profession. All the two unfortunate grapplers knew was that things could be better.

While Dekker was appearing to get vertigo, Waterman was appearing to get poisoned, but neither man mentioned the fact, doubtless hoping that the other man would crack first.

"If the baked beans kick in now, I'm a winner," Dekker mouthed to Chizzie in another aside, "I'll flatten him." He looked down to see if the idea had occurred to his opponent.

It had, or something of the sort had, for the suffering Waterman looked up at Dekker with eyes that said only too clearly, "Break?"

Dekker caught the message and nodded. The two men disengaged.

Next, they circled each other for a while, with Waterman pressing forwards most of the time, and Dekker backing off most of the time, except for the occasional gesture of a swipe at Waterman's ankles. Once again, it became clear that neither man had quite the strength to get the other out of the ring, so this was shaping up for a points contest – a contest that Waterman was sure to win, and everyone knew it. So, no one could blame Dekker for seeking to minimise the loss. Why make it tough for Waterman and risk a bruising at this late stage? He could come to an arrangement with Gentleman Bob, and both of them would retain their dignity.

Dekker cast a long, knowing look at his opponent, followed by a little nod towards the ground. Waterman, getting the picture, returned a long blink. A gentleman's agreement had been sealed – Dekker would take a fall, and Waterman would pin him and take the points. Then later on, in the beer tent, the grateful victor would get the pints in.

Dekker looked to Chizzie and nodded discreetly in Waterman's direction with a pleasant smile that said plainly, "The game's a bogey, but three cheers for Gentleman Bob, if only there were more like him. What a man!" Then with a cheeky wink he indicated, "If he slips up, I'll pin him to the floor."

Waterman came in fast and strong. Dekker, obligingly but convincingly, stumbled and rolled backwards offering the points – an opportunity that Waterman seized with both hands – and that was it; it was all over bar the shouting. Or it should have been, but Waterman had better ideas and the shouting broke out in earnest as Dekker, hoisted aloft, was taken to the edge of the ring and then flung out like a big bag of refuse.

"Well, there you are," said a bruised Dekker later, "you just can't trust anybody these days – and especially not a gentleman! What a bastard!"

Still, on reflection, Dekker was a happy man – when all the wins and points were totalled up, Waterman came out number one, and Dekker came out number two – not a bad day's work for a smelly, old greaseball.

CHAPTER 40

"Hey, there's a penis in my programme!" Ludo shouted pointing to a name in his programme. "Look, P. Ness; he's in the high jump!"

"He should've been in the pole vault!" chirped Crispin.

"What's a penis?" asked Archie.

"Never mind," said Lady Hawkshaw, with a shudder.

"No, no, he asked politely," insisted Crispin, "he's entitled to know. Tell him, Father."

Sir Hew struggled to find words. "Well, it's… it's…"

"It's the hose between your legs," broke in Lady Hawkshaw. "Now be quiet."

"You… you pee from it," advised Sir Hew finally.

"And you have sex with it," added Crispin.

Lady Hawkshaw clenched her fists. "Cut it out, will you? No filth! No more bad language!"

"It's better he hears it from us than in the playground," insisted Crispin.

"Quiet!" bawled Lady Hawkshaw. "No more gutter talk."

"This is the gutter," opined Weever quietly.

"Penis! Penis! Penis!" chanted Archie, drawing wide-eyed astonishment from all within earshot.

Weever turned on the boy. "*Shut up, will ya?*"

"Don't talk to him like that," demanded Lady Hawkshaw.

"Look, lady," said Weever, turning round, "he needs to learn a thing or two. He ain't the centre of the universe. He isn't even close. When I was his age, I was doing deals; I wasn't going crazy over the word 'penis.'"

"I was frozen sperm once," Ludo announced.

"Who's your father, then? Captain Birdseye?" quipped Weever.

"Shh," whispered Sir Hew, holding a finger to his lips. "Their father left them. He went AWOL."

Weever went pensive suddenly and rubbed his chin, before replying quietly, "Hmm. It's sad that, very sad, but—"

"It's very sad indeed," reflected Sir Hew.

"Yes," continued Weever sombrely, "you bring them into the world, and, come hail or shine, you give your life to them."

"Yes, you do. Many times over. You die a thousand deaths, or the death of a thousand cuts."

"No, what I meant was… Jeezus, I'm goin' nuts here," Weever hissed, shaking his head. "I want to know what's going on out there. Instead, here I am, fighting for my sanity. What the hell is the score, Charlie?"

CHAPTER 41

The hill race was announced: it was Chizzie's hour of reckoning. Butterflies flooded his stomach. He hadn't trained for this race, anything could happen. Thankfully, attending other people's events had kept his mind off his own race; only now did the awesome prospect hit him.

Yolanda came up to him, and calmed him with a hug and a kiss. With determination overcoming apprehension, he took off his tracksuit and gave it to Yolanda, then jogged lightly up to the starting line.

The start was straightforward: "Are you ready, gentlemen?" asked the starter, "Go!"

And away they went. Ahead of them lay one lap of the track, then two-and-a-half miles of boggy moorland, followed by two thousand feet of mountainside, and back again.

They were a curious mixture, these rockhoppers, as they were known. Frankly, if your worst nightmare was an alien landing, this was no place to be. At one extreme there was the tall, elegant, out-and-out runner wearing the Findandie colours, and at the other end of the scale came the Altnaclog man, Mr Anthony Swedhed-Fyffe, resembling nothing more keenly than a posh Neanderthal. Every one of them, though, looked a picture of health next to the Oxdale man, a pallid-faced doctor who was like something risen from the pathology slab.

As Chizzie and his fellow rockhoppers made their way round the track, in their own individual styles and savouring the crowd's applause, the Millburgh Pipes and Drums struck up with the old favourite 'Cock O' The North'. Its effect was immediate: Swedhed-Fyffe broke into a spring-cum-bound style of propulsion, which seemed very mannered, but, for him, was said to be perfectly natural.

Leaving the arena for the gruelling task ahead, these brave men of the hills departed with another change of tempo, this time to the tune of 'Marie's Wedding', which propelled the posh Neanderthal immediately into a bounding-cum-canter-with-cheery-smile form of propulsion; again, this was apparently effortless and perfectly natural. The good-humoured crowd, capturing the mood, took up the refrain, clapping in time and singing, "Step we gaily on we go, heel for heel and toe for toe".

Then, out of the showground, the rockhoppers went. They remained together in a tight bunch over the boggy moorland track, but, at the base of the hill, the posh Neanderthal swerved off the main track suddenly and broke free. Selecting one of the many sheep tracks, he began bounding along in his unique style. Then came yet another swerve, and he was scrambling up the hillside – leaping from rock to rock one minute, then down on all fours the next, grabbing at grassy tussocks and hauling himself up the hill. In this improvised style, he began to build a healthy lead – a lead that set Chizzie to thinking that maybe it was time for him to be on the rocks too; he was focussing on conserving energy and losing touch with the bunch very gradually. He made the decision, and off he went after Swedhed-Fyffe, weaving his way along a narrow sheep track and onto the rocky slopes.

Clambering up these slopes was hard work, but it was worth it; very soon he was well above the pack. Tired though he was, seeing the others beneath him lifted his morale enormously.

As any climber knows, there is a very large difference between being the first person up a rocky slope and being second up a rocky slope: namely, the first person dislodges debris and the second person gets it. And down it came; a perpetual stream of debris came tumbling towards Chizzie: chunks of peat, tufts of grass, rocks, pebbles, grit and even the odd boulder. A less desperate head would have altered course, but not Chizzie: he was now so tired that his head was a province ruled by his muscles, the mob of the human body, and they were in no mood for extra mileage; they were for easing their pain by keeping things simple – very, very simple.

As he hauled himself up, inch by inch, higher and higher, the fatigue set in deeper and deeper, and a kind of delirium overtook him; even the odd passing boulder lost all significance until one small boulder came bounding down out of the blue, heading straight towards him. Luckily, his reflexes were still keen and they jerked his head away as the boulder shot past his left ear.

But the Tottiepans man was not so lucky. Unseen by Chizzie he was close behind, and the small boulder grazed the man's head, forcing him to make a loud yell that nearly sent Chizzie tumbling backwards, before he managed to grab a tussock and steady himself. When Chizzie looked behind, it seemed for a moment that he was on the slope with a waxwork. As if frozen in time, the Tottiepans man stood utterly motionless. It was a worrying sight.

Then, even more worrying, there suddenly came a song as the Tottiepans man hit key of A major and began belting out 'Fly Me to the Moon' in a booming baritone, like a human Wurlitzer. The race-world froze. All running stopped. Swedhed-Fyffe, clinging to a grassy tussock, leaned out from his lofty perch and gazed down, with his mouth agape and his forehead, said to be rarely troubled by thoughts, bearing a look of puzzlement.

The other runners, like a pack of meerkats, were staring upwards as if something very major had occurred; the Second Coming perhaps or possibly some terrible affliction stalking these heights. It was amazement jostled with fear. Could this be contagious? Should they be standing there? Should they not be getting the hell out?

The wildlife had no doubts – they were off. As if a gun had fired, everything that could run was charging up the far slope and over into the next glen: red deer, mountain hare, stoats and a fox were as one. Everything that could fly was in the air, soaring or whirring away, and, doubtless, every creature that could creep, crawl, wriggle, slither or summon a carpet of slime had done all it could to get under a boulder or into a bolthole.

Then, as suddenly as it had come, the musical interlude ceased. The mountain cabaret was no more. The Tottiepans man's brain cells had seemingly rallied and regained control. He looked about him. What had happened, he probably knew not, but one thing he would know: people do not stand and stare at you for nothing. Something from deep within had outed and now everyone knew, whatever it was. He could only hope it was nothing embarrassing. In spite of the graze on his head, he was now good to go, and not only that but he actually looked positively refreshed. His excoriating effects on the ecology of the area had very possibly revitalised it too and benefits would doubtless flow. Certainly, the young grouse would be better off for knowing that humans could be lunatics.

Chizzie responded, thankful for the rest but knowing he had to stay ahead of the Tottiepans man if he were to avoid the same fate, so he turned, lifted his eyes up the hillside and then, lifting his head further to the heavens, he opened his mouth as if to offer up thanks. Then he thought better of it – it was too cheap. He was off again, clambering. Onwards and upwards!

The runners below snapped into action too, and Swedhed-Fyffe burst from his little bubble of semi-concern and shot off again – the race for glory was back on.

Five minutes later, all was not well with Chizzie: he had a chest that was now as raw as a red-hot boiler and a pair of legs seemingly magnetically attracted to the earth's core. The Tottiepans man went past him. Barely able to move now, Chizzie's every step required a huge intake of air. His wheezing got so loud that he even failed to hear the approach of another fellow competitor – the man of the anatomical slab, the pallid doctor. Where had he come from? He must have been obscured in a hollow close by. Had he the strength, Chizzie would have leaped with fright, but his heart and nerves had other priorities: namely, keeping their man upright and conscious.

Evidently assuming a warm welcome, the medicine man came up and laid a hand on Chizzie's shoulder, enquiring very kindly, "How are you, Chizzie?"

"Not bad, not bad," Chizzie gasped sharply, almost passing out with the effort. "Buzz off, ya creep!" was what he really wanted to say, but his natural politeness got the better of him. What on earth was this man doing creeping up on him? Him and his touchy-feely fingers. Chizzie made a big effort and smiled.

The doctor smiled back. "Good, good," he said, "I see you've lost your wingman. I thought we might work together and take it in turns as pacemaker. We can help each other get through the worst."

The only pacemaker Chizzie had in mind was one that would fight off sudden cardiac arrest; the last thing he needed was somebody else sucking up his air and telling him what to do. Anger began to swell within him. Just who did this guy think he was? This presumptuous prat with the big crucifix round his neck? Crucifix! Of course, that's it! He's one of the God Squad, come to win a soul for Jesus; nab a sucker when he's freaked out – easy pickings – that's his game! What a coup: an actual conversion on the mount! Wouldn't that be a sure-fire passport to heaven? Well, if that was his game, the creep was in for a shock. But, then again, maybe not; maybe this guy was the real thing. It was hard to say whether he was a Good Samaritan, or some sneaky creep trying to assert his moral superiority and thereby foist his beliefs on a man so beleaguered that his mind wasn't his own. If it was the latter, the cheapster had better think again, for there – high above them, in the shape of Swedhead-Fyffe – raw animalism was well out in front and going further ahead by the minute. But, of course, the doctor could see all this for himself, and, that being the case, his intentions could only be good. There was no doubting it; he was actually the real thing: a genuine Good Samaritan.

In some ways, though, this was actually worse than being proselytised; at least you could argue against religion, even despise it, but who could argue against goodness? The only thing to do was to thank the good man and send him on his way. So Chizzie politely declined the offer and waved the good man through.

His obligations satisfied, Chizzie sat himself on a large boulder for a moment or two to gather his wits and compose himself. A few minutes later, he looked up to see his way ahead – and what a shock! There, on the path crossing his own line of travel, was the pack of three, not only had they caught up with him but they were ahead of him. He was last!

The silence and the isolation now descended upon him very heavily. His presence seemed to shrink almost to nothing

398

in the vastness of the great space. All alone now, he knew only humiliation loomed.

But, no! No. All was not lost; cramp, a fall and 'hitting the wall' – all of these things and more could take their toll. This was a mountain race, and things happen. Being last was not a done deal; not yet. The path taken by the pack would take a long, clockwise loop round a massive crag; if Chizzie could scramble round the much shorter, but uncertain, anticlockwise route, there was an outside chance he could catch some of them up. Almost certainly, he could catch the Good Samaritan, for that zombie looked worse than Chizzie ever had, even when floored by the flu.

By the time the pack got round the crag, Swedhed-Fyffe had a lead of about three hundred yards. Chizzie – though very, very tired – had profited dramatically from his gamble and got himself into third place, about eighty yards ahead of the pack of three and a hundred yards behind the Good Samaritan, who – very annoyingly – showed no signs of collapsing.

The next mile presented a gently undulating plateau of dry, springy peat carrying a fine, wide track – it was perfect for fast running. And, in no time at all, the pack was at Chizzie's heels. The inevitable happened. Going past him, one of the runners muttered indecipherable comments before leaving him for dead – dead being the apposite word for Chizzie's condition now. The toil and the heat had ground him down, and his mouth felt dry and dusty; foolishly, he had failed to avail himself of the water tumbling down from the many streams. The other competitors all had plastic mugs clipped to their waistbands, but not Chizzie, he had forgotten to bring a mug and now he felt an overwhelming need to plunge his face into cool water and gulp it down in bucketfuls, which he did, leaving himself yet further behind and hopelessly waterlogged.

Things were now desperate. Even Swedhed-Fyffe was being overhauled by the pack as they approached the final brutal slope. But Swedhead-Fyffe worked hard, regained his lead and was about fifty yards clear by the time he got to the bare summit, where he rounded the official stationed there. He would need all his lead, though, for the out-and-out runners would do well going downhill. Indeed, as the pack of runners pattered along the track on their descent, they all but ran down Chizzie, who was still making his way up. The red-faced Tottiepans man swept by without a word, followed closely by the pale-faced Good Samaritan, who wished him luck.

At the summit, the official hung on, glancing impatiently at his watch and peering down at the lumbering Tannadee man. Probably as much for his own sake as Chizzie's, the official made the struggling rockhopper an offer he couldn't refuse: "*On ye go back down again, son!*" he yelled through cupped hands, "*I'll clock ye as havin' got here! On you go down now! On ye go!*"

It was a sensible move, since there was absolutely no chance that it would affect the outcome of the race, but Chizzie was having none of it. Having compromised on the cycling fix, he wasn't shirking on the mountain. This was a sort of penance. He was nothing if not a man of honour.

The official was now a man of fury, and it was clearly all he could do to prevent himself running down and kicking Chizzie's backside straight down the hillside where it belonged. But, of course, you must never kick a man when he's down, not even when you're an official on the top of a mountain, for who knows? The man might just have enough strength to kick you back, and who's going to pull him off if he finds the strength to completely lose it? Even a man in

Chizzie's desperate state has been known to find the strength to get in a good whack.

"I have never ever seen a man so near death in all my life!" the official was later to report after seeing Chizzie rounding him eventually. "All the flies on the hill were onto him, and the buzzards had their eyes on him," he added perceptively. A moveable feast then, but only just. As soon as he was out of earshot, the official got on his walkie-talkie and alerted the mountain rescue team to Chizzie's plight.

The words were barely out of the official's mouth when he was looking at something even worse: Chizzie had stopped and was standing above the scree slope. Unbelievably, he was looking all the way down to the bottom. The Tannadee man it seemed was weighing the odds.

"No! No, for God's sake!" shouted the official. "Not the scree slope! It's suicide, man! It's suicide!"

But Chizzie's mind was sold. He would take the risk. He would take the infamous scree slope – the Devil's Ride, as they called it – for on this scree lay his only chance of not being last. This seven-hundred-foot curtain of hanging rocks, stones and grit, known to be a destroyer of men, bristling with awesome reputation and with the careers of many a famous hill runner lying shattered at its base. These were men who'd thought themselves equal to the scree and found to their cost they were not; men, it has to be said, who were in far better condition than Chizzie Bryson was.

"No, man! Don't do it. Don't do it!" the official yelled, hurrying towards Chizzie.

But that was the trigger. Chizzie crouched, then tilting his head to the heavens for a moment, he paused as if surrendering himself to the arms of fate. Then he rose, and shuffling forwards, he eased himself onto the edge. Here, he hesitated, but only for a second, then he stepped into the open air and his feet met the scree. The shifting ground caught his feet gently. For a second, he felt as light as air. He was on his way. On his way to either glory or oblivion.

Moving at exhilarating speed, his feet sank into the loose-flowing stones and the coarse sand. It was almost like speed skating. Seconds later, he was going so fast that he was even feeling a breeze on his face. The sound of the rushing stones drowned out the gasp from the arena when the news hit that one of the hill runners was on the scree. But he was okay, the scree was dry and fluid; he was doing well, and even beginning to feel a bit cocky; it wasn't so bad after all. He was lucky; he'd got the scree in good, dry condition. *This is the way to travel!* he thought.

Then he felt a slight strain, and his ankles begin to hurt a little. All that movement and the bumping of the stones was bruising him, and there was a big spread of boulders ahead; he'd have to clamber over these very carefully or risk a fracture. With his ankles getting more and more painful, he was beginning to have second thoughts and was wishing he was back on the path; this was beginning to feel like a terrible mistake. The track might have been long, but at least it was smooth, and running downhill would have been a lot easier than clambering uphill, even if it was hard on the knees. But it was too late; he was committed now and, frankly, in a bit of a mess. All the more so because the niggle in his back had returned and would very likely get worse.

Clambering over boulders on all fours was as humiliating as it was slow; it was much, much slower than if he'd taken the track. Realistically, it might even be nightfall before he got finished – if indeed he ever got finished.

By the time he got to the end of the boulder field, his back was aching so much that he could hardly straighten up. And he knew full well that his ankles just couldn't take any more hits – they were just too painful. Tired, angry, sore and longing for respite, he stopped and stood up straight with a struggle. After taking a deep breath, he gauged the distance he still had to cover. It looked a long way, but the air was good, it was refreshing and it lifted his spirits. Then he took another look down. This time he saw for certain what lay below, and the hairs on the back of his neck stood up. They stood not in fear, they stood with hope.

A masterstroke had flashed across his brain. The remaining scree consisted almost entirely of light pebbles and coarse grit. He needed only to become a wheel and he could roll all the way down! There was nothing in his way except a crop of small boulders, and there weren't many of these, hardly any at all. Without a second thought, as the idea was that good, he tucked his head between his knees, curled into a ball and off he went – the human wheel was on its way!

Whether this course of action owed anything to oxygen starvation, vertigo or any other affliction, no one could tell. All that can be said for certain is that Chizzie Bryson went hurtling down this fateful slope, bound for stardom or the crematorium. Down the slope he went, glorying and dooming, puffing and bouncing, rolling like a punctured beach ball, and squeaking loudly and yelling, "*Ooyah! Ooyah!*"

Standing by, their eyes glued to the scree slope, the mountain rescue team took the news with a slight movement of the eyebrows – their way of expressing surprise. Not that they would be entirely surprised to hear of some punter hurtling down the scree slope masquerading as a wheel – nothing humanity could throw at these men could really surprise them. These were men who had seen it all: people strolling through snow-clad hills with nothing more than a lunchbox and a wall map, and people pushing bedsteads up the highest mountain tops for, of all things, life-saving charities. No, the concern of these mountain men lay simply in logistics; they doubtless knew that by the time they got into their Land Rover, the human wheel – or what was left of it – would be a subject not so much requiring their life-saving skills, but more a matter for the funeral director. Anyway, being the obliging souls that they were, they drained their tea cups swiftly and set off for the scree slope.

Meanwhile, Chizzie – having miraculously evaded the boulders at the bottom of the slope – was still alive, though not exactly leaping for joy. He lay in the big, grassy tussocks that had buffered his carcase to a very gentle halt close to the moorland path. Flat on his back, spreadeagled and extremely dizzy, he saw the sky spinning round and round a thousand times faster than he had ever seen it before, even on his most drunken spree. What thoughts he could muster, he gathered, and – after a few minutes – he made a valiant effort to get to his feet, but he was so dizzy he hardly knew which way was up and which was down. He got upright only by first bending over on all fours. Then, trying to move forward, he succeeded only in staggering a few steps before falling over a tussock and landing flat on his face.

After what seemed like an eternity, his head eventually cleared enough to let him stand up, and through his whirling, blurry vision he could just make out Swedhed-Fyffe in the distance coming towards him, and not far behind Swedhed-Fyffe came the other runners. Desperate to get under way, Chizzie pointed his head in the direction of the showground, almost falling over in the process. Through the warm, shimmering air he could just make out the showground; it appeared to be about half a mile away, but it was hard to be certain with it swirling round and round. If he could just stay on his feet and get going now, there was a chance he could actually get there first. His heart skipped at the thought. And, pursing his lips, he lifted up his left foot, then his right foot, and, though racked with bruises and with shoes full of grit, he staggered towards the track. In the corner of one eye, he could just see Swedhed-Fyffe getting ever closer. So, raising his game, Chizzie tried to lift his knees higher; but in a flash, his feet slipped from under him and he thumped face down into the peat bog.

Fortunately, the bog was shallow. With a mighty effort amid slurping and sucking sounds, he got to his feet again and, pulling his left foot up, he held it out in the direction of the firm track. But, in planting it, he wasn't quite there and he felt his right foot slipping away ahead of him as the rest of him descended slowly back into the peat bog. Performing the splits, he keeled over sideways into the now much visited bog.

The sky, beautifully blue and white though it was, was rapidly losing its appeal for the man. Half-paddling and half-crawling through the black, sloppy peat, he struggled onto firm ground finally, and hauled himself and his cargo of peat to the vertical. The peaty stuff was everywhere – in his shorts, his shoes, his mouth, his ears, his nose, his eyes and his every nook and cranny; he was completely covered in it. And though it wasn't too pongy, it wasn't exactly fragrant either. On a positive note, there were other properties – like some herbal poultice, the clinging peat had seemingly put a brake on the spinning in his head and had helped to steady his vision. By then, he was able to move forward with at least some degree of confidence, albeit carrying something like twice his normal weight, or so it felt. At a half-gallop, half-stagger, he squelched his way onto the moorland track.

As the men of the mountain rescue team drew up in their Land Rover, this was the slimy, gyrating spectre that met their eyes. They had seen it all, these men, but never, even in their wildest dreams, could they have imagined anything like this:

a peat hag on the move! What do you do? Do you take a risk and haul it in? Or do you get the hell out? They did what most people would do in the circumstances: they remained in the vehicle and let the thing pass. In jaw-dropping amazement, they looked on as the freaky figure lumbered past in a sort of waltz step – roughly four steps forwards and one to the side.

Over the public address system, Frank Tosh broke the news that Chizzie, the human wheel, was now in the lead. The crowd responded first with a huge gasp of amazement, and then with a great cheer and thunderous applause. Chizzie heard it all – his name, the cheer and the applause – and his spirits soared above all the strains and pains of his body. It was mind over matter now, though with the amount of matter he was carrying it was never going to be easy.

The soothing effects of the peat were working their magic. They kept him in the reckoning. Even his backache had abated. Buoyed up now, he even got to thinking that there was a business opportunity here. His hotel could feature a health and recuperation spa founded on the salving properties of the Highland quagmire. Alternative therapies were all the rage, after all, and this stuff was nothing if not alternative.

Frank Tosh's voice came wafting through the heat haze and the swarms of flies to greet Chizzie's ears again; this time, though, it was not good news: Swedhed-Fyffe was only three hundred yards behind him, and close behind Swedhed-Fyffe was the Garthbay man.

A flutter of panic raced through Chizzie's body. Desperately, he tried to summon up more speed. But though the spirit was willing, it was the only thing that was, and he was actually getting slower. The heat of the sun was baking the peaty slime on him, and it was getting crustier and harder by the minute. It got harder and harder for Chizzie to move. From a distance, he could have been mistaken for a giant beetle fleeing from its under-a-boulder home. No one knew quite what to make of it, as Swedhed-Fyffe, puffing and blowing, arrived at Chizzie's shoulder and then went past him, followed a few seconds later by the Garthbay man. The crowd, ever for the plucky underdog, groaned at the news. But, when Swedhed-Fyffe entered the showground for the closing lap, they cheered politely, and the sound of it almost sank Chizzie to his knees.

Third place was still up for grabs, though, so Chizzie, battling on, went for it – cracking and flaking, grinding and scraping. Alas, with only fifty yards to go to the showground entrance, the other runners, including the Good Samaritan, caught up with Chizzie and went past him, sending a shudder through his flaking carapace. Another shudder struck when Tosh's announcement hammered home the news that now he, the Tannadee captain, was last. Then he heard the applause for the winner of the race, followed by the announcement that Garthbay had won. It was almost too much to bear. How many hammer blows can a man take? But Chizzie was no quitter. Dignity was on the line here. If he came in not too far behind, he could still salvage his pride.

As he struggled on and entered the showground, with the applause for the fourth and fifth men just tailing away, Frank Tosh announced Chizzie's arrival. The sight of him cut the applause like a knife. People gasped in horror. But what on earth could they expect? The man had just rolled down a mountainside – he wasn't going to be coming in dancing the Watusi!

The crowd knew guts when they saw it, and the sheer guts of this aching man brought them to their feet; they cheered and roared him on, ten times louder than all the applause for the other runners combined. With plates of peat cracking and peeling off him like some half-finished robot bolting out of a space lab, the doughty, clay-pot figure staggered and jolted his way round the final bend.

Spontaneously, moved by the man and all he stood for, the pipers struck up 'Scotland the Brave'. They, too, knew guts when they saw it. The crowd went wild, and – cheering him to the hill tops – they got their man home! Last he may have been, this knight in lustreless armour, but as love even more than fortune favours the brave, the real victory – the moral and lasting victory – was his.

The brave, the redoubtable, the one and only Chizzie Bryson fell into the arms of his beloved Yolanda.

"My hero," she whispered as she cuddled his crusty cheek.

But Chizzie was far too spent to respond: his head simply flopped onto her shoulder until Johnny supported him by the left arm while Sven took him by the right arm. No one knew quite where the priority lay: Johnny and Paw suggested the recovery tent, while Sven insisted on the changing room, and Dekker was for the local carwash. Chizzie, in a whisper, insisted on the changing room, where he could soak in the bath, so that's where the ordeal ended. The now legendary rockhopper began his road to recovery in an old-fashioned bathtub, soaking up to his armpits in gravy-coloured water and groaning like a rut-spent stag.

The groaning only got worse when his mind cleared to remind him that he might be spent, but he still had a job to do.

He had to get to Yolanda right away. He took several deep breaths, then hauled himself slowly and awkwardly out of the lukewarm but very soothing water, which was the best place in the world for him right at that moment. Aching all over, he dried himself off as fast as he could manage before putting on his tracksuit and easing his way to the warm-up field. With every muscle tight and sore, and his head buzzing, just as it was on the hill, he was nevertheless determined to be with Yolanda.

CHAPTER 42

Weever leaned back and breathed a sigh of relief. Finally, the G&Ts had kicked in and Sir Hew had fallen asleep, with his head slumped over his right shoulder. When his cap fell off, he didn't even notice and his lights were still out when Lady Hawkshaw put the cap back on his head.

"Once he nods off like that, that's him gone for a while," she said quietly.

"Thank God!" muttered Weever.

"Pardon?"

"Land of nod."

"Yes, he doesn't sleep well at night, so I'll just leave him be for a bit. No one will notice."

Weever nodded gently.

"Aw, the dear man," said the lady sitting next to Lady Hawkshaw. "He works so hard; he deserves his little rest, and what a magnificent head of hair he has."

"More like loft insulation," whispered Weever to Fairfoull.

Lady Hawkshaw smiled affectionately. "He makes his own hair conditioner – enriched with turnips. 'Turnip strong!' he likes to say. He loves turnips – can't get enough of them."

"Yeah, and we know where they go," whispered Weever.

"Straight to his head," suggested Fairfoull.

"They drilled four holes in that skull after his accident," said Lady Hawkshaw. "And he still wasn't right."

"Not deep enough?" enquired Weever.

410

"Then they put a metal plate in his head the size of a Jaffa cake," continued Lady Hawkshaw. "You can't see it unless I—"

"No, no, please don't," cried the other lady, holding her hands up in horror.

"You hear that?" asked Lady Hawkshaw, tapping the inclined head. "Metal."

"Mental more like," suggested Weever quietly.

"He picks up radio waves, he says. He got Radio Botswana last week. Either that or hailstones," said Lady Hawkshaw.

"It must've been quite an accident," said the other lady.

"Oh, yes. Oh, yes," agreed Lady Hawkshaw. "He was hoping to smash the world land speed record on a lawnmower, but he smashed his head instead. Thank God for the turnips. It could've been much worse. The record stood at eighty miles an hour; he was going for one hundred miles an hour. And it still had to be able to cut grass! So he went for it on a beach up north, and at sixty miles an hour a gull pooped on his goggles, and in the whiteout he hit a rock and was punted through the air into a rock pool."

"Aw, God!" groaned Weever. "Now *she's* at it – yakety, yakety, yak."

"And that's how it happened," continued Lady Hawkshaw. "He's never cut grass since. Actually, I think people will notice that he's nodded off. I'd better wake him."

"No, no, no, think of his health," pleaded Weever. "Just put a programme in his hand and make it look like he's reading."

"But his head's at an angle," Lady Hawkshaw remarked.

"He's a deep sleeper?" Weever queried.

"Yes," confirmed Lady Hawkshaw.

"Right, we lift his head up." Weever pulled Sir Hew's head up by the ears to a reading position.

"Careful, that's his ears you've got," complained Lady Hawkshaw.

"I know ears when I see them. There now, cap on and he's back in business," said Weever, looking pleased.

"He's dead," said Ludo.

CHAPTER 43

The high jump went off relatively smoothly except for one small matter: a big tear in the landing mattress ran about two feet up the middle from one end, and every time it was the turn of the Tottiepans man, the only jumper with a left-sided run up, the mattress had to be swung the other way round to prevent him disappearing through it. But apart from the dust and the faint odour of mature sweat, it was perfect, or at least as perfect as you can get with no one watching. In the silence, Garthbay triumphed and Tannadee came last.

Next, came the half-mile race. Chizzie got to the warm-up field just in time to kiss Yolanda and wish her luck before she made her way to the track. Among the runners, her presence received a mixed reception: some seemed pleased to see her, no doubt thinking that their own chances had just improved a notch; while three others looked decidedly peeved, perhaps perceiving that the status of their race had been lowered by the presence of a female in what, strictly speaking, was a man's race. But Yolanda looked quite unperturbed by the coldness of some.

They drew lots for lanes and then they were led up to the line to be introduced to the crowd. Again, there was a mixed reaction. First, there was a note of surprise when the crowd caught sight of a female lining up with the men, wearing the Tannadee card on her purple running vest. Then came a swirl of intrigue as the name 'Weever' was announced. The sound of the crowd rose, the excitement built for a moment, like an on-rushing wave, then it faded gradually away, like the wave had swished up the beach and dissolved into the sand. A hush descended.

In the grandstand, Fairfoull was the first to react. "Yolanda's in the race!" he yelped, startling a sleepy Weever. "Yolanda's running for Tannadee!"

"She's what?" exclaimed Weever.

"Running for Tannadee!"

"How? What?" spluttered Weever. "What's she doin'? She can't do that."

"It looks like she can, and is," said Fairfoull.

"Goddamn! I gotta get her outta there." Weever leaped to his feet.

"It's too late, Gordon."

"For Chrissake!" exploded Weever. "She's crazy!" Desperately, his eyes swung from side to side and his hand went to his chin as he thought for a moment. "Right, just make sure she wins," he declared. "I don't want her beaten."

"If she wins, we lose," Fairfoull reminded him.

"Well… get her in the middle somewhere. She's up against men, and that's not right! It's a disgrace! Jeezus!" Weever leaned forwards and accosted Frank Tosh in the aisle below him. "Hey, Froth! Tosh! Whatever your name is! Cancel this race. There's been a mix-up. You can't have men against women."

Tosh, somewhat bemused, simply shrugged. "There's nothing I can do," he said quietly.

"Gimme the mic; gimme the mic," demanded Weever.

"I can't do that, Mr Weever. I'm the official presenter," explained Frank.

"*Gimme the fuckin' mic, will ya?*" Weever yelled.

414

Lady Hawkshaw gasped. "Mr Weever!"

"Excuse my French, but I need to stop this now. It's urgent." Weever reached for the mic, but Tosh pulled it away, asking for calm.

Sir Hew, rubbing his sleepy eyes, joined Tosh in asking for calm. "Sit down please, Mr Weever," he pleaded.

"Oh shut up, you old babbler!" ranted Weever.

"Mr Weever! Language!" cried Lady Hawkshaw.

Sir Hew was more philosophical: "No, no, he's right, dear. I do rattle on a bit. In the open air, I'm like a wind turbine. I just go on and on and on and—"

"Shut your goddamn face, *will ya?*" barked Weever. "Let me think. I need that mic, gimme it now! Gimme!"

He reached further over, almost getting his hand on Tosh's shoulder, but Tosh saw it coming and leaned away, causing Weever to overreach. And though Weever arched his back desperately to regain his balance, he was too late. With his arms flailing like an electrified octopus, Weever twisted and toppled forwards. With a fleshy bang, he hit his head on the handrail and crashed to the floor. Lady Hawkshaw screamed. Fairfoull jumped up then fell to his knees and asked the great man to respond, but there was no response.

"Is he dead?" Ludo enquired casually.

A groan from Weever confirmed life yet remained in the great man.

Fairfoull looked up anxiously. "Get the doctor!"

Lady Hawkshaw turned away as Sir Hew beckoned to the steward before leaning over Weever to take a good look at the stunned billionaire, who, though a little groggy, was attempting to sit up supported by one of his security men.

Sir Hew smiled. "He's fine. He'll live. It was just a little thud. I'll wager he'll be tickety-boo in two days. Say, is that a wig?"

"Wiggy! Wiggy!" chanted Ludo quickly.

Weever groaned again.

Sir Hew gazed at Weever's head for a moment, then, with all the authority of a senior consultant, pronounced: "He should try turnips."

Unaware of the turmoil in the grandstand, the starter called the runners to the line for the half-mile race. They took their positions and braced themselves for a quick start.

"On your marks, get set..." declared the starter.

Bang!

They were off!

But, after only fifty yards, the runners looked like they were treading on glue. Everybody, it seemed, wanted to be in last position, right at the back of the pack. The mile race had evidently struck a note of fear in them all: it seemed the loud and clear message was to keep out of the pack! There would be no rumble in the jungle for them, there simply wasn't enough time to recover. If you went down in this race, you'd be out. So, no one was tempted to lead. Everyone, it seemed, had total faith in the power of their own fast finish. As they reached the first bend, they were almost tiptoeing in trying to out-slow each other.

Then, suddenly, there was a purple flash: it was Yolanda. She'd broken free, accelerated away into the bend and headed off down the back straight. The men watched her go, seemingly bemused or simply discounting her; they did not respond. After one lap, she was nearly sixty yards ahead and looking strong.

Then, the other runners became seriously alarmed, and – with a quick change of mind – they threw caution to the wind; the female was much stronger than they'd thought. They were going to look like idiots. They were going to lose to a woman. So, like hounds on the scent of a fox, they went after her. They made inroads quickly, and the gap shrank and shrank.

Yolanda was beginning to slow, and the gap was closing faster. With two hundred yards to go to the finish, they were on to her. As they went into the final straight, one man went past her, then another and then another. But Yolanda was no Dalrymple, she kept her form: there were no flailing limbs and no bulging temples. She was overtaken again, but, with forty yards to go, she narrowed her eyes, pushed out her chin, gritted her teeth and gave everything she had. She gained on one runner and went past him, but he wasn't done yet. He fought back and, putting in a burst of his own, he pulled away again.

Yolanda finished fifth. She was completely spent and unable to stand. She dropped to the ground, kneeling and gasping for air, then she rolled onto her back, with her hands slapped against her head.

Chizzie knew how it felt, but there was nothing he could do, so – looking on anxiously – he just waited for her to recover. Moments later, he was relieved to see her get to her feet, a bit wobbly but able to walk, with her hands behind her head and her chest heaving. The other guys went up to her and shook her hand, even the guy she beat. She had saved the race for them; they knew that. Without her, who knows what would have happened? They could have still been out there on the track, scuffling around the second bend.

Then came good news for Yolanda: over the tannoy, it was announced that she'd been upgraded and given fourth place. Plus, it was effectively a double pointer, because the runner from Garthbay – one of Tannadee's main rivals – was the one who'd been disqualified for head-butting and barging. It was a tragedy for the man really, as it had been clearly an accident: he dipped too early for the finish and his fancy hairstyle flopped over his face, blacking out the finish line, and he stumbled into the runner alongside in the blackout. Technically, though, it's a foul. After all, if you can't control your own hair, then it's nobody's fault but your own and you pay the price.

Chizzie could hardly believe it. He hadn't known what to expect from Yolanda, secretly he'd feared the worst – humiliation – so fourth place was a great result as far as he was concerned. As Chizzie made his way to Yolanda as fast as his aching muscles would allow, he wondered why the applause from the crowd was surprisingly muted for such a brave effort from Yolanda. Possibly, they simply didn't know what to make of her; this view was confirmed when Chizzie passed a couple of beer drinkers.

"Is she a man disguised?" asked one of them.

But Chizzie was in no doubt: even if Yolanda had boosted no one else's morale, she'd certainly boosted his. He felt very emotional when he saw her and reached out to hug her.

Breathing hard and cradled in his arms, she whispered, "Sorry... sorry, I didn't do better. I could've done... If I hadn't gone out like I did, if I'd stayed with the pack... I should've run my own race. I thought getting the jump on the others was worth at least ten yards... but the price was too high. I had to carry lactic acid too long. Ugh!"

"You did bloody well!" insisted Chizzie, misty eyed, "Don't beat yourself up, Yolanda. If you'd stayed with the pack, anything could've happened. You got us some extremely valuable points. I couldn't have done better myself."

"Liar."

"No, really. Honest to God. There were two guys in that race who could've beaten me. Put it this way, if I'd got the points you got and Garthbay got none, I'd be absolutely bloody delighted with myself. You did us all proud. You're an inspiration, Yolanda."

Hand in hand, they walked back to the warm-up field where Yolanda wanted to do some light jogging and stretching before heading for the changing room. On the way, they met Dekker, a man exuberant: "*Congratulations! Great performance, Yolanda!*" he roared as he hugged her. Then, stepping back, he raised her right arm, announcing to all within earshot, "Companion Yolanda! Companion of honour! Yee-hah! Whoopee!"

CHAPTER 44

When Chizzie got word of the points totals, nerves jangled his aching body. Now two were level in top spot, Garthbay and Tannadee, and only one event remained: the one hundred yards. Running for Tannadee was Billy Pung. On the erstwhile schoolboy legs rested the fate of the school and perhaps even the future of Tannadee. As team captain and Billy Pung's mentor, Chizzie knew that Billy would be looking for him. He had to be with the lad, who he feared privately might do a runner, not on the track but clean out of the stadium and into the hills, away from all the hurly-burly that so often upset him.

To his great relief, he found Billy near the start line, along with Paw and Sven. Billy seemed remarkably calm. Chizzie didn't have to look far to find the reason: Billy's eyes kept turning to a young lady in the VIP section of the grandstand. She was none other than Mary Boone, the singer who'd wowed the crowd earlier while the rockhoppers were making their way over the moor and up the hill. She seemed pleased to return Billy's interest.

Hoping this was all positive, Chizzie tapped Billy on the shoulder to wish him luck, but, before he got the words out, Billy swung round and grabbed him in a bear hug, which – though well-intentioned – stung every muscle fibre in Chizzie's fragile body, forcing out of him a moan that Billy seemed to interpret as a burst of emotion, for Billy too moaned. Perhaps the lad's hormones were high. Through the pain, Chizzie put his arms round the lad and hugged him tight, moaning again, this time with real affection. It brought a tear to Paw's eye.

Then the starter took up his microphone, and told the runners to get ready and approach the line.

Yolanda took Chizzie gently by the arm and called for Paw, Sven and Billy to join them in a group hug.

As they linked arms and formed a sort of scrum, Sven shoved his face into Billy's and whispered, "Remember, Billy, we are the Companions! We're with you all the way. We give you our strength. We pass it to you. All our strength is yours. So burn it up, man! Burn it up!"

Billy nodded, his eyes now flaring, seething with energy.

"Burn it up, man! Burn it up!" Sven snarled again.

Paw joined in, "Show 'em, Billy; show 'em what you can do."

Billy replied with a muffled, wolf-like growl. Things were getting just a bit too atavistic for Chizzie; besides, he couldn't help thinking that, far from donating energy, he was likely to be draining it from the lad, so he quickly broke from the group hug and ushered Billy over to the start line.

Everything now hung on this poignant journey of less than ten seconds up the middle of the arena. Any one of four runners, including Billy, could win the race, but the clear favourite was the man running for Garthbay – the renowned Peter Gribben, a Commonwealth Games semi-finalist and Olympic qualifier. No one had told Billy about Gribben's record, but he hardly needed telling; he would see it for himself. When you're looking at a Ferrari, you know it's fast. And when you see a guy measuring out his starting blocks as carefully as a jeweller or you see him shooting away from his blocks in practice like he was catapulted out, you know you've got a job on your hands, and particularly so when you don't have any starting blocks yourself because you thought they held you back.

Billy was told he was in lane six, and an official took him there. Next to Billy, in lane five, was the man himself, the great Gribben, who appeared completely unaware that Billy even existed as he fixed his eyes unwaveringly on the other end of the track. Billy took a look from behind Gribben to see what was so interesting, but, evidently, he couldn't see anything. All the others were also into staring at the far end, except sometimes when they broke the spell and went on to other things, such as slapping themselves on the legs, jiggling their arms about, or wobbling their heads round and round. Few words were exchanged.

No one spoke to Billy except the cringing chap representing Altnaclog, who actually hailed from the Isle of Rocknay in the Outer Isles – a place where you get all the training you need simply by opening the front door and trying to shut it again in one of the many fearsome gales that thrash the place. People there have been known to run a full marathon on their own doorstep. Understandably, the man was the complaining sort. "Bloody sun!" he complained. "It's been hittin' me for a whole ten minutes now. I can't think straight! I can't think straight." But, after successfully borrowing a sunhat from an official, the man went quiet again.

Even Billy, who confessed habitually to feeling abnormal, would have been forgiven for feeling uneasy in such company. He restricted himself to standing still and awaiting instructions.

When the starter called them to their marks, some of the guys started bouncing up and down and blasting big breaths out. Billy looked mystified, clearly wondering if he was really in the right place. He darted a glance at Mary Boone. She smiled. Amazingly, Billy smiled too. He drew a huge breath, held it for a moment, then exhaled powerfully.

Cries of "Come on, Billy!" and "Up Tannadee!" rang out. They were countered with similar cries of "Go, Gribben, go!" and "Up Garthbay!"

The starter raised his gun. The runners raised their tempo, all springing and bouncing, except for Billy and the scowling man from the Outer Isles, who threw off his sunhat.

Barrington crossed his fingers and bit his nails; Chizzie took a deep breath to quell the bellyful of butterflies fluttering inside him.

"On your marks!" called the starter.

The athletes moved forwards and got onto their blocks; all except one, of course – the oddball – the one with no blocks, no jiggle, no wobble and no bounce. He just knelt, his fingers arched behind the line.

When all the fidgeting ceased, the starter called "Get set!"

The athletes, rising slowly, came up to the set position, setting themselves like panthers – poised and ready, tense as thunderclouds, still and breathless. Then they were off!

In a flash, away went Billy Pung! He ripped through the invisible force field that held them all together. Keeping as low as he could for the first five yards, as instructed, and powering away with his legs and driving with his muscular arms, he was as relaxed and loose as anyone can be in a cauldron. Six yards out, he took a slight peek to either side, but there was no one there! It was a dream start, with no one level; he was at least a yard up! He chanced a bigger look and found himself all on his own. It was a false start. He'd gone before the gun.

Two officials came running up to him and escorted him back to the start, with Billy protesting all the while that the gun was late and should have gone off when he did, they'd waited long enough.

Horrified, Chizzie closed his eyes and took a deep breath. His head swam with visions of defeat, but Yolanda rushed from his side and ran over to the officials. With a mixture of explanation, special pleading, flattery and seduction, she persuaded the officials not to disqualify the exuberant Billy Pung. They gave him a yellow marker: one more of these and he was out.

As discreetly as she could, Yolanda took Billy aside and explained that he must wait for the bang; whatever he did, he had to wait for the bang or he would be disqualified. "Are you clear on that, Billy?" she asked, searching deeply into Billy's eyes for a flicker of understanding.

"Yeah, yeah," Billy replied not very convincingly.

The runners were called to the line again. They settled down once more, with Gribben being last to put his fingers to the line – confidence born of experience, no doubt.

Then, with everyone settled, the starter called, "Get set!"

The runners raised their posteriors again. In complete silence, as before, they poised. With their breathing suspended, the air hung taut.

Then, a "Blam!" hit the air. It was like the sound of a gunshot, but not a gunshot. It was a bum!

Gribben was away nonetheless; he leaped from his blocks and off he went down the track, streaking away. Billy went after him. The officials quickly intervened and waved them down. Mortified, Gribben returned to his blocks, looking daggers at Billy. But it was nothing to do with Billy: he wasn't that sophisticated. In fact, Billy was still arguing that Gribben had started it and he was just following, but this time no one was arguing.

The man the officials were after this time was the man from the Outer Isles, who was defending himself vigorously. He explained how the long sea journey to get here had played merry hell with his innards and had thrown them into turmoil. "If you'd been on a ferry for two days wi' seasick sheep and cattle dying all around ye, an' put clean off your meat, an' feedin' on ferry fries an' baked beans for two days and nights, you'd be backfiring too, I can tell ye! Ma guts are in turmoil, man. Turmoil, I tell ye – turmoil!"

It was a point that found ready sympathy with the officials, who, to a man, appeared to have experienced seasickness at one time or another on visits to Highland Games on the islands, and doubtless had no difficulty in recalling the awful experience of leaning groggily over the ship's rail, and throwing up over the wind-tossed sea only for their grub to come flying back at them and plaster their faces. Accordingly, the incident was adjudged an indiscretion and there was no yellow card.

But the islander wasn't the only man in turmoil: far from being supremely confident, Gribben by then looked to be a bag of nerves. After two false starts, he was falling apart.

When the starter called, "Get set!" for the third time, Gribben was the last to rise. His inner calm might have been in tatters, but his experience was still intact: he made sure he kept the others waiting. Billy wobbled slightly in anticipation, so the starter made them wait a little more. He held them and he held them, and then, "Bang!" off they went.

This time they were go! All powered away, except one – Billy Pung; he held back a moment.

"What's he doing?" cried Chizzie desperately.

"Avoiding disqualification maybe," Yolanda answered.

"He's given them a head start!" cried Chizzie.

But Gribben needed no advantage, he was off like an ostrich getting clean out of an abattoir. He was three yards away before Billy got going. At ten yards out, the ground fairly crackled as the athletes skimmed over the cinders of the bicycle track and Gribben was a yard up on the nearest man.

Billy, eating into the pack, went past first one man and then another. Gribben, though, was a sight to see: athletic and balletic, with heels of helium, he flowed over the ground as if on a trail laid by the gods. Billy, on the other hand, pounded along as if on a trail laid by a rhino chasing a cheetah, who'd just called him 'Apeface'. But he went steaming past another two men: with the fury in his legs and the sheer power of his body, he was cutting into Gribben's lead. A pretty sight he may not be, but he was shifting and, at this point, faster even than the great Gribben!

At fifty yards out, Billy took a light shower of manure off Gribben's spikes as they hit some dung left from the Battle of the Tooth. It inspired him, and he came closer and closer to Gribben. But then another ten yards on, Gribben put in more speed and began holding his lead; he had one yard over Billy and he was holding it. Billy just couldn't cut into it – the flyer held the fury, and art defied nature. But Billy threw his head back and drew on every sinew, and at seventy-five yards out, he was gaining again.

The noise of Billy, huffing and puffing, and getting closer and closer seemed to unnerve Gribben and he made the cardinal mistake: he looked round. The sight of Billy on his shoulder rocked him visibly, and the majestic flow all but burst. But bust he wasn't; there was no way he was giving in.

At ninety yards out, the gap between them was no more than a couple of inches. Then Billy came level, but Gribben wasn't done and the lead swung between them: first, it was Gribben ahead, then Billy, then Gribben, then Billy again, then Gribben again, then Billy – it was going right to the dip.

426

Then all of a sudden, he was gone! He was no more! The great Gribben was out! Had he dipped? Had he leaped? No, he'd skidded on a cowpat and was flat on the ground – dazed and utterly undone.

While the others shot past the stricken Gribben, Billy breasted the tape to a deafening roar of "Tannadee! Tannadee!"

The roar hit like a wind on Chizzie's face as he scuttled over to greet his victorious sprinter. In rapture, Tannadee people hugged and danced, even kissed, everything and anything: spouses, partners, babies, strangers, dogs, cars and even a fence post in one case.

But, in sport as so often in life, for every joy there is a sorrow. In a world never more than half in light, there is always darkness somewhere, and on the Garthbay horde the darkness fell. They were sorely aggrieved. Tannadee might be savouring victory, but Garthbay were smelling a rat or, more exactly, a cowpat. An exceedingly suspicious cowpat.

And so began the legendary 'Cowpat Controversy'. When the victorious Tannadee team took their lap of honour, they were greeted at first with great cheering, whooping and applause.

But soon there were jeers, and cries of "Cheats!", "Boo!" and "Fix!" issuing from the mouths of the enraged Garthbay people who, like a terrier with a rat, just would not let go of the idea that a cowpat had been dropped deliberately in Gribben's lane. And so they worked themselves into a scandal – completely lost to them was the fact that the lane order hadn't even been drawn when the cattle were in the arena, and, certainly, if anyone had walked into the arena carrying a cowpat, or had one stuffed up his jumper, someone would have noticed. But no, Garthbay needed an inquiry and they got one – or as near as you'd get to one in that area.

427

Subsequently, after great deployment of the cerebral hemispheres that were still at the command of their owners, a decision was made. The chief referee – Councillor Charles Swetley, cattle trader – mounted the rostrum to make the announcement. In grim-looking mood, one that clearly offered little hope for whining villagers, he made his stand in the face of whistling, and cries of "Fix!", "Cheats!", "It's a disgrace!" and other less flattering concepts.

"What is a cowpat if not natural?" began Swetley defiantly. "A mere call of nature! The smell of the wild! A thing right at the very heart of any traditional Highland Games. And if you think about it for a second, we wouldn't have any grass if it wasn't for cowpats. And, quite frankly, if you can't run your way through a country pancake, you shouldn't be in a Highland Games! You should be in Sauchiehall Street, shopping for thongs or the like. This is countryside, for God's sake!"

Well, the Garthbayers hadn't expected much, but this was more than their flesh and blood could take. Immediately, some of them broke into a frenzy, bawling and gesticulating with venomous language that left little to the imagination. Even some of the more placid Garthbay folk found themselves shouting things, looking incensed one minute and self-conscious the next.

Chizzie, whose nerves were now almost in tatters, joined with the other Tannadee people in applauding Swetley's refreshing candour.

Swetley continued with the words that brought the sweetness of a desert oasis to Chizzie's aching heart: "And so…" declared Swetley, "the decision stands! The winners of the Colonel McBraid Bequest are – fairly and squarely – Tannadee!"

And that was it. Or so it should have been, but Swetley – a man whose willpower came and went with the puffing of cigarettes, and he hadn't had one for over ten minutes – couldn't resist just one more little dig now that he had villagers jumping. "The fact is," he observed, "there's too many bad losers here today! It's as simple as that!" This was a remark designed to hit the whining horde right between the eyeballs, and that's exactly what it did.

As poor PC Tunnock and his sergeant struggled to placate the seething crowd, they flashed a look that said, "Thanks a lot, mate," at the effervescent Swetley.

However, the crowd were not to be placated; they were losing it fast, and some hotheads surged forwards and made to storm the rostrum. PC Tunnock and his sergeant beat them to it and pulled them back valiantly before wiser counsel from Garthbay hauled the hotheads away and others appealed for calm, as, indeed, did Swetley – the peacemaker who had incited it all.

Few from Garthbay were in attendance when Chizzie struggled onto the rostrum to receive the prize, but who needed Garthbay fans? The Tannadee cheers were more than enough, for they hailed their team as loudly and fervently as a body many times their number.

The celebrations began immediately, with no speech from Chizzie. Not wishing to tempt providence, he hadn't prepared one. Counting himself very lucky and being too tired to protest, he was carried away at shoulder height to that great Valhalla of the showground: the beer tent.

All the Companions went too. Jim and Johnny were there; the former on orange juice along with Sven. Even Dalrymple was there, with a pallor almost whiter than his teeth, but nevertheless joining in the celebrations and managing a rare smile as he introduced his new friend, the young ambulance lady, to the Companions of Tannadee. She wasn't the only young lady being introduced, though: Billy Pung was every bit as pleased as he introduced his new lady friend: the singer Mary Boone.

The Companions and their partners put two big wooden tables together and sat around them before ordering more refreshments, ready, it seemed, to reflect loudly on the day's events. But there was to be no reflection; that would come later, in the next few days. Just then, it was a quiet air of high achievement and some amazement that settled over the company as the adrenalin and euphoria that had driven Chizzie and his Companions to new extremes ebbed away. At that time, the aches and pains returned and Chizzie began to feel like an assemblage of butcher meat hanging from hooks, though exhaustion helped to numb the aches and brought about a quaint, warm happiness.

Too happy and too tired to feel self-conscious or any sting of refusal, Chizzie made a big decision, and, turning to Yolanda, he tapped her on the shoulder. When she looked him in the eye, he whispered, "Yolanda Weever, will you marry me?"

Without surprise and with no hesitation, she whispered gently, "Yes."

They gazed at one another for a moment, almost stunned by the momentous simplicity of the exchange. There were no fancy words and no ring. They simply knew the love and the worth of the other. She took his hand and squeezed it, and they sealed their fate with a kiss that Chizzie was too ecstatic to rate, but it was certainly up with the best.

No one was in any doubt about what had passed between them. Applause hit like a thunderstorm. Dalrymple took a chance and kissed his lady. Mary Boone kissed Billy. It was a golden day – a day when Chizzie, feeling not the slightest bit cheesy, surrendered completely to love and fatigue. So overwhelmed were his feelings, that he became dizzy and only faintly did he hear a helicopter somewhere above.

In the helicopter was Gordon Weever, who peered out of a window before leaning over and speaking into Fairfoull's right ear. "You know what?" he shouted. "Those people down there – they're my family. For thousands of years, they've been here and with my folks nearly all that time. The fact is, we're all jumbled up – them and my folks and me. What's in me is in them."

"Not all of them," stated Fairfoull.

"Most of them. Most of them are Clan McShellach. And if I'm clan chief, these people… they're my children. That's what 'clan' means right? Clan is 'children' in Gaelic. Am I right?"

"I think you are, Gordon."

"And they're sure gonna love me cos, you know what? I'm gonna be the best clan chief ever. They're gonna love me like their daddy."

"Love you?"

"Absolutely. What's not to love?"

 Matador

For exclusive discounts on Matador titles,
sign up to our occasional newsletter at
troubador.co.uk/bookshop